Heart
of the
Witch

JUDY GOODWIN

Diamond Print
Press

DEDICATION

I would like to dedicate this book to my partner and family, who assisted me, supported me, and helped me keep faith in things. I would also like to dedicate this book to my daughter Vanessa, may she read as many wonderful tales as I have.

Zerrick Dhur

Book One: Witch Hunt

Chapter One

"The guilty cannot escape punishment; they are their own tormentors."
-II Ja'hal, 51:14

Zerrick tore through the jungle, heart pounding as he leapt over vines and tangled roots of cypress trees. His pouches--full of herbs he'd been collecting since daybreak--slapped his sides as he ran. Ahead he could see the slowly turning vanes of the town's windmill near the banks of the Divenen River.

"For pity's sake, Zerrick, come out! Something big is happening in town!" His brother Dellin's voice cut through the dense foliage. Too close.

Zerrick wasn't going to make it to the fields before his brother caught him. He could see his brother now, at the edge of the jungle where civilization began in the form of rye crops struggling in this wet foreign soil. As usual his brother wore black, his dark brown hair tied back in a queue, with a pressed white collar falling neatly over his doublet. His heavy brow, so like Father's, was deeply lined, youth quickly melting away into stolid adulthood. He paced at the edge of the rye field, dark eyes trying to bore a hole into the jungle. Zerrick came to a halt, panting.

Should he make light of it, say he was just pulling a prank? Or could he sneak by, get to the Old Mill where he'd said he'd be studying? Zerrick pulled out his book and quill from his knapsack--brought along just in case--and dusted dirt and an errant herb from them. With a prayer to Iahmel, Zerrick pulled his own black hair to a pony tail, hoping Dellin wouldn't notice he was wearing a leather jerkin rather than the usual attire Mother forced him to wear.

There were sugar fields to the left, just a hundred yards away. He might be able to sneak into them, claim he'd been sampling some sugar cane--a reward for study. That sounded good.

He walked quickly but cautiously, lest he give himself away with a snapping twig. Dellin growled, crossing his arms. "Zerrick, for mercy's sake, act your age! You're not a boy any longer, and you can't simply leave town like this! I don't have time to wait for you. The witch trial is under way right now."

Ugh. The poor girl, Zerrick thought, his insides twisting. He wondered if Alden was there at the trial. Probably not. What place would an old herbalist have in a courtroom? Zerrick just hoped he got a chance to see the old man before all the herbs he'd collected dried up.

With a whisper of rustling leaves, Zerrick slipped into the cane field. Once he'd gotten a fair distance from the jungle, he called out, "Hey Dellin, over here! Shh, don't let the slaves find out!" The last was hardly necessary. He hadn't seen any of the red-skinned slaves in the field all morning. Probably they were with everyone else, watching the trial.

Sighing with exasperation, Dellin walked over. Zerrick left the cane field for one of the many pathways leading into town to meet him, snapping off a piece of cane as he went. He hurriedly cracked it open with his knife and began to chew on it.

When Dellin approached, Zerrick offered him the cane. "I . . . uh, was in the middle of the field. Just a reward for studying. I didn't want to reveal myself in case the workers heard." Zerrick tried to look shamefaced. Hopefully being in the field would also account for his bedraggled state.

Dellin dismissed him with a hand. "Fine. We'll talk about it later, when you show me what you learned. For now, we've got to get to the courthouse. Father's addressing the town."

He began walking, long strides made only more solemn by black hosen and heeled shoes. Zerrick struggled to keep up with him. He tucked away his book and made sure none of the plants peeked out of his pouches. By the westward sinking sun, he realized it must be mid-afternoon. Far longer than he'd planned on being out.

That was the spell the jungle put over him. To lie on the roots of ancient mangrove trees, gathering lilies from the slowly swirling waters of the Divenen River--ah, that was the life! He'd even found some odd tracks and a few blue scales by a cluster of orchids. Alden would recognize them, if only he could find a way to slip away and show them to the old herbalist. Zerrick sighed.

They passed more fields, these of coffee and tobacco, and as they drew closer, Zerrick began to hear a roar of voices spilling out over the wooden palisade wall. He glanced at Dellin as their father's stern baritone became discernible over the roar.

"We're too late," Dellin muttered, his brows knotted. He quickened his pace, thin lips pressed together. Zerrick almost ran to keep up with his taller sibling, passing through the gatehouse and hurrying towards the center of town.

Zerrick paused as they neared the square of the town, which was bordered by the four most important buildings in town: the courthouse, church, gubernatorial lord's hall, and the clock tower. A mob had gathered. Farmers stood armed with axes and hoes, and small boys threw rocks at the pillories. Women who normally coddled their children were red in the face from screaming. Mr. Edelson, the tailor, a normally quiet man, brandished his scissors and shouted out condemnations in a voice gone hoarse. The only quiet ones in the crowd were the slaves, on the fringes of the crowd, muttering amongst themselves in their strange tongue, dark heads huddled together, sun shining on their reddish skin.

Dellin plunged into the maelstrom. Zerrick hung back, instead climbing the courthouse steps to get a better view. Directly across from the courthouse, on the top steps of the steepled church of Our Lord Iahmel, stood Zerrick's father, the town pastor, the Reverend Delwar Dhur. He paced before the crowd, dressed in black silk with a crimson-lined cape, his dark brown hair slicked back to fall unbound down his shoulders.

He called out to the crowd, raising high his silver-studded walking stick. "We cannot let such wickedness continue! I sat before dear Vera

Smith, clasping her hand, and prayed to the Almighty to show her salvation, let her confess her heinous ways, and confess them she has! Praise Iahmel, praise the Lord, for He has driven out of her the seed of vilest sin, the contract she made with the evil Angist himself!"

Zerrick shivered, entranced by the sheer power of delivery. Such was the gift of his family: theatrics. Once his father's speech would have spurred him to go down and join the crowd to raise his voice with the others. Now, it only filled him with dread.

"Burn the witch!" the baker's wife called, balancing a toddler on one hip.

"Cut out her tongue!" cried Mr. Edelson with a snap of his scissors.

"No more curses!" shouted several boys in unison.

Zerrick spotted his brother climbing the church steps to join his father, and hunched his shoulders so the two wouldn't see him. There were enough people on the steps that he could hide among them, not that he need fear. When Father began one of his sermons, he'd ignore the Savior Ja'hal himself standing before him.

"Yes, my children, we must punish sin, that we should abolish evil from the minds and souls of mortals. But Iahmel is merciful in His ways; He protects those who confess to Him and are repentant." Reverend Dhur reached out a white-gloved hand towards the pillories, his features softening.

"She's a whore!" the tanner's wife screamed. "She'll try it again!"

Reverend Dhur raised his hands for silence, and reluctantly the noise settled. He leaned over and conferred with Dellin, and in that moment where pitchforks were lowered and people hushed to listen, Zerrick caught a look at the victim of this fury.

He'd seen her only a few times before. She was a few years older than him, in her early twenties, with a square jaw and brown hair wrapped in a kerchief. Her gaze darted from person to person, while her manacled hands gripped a faded shawl.

Zerrick knew only a little about her. She tilled Lord Hennaker's land to pay for room and board at the House of Labor. Only the more wretched sort lived there, like indentured servants who'd paid for their passage from the Motherland of Endersey with hard labor, or penniless orphans, or women without prospect. Vera was one of the latter--her father had nine other children to support. Unable to find a husband, Vera's only choice was the House of Labor.

There were rumors that she supplemented her income with less honorable work, though she was no beauty. She'd been seen cursing farmwives and children who dared call her a woman of the night, and people said her manner was rude and volatile. But Zerrick felt disturbed, watching her pain and the fury of the crowd. He knew she was no witch.

Their conference over, Reverend Dhur placed his white-gloved hand on the woman's dusty kerchief and spoke in a steady voice. "I have listened to this sinner's confession, and I believe she will keep her word and stray never again to the Dark Arts. Nevertheless, her soul has been marked, and her family name tainted--"

"How could you! My own daughter!"

This last came from the blacksmith, a large bearded man with tears streaming down his face. The Reverend silenced him. "Now Kimball, it is known that the young, unguided female is the prime target for Angist's lies." He addressed the crowd again. "But because she comes of such good family, a family which looks after our dumb animals in their haltering and shoeing, she herself will be punished as would a stray horse. As her soul was branded eternally by the mark of Angist, we will try to counter that with a mark of our own. Upon her upper arm, she will be branded with the holy seven-point star, the mark of our Savior, Ja'hal." The crowd broke into shouts of approval, but the blacksmith cried out. Zerrick wondered if he was thinking he'd be the one to perform the deed; he was, after all, in charge of forging brands.

Again his father's voice somehow rose above the noise. "I have consulted with the prosecutor and judge, and we have all agreed on this punishment. She will be marked in pain for her sin, yet the mark will protect her, remind her to whose flock she belongs. If she lives forever more in strict obedience of the Lord's ways, He may show His favor for the one who bears His mark." Sound reasoning, Zerrick thought; yet why did it feel so wrong?

Around him, the opposing voices dwindled. Though the black-smith hung his head, it was obvious he agreed with what must be done. Reverend Dhur gave the task of forging and applying the brand to the blacksmith, and scheduled the branding for the coming Thursday. The crowd began to disperse.

Zerrick considered joining his brother and father, but even as he descended the steps of the courthouse, the two of them disappeared into the church without a backwards glance. He told himself he was not going to feel hurt; it was not the first time they had forgotten him. This was better, actually. Now he had a chance to see Alden.

Avoiding the townspeople, Zerrick ducked into the alley behind the courthouse and with a stealth long practiced made his way to Alden's home. Vera's red-rimmed eyes haunted him. He would find some excuse to be away from the square the day of the branding--he didn't think he could bear to watch some poor innocent woman struggle as her father placed a glowing hot brand to her skin.

By the time he reached Alden's cabin, Zerrick's nerves had settled. He opened the iron gate and crossed the garden, overgrown with vines climbing the walls. Alden's house, though within the town walls, managed to create the illusion of sitting by itself in a secluded glen. Trees that must have been planted before Zerrick was born lined the fence, and everywhere things flowered and bore strange fruit, all specimens from Alden's travels down the coast of Argessa. Before he had settled down to become town healer, Alden had been a great explorer. He had lived with the natives and seen magical creatures that lived in the jungle. He taught Zerrick herb lore, among other things that Zerrick hoped Father never learned about.

Zerrick stepped over a potted palm by the steps and rapped on the door. He heard a low mutter on the other side, then Alden opened the door and pulled him inside, saying, "Come, come, don't just stand there--lot of commotion around town today, eh? Let's see what you've got for me? Oh, full pouches, very good, good!"

Zerrick blinked at the speed of Alden's excited speech, but as he breathed in the house's exotic scents, he relaxed somewhat. He found a chair as Alden went on, "Pitchu for open sores, Javanica pods for malaria, mangrove, curry orchid, tree fern, brown spotted orchid . . . ah, Argessan Lobelia!"

The old man grinned like a child as he emptied Zerrick's pouches, stuffing plants into glass jars which must have cost him a fortune. Zerrick was pleased to see most of his gatherings went into the proper jars, although a few specimens were thrown into the poison jar and quickly corked. Well, he was only an apprentice. He sat back and stretched out his legs.

The house was cozy, the walls decorated with paintings from Endersey as well as artifacts from local tribes. Almost the entire downstairs was taken up by the research laboratory with only a small kitchen and dining area and no place to receive guests, not that many came to call. It had been different when Alden's wife was alive. She'd kept a little corner for sitting and chatting by the atrium where Alden grew his ferns, off from the main part of the house. Now, however, every table and chair had plants growing in pots upon it, or glass jars of herbs, or a carefully wrapped book, or strange tools of wood and stone.

Master Alden finished his sorting and returned Zerrick's pouches. He sat back in his faded red velvet chair and regarded Zerrick with watery blue eyes.

Zerrick gazed back at him, forcing himself to be patient. Alden often did this--went from childishly excited to ancient and solemn in a breath. He had to talk to him about the branding, and now Alden would be in the mood to listen. Zerrick glanced at the water clock on the mantel, calculating; he had an hour or so before his family would expect him home for dinner.

Alden ran a hand through his gray hair, leaving a brown streak of dirt. He spoke in a much slower voice. "So, how was your sojourn into the wilderness? I noticed a few interesting scales in one of your pouches. Karuneeb, I believe. Did you see any sign of it? They are quite shy, you know. Usually don't come close to civilization."

"I saw its tracks," Zerrick said, dusting a little leftover soil from his clothes. He'd have to change clothes before dinner of course, but hopefully he wouldn't have to order a bath.

Alden nodded. "It looks like a large rodent with intelligent eyes, blue scales, long prehensile tail, and the most beautiful voice you've ever heard. Magical, naturally. I'm surprised you didn't thrust those at me the moment you came in. You seem distracted--did something happen today? I heard quite a noise from the square." Alden began writing notes in one of his books, glancing up at Zerrick occasionally as he spoke.

Now Zerrick could bring up his concerns. "Master, do you remember Vera Smith? She was accused of witchcraft. Today my father encouraged her to confess, and now her punishment will be a public branding of the Star of Ja'hal on her arm!"

"How gruesome! And unnecessary. I've met the girl; she doesn't have the brains to become an apprentice of magic, much less a full witch." Alden's mouth set into a grim line as he wrote, a slight tremor in his hands the only clue to his feelings in the matter. Was he denying the state of things? Zerrick wondered.

"Are you sure?" Zerrick asked.

Alden looked offended. "Of course! I know all the spellcasters in the colonies, except those terrible renegades in the wilderness, and she could not have trained with any of them. Knowing your father, he probably convinced her she was a witch and was hiding the fact from her own little mind. He seems quite good at inspiring guilt." Alden looked Zerrick up and down and Zerrick flushed. It was all too true.

Alden patted Zerrick on the knee. "Oh now, don't fret. If there's one thing I can't stand, it's you fretting at every little thing. Relax! This whole trial means nothing. It's just a few folks upset over the malaria outbreak. It will pass." He closed the notebook, setting it aside to study some of Zerrick's findings. With a flick of his fingers, he lit one of the candles to bring more light into the dark room.

"I don't think so," Zerrick said, leaning forward to keep his master's attention. "You should have heard them in the square. Witch fever--like the kind you described from Endersey--has reached Harrow. They were suggesting she be burned alive!" Zerrick's hands clenched the armrests. A trickle of sweat ran down his back beneath the linen shirt.

"Ridiculous," Alden said, waving him off.

"No please, listen to me. It's been coming for some time. First those whispers they used to make about your wife whenever she lost a child--"

"She was the best midwife in town."

"I know that, but her death was unusual. Being struck by lightning? Then the diseases started growing worse, then Father began preaching about the troubles back in Endersey, then this Smith woman, saying curses to children, or so they say--"

"You're fretting again. We've already got the cure for the current diseases and simple words can't hurt children."

Zerrick let out an exasperated sigh. "But they think they can. So what happens if someone catches me making trips to the jungle, or what if one of your cures doesn't work?"

"Is that what you're worried about? Well, you needn't. You're the pastor's son. Who would suspect you? And I'm just an eccentric old man, but a man with some mighty helpful knowledge. No, I don't think they'll challenge either of us." Alden placed a potted fern in Zerrick's lap. "Now, let's get on to the lesson, shall we?"

Zerrick resisted the urge to shove the plant away. "I don't know if I should continue. I'm not sure what is right any more." He glanced around, noting a tribal knife on the bookshelf, the watchful eyes of a stuffed hawk on the table. He thought back to the sentencing, feeling once again the fear, the unease at his father's words. "Father spoke of souls being branded. Is my soul branded with evil? Because I practice witchcraft?" He whispered the last word; even so, it seemed terribly loud. He fought the urge to touch his temple in a sign of protection.

Alden looked weary, as he rose to go to a leather-bound tome on a wooden stand by the door. He leafed through it and came to a page marked with a faded ribbon. "And he spake against the people, saying 'Blame not the craft for the errors of the craftsman.'" He closed the book and turned to Zerrick. "Many think Ja'hal was referring to the innocence of material things and the evil within the human soul, but if you read it within context, Ja'hal was addressing the mob after the warlock Herfastis was caught committing the slaughter of the seven cities with his spells. Ja'hal was not simply speaking of crafts and matter; he was referring directly to the innocence of magic as a primal force."

Zerrick was still unsure. Ever since he'd learned of the works Alden did, he'd wondered where his curiosity would lead him. Master Alden was a good man; he had saved lives with his magic, including Zerrick's, but magic was difficult to place in the moral scheme of things. Wasn't all power evil?

Alden returned to his seat and clasped Zerrick's knee. "Young man, magic *is* dangerous. Nobody ever disputed that. But it has no taint in and of itself. It can do great good in the right hands. You're just the sort to use it, because you worry about the right of your actions. That's why I chose you for my student."

Zerrick held tightly onto Alden's hand as he tried to understand. "Magic comes from the Goddess; you taught me that, but my father says the Goddess is evil, almost as evil as Angist."

"That is from a very biased look at Creation. The Goddess and God were once one, and regardless of how the error occurred, after Angist separated them they were still two halves of a whole, and that whole is good. The Goddess may be buried beneath Angist's lies, but that does not make everything that She created in the Beginning evil. I refuse to believe it." With that, Alden sat back, glancing over at the water clock.

He sighed. "It's late. Go on home, and think about what we've discussed. You'll find I am right in the end. Practice your studies, and see me tomorrow." He made a gesture to dismiss Zerrick and settled in to his books. Zerrick hesitated a moment, but when Alden showed no signs of responding, Zerrick slowly went to the door.

He wished he'd never seen the mob. All the commotion simply made his conflict worse. And it wasn't the sort of thing he could discuss with people, not that he had any friends to discuss it with. All he had were Alden's words against his father's. He couldn't choose which to believe.

Chapter Two

"Among the greatest of sins is vanity.
-I Ja'hal, 24:13

Deep in thought, Zerrick left Alden's place and walked in the lengthening shadows to his house on the other side of town. It was a beautiful white-painted mansion, with real glass windows imported from Endersey and a courtyard with clipped grass and palm trees. He entered by way of the kitchen, holding his finger to his lips as the cook, Maureen, started to scold his appearance. She humphed and threw a towel at him.

"I don't want to know," she said, crossing her arms over her chest. She was a large woman with a gray bun drooping down to one side of her head in the heat, and her cheeks, as always, were rosy, belying her age. Despite working with foodstuffs and sooty tools for the fire, her apron was clean.

Zerrick tried not to smile as he explained, "Got caught sneaking sugarcane."

"And I'll bet that's all you've eaten today." Maureen wagged a finger at him.

He grinned, shrugging, and Maureen threw up her hands. "How am I ever going to put meat on your bones if you never eat? Women hate skinny men. You'll never get married looking like you do!" She chuckled, her eyes sparkling.

His looks were the common joke. Mother had fussed and fretted over him since before puberty, shown him off at any local gathering, then berated him for any scratch or scrape that could damage his precious good looks. It hadn't helped that her attentions had made him the fop around town, the one who got beaten bloody by the local bullies. Maureen had always been the one to put herbal compresses on his bruises, protecting him from his mother's ravings.

He gave her a quick hug and asked if his father was home.

"Your parents are upstairs in the study--I believe your father is preparing his sermon. Dinner will be at six. You'd better wash up here." She went over to the huge fireplace to turn the roast then pumped him a basin full of water from the sink.

He washed up while she bustled about to stir the soup, cut fresh fruit, and put something that looked highly promising--tarts, perhaps-- into the baking oven adjoining the fireplace. When he was done, he asked, "Is Grandmother coming?"

"Yes, with Ingar. Your brother and his wife will stop by afterwards. You'd best wear your green velvet doublet and cape. Your mother wants you to look like a gentleman tonight."

Zerrick groaned. "Why must we conform to Endersian fashion when we live in the tropics? It's ridiculous to wear a cape in this heat."

"Well, that's your grandmother for you. Best get along now. I've got to cut the roast." With a wave of her apron, she shooed him out.

Zerrick went up to his room to avoid being spotted and shut the door. He didn't know if Dellin had told his father of this afternoon's mischief out in the sugar field, but either way his father would deal with him more kindly if he looked civilized. He lived in what had been Dellin's room, and while he had tried to soften the barren space with new bed curtains and a rug, it still kept the stark look of its former occupant. The only area of true color was in the wardrobe which held the array of clothing Grandmother Celinda had given him. A full sized mirror, a desk and chair, and a trunk at the foot of the bed for his more precious belongings rounded out the furnishings.

He went to the trunk and pulled out the sword that his grandfather Ingar had given him for his fourteenth birthday, and his black shoes with the brass buckles. He quickly changed shirts and stockings, pulled on the velvet breeches and doublet, and smoothed out the lace falling band collar.

After the talk with Master Alden, he would have liked to call for dinner in his room, but with his father's performance today there would be lots of visitors. Tomorrow was Sunday. He'd have to attend church, read over his lessons with his brother or one of the clerks, and

14

then he could slip away to Alden's if he didn't stay long. Sunday was the day he was most watched, if not by his father, then by the community in general. As the pastor's son, he was expected to adhere to all the day's laws.

As he was combing his hair out to let it flow loose down his shoulders, a knock sounded at the door. He opened it to find his mother, Emilia Dhur, in her best evening gown of deep turquoise blue.

"Ah, I see Cook told you to wear your velvet. It sets off your eyes, gives them more color. Did you hear Delwar in the square today?" Emilia swept into the room, pausing at the mirror to straighten hair black and thick as Zerrick's, gently patting it into its carefully arranged bun and side ringlets. Her lace neckerchief hid the fact that the décolletage of the gown was settled quite low on her bosom and her padded sleeves disguised her slender arms, yet still in the voluminous gown she looked tiny and fragile.

Zerrick had been told many times that he took after her, with her high cheekbones and pouting lips. If they looked so much alike, why couldn't they achieve anything more than a coldly dignified relationship? Her mere presence cooled his room.

"I did watch the end of the proceedings," he answered, tying the bows of his breeches at his knees.

"Yes, I was at Grandmother's--trials are no place for a lady of quality--but even there I could hear the shouts. I understand it was impressive, but witches! Ugh--what a disagreeable lot. Rather like that old herbalist's woman--whatever her name--"

"Lobelia," Zerrick muttered, wondering if she brought up topics like this just to punish him. He fingered a small red ribbon, debating whether or not to tie up his lovelock, the long tail in his hair. He decided to let fashion be hanged; he wasn't submitting any further to Grandmother's ideals.

"Yes, yes, brutish sort, should have been killed after her mistake..." Emilia trailed off, staring at her reflection in the mirror, face impassive, but Zerrick winced. It seemed his mother could never forget how he had spoiled her as a childbearing woman. At birth, he had been turned wrong; it had taken all of Lobelia's skill to save both him and his mother . When they visited families with six and seven children, his mother would sit quietly, giving Zerrick smoldering glares.

"Well," Emilia continued, "this girl will be properly punished, and this incident should bring more of the town to church tomorrow, so it is all for the best." She gazed at Zerrick's reflection and their ice-blue eyes met.

The moment broke as she patted his arm, smirking. Gathering her skirts, she floated past him and out the door. "We'll be expecting you downstairs," she called as she glided down the hall. "And do wash your face. There's a smudge on your left cheek."

Zerrick did so, making sure to remove any trace of his morning's activities, then he pulled on his gloves and left the room. He was halfway down the stairs when he remembered he had left his cape on the bed. Sighing, he went to retrieve it.

When he entered the dining room, his father and mother and his mother's parents were all chatting at the dinner table, waiting for him. As they saw him, all conversation ceased, and his father's black eyes bored into him from the head of the table. He hurried to his place and they all rose to give grace.

His father led them. "Thank the Lord Iahmel for this food He hath provided, that we may be strengthened in our beliefs from His nourishment. Amen."

"Amen," they all solemnly repeated, then they sat down and began. Zerrick sipped at his soup, listening to the chink of silverware and the blessed quiet of everybody eating. The table had been covered with their finest lace cloth, and new sweet-smelling candles were lit. His grandmother Celinda sat beside him, picking daintily at the roast, while Grandfather Ingar sat across from him, speaking quietly with Emilia. His father, between bites, flipped through his sermon notes.

Zerrick froze as his father suddenly addressed him. "Well, young man, you managed to make yourself scarce today. I didn't even see you at the trial."

Zerrick tried to keep the guilty flush from his face. "I was there part of the time, sir. Most of the day I was trying to read those lessons for tomorrow. I found a wonderful secluded spot by the mill." There; that should corroborate with Dellin's tale.

"Upstanding young men should not endanger themselves by leaving the town walls," Celinda stated, dabbing her berry-stained lips with a napkin. "Also, don't you grow lonely, studying by yourself all the time? You should be out courting, especially on a lovely day like today." She regarded him primly, her hands hanging in the air like unfinished thoughts. She was dressed in deep royal blue, in which she had probably looked stunning in her youth. Now, with her hair turning gray and her pale face lined with wrinkles, there was too much contrast between the vivid gown and her skin. It made her look bleached out, a remnant of past times in another country.

His father continued as if she'd never spoken. "It is good you are sticking to your reading. I understand it is difficult for you, but you shall never amount to anything unless you keep at it."

Zerrick flushed. He'd never been able to read very well. The letters seemed to misbehave for him, moving around the page to places they didn't belong. It was why his father had given up on teaching him to preach or govern the church, while his brother became a deacon. If he was lucky, his father would grant him work as a lowly clerk.

Once his father had made the obligatory exchange with him, he turned to Ingar to ask how the slave trade was going. While Grandmother embodied the absolute vessel of grace and dignity, her husband was coarse and rugged, like the land. He had come here with Celinda and Emilia to find a fortune, and he had succeeded by shipping captured natives to Endersey and selling them as slave labor.

The natives were said to be wicked, possessing the minds of children and no souls to speak of, though they looked human enough to Zerrick. Their skin was something of a reddish-brown which matched the river mud when the floods came, and their hair was black and curly, flowing free down their backs. The men refused to shave their beards, which they adorned with feathers.

Grandfather Ingar kept twenty slaves of his own, and most people in town felt he ran a respectable business, but it had always bothered Zerrick to visit his house and see the men, women, and children caged like animals, their eyes dull and unseeing.

As for Grandfather, he reveled in the mastery of a valuable trade his many trips inland had brought him, and his ruggedness showed in his gray hair held back only by a leather strip, and in his thigh-high boots. He was the only one at the table slurping his soup.

While Delwar and Ingar discussed slaves, Grandmother and Emilia chatted about the current shortage of available ladies in town, and how Zerrick was wasting his best years by not pursuing one. He sat and poked at his food.

"Well, it's dreadful, Mother. The men are getting so competitive these days, and Zerrick's not much of a fighter, I fear. But things should get better. He's going to finish his studies and start his journeymanship in Questin; there he can compete for attention. If he can finally stand up for himself."

Zerrick sat hunched over, his appetite lost after hearing his mother's words. Sometimes he wanted out of this town and away from the people who tormented him, but that would mean losing Alden, and he wasn't ready for that. He needed his one friend; it was his only escape to hear the old man's tales and lose himself in lessons about fascinating plants and wondrous deeds done by magic.

He was glad when dinner was finally over, but now it was time for guests to arrive, and Zerrick knew one particular guest he would have to face: his brother. He led his Grandmother to the sitting room. She complimented him on his remembering to wear his cape then berated him for forgetting to tie his lovelock.

Only moments later there sounded a knock at the door, and he stood to greet Dellin, Delin's wife Ivie, and their two children, just four and two years old. Maureen hustled the little ones off to the kitchen for tarts and Zerrick watched them go with envy, wishing he could go play with them rather than endure what was surely to come. He schooled his features into what he hoped was a pleasant smile, and nodded to

Dellin. Dellin didn't smile back, but that was hardly unusual. He looked solemn, dressed all in midnight blue, his hair pulled into a very tight queue. He seemed about to say something, then Delwar entered with Ingar. Delwar and Dellin actually smiled as they clasped hands, then they launched into a discussion of the ramifications of the day's events. It seemed Zerrick's escapade was forgotten.

Instead they planned how they would help the town from this growing threat of witchcraft. Zerrick crossed the room to stand by Ivie, who never spoke unless spoken to, and together they stood, silent, as more guests came: Grandfather Telrick Dhur in his official robes of the church as Honorable Curate of the province, and Judge Inister, a tall thin man whose heavy brows always left his eyes shadowed.

Telrick added his rhetoric to the discussion and Zerrick wondered if he could slip away unnoticed. Then he heard something of interest.

"Vera Smith is not really a bright enough girl to have caused such a plague by herself, you know," Dellin said. "I think she represented only one minor player in a greater scheme."

"Yes, I agree," Delwar said, nodding gravely. "The child was being used. She admitted she wished evil on the children, but she said she did not know how her curses came to actually work. It is possible she was ensorcelled." Zerrick shivered at the intimate tone of his voice, so expertly controlled to punctuate every word, let it sink into the listener's mind as if meant for their ears alone.

"There must be at least one other witch, then, an old, powerful one, who led her to Angist." Judge Inister had a thin reedy voice that matched his thin lips which seemed to curl around the words.

"We'll have to organize a search, then," Dellin suggested.

"Of course. And tomorrow's sermon will be the first clue," Telrick said, fingering his robes. "All concerned citizens will be there, but it is known that devils feel uncomfortable in a House of God. Those who don't attend tomorrow are suspect."

Master Alden often skips church, Zerrick thought, feeling the blood draining out of his face. For once he was glad nobody in his family ever took notice of him. Alden was right. No one would ever suspect Zerrick of anything, but how many others would be tried after this?

They continued, deciding how to approach the suspects and going over what traits marked magic use and how to recognize magic when they saw it. They talked of devil marks, familiars, kinship with nature, and worship of the Goddess. Alden didn't have any pets, thank goodness, but he did have a small scar beside his nose from a tribal initiation, and he had his gardens, and his powers. Zerrick began to feel nauseated, imagining what could happen if his father confronted Alden. What would he do? Defend Alden against his father? Die for something he wasn't even sure he believed in? Maybe Alden would sense the unrest and attend church. Or maybe Zerrick could get word to him, somehow, before the sermon began.

He jumped as Ivie suddenly spoke to him. "Are you feeling all right? You look rather pale. Perhaps you should lie down." She wouldn't look at him, opening and closing her lace fan.

He could have kissed her. "Yes, I am feeling a bit off color. Please tell my mother I went to bed. I certainly wouldn't want to miss the sermon tomorrow." He bowed and slunk out of the room, wishing he did not truly feel so awful inside. He needed sleep, blissful, uncomplicated sleep without worries or regrets.

As he made his way up the stairs, he heard his father describe the terrible deaths the malaria was causing, how people saw visions in their sleep, visions of black wings blotting out the light. He waited in his room, intending to stay there only until Father was asleep, until the house was quiet, so that he could sneak out and warn Alden.

Instead, Zerrick fell asleep.

Chapter Three

"The sweetest voice hath oft been the seed that sows poisonous unrest."
-I Ja'hal, 35:22

Zerrick sat up in the bed with a jolt, aware that he had just escaped a nightmare about flames and smoke, but the dream was already fading, sinking back into the murky depths of his minds. Pale morning light lanced through cracks in the shutters of the room's only window. He yawned and massaged an ache at the back of his head. Then he remembered Alden.

I've got to somehow warn him, he thought, and pulled on his shirt from last night, stumbling over to his wardrobe for his Sunday black. He dressed quickly, not bothering to check if all his bows were correctly tied, and swiftly washed his face and wet back his hair.

He flung on his black silk cape, then went downstairs, taking the steps two at a time to check the house's only clock with springs, a new design from the homeland. A little after five--less than an hour before the early sermon, which Zerrick would be expected to attend, as well as the midmorning sermon for the lazy.

As he stood wondering how to slip away, Delwar came down the stairs, reading his notes and sipping a cup of tea. He stopped as he saw Zerrick. "Finally up, I see," he said, staring at him.

Zerrick tried to speak past the sudden knot in his throat. "I'm after some herb tea. Is Mother up?" His father rose early every morning, but Mother generally slept in until later, even on many Sundays when she would spend the morning perfecting her hair and dress for her appearance beside her husband at the later sermon.

"Yes. Her handmaiden is plaiting her hair. We're going to make our appearance as a family today. Even Almieta will be with us for the dawn sermon. Stay nearby so we can leave on schedule and arrive together." This morning he seemed to glow, suffused with inner wisdom in his simple white robe over which he would later don his habit, back straight and proud. Delwar had always enjoyed his power; the current situation must be a dream-come-true for him, Zerrick thought. It was a chilling thought, but he didn't have time to add any more worries. It was going to be next to impossible to warn Alden.

He assured his father he would stay close and went to the kitchen to grab a tart from the breadbox. As he scarfed down the tart and drank his tea, he contemplated the servant's entrance, warring with himself over whether he should break away. Maureen entered and stalled his decision.

"All ready, Zerrick? You look quite mature today, or maybe it's just me. Have you already eaten? I've fresh mangoes and leftover tarts." She bustled about the kitchen, piling up a tray of food for his parents and trying not to stain her Sunday dress. Zerrick held up the half-eaten tart and she nodded then hurried out towards the sitting room.

Now was the time. If he sprinted both ways, he might make it. He popped the last bit of tart into his mouth and gripped the door handle, ready to make a run for it.

There was a knock at the front door.

Let the maid get it, please, he thought, but he knew who it was and that he would be expected to act as host until his mother was ready. With a longing look at the back door, Zerrick wiped off his hands then went to the sitting room off the foyer.

The maid was taking Almieta's shawl when Zerrick entered, and Almieta waved a milky white hand to acknowledge her brother. Her husband, Hilliard Inister, was already seated, smoking a pipe and glaring at him through the puffs of smoke. Zerrick felt about as comfortable around Hilliard as he did his father, Judge Inister. Hilliard was the open embodiment of that dark glint in his father's eyes; he was a giant bully of a man with dark hair always in disarray and a mottled red complexion hinting at anger just under the surface. His eyes, however, were open and honest, a sort of hazel brown which changed to reflect his mood. Right now they were green with discontent. He and Delwar didn't get along. Zerrick knew his mother thought Hilliard handsome but a little frightening; he'd never understood why his parents had given Hilliard consent to marry Almieta. They were an unlikely couple.

Almieta stood behind Hilliard's chair, a wispy aspen next to a thick gnarled oak. Somehow she'd escaped the somber tones of her parents' hair color; her golden hair was tied back, ringlets falling softly onto her shoulders. Her eyes were pale blue like Mother's but timid, haunted almost. She had always been the shyest of the family.

Zerrick glanced around to see if they had brought their daughter, now four years old, but apparently she had been allowed to sleep in. Her nursemaid would probably take her to the later sermon. He decided he had better at least make an attempt at entertaining them. "Well, this should prove quite an interesting morning, don't you think?"

Hilliard gave an ungracious cough, waving at the air with his pipe. "Bloody nonsense, dragging everybody to church for a sort of mock-trial. No guilty person would be stupid enough to miss today. Your father and mine are both fools."

Zerrick wondered if he would utter such words if Delwar were present and decided he probably would. Hilliard was known for his blunt honesty and general lack of fear. It made him a shrewd prosecutor.

He decided to try his sister instead. "Will Flora be joining us?"

"Yes, she's been down with a little fever, but she'll make the second sermon. She's excited to see you." Zerrick had to strain to hear Almieta, though he stood only a few feet away. He smiled at her words; Flora would make this whole terrible business a little brighter. She was a lot like him: imaginative, curious, a regular little sprite full of potential.

They discussed a few inane topics as the hand on the clock slowly moved towards six, then Delwar and Emilia came down arm in arm. Emilia floated over to Almieta and hugged her, gushing over how lovely she looked and how awful she was for not coming to visit more often. Delwar shook hands with Hilliard, the maid fetched hats and capes, and they all prepared to leave. Emilia took one look at Zerrick and told him he'd missed three bows. He tried to contain his ire as he tied them, and followed the two couples out the door into the early morning coolness.

The streets were still empty except for a few early risers: a fisherman on the way to the river, a patrolman who waved hello at them, and an old couple also making their way to church. Dew covered the street lamps and misted windows and doors, and overhead heavy clouds gathered. The rising sun was visible, however, and its light wreathed the clouds in golden fire.

A small group gathered inside the church, mostly members of his family he'd seen last night, plus some of the more devoted worshippers. Young clerks lit candles in the wall sconces, and Dellin was busy directing things, a ghostly figure in his white deacon's robes. Zerrick took his seat in the front row of the pews as Delwar went to an antechamber and returned with his long sleeved yellow robe and the chasuble Grandfather Telrick would wear. Grandfather no longer preached, but he was Curate, the link to the Church and King back in Endersey. He had also built this church. With a nod to Delwar, Telrick donned his chasuble and took his place in a seat back behind the podium. The rest of Zerrick's family sat, and Zerrick found himself wedged in between Almieta and Grandmother Celinda, who took one look at his sloppy bows and refused to speak to him.

People continued arriving. Zerrick turned his head every time he heard someone enter, trying to see if it was Alden. He stopped after Celinda growled at him to mind his manners.

The place was surprisingly full by the time they closed the doors. Families who usually only attended the later sermon were there, even the gurgling babies and querulous schoolboys, the latter seated in the back, watched over by Dellin with his burning stare and his switch swinging mesmerizingly from side to side. One of his duties in the small town as deacon was to act as schoolmaster.

Everyone seemed pensive, their gazes turned inwards as they sat in stiff gowns and breeches, the younger men trying hard not to scratch at their starched collars. The blacksmith was also present, with his wife and every one of his ten children, though Vera sat off to one side, ostracized by her younger siblings. Zerrick couldn't look at the misery on her face for long; he turned his attention back to the podium as his father took his place and directed them to the first hymn.

Everyone rose and sang, and Zerrick sang a little off key, trying to see the rows of pews behind him out of the corner of his eye. Alden wasn't here. He hoped he would make the second sermon.

The song ended, and Grandfather Telrick took the podium. He made a few announcements about news from Endersey and the affairs in nearby towns. "And in Questin, there has been a strange behavior seen in children, who said they dreamt of a lady clad in green plantlife. Questin officials have been searching for the evildoer causing these dreams, but to no avail."

He continued after a rumble of discontent, echoed in a distant rumble of thunder outside. "The priesthood in Endersey has noticed a great movement of witches into the New World of Argessa. They are alarmed at this trend, and have advocated that the townships do whatever is necessary to stamp out the threat."

That caused a greater stir than the first statement, and Zerrick heard behind him the blacksmith whispering a fervent prayer.

Telrick concluded his announcements and they stood and sang the second hymn. Then Reverend Delwar stood up. As he came up to the podium, the rain began outside, pattering on the high vaulted roof and against the single stained glass window above his head, which threw its muted orange and red light on his robes, coloring him like the dawn. Or like fire.

Delwar stood straight, hands folded in front of him, and when he spoke, his voice was low but heated, impossible to keep out, like the sun's rays. "In the Beginning, unorganized, chaotic, searing Light and Energy surrounding the spirits and the dual God, Iahmelainéra. He and

She observed the Light, and it was good, yet it was without mind, without form. So Iahmelainéra decided to shape it."

So it was the creation tale he was starting with today, Zerrick mused, interested despite his anxiety. He remembered long discussions with Alden, picking over the details as it had been described by the prophet Kazimir. In the Beginning, everything had been One, and good, pure. He wondered why it had been changed at all.

Delwar continued, "From one third of the Light was created the Heavens. From the second part of the Light created they the world. The towering mountains, the land, were created by the Iahmel aspect of the Supreme Being; the rivers, oceans and springs were created by the Ainéra aspect." Rain ran in rivulets down the stained glass window.

The first separation of the One into Two, thought Zerrick mournfully, almost hearing Alden's impassioned lecture about how just by creating different parts of the world, the deity had been doomed from the start. And how clever his father was, he thought, using the weather outside. The early morning showers were common this time of year.

Delwar described the creation of animals and birds and plants from the waters, and then his tone changed from wonder to foreboding. "But the third part of the Light was still unconquered; it pervaded Nature, and some of the animals mutated into the great dragons and griffins, gargoyles and hydrae."

Zerrick remembered Alden's words, *And it is because of this infiltration that magic exists in the world, will always exist, deep within Nature. That first Light, that Chaos before Creation, was magic.*

Thunder accented Delwar's speech. "Concerned that the raw power of Light might be harmful to their Creation, Iahmel and Ainéra quickly tamed it. The first third Iahmel took and forged into the sun, that its regulated energy could sustain life. Ainéra took the second third, and created the moon and the stars, to light the world when the sun was away. Then together, They contemplated the last third."

This part should get interesting, Zerrick thought; here different religions argued about the story.

Delwar paced, adding passion to his voice. "The spirits of Heaven suggested a thinking, feeling creature unlike the animals, a being with morals and language to glorify the goodness that was the Dual God. Iahmelainéra agreed. One created man; the other created woman, from the mud where land and water mix. Then They rested. While They rested, Emos the man and Lera the woman gathered food and played among the wilderness, but after a while Lera grew bored, and went to the river to view herself and sing. Her singing awoke the Ainéra aspect, and Ainéra watched her with pride, thinking 'I have created this, I, Myself, and not My Mate.' As She thought this, a pain erupted in Her side where She was joined to Iahmel. A crack formed."

How could the Goddess wake without waking Iahmel if the two were so wholly joined, Zerrick always wondered. Alden said the Nemite religion believed they had both woken and were both contemplating their separate achievements. Zerrick thought that made more sense. Looking around, however, he doubted if anyone else thought that, or anything else. They were entranced by his father's performance.

"In Her ear, a tiny voice said, 'Great are Thy works, Fair One, greater far than the works of Thy Husband. See there the moon, how it sparkles in the streams and oceans. Yea, truly Thou art highest in Thine art!'"

Reverend Delwar's voice rose to a crescendo as he came to the critical part, "And the pain in Ainéra's side grew worse, and with a terrible wrenching, Ainéra found Her face separated from Iahmel's. The crack in Her side deepened, spilling dark blood. Iahmel stirred, and the voice warned, 'Now Thou hast committed grave error. When He awakens, He shall punish Thee.' But She replied, 'It is of no matter. I am the greater. He can do Me no harm.' Yet fear arose in Her heart that the love of Her Mate might falter. And from this fear flowed anger that Iahmel should think Himself master, should take it upon Himself to discipline Her. In sudden fury and terror, She tore Herself bodily from Him; separated neck and torso, leg and arm. The crack became a gaping hole, and as the blood spilled, Angist was born, Father of all

Evil, and darkness eclipsed the moon as his words seduced Her." The storm outside reached its peak, and people murmured prayers, cowering.

The rest of the tale was the same in both cultures, and as Zerrick listened, he tried to consider how the Nemites would have interpreted things. Iahmel either woke or was already awake and partly guilty, and together He and Ainéra fought to destroy Angist, but Angist escaped into the world. As for Ainéra, She was either thrown out or exiled Herself in order to combat Angist's evil in the world. Of course, Zerrick's father insisted on the former, and the townspeople agreed, shouting condemnation for the errant Goddess.

Reverend Delwar turned to the lesson of the tale. "You all know the story of the first tribes, how Angist and Ainéra stalked the wilderness and lured men away from the truth of Iahmel. Ainéra's lies created beast worship and savage barbarians, much like the soulless here in the colonies who have lost all touch with Iahmel and have become beasts themselves. She granted magic to many of these cultures, and to the evil Nemites of the West who sought to take over the world in the time of Ja'hal's First Coming."

Now Zerrick wished he could block out his father's voice. The last thing he needed was more guilt that his experience with magic had aligned him with Angist. Delwar went on to describe the War of Mages, over three thousand years ago, when the boy Ja'hal was born to the Emir of one of the two nations of wizards. Angels visited him and taught him that wizards were all evil, seeking dominance with their power. He managed to convert the Emir after near destruction then defeated the Empress sorceress of Al'Tuon.

"And the horrors did not simply end after Ja'hal's Comings. In Balia, just north of our homeland in Endersey, just ten years ago there was a terrible mage storm caused by a witch who swore he'd seen the Goddess and was acting on Her orders to kill worshippers of Iahmel. And just in the last year, one hundred and twelve acts of magic have been recorded by witnesses here in the colonies and along the coast of

Argessa. One needs only to hear of the Stonefist Gang to know witchcraft is rampant in the New World."

The renegade mages Alden complained about. Oh yes, there were real acts of magic being done, but most of it was hardly recognizable as magic. Mage storms? Curses? *Plagues?!* Such things were possible, but only by incredibly powerful witches, and Zerrick doubted there were any here who cared a thumb's length about the colonies. He had to admit, however, that there were probably more powerful witches here than in Endersey--according to Alden, there was a rich store of magic here that had apparently all been used up back in the Motherland. But *mage storms?* Unlikely. Half these 'acts' were probably natural phenomenon.

"This Creation tale I have told is to remind you that the witch's power comes from Angist, from that first separation, the betrayal of Ainéra and the birth of evil. Only the Will of Iahmel can fight it. Where the Church is strong, as in Endersey, the witches will flee and torment man no longer. We can fight this evil," Delwar concluded, leaving the podium and coming towards the congregation to stand before them, arms upraised. Behind him, the clouds parted, and beams of sunlight shone through the lighter colors of the stained glass, bathing him.

No, that was all wrong, Zerrick thought, anger rising up to his throat. He clenched his teeth to keep quiet. Magic was of the first Light, not the first darkness. It came before the Separation. It was simply that when Angist was born, magic became a power for both good and evil. If he had any of his father's talent, he would have stood up and explained it all. But Father wouldn't have listened.

The people nodded and slowly they began to stir, slowly transforming into yesterday's mob. Zerrick sat up, as restless as those around him but for different reasons. He found himself glad Alden wasn't there. The old man would be livid at the things Father was describing; he'd be standing up and arguing, and that would be worse than missing.

"Remember the signs of a witch! It is written in the Tylander Chronicles that witches are always close to untamed nature. They carry pieces of it with them: dried plants, live fronds, a crystal, sometimes even the soil itself to draw power from, and they often have pets, like the cat or crow. Iahmel or nature often marks them with witch marks, or scars, and they shun all things holy." Eyes afire, Delwar strode out into the pews, touching the heads of his worshippers.

"You, my flock, you shall be the eyes and ears of the Lord Iahmel! Seek out witches, capture them, but do not kill them, that they may receive judgment by the Law and by the Church, and be sent into Hell in a fiery blaze!"

The response was incredible. Farmers and fishermen, housewives and elderly widows, all stood up around Delwar and prayed aloud in glory to the Lord Iahmel, reaching out hands to touch Delwar as he passed through the pews. He blessed them and told them their faith would be their greatest weapon. Emotion seemed to whirl through the room, like a great hurricane, and Zerrick was tempted to be swept along with it, dive into the center of the maelstrom where his father called him . . . but of course, it wasn't he that was being called; it was the nameless people, never him, that mattered to Delwar. His father's eyes swept over the people then gazed up to the roof above, but they were unfocused, almost all pupil.

Zerrick shivered in the humid air, smelling the stench of too many bodies, his ears ringing with their fervent cries. Delwar went on to tell them what he and the others had discussed last night, that there was at least one master witch in town and they must all be watchful and not stray from their beliefs. He answered a few questions, assuring folks of their safety in the arms of Iahmel. Then the sermon ended and everyone sang the last hymn.

As the door opened, Zerrick breathed deeply, trying to dispel his tension. A cool wet breeze hit his skin and he heard the schoolboys shout with glee as they ran to play in the puddles, only to be scolded by their mothers. Other than the boys, however, people seemed reluctant to leave, and he wondered if they would actually stay for the second sermon. It seemed many would; people stood to stretch and greet each other, but only the fishermen and farmers left. The rest chatted away, mostly about innocent subjects, but every once in a while Zerrick heard the word 'witch'.

He was kept busy taking Dellin's place to watch the schoolboys as Dellin attended Father and the clerks tried to organize people into sections so that seats could be opened up for the next group. Delwar looked positively ecstatic at the devotion of his people.

After an hour of trying to keep fidgety boys in line, Zerrick was ready to throw down the switch and stomp outside--he was no disciplinarian--but a clerk came to relieve him. He went back to his seat to find his niece Flora and her nursemaid had arrived.

He sat down and Flora scrambled up onto his lap to hug him, wrapping tiny arms around his neck and burying her face in his hair. He laughed and gave her a kiss on the forehead. Her eyes were so blue, brimming with color. She settled down and spread her skirt on his knees, saying, "Mama got me a new dress, see? Not a baby dress. A *lady's* dress!"

It was a beautiful gown of pink rose with bows of crushed velvet and padded sleeves, probably even with a corset underneath, which must have been very uncomfortable for Flora who was used to loose toddler gowns to run around and play in. They were already preparing her for maidenhood.

"It's beautiful, Flora! And such a lovely color," he said, starting to feel claustrophobic. Alden couldn't possibly miss the second sermon, could he? Not when the entire town was here. He tried to remain calm, even though his heart was thundering in his ears.

Then he caught sight of someone in the corner of his eye, waving at him. He turned to see Alden in a faded and dated suit of gray silk, coming down the rows of pews to sit right behind him. Zerrick turned his head to the front again, trying to ignore the herbalist. What had possessed the man to sit so near his family? He flinched as Alden's hand came to rest on his shoulder.

"Who is this adorable little woman in your lap, eh Zerrick?" he asked amiably, as if people weren't turning to stare uneasily at him.

Zerrick considered shunning him, but Flora peeked over his shoulder, grinning and laughing at the old herbalist. "Mr. Alden, this is my niece, Flora. The *prosecutor's* daughter," he answered, turning and nodding his head towards Hilliard who looked at Alden in distaste. Almieta sat beside him, her face anxious.

"Ah," Alden said, smiling and removing his hat as he sat down. Zerrick sat ramrod straight, concentrating on the podium and clutching at his niece as if she could protect him from unwanted attention. He was breathing fast and shallow, and the church had turned stiflingly hot. He must look odd to his relatives, even to Flora who tried to wiggle out of his grasp, but he couldn't help it. He felt trapped.

More people showed up; Zerrick was positive just about every person in Harrow was there. Even Lord Hennaker and his Lady were present with their servants and three of their four children, the last apparently having taken ill. People sat crammed together--the walls were lined with worshippers standing to watch the sermon and the heat grew as the clouds cleared and the sun shone down through the circular stained glass window. The doors shut, entrapping the heat. Telrick repeated his announcements, and then Delwar took his place in the circle of sunlight on the floor.

He didn't repeat exactly the same sermon; Delwar always made a few changes for those who had to watch both, but his message remained the same. He was enlisting Harrow's help in capturing witches.

Zerrick sat feeling Alden's presence behind him, sweat trickling down his neck. Flora had settled against him, snoring quietly. He kept waiting, through the creation tale and the chronicles of the mage wars, to hear a muttered retort from Alden, an outburst, anything. He only heard the gasps of the other townspeople, their murmured words about the evils of magic. When he finally dredged up the courage to look behind him, in the middle of his father's speech on the signs of witches, he could see Alden was deathly still, his eyes fixed on Delwar, narrowed, concentrating, but inscrutable. Zerrick relaxed. Of course Alden was too smart to draw any attention to himself.

After the service ended, people again crowded around Delwar, chanting prayers and touching his robes for a blessing. The clerks opened the doors, letting in rays of sunshine which blanketed the crowd and Delwar in an eerie glow. Slowly, people started leaving and Zerrick edged over to the wall as townsfolk came to greet his family and praise Delwar's sermon. Alden wandered near him, and their eyes met.

"Not a good idea, today, I think," Alden said in a light-hearted voice, but his face appeared gray, aged by several years.

"No, I need to talk. After lessons." Zerrick spoke as if it he were discussing the weather, but he held Alden's eyes a moment to drive his point home. Then he glanced away and started to make his way back to his family.

Alden caught hold of his arm."Yes, I suppose we must--you're at a critical point, and it would be dangerous to stop now. But I understand. And I'm sorry."

Zerrick shrugged off his grasp and whispered, "It's all right. I'll see you later," then hurried back to watch over his niece as people swarmed around them, chattering and congratulating them as if holiness were a family trait. Zerrick endured the hand shaking--there weren't too many interested in him personally--but he found himself glancing around for Alden. He was gone.

Sighing, he watched instead the antics of his mother and grandmother presiding over their gaggle of women, and again noticed there was no real emotion being expressed. It was all theatrics. He felt an irrepressible longing to get to Alden's, discuss all the things he had seen today, to tell him he was ready now. His father was wrong. He had to be. How could he speak objectively? He had never even seen real magic, never felt it, and he had his Creation tale all in disarray. Magic was chaotic, but it wasn't created by Angist.

Eventually people left, and Zerrick went into the office with Dellin to study. The lesson was long and frustrating; Zerrick felt like a fool, trying to read aloud chapters from Kazimir and Hergendes the prophets. He kept losing his place or reading words wrong, simple words like "saw" and "was" and "dumb." Then he had to write, and that was an even greater disaster, for half of his lettering was backwards, and all of his spelling was wrong.

Finally Dellin told him to copy a brief note five times and leave. He did so, then escaped out into the afternoon warmth, his fingers aching and his eyes tired. After the dark confines of the office, the sun felt wonderful, slowly warming his black breeches, soaking into his skin.

Zerrick slipped into Alden's house.

The herbalist was engrossed in study, sitting in his favorite old chair, open books surrounding him in a nest of knowledge. His hair flew loose in wild wisps down his shoulders, and he had two volumes perched on his lap. He looked up and waved for Zerrick to take a seat at his feet. Carefully setting aside a book, Zerrick did so.

"Very interesting things going on today," Alden mused, skimming pages.

"You should have been at my house last night. You're in danger, you know. Everything about this place screams 'witch!'" Zerrick said, looking wistfully at the books. So much knowledge, locked away from him. Maybe he was destined to be inept at everything.

"The mayor called me to his house after church. His youngest son, Astor, has taken ill. High fever, vomiting, all the symptoms of malaria, but it's not quite the same--he's coughing up blood--there's complications." Alden spoke into his book, flipping pages. He paused, reading, and looked at Zerrick. "I'm trying to decide what to use to cure the boy."

"Coughing up blood," Zerrick murmured, echoing Alden's distress. He gripped Alden's arm to pull his attention away from the books. "I've come for my lesson, since today may be the last time I can come for a while."

Alden nodded and closed the book. "I understand. Believe me, when I brought you into this, I never expected such a--" he wrinkled his brows, "--a fury. People have always been a little fearful, a mite cautious, but what hatred! I've never seen the townspeople get so worked up before."

"Yes, and it's mostly my father's fault. Could you believe that sermon? I see now what you mean about a biased view. But I agree with you. Magic isn't evil." His stomach gave a lurch, but Zerrick ignored it. Alden wasn't evil, he told himself. He had to believe in that, if nothing else.

"Hmm," Alden said with the hint of a smile. "All right; you're a bit out of practice. Come follow me," he said, rising and leading Zerrick over to the atrium. He cut a small frond off one of the ferns and handed it to Zerrick, then led him back to the table to sit. From the clutter on the table he uncovered a small candle, and placed it before Zerrick.

"Make me a light. Feel the candle, the wick, the energy flowing out of that fern in your hand, and reach out to light the candle," Alden said.

Zerrick breathed in deeply, and slowly released the breath, banishing all thoughts from his mind, letting his instincts take over. In the back of his mind, he heard Alden's words: *Magic is of the first Light, which was Chaos: pure creative or destructive energy. Chaos cannot be controlled with orderly thinking. Let your imagination rule.*

He did just that; blanked out his senses of the physical world around him, and let his senses touch the energy in the fern frond. The energy was weak but pure. Living energy. Easy to reach and tap into.

There were echoes of other energy fields around him: a bright yellow-colored pool from the ferns in the atrium, a dimmer tan-colored residue over the wood furniture, even a deep blue, heavily buried sprinkling in the ground beneath his feet, but these energies were inaccessible to him. Either they were too deeply buried for his understanding to grapple with, or too bright and powerful, threatening to overwhelm him. The danger of magic occurred when trying to learn too quickly, trying to gain more power than the mind and body could handle. A spell out of control could be devastating, especially to the caster.

He focused more deeply on the tiny green light of the frond in his hand, soaking himself in the tingling pool. Then he gathered it up with his willpower and reached over to transfer the energy to the candle. A charge, like the air before a thunderstorm, went through his fingertips, made his hair stand on end. Then he was aware of light--real light, not imagined--breaking through the barrier of his closed eyelids. He dropped the remains of the plant, withered now with the expenditure of its magic, and opened his eyes.

Oh no, I've done it again, he thought, gazing at the candle. He had provided a light for Alden, but not in the way he had intended to. Instead of lighting the candle's wick with fire, he had changed the wax somehow. The candle was unlit, and it was glowing a pale green.

"Well, that wasn't quite what I had in mind, but you did produce a light. Very good." Alden patted him, dusting off the remains of the frond from the table.

"I thought colors rather than fire," Zerrick said, scowling at the candle. Why did he have to be so stupid?

"Yes, you lacked control, but you were very quick about reaching the magic. I remember when it used to take you half an hour to find that energy. You can pull the magic; now it is your task to control it." Alden took the candle and placed it within a lantern, and it glowed brighter, as if it were a flame, sheltered by the glass from crosswinds. "It is a lovely shade," he murmured, holding the lantern up to his face. "About the same shade as the fern was."

Zerrick let himself smile a little; Alden looked elfish in the green glow. Zerrick cleared his throat. "Let me try again."

Alden cut another frond and set a second candle in front of him. Zerrick closed his eyes again, taking the fern, feeling it, letting his senses expand again as Alden explained in a soothing voice, "Man was created out of that Light which is magic. That's what gives us the ability to reach and control otherwise buried energy. Merge with the magic. Let it surround you and absorb your will; that is the communication with the energy. Then, release it to do your bidding."

Zerrick did so, feeling the world around him blur, trying to focus on what he wanted, trying to ignore the glimmerings of energies around him, like stars in a purple night. Again he found the spark within the fern, tapped it, enfolded it around him, and then reached out to transfer it to the candle. A flash of light and the smell of smoke told him he had succeeded.

He opened his eyes, but was forced to half close them again against the brightness of the candle. "Not again," he said, groaning.

The flame sizzled white hot, throwing off sparks as it speedily consumed the wick and candle. The whole room was brightly illuminated, as if a star had descended from the heavens to land right in the house. The sparks made shadows dance in corners as the flame sputtered noisily. Finally the candle exploded, and the green light from the first candle dominated again as the new fire fizzled out. All that remained of the candle was a blackened puddle of wax.

Alden's eyes were wide. "You must have pulled a lot of power for that." He sounded frightened, though he seemed to be making light of it.

Zerrick found nothing but dust in his hand where he'd once held the fern frond. He let the dust fall between his fingers and swallowed in a dry throat. "That could have hurt someone," he whispered.

"Perhaps, but it was well contained by the candle. You were quite accurate in where to transfer to, but not in what exactly you were transferring. No harm done; just lit up the place a bit." Alden set to cleaning up the burnt wax, not looking at Zerrick.

What about outside the house, Zerrick wondered. Could they see the flashes out there too? Hear the small burst of the explosion? As if to answer his question, there was a knock at the front door. Zerrick clutched at the chair, his heart lurching, but Alden simply looked annoyed.

"In the kitchen, quick. I'll handle this," he ordered, handing Zerrick the green candle to take with him.

Zerrick hurried over as Alden lit new candles. When Zerrick reached the small kitchen, he squatted in the corner by the pantry across from the doorway into the main house. He faced the wall, holding the green candle trying to block the glow with his body. His teeth chattered; he clamped down on them, biting his cheek to keep silent.

He heard Alden open the door. "Yes, yes, what can I do for you? Ah, Miss Stonecraft, I hope all is well?"

Maisie had the wits of a steel trap; she'd caught Zerrick a time or two when he was younger, sneaking berries from Lord Hennaker's garden and playing hoops on a Sunday. He wondered why she was here, then remembered Astor's illness. Maisie was Lady Hennaker's handmaiden.

"Mr. Alden, I didn't want to disturb ye, but it's Astor. He's grown worse since ye left. The medicines--they don't work--the poor lad's coughing up his lungs. By the way, was ye burning anything just now? Coming up the path, swore I saw a most peculiar light coming out your window." Zerrick heard her sharp voice, the rustle of her dress as she entered, probably around Alden's body. Alden tried to protest, but the words fell on deaf ears, and Zerrick could hear a plop which must have been her collapsing into Alden's chair. Pages hissed as her careless feet brushed over them.

"Madame, I will certainly come, but you'd best go on ahead. I was, in fact, in the middle of an experiment--ah--creating ashes for the treatment of open sores. Indeed it was that burning which you saw on the way here."

"I can smell it," Maisie said, and Zerrick sniffed the air. It did smell of smoke, but not wood smoke. It smelled more like smoke from a fired pistol.

"Yes, yes, even so. Now I tell you, I will be along shortly, but you mustn't rush me. Hurry back to your mistress, try to calm the boy. Tell him I'm preparing a remedy. Go along now, there's a girl." Zerrick heard a scuffle of papers, and a rustling of skirts--Maisie leaving her seat, hopefully--then her assurances that she would convey the message.

A long pause followed, when it seemed she should be near the doorway. Zerrick held his breath. He could feel the tension building in the air as the silence dragged on and on. *She senses something,* he told himself; *she can see something she shouldn't.* But then she humphed, and the feeling passed.

"Good day to you, Master Herbalist."

"Good day," he said in a subdued voice, and closed the door.

Zerrick breathed a sigh of relief, clutching the candle to still his shaking limbs. That had been much too close. He'd have to end the lesson--it was getting late anyhow, and he'd be expected home. When all of this witch fury was over, he'd return to continue the lessons. Until then, he couldn't risk this again.

He rose and turned to go, watching his shadow move across the doorway and the walls from his strange candle. In the main room, Alden was busy with his notes again. Zerrick thanked him and left, leaving the candle on the table.

Things were quieter that evening, and he had no trouble keeping to the shadows on his way home, or of complaining of a headache and calling up for dinner.

It was later that evening, as he bent to blow out the candle at his bedside, that he realized that even with the door closed in Alden's kitchen, light would have been spilling out underneath.

Visible to anyone who sat in Alden's chair.

Chapter Four

"Magic is the mark of madness."
--The wizard Herfastis, just before execution. II Ja'hal 45:15

Flames burned before him; a wall of heat through which he could not pass. The fire licked at him, devilish fingers curling to coax him to his doom. Behind him was darkness, but in that darkness, like many lit candles, glowed the eyes of watchers. Their voices hummed just lower than his ears could distinguish. He couldn't make out their words, only their tone: judgment. Zerrick stared into the flames, breathing hard against the seething air.

Beyond the flames he could see a ring of mountains, a cage of earth and granite touching the misty clouds above. Within the mountain ring was a woman--his mother? No, a queen, or perhaps a sorceress. The woman called to him, softly whispering his name to the wind: Zerrick, Zerrick. He shut his eyes but he could not shut out her voice.

A figure emerged from the darkness behind--Judge Inister, but then the figure blurred, and he became his father, then Alden. Alden came to stand beside Zerrick and said in a stern voice, "You must go through the fire."

"I'm afraid," Zerrick whispered, and cringed as the man--now Judge Inister--laughed cruelly.

"You have no choice! In you will go!"

Judge Inister suddenly became Delwar, and with a shove, he thrust Zerrick head first into the fire. The murmuring voices broke into hideous laughter, but the roar of the fire soon drowned them out.

Zerrick screamed as tendrils of flame snaked around him, wrapping him in agonizing heat upon heat. His skin cracked and bled; he sucked in a breath only to cough as plumes of black smoke encircled him; his hair was ash. Despite the pain, he tried to move, to lunge forward and break free, but he found no ground to support him. He was falling down into a flaming pit, his eyes becoming fire--

Zerrick woke, sucking in gulps of air to find he had rolled off the bed. Sweat plastered his hair to his skull, yet he was shivering violently. He crawled back into bed and worked to untangle the sheets, forcing himself to calm down. The flames--they had been so vivid! He rubbed his head to dispel the image.

Outside it was dark. He had left his shutters open to let in the pale moonlight, a practice of which his mother disapproved. She'd warned him that moonlight caused delusions, nightmares, even madness. He was beginning to believe it.

He'd slept less and less over the past few days since his father's sermon. The town felt like a branch ready to snap, or a brittle pile of tinder, needing only a tiny careless spark to set it alight. He'd heard rumors that Astor's sickness was worsening, and that Alden was only helping to prolong the ordeal. The boy was supposedly in great pain, and townsfolk whispered that his parents wanted to bring Reverend Dhur to say last rites over him, let him die in peace. Zerrick knew Alden, never one to give up, would fight such notions.

Meanwhile, things at home were becoming stranger. Judge Inister and his sons visited nightly. Some nights Dellin would come as well; Delwar would greet them, then they would disappear into his study for hours. Delwar had given Zerrick the most peculiar look one night--a look of sadness, or of confusion? That look had singed Zerrick; he'd tried to avoid his father after that. What was stranger was that his father seemed to be noticing him now.

It almost made him laugh--for years he'd tried to get his father to see him, to listen. Now his father perhaps felt guilty about Kimball and his daughter Vera, for he was having actual conversations with him. Last night they'd talked about where Zerrick wanted to complete his journeymanship. They'd discussed different towns and their advantages and disadvantages. Somehow Delwar had known Zerrick had been spending time at the courthouse looking over maps of the region. Zerrick felt guilty, tricking his father into believing he'd been there contemplating his journeymanship. He'd actually gone there, plagued by the foreboding thought that if anything should happen and he should have to run, he'd better have an idea of where to flee.

None of this was conducive to a good rest. And the worst was yet to come. Last night after their discussion, Delwar had announced that

Zerrick would start his clerical duties by attending the branding and acting as church scribe, writing down what was spoken at the event. He would sit by the court scribe to his father's left.

He should be wary, even suspicious, but he'd seen no evidence to make him believe his father suspected anything. In fact, his father had hardly spoken of witchcraft since the sermon.

His mind too active to sleep, Zerrick sat by the window, looking out on the courtyard and his mother's tidy rose garden. In the peace of the cool night, he settled into a soothing calm, letting the silvery rays bathe him in soft serenity. He closed his eyes, emptying his mind of all thoughts as he did when performing magic, and concentrated on the glimmer all around him, not trying to do anything, just perceiving, feeling. He saw the magic sleeping everywhere, sparkling in little puddles around every living thing. Such a natural and life-filled energy could not be evil, he thought, his heart aching with the beauty of it. He laid his head to rest on the sill.

A slamming door jerked him out of his reverie.

Zerrick strained his ears, and heard voices down the hall: his mother's voice, laced with worry, and his father's, heavy, urgent.

"I must go. They say he won't last the night, and he hasn't made final confession." Delwar had on his boots, and Zerrick heard the rattle of his walking stick as he passed down the hall.

His mother's voice sounded softer, more distant. "There's an evil moon out--be careful."

"I am protected. Go back to sleep. I'll be home shortly." With that, his father descended the stairs, his footfalls becoming faint. Zerrick couldn't hear his mother but he could picture her, gliding silently back to her bedroom. He closed the shutters and went back to bed.

In the morning Zerrick found his father brooding by the fireplace in his padded chair, a steaming cup of tea in his hands. His father was dressed in somber violet robes for the station he would be taking today as a giver of penance. Delwar raised his eyes to look at Zerrick, and

Zerrick was startled to see moisture at the corner of his eyes. Zerrick swallowed in a dry throat. That could only mean Alden had failed. Lord Hennaker's son was dead.

Delwar's eyes focused on him suddenly, as if noticing him for the first time. "Are you ready for the day's trials, son?"

Zerrick wasn't sure exactly what his father meant. "I believe so," he said, quelling a surge of uncertainty. Delwar continued to stare at him, saying nothing, and again that strange look entered his eyes. Was that sadness making the lines around his mouth deepen? Despair? Zerrick almost thought he saw a trace of anger, although it didn't really seem directed at him.

It took every ounce of his courage to force words out of his mouth. "Is everything . . . all right, sir?" His voice faltered at the end, but he did not lower his head.

His father looked away. "Far from it, I fear. Lord Hennaker's son Astor has passed on." He seemed about to say more, then rose, turning his back on Zerrick as he gathered up some books on the hearth and his walking stick. "I have work to do. Go to your brother's; he has the robes you will wear, and your instructions. I'll see you in front of the courthouse before noon."

He paused and reached out a hand to halt Zerrick as he turned to leave. "Do not tarry," he said, his voice becoming sharp, commanding. "Stay close by Dellin today--this is not time for one of your wanderings." Delwar gave Zerrick a hard look, then brushed past him to go to this study. The door closed, and Zerrick heard the brittle click of the lock.

Zerrick wasted no time in getting over to Dellin's place near the center of town. He spent the morning in the study, trying to at least make an attempt at correct spelling, while Dellin stormed around in a silent fury and Ivie sat knitting. It seemed Dellin could not find the right gloves for the occasion. Zerrick welcomed the messenger who came to tell them it was time to go.

Zerrick walked behind Dellin in his new clerk robes as they made the short trip to the square. A crowd was gathering, but he couldn't identify who was there, because he suddenly found walking in a floor length robe more difficult that it appeared. He only narrowly missed tripping as he climbed the stairs to the courthouse.

A long table had been set up before the entrance at the top of the stairs, the chairs facing into the square. Judge Inister sat in the center, Delwar to his right, next an empty chair where Dellin would sit, then Hilliard Inister's chair. On the Judge's left sat Lord Hennaker, looking weary and ill prepared. He was a plump man by any account, and usually merry, but today he held a white handkerchief and used it often, dabbing at his eyes behind thick spectacles. Next to him sat the Judge's second son, Marvis Inister, who was the master clerk for the courthouse, and finally Zerrick's chair.

Zerrick sat down, eyeing the master clerk who returned a sullen look. He would be keeping the court's official copy, while Zerrick produced the church copy. He sneered at Zerrick, and it was obvious he thought even this small task was too great for him. Somehow he was the most frightening of all the Inisters--he appeared thin, almost emaciated, but frail was definitely not the word Zerrick would have used to describe him. Sinuous, maybe; better yet wraith-like, ghoulish.

Vera Smith sat with her father on a bench at the foot of the steps, four patrol officers standing by to keep close watch on them and holding back the crowd filling the square.

In the center of the square burned a small bonfire into which someone had stuck a small iron stake with a little wooden doll, now blackened and burned. People kept back from the fire whose sole purpose today would be to heat the iron for branding.

The sun blazed overhead, and that glare combined with the fire and smoke made the air hellishly hot. Zerrick squirmed inside his robes, trying to release the heat gathered in every fold. Despite the heat, his heart was cold with dread.

A bell atop the church began to ring, a loud, jarring sound which echoed off the recesses of the courthouse doorway. It sounded twelve times, then fell silent. Judge Inister rose and thanked the people for coming but warned them to stay clear of the fire and the prisoner. He made a short account of what had transpired during the trial, then concluded, "With all speed, we will now complete the sentencing of Miss Vera Smith, accused and found guilty of witchcraft last Saturday, the twelfth of Siebenmont, in the year of Ja'hal's Second Coming 1640. Reverend?"

Delwar rose as Judge Inister sat down. "As I previously stated, the punishment for witchcraft is commonly to be burned alive at the stake."

He was forced to pause as a group of farmers began to chant, "Burn the witch!" He gave them one of his stern looks, and they subsided.

He continued. "In light of the girl's previous good standing and her willingness to confess and do penance for her sins, it was agreed that her punishment would instead be the branding of the star of Ja'hal on her arm. As he is her father, Mr. Kimball Smith will perform the branding."

He nodded to Lord Hennaker who gave the command, "Lead them to the fire."

The guards arranged themselves around Vera and Kimball, and the group slowly walked to the fire, the crowd parting for them then closing in behind, swallowing them. Zerrick wondered how Vera could walk so calmly to her fate, and then saw the glimmer of chains binding her. She glanced around her, her head jerking back and forth from the people's jeers to the bits of garbage flung at her, and Zerrick wished he could talk to her, tell her to fight back, not give in. Those kinds of thoughts could only bring trouble for a witch; he gritted his teeth and kept writing, struggling to remember his grammar.

Vera and Kimball reached the bonfire and Delwar called out to them, "Can you do this, Kimball, or do you need aid?"

Kimball shouted up at him, "I will do this alone!" He did not look towards Delwar or at his daughter. His focus centered on the flames, where he thrust his brand deep into the orange coals, turning it slowly.

Zerrick began to feel faint, though he didn't know why. He concentrated on writing the words, but images danced in his head; he felt magic stir in the reed pen in his hand. He clamped down on his wild emotions. This was no time for one of his misfired spells!

He managed to return his attention to the square where they were tying Vera down. Now she writhed and shouted out something garbled, but they gagged her and tightened the chains. After a few moments, Kimball removed the brand. It glowed a deep angry red.

Suddenly, Zerrick heard the blacksmith's thoughts as clearly as if the man were at his ear, speaking in a low voice, *"It's only a horse--not my daughter--only an animal . . ."*

He glanced beside him to see if the clerk heard it as well, but the man wasn't even watching the proceedings, writing away at his account. Zerrick returned to write only to find his pen had collapsed into dust. Still he heard Kimball's thoughts, *"Just got to do it. Don't think, just do . . . almost over."*

Then Zerrick jumped as he heard, or perhaps felt, an inner cry of pain, even as Vera Smith shrieked her torment as the brand touched the skin of her arm. A shudder went through the crowd; like a live thing it flinched away.

Zerrick stood up, though for what reason he could not say, and was about to run forward when he felt his father's eyes on him from the other end of the table. He turned and saw Delwar glaring at him, his eyes saying clearer then words--*don't you dare disgrace me now!* Zerrick sat back down, flushing, and dug his fingers into the folds of his robe as Dellin called out for order and the guards dragged Vera to the steps.

Delwar took over for Dellin in calming the crowd as Dellin knelt by Vera to wrap her arm in damp towels. She was slowly coming to, whimpering in pain. Before Kimball covered it up, Zerrick caught a glimpse of the star on her arm. It was black and bloody.

"Was it a clean branding?" Delwar called out to Kimball who remained kneeling by the fire with his head in his hands.

Blinking, Kimball staggered to his feet then turned towards them. "Yes," he said at last, "But--I felt him! Lord help me, I felt the Dark One! Here--" he pointed to his forehead, "inside my head, watching me, listening to my thoughts! Lord save us all, you were right." He stumbled and nearly fell, but a guard helped him up, dabbed his forehead with a cloth, and led him to sit on the steps away from his daughter. The crowd went into another uproar, demanding explanation.

Zerrick sat hunched, his face burning, wishing he were far away . . . but he clamped down on that thought at once. The Dark One in Kimball's head . . . had that been him? Or the power behind his magic? He glanced at Marvis and quickly looked away. The man smiled at him, a cruel, humorless smile that made his hair stand on end.

"Please, everyone, calm down!" Delwar shouted. The noise died down, and the people stared up at him. He smiled. "Now you see the truth. Vera was indeed in league with Angist, but Kimball defeated him by completing the task which freed her from that terrible grasp." He strode over to Dellin and murmured something to him, then helped Vera stand.

"Now we will consider this affair at an end for Vera, if she will try, now that the evil influence is gone, to remember who it was that taught her." Again he murmured, this time to Vera, who shook her head in weary confusion.

He addressed the crowd again. "Alas, she does not. It is of no matter, however, for I believe I know the man which brought such evil upon her." He turned to the table. "Hilliard! Bring the old sorcerer."

Judge Hilliard rose and went inside the courtroom. A moment passed, long and eerily silent, during which Zerrick dared not think, dared not even move. Hilliard emerged with several guards and a heavily bound prisoner. It was Alden.

"No!"

It was a half-choked, strangled cry, and Zerrick realized, as everyone stared at him, that it had come from his own lips.

"Marvis," Delwar's voice sounded heavy, but terribly stern, "Go ahead."

Zerrick only caught the blur of movement as the clerk leapt up and grabbed him, pinning him arms to bind his wrists with rope.

Zerrick kicked as Marvis dragged him from his chair, but then a guard grabbed his legs and slapped on iron manacles. He howled in fury.

"Silence!" His father's voice stopped him cold, running like ice down his spine. His captors shoved him upright to face his father, the rage and despair boiling inside to escape only in two hot tears sliding down his cheeks.

Delwar's face betrayed no feelings. He faced the stunned crowd and explained, "I came to Lord Hennaker's last night to hear young Astor's confession and perform last rites. I suspected the herbalist of peculiar doings, but I had no proof until last night. Upon entering the boy's room, I saw Alden conjuring magic, trying to steal poor Astor's soul!"

Alden squirmed in his bonds and tried to shout out something, but his gag muffled the words. It was obvious; he had come to the end of his herbal lore and had tried to save the boy with magic, Zerrick thought. He wanted to say this out loud, but his body wouldn't obey. It was as if his father's command had frozen every last ounce of his will.

That deadly voice continued. "I saw with my own eyes the glowing form of Astor and the herbalist. I called on Iahmel and tore the man away in time to stop it, but alas! The boy died then, in much pain. It is now clear to me that all along Alden has been creating plagues which only he himself can heal, bringing misery and death to the inhabitants of Harrow. He thought his 'healing' powers could disguise him as a valuable member of the community, but he has been discovered. He and those young ears he corrupted with his teachings: Vera, and now, the cruelest stroke of all, my own son!" Delwar no longer concealed his emotions but let the rage and indignity burn in his voice, and every word struck Zerrick like a blow. He closed his eyes and fought to remain standing, the shame and guilt a black weed in his throat, strangling him. He felt tears slip down his face but he no longer cared. He was going to die, if not in flame, then by the coldness of his father's scorn.

He felt grateful that his father kept his back to him. "I was not sure of my son's involvement until just now, but there is one witness who said she saw signs of him inside Alden's abode, and others who saw him leave there last Sunday. It grieves me deeply that he proved so weak, but such is the might of Angist. Though he is my son, he shall not escape justice. I shall pass this test of my faith and bestow punishment even upon my own blood; thus shall Iahmel know that this is a town which truly follows His Law." He paused, as if weary, and Zerrick forced himself to tear his eyes away from him and look about.

The crowd was silent, amazed and horrified, staring at him and Alden. Vera, gazed glumly at him, perhaps in understanding. Alden's face was the most terrible to behold--his eyes were filled with sorrow and he looked ancient and wise, peering out at the crowd. He shifted his focus to Zerrick, and now Zerrick had to close his eyes or risk a total breakdown. It was the only look of compassion he had received.

"Now, this affair is by no means over. We must question the guilty and try to save any that can be saved. However, your part, faithful followers, is done. Return to your homes, and be at peace; the enemy has been found, and we shall deal with him. Bless you, all of you, for your faith. Tomorrow, Judge Inister shall announce the verdict and punishment for the witches. Until then, pray, that your hearts be free of the spells that have held this town enthralled. Also pray for these two, and their wretched souls."

With that, Judge Inister declared an end to the gathering and ordered the people to disperse. Zerrick and Alden were taken inside the courthouse and put inside a small chamber with a table and benches, no windows, and only one door. Two guards posted themselves at the door.

Alden hobbled over to the bench and sat down. Zerrick glanced at him, and turned away. He stared at the door, willing himself not to feel.

Some time later they removed Alden and a stone-faced guard fed Zerrick a simple meal of bread and sausages. After that came silence, ringing in his ears, as he sat, trying to combat a morbidly vivid imagination.

He jumped as the door opened and his brother came into the room. Emilia entered alongside him, dressed in her most somber shade of indigo, shaking rain off her velvet skirts. Dellin refused to look directly at him, but Emilia stood with folded arms, looking down at him with her glacier eyes.

She spoke first, as Dellin hovered near the doorway. "Your father has much to do attending the warlock, and he is in no mood to see you. He asked, however, that we try to talk some sense into you." She went to stand across the table from him. "I always thought there was something wrong with you, from the time you were born. You were always a backwards child, learning everything in a backwards fashion, and now? I shouldn't even be surprised! You've gone and worshipped the wrong god."

"Goddess!" Zerrick hissed between his teeth. He was in no mood to sit meekly under her criticism now.

"Whatever. I don't know how much hope I have. Obviously the beauty I tried to bring out in you has all been in vain. We never expected you to be like your brother, but you had to have power too, was that it? Disgraceful!" She plucked out her fan to cool herself, leaning against the wall as if this little speech had exhausted her.

Zerrick held onto the bench, gripping it until his fingers cramped, telling himself *don't react, don't shout back; it's just what she wants*. He gritted his teeth and held back the hurt and rage that boiled just near the surface and made him shake. Only Dellin's intervention kept back his retorts.

"Mother, please." Dellin finally entered the room and crossed to stand beside Zerrick, facing Emilia. He took off his hat and set it on the table, seeming to take great interest in it.

"I really don't know what to say," he began, glancing at Zerrick. The usual harsh lines around his eyes had softened, making him look closer to the brother Zerrick had known not so long ago. Yet his voice had aged.

He began again. "When I saw you react to the old warlock being brought out . . . well, Father may have had suspicions, and Mother may have expected his, but I was shocked."

"I don't believe you. What did you discuss with Father, locked up in his study? I think all of this is just an act," Zerrick retorted, his head beginning to pound.

"We discussed Alden, and a few other suspects. He never mentioned you, I swear it. The witnesses came to him alone, and I only just learned about it." Dellin leaned closer. "It doesn't matter. You made a mistake; you joined with the enemy. You've condemned your soul to eternal damnation! Still, it doesn't have to be that way, even now. It's not too late to turn back, to the right path--"

"Wait, let me finish for you," Zerrick said, rising as far as he was able to with the ropes and shackles, bringing his face level with Dellin's. "I confess all my crimes and you allow me to rescue my pathetic soul and bring me back to my sorry position as the fallen devil in a family of angels. But first, of course, the punishment! What will it be, another branding? The removal of my tongue? Torture?"

"Oh stop it!" Dellin snapped, retrieving his hat and stepping back to stand beside Emilia. "You just don't understand, do you? I'm trying to help you, but you won't let me. What, are you jealous? Because I am what you cannot be? Did you ever try to follow the right path, I mean really try? I don't think so. You chose the easy path, to Alden and his enchantments."

"He gave me love and respect--something neither you nor Mother nor even Father ever gave me." Zerrick sat back down, sucking at his wrists, raw from the stiff ropes, and staring at the table. Why couldn't Dellin see how useless this was? At Alden's place last Sunday, and again this morning, staring at the moon, he'd learned he couldn't turn back. If he was fallen, he had been born that way; there could be no 'saving' him now, especially after Alden and his kindness . . . and the wild beauty of magic.

"I'll not stand here and listen to this," Emilia cried, closing her fan and going to the door in a flurry of skirts. She whirled to face Zerrick. "Why would I try so hard to rear you properly if not for love?"

Perhaps to create a showpiece, Zerrick thought, but he said nothing.

Dellin took up where she had left off. "As for respect, that has to be earned. You always told us how hard you were working at your studies, yet still you can barely read. I know you're not slow, so therefore you must have been lying to us, concentrating on magic rather than the words of Ja'hal. Come learn to read, know the words of righteousness, and I'll respect you. But enough of all this! Will you confess now, willingly? It will go harder on you otherwise."

Zerrick remembered the stories of torture and 'purification' of suspected witches. He shuddered. Then he remembered Alden, what might happen to him if he remained silent and they continued to think the worst of him.

He decided to speak. "I am a witch. I have performed magic with my own hands on several occasions. However, I have never hurt anyone. I don't know how to work magic on people, only on things. I can light a candle, or dust a shelf, or make an ink bottle float. I'm only an apprentice."

A light came into Dellin's eyes, and he came forward. "And Alden is, or rather was, your teacher? Did he make you sign any contracts?"

"What? Of course not," Zerrick paused, recalling the very first time he had seen Alden perform magic, when Zerrick was fourteen. The herbalist had been in his garden, creating a focus crystal--a stone into which magic from living sources had been fed. It was a very delicate process, and Zerrick had tumbled into the garden after trying to escape the town bully, right into Alden. The crystal released the magic with a burst of light, and Alden had been ready to enchant him and make him forget what he'd seen, but he had begged Alden to learn this wondrous mystery. Alden had made him promise to keep it a secret, had made him swear on Iahmel's name not to perform magic where others could see, or tell others Alden performed such works. Would a verbal agreement constitute a contract?

"All contracts are not evil, in any case," he said, blushing slightly. "Also, Alden isn't evil. He uses his magic to save lives, not curse them. He was trying to cure Astor after the herbs failed, I know it. After all, he saved my life when I was born, remember?"

"Any agreement to learn magic is a contract with evil. He cursed you when he saved your life, made you fit for nothing but witchcraft!" Dellin said with feeling, in his element now. "Angist can be subtle and patient, slowly drawing the unwary to his darkness until there is no escape. You're addicted to it now, aren't you? To this magic."

Zerrick had no reply. He was so tired of all of this. He wished they would just leave. He had no more anger to fight them with, and their words were beginning to hurt. He made one last attempt to make them understand. "You don't have any idea what you are condemning. Magic isn't some intoxicating sin! It's merely a part of Creation which has never been studied, but which exists all around us. There's a science to this. It's the use of natural energy, making it useful to mankind. It's like alchemy, biology, the study of heavenly bodies--"

"Blasphemer!" Emilia shrieked, rushing forward to cuff Zerrick across the cheek, sending him reeling. Zerrick put his hands to his burning cheek and said no more. Dellin nodded to himself and opened the door, motioning to Emilia that it was time to leave. He gave Zerrick one last look, a look Zerrick would always remember, full of pity. Dellin turned and the guards closed the door with a thud.

Silence enveloped the room. Zerrick rested his head on his arms and let out a weary sigh.

Chapter Five

"Hath fire the power to destroy--or to redeem?"
--Kazimir 35:12

Some time later, a guard led Zerrick downstairs to a small row of cells. Zerrick noticed Alden's cell immediately, bare of any furnishings with only stone walls and iron bars. Alden sat on the floor, gagged and bound.

The guard led Zerrick to a cell right across from Alden with a straw pallet and a copper chamber pot, and shoved him inside, slamming the bars shut. Two guards stayed by the stairway to the courthouse, talking softly. Zerrick contemplated the straw for magic potential, but it was dead, crumbling to dust even as he touched it. He sat on the floor facing Alden, wondering whether to speak, when something gleamed in Alden's hand--a quartz crystal, shielded from view by his robes.

"Ah, I wondered when they would bring you down here." The sound of Alden's voice heard inside his head made Zerrick start and nearly cry out. Magic! But how, he wondered? Surely his father would have searched Alden before binding him.

"They missed a crystal in my stocking, and was it ever a trial, extracting it! Well now, things couldn't be worse, could they? But I see you're wondering why I wasted magic on this when I could be opening the cells, putting the guards to sleep, right?"

Zerrick had been wondering just that, and he was suddenly chilled. To read thoughts so easily!

"I could do that, but there are patrolmen in the square, plus of course the entire town is against us. Where would I go? I'm too old to live a life on the run. You, however, are not. That is why I must speak with you, quickly, before the spell runs out."

Zerrick glanced up at Alden, trying to read his expression, but Alden shook his head slightly, warning him not to look. Zerrick turned to the wall and closed his eyes, so that he could listen better. "What's your plan?"

"Well, what would be your plan if I helped you escape? Don't answer 'to help you', because that would only waste the effort," Alden said, and Zerrick marveled at how the exact tone and quality of his voice expressed itself in thought; even feelings, which at present were falsely cheerful.

Realizing any speculations he made about Alden would show in his thoughts, Zerrick hurried to answer, *"I'd leave Harrow, travel down the coast perhaps, or flee to a town far in the interior like Depin."*

"The moment you disappear they will search every town within a hundred miles of here. You forget how powerful your father is. However, there is a more important consideration." The notion that he had nowhere to run nearly caused Zerrick to push Alden's voice away; he clamped down on that impulse. Somehow he knew that would break the spell.

"Ah, good control there. Now, I've noticed a pressing problem with you. You completely lost your control at the branding! That is dangerous; it makes you perilous to be around. From within the courthouse I saw you reach into a near-dead reed, which is the greatest pull you've ever managed, but it was totally out of your conscious guidance. If this continues, you'll be able to pull more and more power, but you won't be able to control it. It will control you, until it destroys you."

Just when he didn't need another complication! And this he feared the most: losing control and hurting someone. *"What do I do?"*

"After you escape, travel inland. Across the mountains west of here, there is a tribe of the Put-na called Besprii, which has knowledge of magic--enough to help you gain the control you need. There is one in the tribe, Mok, who speaks our language."

Join with the natives? Images of naked bearded men with scars on their bodies flooded Zerrick's mind, drowning out Alden's voice for a moment. He had nothing against the natives, but to live with them? He wasn't sure it was possible.

"I'm not asking you to be adopted into the tribe, merely to live with them while you learn. It'll do you good. Get rid of that silly vanity of yours. Now picture

for me where you keep your things. Have you any kind of a small trunk to put things in?"

Immediately Zerrick thought of his trunk with his Sunday silk and the sword. There came a sort of mental nod from Alden, and Zerrick proceeded to list what was in the trunk, his wardrobe, the linen closet and pantry--he would need food as well. Alden asked a few questions . . . did he own a machete, salted beef, some rope? Zerrick continued to send images until Alden was satisfied.

Then Zerrick tried to frame the question, *"And what of yourself?"*

"Never mind me! I can take care of myself. You must concentrate on your escape. Promise me that right now."

"Of course, Master. I promise," Zerrick immediately answered, though his heart gave a little tug at him.

"All right. I'm going to use the rest of the magic in the crystal. All I will be able to do is send you what you need to survive in the wilderness. You'll have to do the actual escaping. I imagine you'll be given a fair chance either at the trial or as they take you to sentencing."

Fear rose up in Zerrick again, threatening to cut off Alden, but he dug his fingernails into his palms and used the pain to concentrate on the words. Alden's voice grew fainter, *"Remember, all you need is a plant, cut flowers; anything to touch your skin so that you can break your bonds. I know you can do it. I have faith in you. But right now I need a distraction so I can work . . . my . . . magic . . ."* his voice faded away altogether and Zerrick opened his eyes. A distraction? Well, he would do his best.

He glanced quickly at Alden, and noted he was still in a trance. With a lurch, Zerrick grabbed the copper pot and began banging it against the iron bars, assuming his most snobbish pose. "Excuse me guards, excuse me!"

"Shut up, witch," one man snarled at him.

He continued to bang the pot. "I haven't been fed an adequate dinner and I never had lunch." He kept banging until they were almost at his cell, then he backed up as they brought out whips.

"Come here, little prig, and I'll take care of that hunger," the taller one jeered, cracking the whip through the bars. Zerrick thought he recognized the guy as Ned Smith, one of the bullies who used to throw him into the mud when he was little.

Zerrick flinched as the tip of Ned's whip flicked across his knee, but he only said, "Is that any way to treat an untried suspect? My father will probably acquit me, you know."

Both the men laughed. "Not likely! He'll send ya to Hell, disobeying him like that. Little ungrateful wart; you'll burn in the square," the second one said in an accent that marked him as the son of a fisherman.

As they were speaking, Zerrick began to notice a faint glimmer in the corner of his eye, slowly growing brighter. He hurried to keep attention to himself, saying, "You can't speak to me that way! If I had any components on me, I'd turn you both into insects!"

That got their attention--they tried to reach in and grab him, holding their whips ready, but Zerrick hobbled back to the wall, making little gestures in the air at them. A flash of light momentarily blinded him, and for a moment the two guards covered their eyes and stumbled, crying out in fear.

Zerrick blinked away the red spots dancing in his sight and saw a tiny miniature trunk resting on his pallet, no larger than a jewelry case. He dove to cover it with his body and risked a glance at Alden. Alden mouthed his name and pointed to where the trunk lay beneath Zerrick. He then mouthed another word that looked like "trigger." Zerrick peeked at the miniature and realized it was his own trunk, exact in every detail.

He nodded to show he understood. He would use Alden's name as the trigger word when he wanted to return his trunk to normal size. He pocketed it and stood, glaring at the guards who were slowly recovering from their fright.

"Get back, demon! Reverend Dhur gave us protection against you. You just wait for your execution," Ned said with a snarl, but he backed up as he spoke, retreating with the other guard back to the stairway. Zerrick didn't have to pretend his anger, though he did have to struggle to keep shadows of fear and exhaustion from crossing his face. Tired of standing with his bonds, he sat with his wrists on his knees, then leaned his hot forehead against the cold iron bars.

It was morning when he awoke, or so he assumed from the clatter of an empty plate by his head on the hard earthen floor. He stretched as well as he could, scratching at the red creases the ropes had left on his arms. The guard, a different one from last night, watched him silently as he contemplated the plate, then threw him a waterskin from which he quickly drank. He motioned for Zerrick to raise his wrists. Zerrick did so, and sighed in relief when the ropes were cut. His comfort was short-lived; there was no time to rub his chafed wrists before the guard clamped on iron shackles. He was kind enough to leave his feet unfettered.

"Time for your trial," he said, then led Zerrick up to the courthouse. Apparently Alden had gone before him, for his cell was empty.

Upstairs, Zerrick confirmed his suspicions as he heard the conclusion of Alden's trial. As they rounded the corner and came down the aisle, Zerrick saw Alden's form, slumped and shrunken. A hard lump of worry settled in his stomach. They were pronouncing maximum sentence, "In three days time, you will be put on display in the square, and there you shall be burned alive at the stake, as a warning to other evildoers." Judge Inister glared down at Alden from the bench. "I hope you suffer on your road to Judgment. Case closed."

The guards led Alden away and as Zerrick approached the stand, he tried to catch his gaze, impart to him all the emotions churning inside of him, but Alden kept his eyes lowered, almost as if in prayer. A deep crease cut between his brows, and the flesh around his mouth sagged, making him look ancient and sorrowful.

Zerrick fought against despair as he stood before the judge's bench, keeping his face rigidly composed as the captain of the guard read his charges. "Zerrick, son of Delwar Dhur, you are hereby charged with the willful heresy of practicing witchcraft in this town of Harrow, in the colony of Argessa, of the Holy Motherland Endersey under his Majesty, King Rannow IV. By the law of the land, you are allowed testimony and the calling forth of any witnesses there may be to dispute the charges laid against you. What say you? Have you any supporters?"

Zerrick looked around the courtroom, at the familiar faces of family and townspeople who were witnessing this, his final humiliation. His eyes locked for a second with Maureen's; there were tears in her eyes, but she quickly looked away when he tried to make contact with her. He then saw his brother, sister, and mother in the front row. His mother was wearing black, probably the first time she had worn that shade since the death of the old Lord Hennaker some ten years ago. His sister gazed at him with a look of sorrow, but that could simply have been her usual look of melancholy. His brother kept his head lowered. He too was all in black.

Zerrick turned back to Judge Inister. "I have no supporters, Your Honor. Nor do I have any statements to make. I made a confession--of sorts--to my brother Dellin with my mother in attendance. I stand on the statements I made then." His hands shook as he spoke, but he kept them firmly by his side and hoped the chains hid his trembling.

Inister called up the prosecutor, represented by the Reverend Dhur as it was a religious crime. Delwar demonstrated only too easily the proof of Zerrick's guilt, first with a testimony by Maisie Stonecraft who described seeing a man's shadow in an eerie green light at Alden's, then a farmer who saw Zerrick leave the house in stealth that same afternoon. Dellin spoke of his short confession, and when pressed by Delwar, admitted he had seen no remorse in Zerrick for his transgressions.

Delwar listened to Dellin's testimony, eyes watching Zerrick from beneath his dark brows, and it seemed to Zerrick that the veins of his flesh stood out, showing angry red beneath the surface of his seemingly placid features. Zerrick stood twisting his hands, which had grown ice cold as the hard metal cut off the flow of blood through his wrists. He began to shiver violently.

Finally, Dellin concluded his testimony. Delwar nodded to him and strode up to stand directly before Zerrick. "You say Alden gave you love and respect. How do corruption and the engendering of damnable sin constitute love? And you, who were raised with the truth, how can you equate utter degradation with respect? Have you listened to none of my sermons, my son?"

His voice carried such emotion. Zerrick wished he could let go of the past and let himself be enfolded in the arms of a loving father--but this father was not offering love, only a cold moral pity beneath a vain show. He breathed hard to make the hurt stay down. "I have listened to every word you said, Father," he said, his voice remarkably calm and steady, "And I have listened to Alden's views also. Between them, I choose his kind and gentle goddess over your cruel and unmerciful god. You have never led me to believe there is anything of worth in the Kingdom of Heaven. Therefore, I'll go to hell."

There was only the slightest change in his father's expression, a flaring of the nostrils, an almost imperceptible widening of the eyes, but his voice became cold and leaden. "So be it, then. As your soul is already lost to me, I shall recommend maximum sentence."

Zerrick took some satisfaction in hearing those words, thinking, *Now you are finally paying attention to me!* He told himself that the pain in his chest was merely his soul breaking free of the bonds that had held it so long in misery.

Judge Inister rose and sneered at Zerrick. "The choice is obvious, then. Concurrent with the burning of the witch Alden, there shall be a second burning of the witch Zerrick. Case closed."

The guards led him out of the courtroom, but before he had gone far, his brother came up, blocking his path. "You are a stubborn fool," he stated, "but I haven't given up yet. I'll petition Father and the judge to postpone your execution, convince them you can be saved. Come to reason! Renounce this ridiculous nonsense." He started as Delwar called to him, and left, giving Zerrick a hot look of reproach. Zerrick tried to follow his path with his eyes, but the guard shoved him onwards.

Strangely, Dellin's words calmed him, though of course he knew no appeal would be accepted, or even if it were, he would still leave them. He had failed his family, and they had failed him. Now there was only the image of a burning inferno of a witch's pyre towering in his mind--that must be avoided. In his pocket Zerrick felt the small, reassuring bulk of his trunk, a reminder of plans he must make to save not only himself, but Alden. He had little time.

The day of the burning seemed to pounce on him; in his cell there was no day or night; just endless, immeasurable time which flowed quickly, a river he could not stop with his hands. Still he was not sure what to do. They kept Alden in his cell gagged except for meals, carefully searched for even a scrap of material useful to him, and he remained almost constantly in trance, allowing no communication between them. It was maddening, how close they were, but Zerrick could not reach him, and suddenly the three days were up, and they were finishing their last meal. The patrol that would lead them to their execution stood just outside the cells, waiting.

Blinding sun and the heat of a crowd of sweaty bodies beat at Zerrick as he descended the steps from the courthouse, surrounded by patrolmen. Again as in the punishment of Vera Smith, the council had set up their table on the landing of the courthouse steps, and Judge Inister was presiding. Down the in the square was the makings of a huge bonfire, not yet lit, but waiting, grimly, with two poles jutting up through the center.

Alden walked just ahead of him with three guards monitoring his progress. Zerrick quickened his pace to catch up with him, and as they descended the last step and entered the narrow pathway cleared for them through the crowd, he managed to touch Alden's shoulder. He heard the jeers and shouts all around him, feel the sting of rotten greens hitting him in the back, but all he could think about was somehow communicating with Alden, just to say something, anything, before it was too late. Alden turned his head, just enough to make eye contact. He gave an encouraging nod, and then a guard came between them, blocking Zerrick's view.

It hit him then, finally--he was traveling through the crowd to what might be his death! And he hadn't yet figured out how he was going to escape, everything was happening too quickly; he couldn't think straight. In the back of his mind, he remembered wanting to shout out to Vera, "Fight them, resist!" Now his body suddenly refused to obey him. He walked through a swarm of catcalls and jeers, and he winced as a sharp rock glanced off his brow. More garbage was thrown at his back, clinging to his neck in wet little heaps.

Then he was clear of the people. Before him rose the pile of dead wood and thorny kindling. The guards started pulling him up the mound to one of the poles, but finally he began struggling, with strength born of panic.

"I don't want to die," he found himself saying as he shoved back against his captors. He wrapped his chains around one of the guard's necks but before he could make use of that the other one was grabbing his hands and wrenching him away. He hooked a foot behind that one's foot and tripped him, but that caused him to lose balance as well. He fell down in a heap at the base of the pile, entangled in thorny branches.

The guards yanked him to his feet, but as they dragged him up the pile again, Zerrick heard a shout from the crowd, "Halt!"

Dellin pushed his way through the crowd, holding high a piece of parchment with the Judge's seal. Wiping sweat from his forehead, he strode up to Zerrick and informed the crowd, "I have here a stay for the execution of Zerrick Dhur, convicted witch. I petitioned for the right to prove myself a true member of the long line of successful preachers in my family by attempting to save this, my brother's soul. I have been given one month to do so."

There were murmurs of admiration for Dellin as well as a few mutters of disappointment, but in general Zerrick saw the crowd was nonplussed as to what became of him. Now even his brother had turned from saving him for his own sake to saving him for a higher place in the Church. The whole thing disgusted him.

"We shall, of course, carry on with the execution of the wizard Alden," Dellin concluded, this time drawing cheers from the crowd. He went over to stand clear of the pile.

Zerrick allowed himself to be led over by the guards, but he kept watch on Alden who was secured to his post and making no moves to escape, even though he was now surrounded by wood. It was dead wood, but there was enough magic there to at least break his bonds. Zerrick felt a chill. Alden wasn't going to stand there and let them burn him, was he? There was nothing he could do at this point; it would be hard enough to arrange his own escape. Now he had a little time, hopefully.

Four more guards entered the cleared area around the pile, bearing brands of fire. Zerrick squinted against the glare of the noon sun to watch Alden's face. Even with the gag in place it was obvious he was in deep concentration. Good. Behind him, he heard his father making a last statement to Alden, condemning for his evil actions and influences. *He doesn't even hear you*, Zerrick thought with satisfaction. *He's about to escape.*

Delwar concluded his speech, "And so without malice, but with satisfaction and faith in our Lord's omnipotence, I send you to your final judgment. Proceed with the burning."

Zerrick glanced anxiously from brand bearer to Alden, hoping to see a sign, any sign. Everything stilled--the crowd hushed in anticipation, the guards standing nearby, silent and watchful, as the fiery torches were thrust into the depths of the pile. There was a crackling sound, a few puffs of smoke, then the tiny orange flames emerged from the tangle of thorns, growing steadily larger and brighter.

Within seconds, the lower half of the pile was in flames, but as the flames began licking up at Alden's feet, a glow began to spread from him; not the orange glow of the fire, but a pale lavender one, emanating from his skin, growing brighter and brighter until it blazed pure white. Within this glow, his body began to change form.

"He's spellcasting! Somebody stop him!" Dellin shouted, rushing to the base of the pyre.

The crowd shifted nervously and began backing away in a confused mass. Alden's body shrank, becoming avian in shape as white feathers burst from his skin. The guards circled the burning pyre, wavering, but Dellin strode up to one and grabbed his flintlock pistol. "Shoot it! He's changing form to escape!"

"Alden!" Zerrick shouted, watching in horror as Dellin, unused to firearms, struggled to cock the trigger.

Searching frantically for some way to break free, Zerrick felt around, and found half a head of wilted lettuce--some of the garbage that had been thrown at him. He plunged his senses into the realm of magic and demanded, *"Free me!"*

There was a wrenching inside him, as if his insides had been pulled two different directions at once, then the metal broke apart, smoking with the violence of the magic pushed into them. Zerrick grabbed the chains and swung them into the face of his guards, dodging between them to grab Dellin. He took a second to glance up. The flames were growing fiercer, but Alden's transformation was nearly complete. He had become a large albatross.

Dellin fought with him for the pistol, wrenching his arms backwards as Zerrick tightened his grip. With a shove, Zerrick knocked Dellin to the ground and held aloft the pistol.

"You can't get him now," he said, exultant, but even as he spoke he heard the explosion of a gun being fired. The bird, which had been spreading its wings to fly, screeched and fell back down into the fire with a horrible crunch, the white of its wings quickly turning black with smoke and flame. Beyond the burning pyre, a guard smiled with satisfaction, holding his smoking flintlock.

Zerrick cried out, dropping the pistol, but now the guards were stalking him as his brother rose to his feet.

He watched in anguish as flames began to consume Alden's form, which had changed back as the spell was interrupted, and the stench of burning flesh assailed his nostrils. Dellin grabbed him, but he slithered free and started running into the panicking crowd. Tears blinded him as he started fighting his way through the people.

Several of the local fishermen grabbed him, and he turned to them and howled with all his rage and loss, "Leave me alone!" He felt a spark of magic somewhere, traveling through him, and suddenly the men were running away from him, screaming.

He whirled, and the people before him also cried out in terror; clambering over one another to get away from him. He felt his face to see if there had been any change. His features felt normal.

He stood trying to collect his wits, but Dellin was gathering the people again as Delwar came down to help him. Delwar's voice washed over the crowd, "It's an illusion, only an illusion meant to frighten us. Don't be fooled! He cannot hurt you--he is weak, and Iahmel is strong. Get him!"

Zerrick began running again, this time for the back of the courthouse and the main road out of town. His fear lent fire to his muscles as he heard the townspeople following behind. The light from the bonfire threw shadows along the walls ahead of him, keeping pace with him.

He caught sight of the town gates closing, rusty iron hinges groaning as the watchmen pulled the ropes to shut them. He managed to squeeze his body through as the heavy doors closed with a thud. Ahead of him were the fields, then the jungle. Freedom.

"Through the side door, quickly!" he heard Dellin cry, and knew he had only a few minutes head start. He ran, sucking in great gulps of air as he forced his legs to keep moving. A slave out in the field glanced curiously at him before the slavemaster forced him back to work. Only a hundred yards or so lay between him and the edge of the jungle now.

He heard a shot behind him and something whizzed by his ear his as his heart clenched in fear. He reached the cover of the first trees and began clambering through the thick foliage, keeping low, afraid that any second another bullet would find its mark.

He leapt over mossy logs and ducked through ferns sprinkled with dew, keeping low to the ground in an effort to lose his pursuers. For several minutes he made his way through the jungle, trying to put as much distance between himself and the town as possible, but it was hard; here at the edge the growth was thick and tangled, impossible to run through. Just as he reached the riverbank a rotting carpet of herbs and fungi gave way under his feet. He slid into a muddy ditch, cursing as a rustling in the brush behind him warned him that his pursuers had nearly caught up. Looking around, Zerrick spotted an overhang of earth and roots under one of the mangrove trees. On his belly he crawled below the thick underbrush through the mud, then slid between the roots into the shadows beneath.

Something splashed through the water behind him. A moment later, he spotted Dellin and Marvis Inister standing on the bank of the river above the mudflats, only a few feet from where he had slipped. He held his breath as they scanned the river and more searchers gathered around them. Zerrick heard his heartbeat thudding in his ears. There was a small plop from the roots above him, and something wet landed on his leg. A leech, probably, but he couldn't worry about that; Dellin was staring right at his hiding place.

The others left to continue the search, but Dellin stayed, one foot resting on the root of a tree as he leaned forward to peer into the sunlit riverbed. Zerrick felt his brother's eyes trying to pierce the shadows, trying to find some trace of him, but a familiar voice called Dellin away. Delwar had arrived.

"Any sign of him?" Delwar's deep voice made Zerrick's hair stand on end. He wriggled deeper into the shadows.

"I think he's along the river--there are fewer obstacles there, and the water can wipe out his tracks. Or he may be hiding. There's certainly places enough for that."

Zerrick held his breath as both his brother and father came back into view, standing on another outcropping and earth less than twenty feet from him.

Dellin continued, "We can keep searching, but the townspeople refuse to go much deeper into the jungle."

"Yes, that's wise. There is too much evil out here," Delwar said, flinching as he pricked his hand on a thorny vine, "Well, no matter what dark help he has, I don't think Zerrick can survive long in the jungle. We'll keep a watch for him. I also think it advisable to continue studying Alden's home."

"What have you found there so far?"

Delwar pulled from his pocket a small book bound in red, with one of Alden's faded green ribbons holding a place. "A book of pure evil. It is a study made by Alden during his travels, in particular, detailed descriptions of tribal devil worship and cults dedicated to beasts. There is even a glossary in back where you can find Angist's name in each culture. I can only assume it is filth like this he was using to corrupt Zerrick." He returned the book to his pocket, wiping his hands on a handkerchief.

The two of them were silent a moment. Zerrick was fuming. Was this a trick, merely to turn his loyalty from Alden, or was it real? Why would Alden make such references? Accounts of tribal ways . . . that sounded like him. Zerrick wished he could see the book himself--was Angist's name really written down? Or was this his father's interpretations again?

He was given no more time to think things over, however. Delwar and Dellin started walking towards him, and from their position they would soon be able to see his skid marks. He had to get out of here.

The slow moving river was only a few feet from his hiding spot, but it was a muddy area without cover. The tide affected the river here and it was low, so the river was shallow and parched, easier to swim, but he would be seen crossing over to it. He could try instead to climb back up the ridge, but that would mean traveling through territory being actively searched by the townspeople.

Suddenly there was no more time to plan. With a shout, Dellin pointed out the mossy area broken up by his fall, and the two of them clambered down the ridge and started towards Zerrick's tree, shoving ferns and young palms out of their way.

He panicked, scrambling out of the roots and throwing himself into the deep wide river. He wasn't a great swimmer, but he'd rather take his chances with the river than his father.

He swam with all his might, certain that he'd soon have his ankles grabbed from behind by his father's strong hands, but while their angry shouts echoed in his ears, he heard no splashes behind him. He paused, fighting to stay afloat in the slow but strong current, and saw Delwar standing at the water's edge, fists clenched in fury.

"Stop this foolishness at once!" Delwar shouted, and for a second the sheer will behind that voice made Zerrick pause. A small wave splashed his face; he coughed and sputtered, then kicked harder to stay afloat. He wasn't going to listen this time.

"You will be hunted like an animal," Dellin warned, but his voice did not nearly match Delwar's in strength or conviction.

His warning did make Zerrick glance around. Hunted like an animal, by other animals. He hoped there weren't any crocodiles nearby. His leg brushed something--a fish, maybe--and he jumped. A little further now and he'd be around the bend, out of sight. After that he could go back to the jungle and circle around the town, towards the west. That way lay the untracked wilderness.

Then, out of the corner of his eye, he spotted a long, black ribbon slicing through the water, moving in a swift silent course towards him. It was a python, he realized, nearly twelve feet long, with glassy eyes and a small black tongue, sniffing the air as it swam.

No time to get around the bend now--with new fear to spur him, Zerrick kicked and shoved at the water, scrambling to get to the riverbank where he could outrun the snake. As his feet hit the bottom, the head of the snake disappeared underwater, only a few feet away from him. He stumbled and crawled through the muddy, shallow waters, feeling something slick and scaly touch his ankle as he clambered onto the shore.

He immediately sank to his knees in the reddish mud, but he managed to grab hold of a palm frond and pulled himself onto the bank covered in roots and vines. As he struggled to stand on the leafy embankment, the snake's head rose for a second, contemplating him,. Then it dipped its head under and swam away.

Zerrick leaned against a palm tree, wringing mud from his hair and pulling off a few stubborn leeches from his legs. From somewhere in the green tangle he heard the sound of his pursuers, not so close now, yet still too near. He set off again. As he ducked under a thicket of twisting vines, he heard his brother frantically calling his name back towards what must be the river's edge. So they'd seen the snake, apparently. Or they thought he'd panicked and run.

Either way, they knew the direction he'd gone. He contemplated hiding in the vines, then shook his head. He wasn't going through that again. Peering through the dense foliage, he measured a pathway of least resistance heading in the right direction. He wished he had the time to retrieve his knife from the trunk in his pocket, but perhaps it was better this way. He would leave less of a trail. As he thought about it, he realized he'd be better off doing as wild things did, scrambling hand and foot over root and vine.

Shouts sounded somewhere nearby; Zerrick ducked under a group of sapling cypresses, running quickly in the low clearing beneath their canopies, letting the shadows they cast cool the exertion from his skin. His path led him through a tangle of thorny blooming vines, over a dense mound of dead and rotting mangroves, and then into an area of more mature cypresses where the ground was half swamp. Once through that, the shouts were more distant, but he did not let up his pace, hiking into the afternoon, doubling back a few times to confuse any trackers who followed him this far. He climbed up a small ridge of lichen-covered rocks and skirted around a muddy pool, satisfied to hear the shouts fade away. As he walked, the sun's rays slanting through the treetops began growing fainter and redder. Sunset was coming, and with night the search would be called off. He'd be free.

As he traveled farther from the river, the ground became somewhat clearer, full of broad-leafed plants and herbs struggling in what patches of sunlight that managed to hit the forest floor. Shadows here were darker, and Zerrick had to watch his step for the moss and mushroom forest beneath his feet. Vines were even more numerous, growing along the trunks of impossibly high trees, hanging like green twisted robes from their limbs. Far above him he could hear the living things of the forest--a constant chatter of monkeys, flying foxes, and birds. He could no longer hear any sound of humans, not even the church bell which must be ringing out the hour.

The last gleams of sunlight fled, and a light shower began to fall, pattering against the leaves above him to fall in fat drops into little pools among the rocks. Zerrick sighed, sitting down on a rock next to a tree trunk speckled with orchids, reveling in the peaceful evening, far from angry looks or harsh words. Above him, the cries of birds were quieting down, as the day creatures settled into their homes and the silent predators gained rule of the sky. A flock of something dark flew past--bats, he realized, hearing their high-pitched squeaks. He felt alive, a part of the wonder around him.

And the magic! Never had he felt such richness, a low humming of earthly power all around him, singing in the air, rumbling in the rocks beneath him. He breathed in the scents of moss and wet leaves, imagining that pure essence pouring into him, a sizzling energy of life. He wished he could sit here contemplating it all night.

But now he needed rest. Night had fallen, and it was completely dark, the stars and moon blocked out by the trees. The rain still fell, but it was only a light drizzle, more of a mist, sending trickles of moisture down his face and body. His limbs shook with fatigue.

It wouldn't do to stumble around in the dark. Setting down the tiny trunk a few feet away from him, he said in a clear voice which sounded much too loud in the darkness, "Alden."

The trunk began to glow faintly, and as he watched, it grew quickly, scraping against the rock he was sitting on as it became life-sized. The glow faded, and there was a click as the lock opened.

Zerrick opened the trunk and began feeling through the clutter inside, all the more blind after that faint flare of magic. He found something glass wrapped in cloth--his lantern, he realized. He drew out the little drawer where the starter kit was located, then pulled out a bag of candles from the trunk. It took a few moments to light it in the dampness, but his determination eventually paid off. As the spark settled into a warm glow, he hung the lantern from a hanging tendril of vine and returned his attention to the trunk.

He started sorting through things, taking a general inventory: clothes, blanket, sword, water, food . . . some of this he ate, realizing how hungry he was. Then he reached down into the bottom and found items he'd never seen before. One was a leather backpack. He would need that, because it was beyond his skill to do as Alden had done, shrinking the chest. A shame, but he'd have to leave the chest behind.

The backpack was old and faded and smelled of oils which made it waterproof. Zerrick turned it over in his hands and discovered a mark burned into the leather. It looked tribal, and he realized he had seen it somewhere before, on some of the objects Alden had collected. This must have been his when he traveled through these parts. He hugged it close, waiting for the tears to come, but they only stuck in his throat. He still couldn't believe Alden was dead.

Next he brought out a small axe for chopping wood and a long machete, obviously well used. He continued to bring out things: rope, a pistol and horn of gunpowder, a pouch full of lead balls, and two pouches filled with bandages and herbal remedies. Last there was a braided leather necklace with a little pouch decorated with tiny quartz crystals. Again, blazed on both sides of the pouch he found that strange symbol, something of a triangle within a triangle with a stylized pair of trees.

With reverence and a heavy heart, Zerrick put on the necklace, crying freely now. The pouch was more ornamental than useful--all it contained inside was a faded drawing of Alden's wife, a primer with a few prayers, and a large oval-shaped piece of polished amber.

After packing his things, Zerrick doused the lamp. He eased himself into a bed of vines, one hand resting lightly on the worn hilt of Alden's machete. The other hand softly stroked the odd necklace.

Chapter Six

"Go ye out into the wilderness, but beware ye the shadows of the soul."
--Kazimir 98:12

Zerrick was back beside that circle of mountains, a band of shadowy purple rising towards the sky, beckoning him. That woman was still there, waiting for him, her soft voice singing to him, like a mother humming a lullaby. He needed to reach her; she was pulling him across plains of brush to the circle of mountains. He followed a narrow winding riverbed to its source in the mountains, always walking, never resting. The sun blazed overhead like a ball of fire . . . fire . . .

Yes, there it burned, as before, the bonfire, blocking his way into the mountains, burning fierce and strong, ravenous. He glanced around, but there was no one around this time to push him in, no humans anywhere. He was lost in the wilderness.

A low rumble sounded off somewhere nearby, setting his teeth on edge, causing a shiver to slide down his neck. The rumble became a growl, and a sharp-toothed, canine beast emerged from the brush by the river, eyes glowing red with the reflections of the fire. It snarled, curling its lip and revealing a mouth full of jagged fangs.

Zerrick backed away, but the heat of the flames beat at his back. He couldn't possibly go through, not again! He considered dodging but the beast made a leap towards him on powerful, rabbit-like haunches. It snapped at his foot, causing him to stumble back, into the flames. Then the beast rose up on its hind feet, like a man, and with its breath hot in his face, placed its paws on his chest to shove him into the heart of the fire which would consume him utterly . . .

A snorting grunt right next to his ear woke Zerrick with a start. For one wild moment he thought it was the beast in his dreams; all he could see was a great snout with two yellow tusks, then he heard the animal grunt again. He lifted his head slowly, watching the wild pig as it burrowed into the earth with its snout, looking for tubers. It didn't seem concerned with him, so he slowly got up, hanging up his pack on a nearby vine. He hoped it hadn't raided his food supply.

His back ached with fatigue and from lying on vines. Zerrick stretched, scratching at a few mosquito bites. He had no idea how late he'd slept. It was still dark and shadowy under the green ceiling, but patches of sun shone through, hitting little beds of fern and palm plants. After moving out of the way of the pig, he retrieved his things and went over to a sunny spot to eat breakfast.

From his vantage point he could see that the ground sloped upwards back the way he had come, and recalled there being a relatively good sized hill a few miles out of town; this was probably the base of it. He could climb that, hopefully find a clearing, and be able to determine his location and direction to travel. He wished he had a better idea of where to find Alden's friendly tribe. He wondered, after his father's words about devil worship, if he should even try to find them. Probably the best thing right now would be to head for Depin. Even if it was too dangerous to stay there, he could use the town to stock up on supplies. What he had now would last maybe two weeks.

Finishing breakfast, he packed up, took out the machete, and began climbing the hill. It was both rocky and slippery with moss and lichens, and far harder work than he'd imagined. He kept his eyes to the ground and his immediate area; the constant movement of swaying leaves and the endless chatter and rustling of birds and other creatures dizzied the senses. After climbing a particularly steep bluff, he stumbled over to a small creek splashing down the hillside and bent to take a drink. When he looked up, he could see clear sky and an incredible view of the valley below.

For the first time he could see where the sun was and see a narrow strip of the jungle below, stretching on for endless miles. He stood at the edge of an enormous valley which stretched as far as Depin, broken only by small hills and many rivers flowing to the sea. He squinted, trying to see the mountains which supposedly cut off

Depin from any expansion further west, but the air was still thick with morning mist. At least he now had some sense of where he was heading.

He descended the hill, moving away from the sun, letting the canopy become his sky once more. He kept his ears open for any sounds of his pursuers, but he heard only the cackle of birds and the rustling of leaves. He thought he heard a harsh human laugh once, but it was only a large brown and white bird.

Zerrick stopped by a stream for lunch, rubbing herbs on his hands which were beginning to blister from chopping so many vines and branches. His boots were covered with mud, and the toes were already stained green. He took them off to let them dry in a patch of sun, and bent to wash himself, keeping watch for snakes and parasites.

He was pulling on his boots, ready to tackle more underbrush, when he caught movement of the corner of his eye. Slowly turning his head, he caught sight of a very unusual creature.

It was crouched down to drink, but it had spotted him and was carefully watching him as its long tongue lapped at the water. Its head and neck were that of a deer, but the rest of the body resembled that of a gigantic rabbit, with powerful thrusting hindquarters. The oddest thing about it, however, was that while it appeared to be a mammal, with a white furry underside, the back of it was covered in feathers, mottled brown except near its head where it became a pale salmon pink. It had wings, also brown but with a brighter salmon underside.

Zerrick watched, amazed, as it decided he was no threat and began eating the leaves off a small sapling growing by the creek. He could see it had a tail like a rat, but adorned with feathers, especially where it joined to the animal.

He understood such a creature was not possible in nature. Alden had read to him books by famous naturalists from the Motherland who discussed the impossibility of mixing two creatures of different elements, such as a water creature like a fish and a land one like man. Birds and land animals weren't supposed to be mixable, either.

That meant this must be a remnant of one of the first creatures transformed by the unorganized Light--a magical beast! Such creatures were said to possess powers. It was an herbivore, obviously. Hopefully that meant it wasn't harmful to man.

The creature stretched out its wings a little, and then hopped a little closer to Zerrick to munch on a bed of tall grass in a little patch of sun. Zerrick gulped; those wings had to be eight or ten feet across, and very powerful to lift such an apparently ungainly creature. He sat and watched it a few more minutes, then decided he had best be moving on. As he stood up, however, the beast suddenly turned in fright, eyes widening. It stretched out its long neck towards him, gave a flap of its great wings, and blew at him.

He could sense the magic even as it engulfed him in a glittery cloud. Then his eyes were closing and the world tumbled down around him. He hit the ground with a thud and knew no more.

When he awoke, the creature was gone. He looked around groggily, but he was alone, his things lying where he'd left them. How long had he been asleep? Five minutes, ten? It was impossible to tell. He was lucky he was still alive--that spell had been a powerful one, and in a jungle with so many dangerous creatures, well, he was thankful he hadn't woke up in the coils of a hungry boa constrictor.

He gathered his things and set off again, telling himself if he saw any more flying deer-rabbits, he'd stay well away from them. The rest of the day went by smoothly, except for a near miss with a poisonous lizard which spat venom at him while he clambered over a dead tree. His tough boots saved him. Then later, a swarm of strange glowing beetles had dived at him, and he'd been forced to hide behind the wide fronds of a young palm tree. Their bites had been magical--at first he'd had the impulse to run screaming, but when he realized the fear wasn't really his own, he'd been able to lessen the effect with a little magic of his own. He still jumped at shadows a little, but the bites seemed to be healing, especially with the help of Alden's herbs.

He found shelter for the night in a hollow created by a strangler fig. Lying on a bed of leaves, wrapped in his blanket, he wondered about these magical beasts he was encountering.

In the Motherland there were legends of magical creatures but they were all old stories. No one had reported finding a griffin or a dragon in over a century. Were they all gone, destroyed by man? Or had they merely fled somewhere, perhaps here? After all, the witches were also here, and there seemed to be an amazing abundance of magic in this land. Was it the untamed wilderness? Or something deeper?

He had no answers. All he knew was that he wished Alden were still here, so that he could tell him what he had seen today and get his views. He had thought he knew the jungle, understood at least the basics of magic, but now he saw that he had only touched on the fringes of both. He didn't even know how far to trust anyone's say on things, especially after hearing about that demon book of Alden's.

As dark fell and the sounds of night creatures hummed and sang on every side, he clung tighter to his blanket, concentrating on its hand-woven threads. Where on the outskirts of the wild the magic had sung to him alluringly, now it hummed all around him in an almost deafening buzz. The magic seemed to beat at his back through the bark of the tree, pulsating to the beat of his heart, trying to draw him into its chaotic state of nature.

If he succumbed, he would become a beast; this he knew instinctively. It would control him, just as Alden said, and he would lose himself. Fighting such notions, he wrapped the blanket all around him, and closed his eyes. He sought for images in his past of human faces, soft warm beds, and a motherly figure tucking him in.

The next three days were much of the same. He pushed groaning muscles, climbing through beds of tangled plants, over rocks and tree roots. Cleanliness was a fond memory; he was always covered in sweat, mud, leaves or spores from the ferns and mushrooms. He had more insect bites than he cared to count. And his hands! He'd done work with them before, cutting wood, climbing trees, but never this much. He had calluses on top of calluses, and they bled until he had to bandage them up entirely.

He still had a fair amount of food, though a monkey had run off with some of it. And he had avoided some potentially dangerous encounters, including one with a large spotted hunting cat of some kind, and another with a strange bird-like creature who could imitate human voices. That one had been a little close--he had almost stepped right into its nest. It chased him nearly a mile. Still, he was pretty certain he was heading in the right direction. He ran across more and more streams which ran southwards, towards the Lyndel River, the main conduit which supported almost all the towns except Harrow.

Of course, he couldn't be sure. He had not run into any sizable hills, and even when the ground did rise for a bit, the impossibly high trees cut out all knowledge of the landscape. He was always trapped into a small dense world of living things. In fact, he wouldn't have been sure he wasn't walking in circles, except he was familiar with the river system, and the stars.

Four days had passed since he'd escaped Harrow, and by his calculations, in two or three days he should reach Depin. He rebandaged his hands, rubbing them with the sap of a medicinal tree, and shook out his blanket. It had rained heavily last night, and even under the palms where he'd slept, he'd still gotten pretty wet.

He used his machete as little as possible, choosing instead to climb through thickets. The blade was growing dull; one of the things he would need in town would be a whetstone. But it was a relatively cool morning and he felt certain he could make good time today, if he could just avoid any unnecessary encounters.

Zerrick stepped carefully over the roots of a tree covered in orchids, trying not to disturb a cloud of small yellow butterflies, then waded his way through a small pond, disrupting a few frogs. It was quieter today--not as much chatter from the treetops. He wondered if another storm was brewing.

He'd been traveling about two hours when up ahead he found a bright light filtering through the trees in a brilliant yellow green. He moved cautiously at first, dreading another encounter with those glowing beetles, but it soon became obvious what he was looking at was not insects or glowing creatures. It was a clearing of considerable size.

Had he made it to the Lyndel River already? He hurried down a net of connecting vines, finding a gully which was the clearest route to the painfully bright clearing. He wondered how long it had been since true sunlight had fallen on him--he could almost touch the beams as he passed through the last trees. Then he entered the clearing and drowned himself in sunlight.

The clearing was thick with life: herbs growing rampantly, grasses, tree ferns, low palm plants and saplings and flowers of every kind in bloom. Butterflies and other insects flew lazily through the air while a number of brightly plumaged birds flitted from plant to plant, looking for fruit, seeds and nectar. Zerrick noticed the lack of trees, and wondered if this was perhaps tribal land or a failed attempt at land clearing by the settlers. He saw no river, nor sign of any habitation, but as he lifted up a plant to look for signs of humans, he saw that the earth was blackened. A great fire had created this clearing.

But what of the trees, Zerrick wondered. Surely they could outlast a fire--and when had this fire occurred? There were dry seasons, certainly, but even then it rained every few days. How could anything have been dry enough to burn completely away?

He studied the shape of the clearing carefully. It was rounded but narrower at one end. As he searched the ground there he found arrow tips, the kind made by his people, bent as if they had struck something, lying scattered on the ground, almost buried by new plant life. They hadn't rusted away completely, meaning the encounter had been fairly recent--a year, maybe.

Perhaps there had been a failed attempt at lumbering here, then, or a permanent camp of some kind. There had obviously been a conflict. So where were they now?

Zerrick continued to search, but plants had covered up and broken down all other signs. Then he found one muddy patch where recent rains had washed away the moss and seedlings. Imprinted into the dark mud were human footprints in the outline made by a boot. These were fresh.

Zerrick bent closer to study the prints when a low vibration began to tickle at the base of his spine. A smell of musk assailed his nostrils. He raised his head, listening. The low growl was repeated, louder this time. Standing up very slowly, he searched the clearing and the shadows beyond, trying to peer into the darkness with eyes now blinded by sun.

A long snout emerged from the shadows, behind which he could see red glowing eyes. It snarled again, and he gasped at the length of its teeth. It couldn't be, he thought. Not the beast from his dream!

It lunged at him before he could complete the thought. He ducked and rolled, feeling its sharp claws tearing at his clothes. Its hot breath whistled in his ear, and he expected to feel those teeth closing around his neck, when suddenly it yelped and backed away.

He rose to his feet in the center of the clearing, panting and shaking. Something glowed pale blue--he looked down and saw it was Alden's sign on his neck pouch. Then it faded, and he wondered if he was hallucinating. The beast's growl brought his attention back to it.

He could see it clearly now. It was wolf-like with a dark green tint to its shaggy fur, and extremely large, especially its hind legs. The musky smell was stronger now that it was out in the sun. It swished its tail, and he flinched in horror. Its tail wasn't a tail, it was a snake, attached where a tail should be, but with a life of its own and a wide gaping mouth showing venomous fangs. The snake-tail writhed along the wolf's back, hissing at Zerrick as the wolf creature studied him, its pupils narrowing to pin points in the bright sun.

"Are we lost, little white man?"

Zerrick gaped as it spoke to him in a clear, gravelly voice. Its lips had moved--it was really speaking!

The wolf creature paced a little back and forth, its 'tail' always squirming in Zerrick's direction, trying to get at him. "What, monkey steal your tongue, succulent man? You surprised I speak your language?"

"Yes," Zerrick breathed, feeling very much like the mouse caught by a playful cat. "What are you? How can you speak?"

"Magic," it said, curling its lips over its sharp canine teeth, "I am called by the locals *Ashwa-grippa,* the 'death-of-two-evils'. You can call me Death. I have come for you."

It lunged, but Zerrick was ready for him. He kicked at its nose and when he heard it groan in pain, he turned and ran for the trees. As he ran, he fumbled to bring out his pistol, praying he had thought ahead and loaded it. He caught sight of a good tree to climb as the beast's jaws snapped at his leg, just missing him.

Then he stepped in something--rope--and the world was suddenly lurching out from under him as the rope tightened and sent him flying. He found himself hanging upside down by his ankle, swaying precariously. Tilting his head back to look at the ground, he could see the wolf creature a good ten feet below him, laughing at him, its yellow eyes gleaming. The laugh sounded horrible--evil and all too human, coming from the throat of this creature. It crouched down, ready to spring for his unprotected neck. Zerrick flailed uselessly, and closed his eyes to die.

The blow never came. He heard a yelp of pain and opened his eyes, just catching the flare of something orange shooting through the jungle, striking the beast. It whirled, eyes searching, but two more bolts, this time blue, came a different point and struck it in the chest. Howling in fury, it bounded off.

There was silence a moment after the Ashwa-grippa fled, allowing just enough time for Zerrick to come up with some truly terrible images of what could have shot those bolts. Then several humans emerged from the brush, led by what was obviously a witch.

"Cut him down," the witch ordered, and Zerrick could see he was young; no more than five years his elder, with dull brown hair, deep green eyes, and a very thin, wiry body clothed in mottled green robes. He stood legs apart, fists on his hips, and sneered as the other men lowered Zerrick down and cut him loose.

As soon as Zerrick was free of the snare, several men grabbed his arms, and another took his pistol and sword. The men were dressed in mismatched clothing and a few odd bits of jewelry, and were all fully armed with axes, swords, scimitars and guns. They looked none too friendly.

The witch strode up to him, swaggering, and studied his sword and pistol. "Good weapons, there. And your clothes! Nicely tailored, good cloth. What are you, the runaway brat of some rich merchant?" He stuffed Zerrick's pistol in his belt and pulled the sword out it its scabbard, casually pointing it at Zerrick.

"I'm an outlaw. I practice witchcraft," Zerrick snapped, wishing he could reach the low branch of a nearby sapling, use its power to flee this place. He was beginning to suspect he knew who these ruffians were.

The witch laughed heartily, "Oh-ho! Do you now? Beware boys; we've got a young sorcerer on our hands! What, can you mutilate a small fly? Set a cat's tail on fire? Look out men; we'd better let this one go!" He doubled over with laughter, and soon some of the men joined in, chuckling as they poked and prodded Zerrick. He wondered if he'd fallen in with an entire band of witches, but dismissed the idea. It was possible all those bolts could have come from one witch, if he was powerful.

The witch sobered and raised Zerrick's sword at him again, pointing right at his Adam's apple. "So you're an outlaw. This means there's no ransom for you, I take it?"

Zerrick wished he'd been caught bootless, or at least shirtless. The ground was covered in green life, but he couldn't reach it through the thick, dead leather of his high boots. If only a breeze would knock a branch within touch of his skin! "I don't know, really," he answered, stalling for time. "They do want me pretty bad. They were about to burn me when I escaped."

"So, there might be a reward for your return, eh? Dead or alive?"

"Alive, definitely. It's my father who wants to burn me. Personally." Out of the corner of his eye, Zerrick watched a low branch of a sapling as it swayed, coming within inches of his pinned arm. He pushed his weight against his captors, hoping to get closer.

"Oh lovely. We'll keep you alive at least for a while. But only if you behave," the witch said with emphasis, and snatched away the branch Zerrick had been about to grasp.

He held the branch a moment, contemplating Zerrick. The skin around his left nostril twitched once, perhaps in amusement. Then he shrugged and let the branch swing free. "Let him touch it," he ordered the men holding Zerrick, "I want to see what he'll do."

The men loosened their hold. As he reached for the branch, Zerrick searched frantically for the trick which would free him. Illusion? Too easy to see through, especially for the witch. Fire? Too wet. He realized he didn't have the power to affect everyone. Perhaps if he could distract the leader, however . . . He grabbed hold of the sapling branch and concentrated hard, using his fear as a focus. He pictured long hairy legs and venomous teeth, then pulled forth the magic.

The power surging into Zerrick nearly overwhelmed him--he had never tried to pull from this large a plant in this natural a setting. His gut began to twist uncomfortably; a funny feeling washed over him and his teeth began to ache, as if they were growing. His eyes flared open as he realized with horror he was the one becoming the spider! He grappled with the magic running wild, demanded that it go away, sink back into the earth--this wasn't what he wanted of it!

He had only meant to conjure a small venomous spider, not become one! But the magic fought his control, surging violently through him, nearly causing him to black out. He screamed in his mind for it to leave. It finally did so, slowly, leaving him weak and drained.

The dizziness left, but he could still feel his new teeth poking at his lips. Well, it wasn't what he had planned, but it could work. He lunged for the hand of one of the men holding him, opening his mouth to test his new teeth.

"Hold him," the witch ordered, and Zerrick suddenly felt a strange new magic, not flowing within him to respond to his desires, but an intrusion from outside, controlled by another's will. He felt the mind of the other witch in this counter spell, trying to undo his magic. It was a horrible feeling, like a thief's hot breath on his neck, or being doused with tainted water. He had no defense against it, and with a wrenching pain he felt his teeth rapidly shrinking back to normal. He felt his knees grow weak and would have fallen if not for the guards. Then the taint faded away. Zerrick blinked with the aftershock of the experience, wondering if this was how the blacksmith had felt when he was inside his mind. Horrible magic!

"About as I thought," the witch announced, motioning for the men to tie Zerrick up. "You show promise, little witch, but you're hardly a threat with that ghastly control. I still favor selling you for ransom, but we'll have to see what Clint and Madame Lotus decides."

He strolled around Zerrick like a vulture contemplating a kill, and ran a long white hand along Zerrick's jaw. Zerrick flinched as he felt that tainted magic again, but he was too weak to resist.

"I suppose introductions are necessary. I am called Murtis the Crow. Your dashing and quick-fingered captors are Brute and Scissorfists. And you are now property of the Stonefist Gang."

Zerrick felt his stomach drop to his boots and realized just in what kind of trouble he had landed in. The Stonefist Gang--the most notorious bandits roaming the wild. The group Alden had badmouthed so much because of its powerful renegade witches.

"All right, now it's your turn. What's your name?" Murtis the Crow asked, grinning.

Zerrick saw no reason to lie; they would know the truth soon enough if they tried to ransom him, "It's Zerrick. Zerrick Dhur."

Avid interest flashed across Murtis's face. "Not the Dhurs of Telrick Dhur, provincial curate?" he challenged, his thin lips curling into a smile.

"He's my grandfather," Zerrick admitted unhappily. Alden was right. His family was well known.

Murtis clapped his knee. "Oh perfect!" he exclaimed, laughing. "A fallen Melite! Oh, Madame Lotus will love you."

"Who is Madame Lotus?" Zerrick asked, knowing he'd hate the answer.

"My teacher," Murtis said, pulling out Zerrick's gun again. "And a perfect example of what happens to witches like you who lack control. She's absolutely, completely insane."

He made sure the pistol was uncocked, then strode up to Zerrick. "Now, enough talking. I have to take you to camp. Much as I'd love hearing about your crimes and sorrows, I can't have you annoying me with amateur attempts at escape. Therefore, good night."

And with that, he slammed the butt of Zerrick's pistol into the back of his head. Zerrick's eyes flew up to the swirling green canopy above, then he plunged into darkness.

Chapter Seven

"And in the City of Sin, surrounded by dark mist and the cries of lunatics and fornicators, Ja'hal cried out, 'Leave me not, my God, for I fear! I fear!"
-- Dersonial 46:18

Zerrick woke when he realized something hard was boring into the middle of his back. It was night. He shook his head to clear the pain at the base of his skull, but when he tried to feel around for his bag for a sip of water, he found his hands tied behind him, while a length of rope secured his foot to the root of an ancient ironwood tree. His things were gone. By the light of a small fire, he caught sight of the shadowy forms of his captors. The smell of roasting meat gnawed at his insides, and he swallowed hard, realizing how famished he was.

A shadow detached itself from the glow of the flames, and came to stand beside him. In the light hitting the sharp cheekbones and cruel slit of a mouth, Zerrick saw it was Murtis the Crow.

"Are we there yet?" Zerrick asked to break the fellow's disconcerting gaze. He had meant to sound brave, unconcerned, despite the awful truth of his capture. Instead, his voice cracked.

"Patience, my friend. We have stopped for the night, but we should reach the camp tomorrow midday. Hungry after your little trip?" Murtis's white teeth glinted in the firelight as he spoke, then he tossed a piece of meat and bread at Zerrick. The bread landed between his legs, the meat in his lap. He struggled to reach for them.

"Oh, I forgot, you're a little tied up. Oh well, guess you'll have to starve," Murtis said, clearly taking enjoyment in his power over Zerrick. He turned to leave.

"Wait! I need water, please," Zerrick cried, trying to twist sideways to get his hand near the meat. He wondered if ants were active at night.

"Please? Are we begging? Or just being polite?" Murtis turned and stood over Zerrick, arms crossed, a smug leer on his face. "All right, can't have you wasting away completely," he said, and pulled out a water bottle, tipping it over Zerrick's mouth so he had to swallow quickly or drown.

Murtis then took the meat and shoved it into Zerrick's mouth. "Here, eat quickly, so I don't have to watch you too long. I need you walking tomorrow. And don't think of using magic to escape. You'll notice you're tied to a tree. In a tree as old as this, there is enough concentrated magic to completely destroy you if you try to pull any of it. So don't try."

Using his knees to hold his dinner steady, Zerrick ate as best as he could, trying to ignore Murtis's occasional chuckles. He knew what a sight he must look to Murtis--thin, dirty, and bedraggled, in ripped velvet that had once been red and was now brown. He was even beginning to grow stubble along his jaw. He blushed furiously as Murtis produced a rag for him to use as a napkin.

"About finished? I'll untie you for a moment, let you perform your necessary, and then you'll be going to sleep. You have a busy day tomorrow. Hope you survive it," Murtis said in a pleasant voice that simply enhanced the cutting mockery in his eyes.

Murtis kept a close watch on Zerrick, then when Zerrick was secured to the tree once more, he pulled out an orchid which had been torn loose from its tree, roots intact. "No sense in damaging you this time. Good night, and pleasant dreams."

Zerrick tried to resist as that tainted magic swept over him like a chilling breeze, but fighting against an enemy witch was beyond his knowledge. He felt his lids grow heavy, his mind grow numb. Again, he sank into night.

It was morning when they shook him awake, untying him from the tree while they strapped on his pack. It felt lighter.

"No more free rides," the one called Scissorfists said with a grunt, hauling him up to his feet. Two heavy lidded eyes scrutinized him, and Zerrick repressed a shudder at seeing the long jagged scar running from one eye down to the corner of a brutal mouth.

Once he was up and ready, they began marching, keeping him near Scissorfists and Murtis to prevent him from trying any magic. Zerrick could see they were using an animal trail of some kind widened and cleared for human use. The air hung humid and eerily quiet, strangely devoid of the usual chatter of birds.

He wondered at the quiet then realized that even stranger than the lack of wildlife was the lack of chatter among the group. When he tried to ask why, Murtis put a hand to his lips. "Bad area," he whispered. Zerrick wondered what could be bad enough to frighten these ruffians. He took more care to tread softly, keeping watch on the dark rustling foliage around him.

After a while, the men began speaking again, in low tones. Zerrick relaxed muscles he hadn't realized were tense. He asked Murtis what they had been avoiding.

"Dragon," Murtis said, and from the tone of his voice and the hard glint in his eye, Zerrick saw he was being serious.

"A fire-breathing, flying dragon? With scales and claws?" It seemed incredible one could be so near.

Murtis nodded, looking serious. "We fought and killed its mother about a year ago. Her flaming breath killed four of our men. Made a damned hole in the jungle too. Lucky for us, it couldn't fly."

Zerrick thought about the odd shaped clearing. "But that one is dead, you say."

"Yes--Madame Lotus conjured some sort of water creature. With the help of that to quench the demon's fire, we were able to kill it. But she's got offspring--not as dangerous, and generally afraid of men with guns, but a bit more than we would want to handle alone, without Lotus. Best to sneak through that territory."

So that was why they'd needed him up and walking, not burdening some person. He considered this Lotus woman. If she could conjure up a creature to kill a dragon, she must be powerful indeed. Perhaps powerful enough to cause some of the things his father accused witches of doing. Why hadn't Alden told him of this? Why had he been kept in the dark? He knew so little, but what he was learning was making him reassess his skills.

"How much farther?" he asked after a pause, to change the subject. He still couldn't believe his ears. Dragons!

"A couple more hours, and we'll be there," Murtis said. Once again, the smile was back.

As they neared the camp, Murtis gave him a few tips, "Clint hates women and weaklings. Never mention children to Madame Lotus, and avoid her if she's raving and spellcasting at the same time. She loves to cast curses on the nearest bystander."

To stop the quivering in his stomach, Zerrick concentrated on the landscape around the camp. For the last hour, they had come into wetter terrain with larger pools and more streams. His captors probably thought he was simply a rich town-bred kid. He saw no reason to let them think otherwise, but it was hard to hide his growing excitement. They were very near the Lyndel River.

Zerrick paused to see if he could hear the supposedly wild rapids of the river, but he was propelled forward by a rough hand. Then he had no more time for sightseeing.

He had entered the bandit camp.

It was a sprawling site beneath a heavy canopy, relatively clear of brush, and followed tribal ways in that the tents could be packed in a day and moved. There the similarities ended. The tents were of dyed green cloth, not huts of palm leaves or bark, and everywhere there was the sign of his people in the racks of muskets, black iron pots stewing meat, and lines of ragged looking clothing hanging everywhere to dry in the rare time between showers.

He could see a group of men gathered in a circle as a dangerous-looking female dressed in breeches threw a set of bone dice. She laughed harshly at the results, and took her money from a scowling man. Zerrick glanced at Murtis to see if this was the infamous Madame Lotus, but he continued past the group, hardly giving them a glance. They went to a large tent in the center of camp.

"Stonefist, got a ransomee," Murtis called into the flap.

Zerrick gulped as the largest man he had ever seen stepped out, muscles bulging with every move. His face reminded Zerrick of a bull--squarish, with a heavy brow and a mean glow in his brown eyes. His hair was long and twisted in snarls and tangles, thick in back but beginning to thin on top. When he spoke, Zerrick could see several of his teeth had been knocked out.

"What is this, dinner?" He stood right before Zerrick and smacked a meaty hand into his shoulder, sending him stumbling backwards.

"No, a witch--says his town would pay to have him back. It seems he missed his execution." Murtis's tone was dry but respectful, and he kept well away from the giant, Zerrick noted.

"Dammit, not another witch! Have the town contacted, see what they'll pay, and get rid of him. One way or another," Stonefist snapped, and lumbered over to join the gambling circle, shoving aside the woman to take a throw. Despite his rough handling of people, his men seemed to enjoy his company, nodding at him and offering him bread and wine.

"Well, that was Clint, our esteemed, if somewhat simple, leader. He reacted about as I expected. Doesn't care too much for things beyond his understanding," Murtis confided to Zerrick, pulling him along to the other side of camp. A few men were about, cutting wood or sharpening their swords, but this part was less inhabited, and the men went about their work quietly.

After passing through a wall of thick young saplings, they came upon a hut of leaves and twigs, nestled on a ridge over a stream. Zerrick could see a little herb garden on one side of the hut overgrown with weeds and wildflowers. The trees had not been cleared around the hut, so it was shrouded in shadow, vines creeping forth to claim it back into the jungle. He felt a peculiar aura around it, like the air before a storm, crackling with chaotic energy. There was only one person who would live here. The magic in the grass of the hut and the trees all fairly hummed in his veins. He waited for a glimpse of the witch.

Murtis was even more cautious now, and he kept his voice low as he called into the gloom, "Lotus . . . Madame, are you there?"

"Who is it? What do you want? Do I know you?" came a voice not nearly as old as Zerrick had expected, full of fear and suspicion.

Murtis backed away a few steps and cleared his throat. "It's Murtis, your student. I have a young witch we're holding for ransom. He's green, but I thought you might want to take a look at him."

"He's come for me, hasn't he? Well, he can't have any! I gave it all away years ago," Lotus said with a growl, and stomped out to meet them.

Zerrick gulped. Lotus might once have been a beautiful woman, but now she looked like a wild creature, matted brown hair streaked with white feathers and twigs, flying in all directions around her head, like a halo. Her eyes seemed intent on something but were unfocused, almost seeming to be looking at two things at once. Her clothes were nothing but rags, with vines twisting through them and crystals hanging around her neck and waist. Draped over her were pouches stuffed with plants, the roots of which trailed down her clothes and dangled around her bare legs. She squinted, and one eye pierced him with its gaze.

"A gentleman! Take away his sword; he'll not duel with me." Lotus reached out a dirt-streaked hand to stroke the lace cuff of Zerrick's sleeve and he fought the urge to jerk away. He could feel the chaotic magic in her touch working on her, and through her.

Suddenly she grabbed his face and swooped in to stare at him, close enough that Zerrick could smell the soil and twigs in her hair and the bittersweet scent of her breath. "Looking for me? You'll find me soon, that I promise. I gave birth to a monster. He'll find you, you'll find me, and we all three shall join together. Best run away."

92

Zerrick glanced to Murtis for help, but he only smiled, more relaxed now that Lotus's attention was on someone else. Zerrick shivered as she began stroking his hair, taking a few loose strands of it to inspect in her hand.

"I wouldn't let her do that if I were you," Murtis told Zerrick good-naturedly.

"What will she do?" Zerrick murmured. The woman was intent on her hand, smelling and tasting the strands of his hair as she walked towards her garden. She began muttering about monsters.

"As I said before, she's rather famous for setting curses on people. Personal items and bits of hair or skin tend to increase her power. I haven't figured out why yet, but it has to do with her madness. If she believes they will help her, they do."

Zerrick looked askance at Murtis. Strange tutelage, he thought. If all Murtis's lessons were from seeing the twisted way Lotus cast spells, that could explain the awful feeling of his spells. Then again, who was to say Alden had been perfectly normal?

None of it mattered now. "I'm going to be dead as soon as you sell me off. Why would she bother?"

Murtis looked amused. "You question a madwoman's logic?" He leaned in closer, watching as Lotus picked a few herbs and dusted the soil from them onto her already filthy rags. "It's ultimately her decision whether we return you or not. She may decide to keep you."

Zerrick tried to fight the bile rising in his throat. These people followed the ravings of this person? Were they all mad? All he knew was he had to escape soon.

He was thinking of running away right then, while her attention was diverted, but he remembered all his supplies and equipment were on Murtis. He forced himself to stay calm, to use his head, but his thoughts scattered in alarm when Madame Lotus shouted something and trudged back over to Zerrick.

"Can't waste food before it's rotten. Did a bad job last time, but I'll do better this time, I swear. Come with me," she announced, and began pulling on his sleeve with surprising strength, dragging him towards the entrance to her hut.

"Murtis--" Zerrick called in a shaky voice, wondering what he was getting into now.

Lotus cut him off. "You can't come in; I don't remember you," she said to Murtis, then shoved Zerrick inside and pulled close the door.

Zerrick landed in a pile of something soft--Lotus's bed, perhaps. He tried to protest as she shut the door, but his body wouldn't obey. Darkness overcame the tiny room. Either Lotus already had him under a spell, or things were just happening too swiftly. He couldn't react.

Outside, he heard Murtis muttering about going to fetch Stonefist, a brief rustling of plants, then silence.

"There now. No prying eyes in here, I make sure of that! Don't be afraid. Just let the magic take care of you," Lotus crooned, settling herself next to Zerrick. In the darkness, he could hear the rasp of her breathing but he could not see her face. Was she mocking? Or trying to tempt him? All he knew was he needed out of this entire camp. Now.

"I think I should stay with Murtis--"

"Don't talk back to me! Now, focus plants, where are they . . ." Lotus rummaged through the pile beneath Zerrick, pushing him off onto the earthen floor of the hut where he sat, wondering whether he should make a run for the door. What would a crazy witch do if provoked?

"Ah! Here we are," Lotus cried, and again settled herself next to Zerrick, grabbing hold of his hand. He sat perfectly still, lest she suddenly decide to tear him limb from limb. "Focus plants, very good thing, my boy. Take the magic from other plants, focus it in one. Much more powerful," she crooned.

She patted his hand, rocking back and forth on her knees, "So nice of you to come back, after all these years. I knew they couldn't kill you, even though I prayed for your death. Very strong, and perfect for the magic now. Very good."

Who does she think I am? Zerrick wondered. *And how can I use this to my advantage?*

He felt her shift her weight, then felt the brush of her tattered skirt as she stood. "Now, a first lesson before we try again. You think magic is something outside you, distant, strange. Not at all. Magic is you, you are magic, and so you must not fight it, you become it."

But only to a certain extent, Zerrick mused. Unless you wanted to become like this.

"So, try it with me, yes?" she asked in a very sweet lilting voice, the voice she might have used regularly if she were sane. But Zerrick wasn't about to trust her.

"Madame Lotus, I really--"

"Don't call me that! To you I am Mama."

Zerrick tried to gulp in a dry throat. So that was it. He was supposed to be her son, which was why she was acting so civilized towards him. But now what? He had a feeling, if he let her perform any magic, he would regret it. If he stalled her for much longer, however, she might decide he was a useless stranger and destroy him. Or worse.

His answer was provided for him, as the sound of a heavy voice reverberated through the forest. Murtis had returned with Clint Stonefist.

"Madame Lotus! Why are you messing with a ransomee? We could use hard gold right now. Come out and speak to me!" Stonefist shouted, and blinding light filled the hut as the man roughly shoved the door aside. Zerrick wasted no time but flung himself for the outside world, stumbling over Stonefist's boots as he tried to get his bearings. He was pulled up and pushed aside, where he immediately ran into Murtis's strong grasp.

Clint loomed over the small woman, but she stood up to him, a dangerous look in her eyes. "Do not mess with me." She stepped around him into the vines surrounding her hut, taking no more notice of the big man, and returned her attention to Zerrick. "Running away again?"

"I'm not your son," Zerrick murmured, trying to twist free of Murtis's grasp. With or without his belongings, he had to get away.

"Damn, I hate when she gets like this. Go ahead, Murtis, give her the boy. I'll bet he ain't worth much anyway. If we get her too riled up, she'll just give us hives again. I knew I shouldn't have let her stay." Clint turned to go and Zerrick suspected that behind all his bluster and bravado, he was scared of Lotus.

Clint parted the foliage and stepped through, disappearing from sight, but Murtis hesitated, watching Lotus while he kept his hold on Zerrick. Zerrick let his muscles relax in seeming defeat, but inside, his mind raced. Now was the last chance, while Murtis stood between him and Lotus.

"What are you planning?" Murtis asked.

"Something special," Madame Lotus answered.

"Teach me," Murtis said, and when Lotus nodded, he pulled Zerrick over to be delivered to the witch.

Zerrick was ready. As Murtis guided Zerrick towards Madame Lotus, Zerrick suddenly came to life, shoving back with all his might. Murtis fell, and Zerrick began running.

He made it to the edge of the clearing when the ground suddenly grew soft, trapping his feet. He heard Lotus murmuring and froze, waiting to be struck dead. Instead, the earth beneath him suddenly seemed to turn to liquid. He sank to his knees, then to his hips as Lotus opened her eyes, smiling.

Zerrick tried to still the pounding of his heart, afraid to move lest the earth pull him in deeper as Lotus came over to him, Murtis following like an obedient dog. The earth was holding for the moment, and it was obvious Lotus was proud of her handiwork. She came right up to him, walking on the same earth that had entrapped him, and knelt down to fondle his hair again.

He trembled as he stared into Lotus's dark eyes, searching for any sign of rationality he could communicate with. "What did I do to deserve this?" he murmured, thinking back to when his life had made sense, surrounded by normal, logical men like his father and brother. They would be laughing at him now, playing doll to a witch right out of a fairy tale. He winced as she yanked a tangle from his hair.

"I imagine you know the answer to that one," Murtis said as he settled himself on a log some distance from the strange liquid earth. "Don't worry, I doubt she'll make you suffer long."

"What's going on? You say you want me for ransom, then give me to this woman, then sit down to watch her put curses on me? Is this some kind of game?" Zerrick turned to the only logical one he could reach, desperate now for some sense. Magic began to creep into him, up his legs from the earth. It had precisely the chaotic taint he had expected.

"Oh, this is no game. Madame Lotus obviously likes you. I guess you resemble her hanged son, the Killer of Questin--"

"Questin, nasty town, nasty . . ." Lotus muttered as she brought out a couple of thick crystals and a very large weed with strange glowing flowers. "Must remove all that scum. Make us one again."

Murtis's brows went up. "It seems she is going to impress her magic onto you, join her mind with yours, I think. This is most interesting. After observing you, I'll be able to see how to completely subvert another's will and consciousness. It may hurt, of course, but don't worry, once she's done, you won't feel a thing. Ever again."

Iahmel save me! Zerrick thought, realizing for the first time just how little he knew of the world. He had been so sheltered . . . but now was not the time for such thoughts. Now that he understood somewhat, he could try to fight back. He scanned the area for an untainted source of magic. The plants around him were no good; they were being used by Lotus, who squatted in front of him, both eyes locked on him.

As the magic rose like a tide up his body, through his veins, he felt her mind drawing closer, a whirling storm of flashing thoughts and a voice like thunder, commanding him to submit. He shut his eyes, shut out any distractions and clung to himself, trying to build a wall of willpower to keep her out, save his sanity. His hands clutched at the pouch around his neck, and the image of the triangle within a triangle burned like a flame in his mind. He realized there was magic there, in the amber stone within the pouch, but he'd never learned to pull from stone.

The pain shot up his legs, twisting through his gut like a gnawing worm, and he began to see crazy images out of another life, a woman, passionate and creative, experimenting with power beyond her understanding. He clung tighter than ever to that triangle symbol, *thinking I am the triangle within, I am protected, my walls will hold,* hoping somehow that magic would respond, that perhaps the shape was a keyword like Alden had used with the trunk, a shield of some kind.

But his walls were not holding. The storm had reached his head and his heart felt like it was exploding, as he felt energies out of the ground pull at him, trying to suck him into the earth, into the womb of the jungle.

The visions filled his eyes now, memories of Lotus after magic conquered her, when she began raising a son, trying to build her power by extending herself to others, feeding off their energy. He watched the boy grow up, suffer unspeakable torture and abuse, until he too was raving, flying off to commit murder, then laughing as they hung him.

Zerrick felt himself falling, his own memories now flowing out of his mind, into Lotus's. Somehow he knew that with the last memory he would be no more and she would have all his access to magic in addition to her own. But still, in the back of his mind flamed that triangle, and in his pain and disorientation he clung to it with every ounce of concentration, praying to Alden, to Iahmel, to the Lady of Magic Herself, Ainéra.

With that thought, he felt a flame of his own, just a spark of his own untainted magic--from Alden's amber! He pleaded the magic for answers, and for one brief second, saw within the heart of Lotus, her secret, primal fear.

She was afraid of her son, the one who had stolen her flesh, her eyes, her hair, all the most personal things which were her. He had wracked her with the worst pain she had ever known, and drained her of strength, of water, of blood. And despite the fact he had been of her flesh, he had been beyond her control.

And Zerrick was her son in her mind. And he was now almost fully under her control; his body still burned, but it was growing numb, swaying weakly into her embrace. But control . . . that was something which could fail. Or be broken.

He lashed out at her mind again using the magic within the amber, trying to make her see visions which would frighten her, break her concentration. He showed her a defiant youth backed into a corner by the sting of her cane, wounded but unbroken. He showed the man, laughing as he turned himself in to authorities to escape her once and for all, triumphant even as they hung him. And he showed the birth. Her horror at the realization that this child-- this thing was coming, whether or not she wanted it. With a tiny shock of magic, he sent a jab of pain into her abdomen, reminding her of that which had been lost.

The result was profound. He felt a sharp stinging on his cheeks, and opened his eyes to see Lotus slapping him for all she was worth. She screamed in his face, "No, you're part of me, you can't fight me; I have control. I made you!"

A disturbance rocked the earth beneath him, and the pain returned, but with it came a flood of memories--his memories. The magic seemed to surge out of its binding, like floodwaters over a damn, and the area around them shuddered, the vines and other plants whipping about as if in a heavy wind.

Madame Lotus was sobbing now, suddenly weak and pleading, "I'm sorry, so sorry, I didn't mean for any of it to happen! Stop the blood, stop it; it's falling on the floor . . ." She doubled over in remembered agony, and Zerrick began to feel a slight lapse in the fire wracking his insides. He tested his legs, but they were still frozen.

Again Lotus came at him, this time wrapping her long fingers around his throat as fury blazed forth from tear-streaked eyes. "The pain! You did this, you demon! I'm losing myself, you bastard!"

She began to strangle him, and in desperation he tried to nudge the magic holding him, make it set him free, make her vanish, anything. Cobwebs of black began to creep over his vision, then he felt a sudden shift in the magic around them. The spell seemed to be unraveling.

Like a cannonball bursting out of a cannon, the magic surged beneath him and spat him out of the ground, sending him flying into a bed of palms. He landed hard, but safe, feeling numb all over. From behind him, a shriek pierced the air, and with a groan, he rolled over and managed to lift his head above the palm leaves to see the earth dance and churn around Madame Lotus.

Plants reared up to twist around her arms and legs, pulling her to the earth, as she began sinking even as Zerrick had. It didn't stop at her waist, but pulled her in deeper and deeper, leaves flying around in a whirlwind around her head, lightning crackling through the ground and up along the twisted vines. She fought with all her might, clawing at the vines and thrashing to escape the earth's hold, but it was useless, and in her eyes Zerrick could see she knew it.

She glanced once in his direction, her brown eyes lucid and filled with utter horror at her predicament. The vines pulled her down by her arms, until there was just her head above ground. Then, with a loud crash of thunder and a horrible rumbling deep within the soil, the ground swallowed her up.

The storm and wind ceased so suddenly, Zerrick thought he had lost his hearing. The leaves, no longer held up by the magical wind, settled on the overturned earth, and slowly the sounds of the jungle resumed. Zerrick lay crouched in the palms, breathing hard with the shock of what he had just witnessed, every nerve tingling. His head ached as he raised himself on one knee, looking to see if Murtis had escaped the backlash of power, or if the noise had attracted others.

Murtis was still sitting on his log, his face white with astonishment, his mouth hanging open. Seeing the look of horror on the other witch's face, Zerrick realized just what he had done.

He had committed murder.

With that thought, all the strength left him, and he reeled, falling back into the palms. *I have killed, my god, I have truly fallen now--I am a murderer!* Zerrick flailed against the plants and grabbed hold of a root to somehow anchor him from the spinning world. He lurched, standing up, fell, then dragged himself up again, wanting to scream but too choked up to even whimper. He saw Murtis again, standing, ready to flee back to the heart of camp. *He must not warn the others!* Zerrick thought, and ran towards him, staggering, his mind a blur. He couldn't let Murtis get the others. He had to get out of here.

Zerrick ran headlong into the witch, and they both fell, tangled in the upturned earth and wreckage left from Lotus's spell. Zerrick grabbed a small frond and swept the magic into Murtis's eyes, willing it to blind him. The magic obeyed perfectly, and when Murtis grabbed at his eyes, cursing, Zerrick pulled his pistol from Murtis's belt and triggered it, holding the muzzle against the witch's cheek.

"Move and die," he whispered, squeezing away the tears which threatened to spill. He pulled his sword, machete, and pack from Murtis.

With trembling fingers, he secured his things, then stumbled away, trying to get his bearings. Which way was the river? He could hear the other bandits calling for Murtis, demanding an explanation for the commotion. He remembered the stream, and began running along it, his legs unsteady as he plunged into the jungle.

He crashed through the brush, hardly noticing thin sharp vines leaving trails of fire across his arms and legs. In his mind, he could only see that wild magic, sucking Madame Lotus into oblivion. Some part of him had enjoyed that power, the singing retaliation of the earth, responding to his command. He ran faster, to escape himself.

His leg sank into a pool of mud and he was forced to slow down, as he neared what sounded like a churning mass of water. He was almost there! But he couldn't stop now, as the witch bandits were still behind him; he could hear their voices, arguing with Murtis.

Finally his body simply collapsed. He crashed into a tangle of roots by the riverside and lay panting, half sunken in mud. The world seemed to lose focus and blur, the green jungle melting into sky, the sounds of birds and animals mixing with the erratic beating of his heart. His head felt unbearably heavy, so he let it rest on his outstretched arm, wondering why he was trying so hard to fight against the inevitable. There was nothing left for him now. With that thought, he sank into oblivion.

Night had fallen when Zerrick came to his senses, and by the feel of wet clothing and the sharp smell of broken leaves, he knew he was still out in the jungle. No ropes held him; only a root or two, and these he swiftly snatched away. The sound of water called to him and he rose, realizing how parched he was, how groggy and weak, as if he had been bedridden with illness. With hands numb and unwieldy, he searched through his pack and found his waterskin. It was nearly empty; he drank every last drop.

Stepping cautiously through the foliage lest he slip into a pool or sink into more mud, Zerrick made his way towards the sound of water, his throat aching. So this was the price of power. A far greater price than he had ever dreamt of paying. All his hopes, all his dreams of the future now crushed. He had imagined himself following Alden's footprints, meeting with native tribes and discovering new and exciting plants, animals and civilizations. Instead, he had utterly failed. As a son, as a pupil, and yes, even as a witch. He couldn't handle this power; it corrupted all whom it touched. Lotus' face would haunt him forever.

He came to the last stand of palm trees and stepped through to be greeted with the sight of the wild and raging Lyndel River, crashing on its merry course to the sea. Zerrick knelt by a small churning inlet and gulped down handful after handful of water, trying to wash away the nausea. The water was colder than he expected; it must have come from the mountains to the west.

After drinking and rinsing himself of the mud, he felt somewhat refreshed and utterly starved, so he pulled out what little remained of his food and began to eat. He tried to bring out the lantern out for some light, but it was nowhere to be found. Stolen by the bandits, he thought uneasily.

Still, it was probably safer without the light, he reasoned, trying to eat quickly and quietly. He didn't know if the bandits had passed this way and missed him, or if they were following at all, but anything was possible. Best not to seek trouble.

He finished and walked out on a fallen tree extending out over a small waterfall, watching whitewater churn beneath him, glowing faintly by the light of the newly risen moon. The river was much wider that he had expected, and much rougher, perhaps because of flooding from the recent heavy rains. Mist from the violent waters rose up and clung to his clothing, covering him with a fine glittery sheen. He trembled, eyeing the rapids below.

I could end my misery now, Zerrick thought, inching his way to the end of the thick log. The current was too strong--it would pull him down, and that would be it. No pain. And no more mistakes.

He sat down, letting his feet dangle just above the water, closing his eyes and letting the mist strike his face. The water gathered into fat drops which rolled down his cheeks, just like tears. But his eyes were dry. He hated everything he'd become, so why shouldn't he die? He couldn't do it--he couldn't conquer the evil within his gift. Maybe Alden had. But he was dead.

Of course, suicide would add one more sin to his long list, he thought, smiling bitterly. Let his father worry about it. There had never been hope for him in the first place.

He was startled out his debate by the sound of gunshots and human voices. The bandits! He slid back along the log to dry land, poised to run, then realized what he was doing. Running to save his skin again. He glanced once more at the rushing waters, tormented. Why didn't he just jump, right now, before they found him? Or else wait, let the bandits finish him off, forget about saving himself.

He couldn't do it, he realized. *I really must be a coward*, he thought, angry enough to fling himself into the river just to prove himself wrong. But he knew he wouldn't. *There's got to be another way*, he decided, checking his pack to be sure it was well secured. *I'll go to Depin, turn myself in, join a monastery, something. I just have to get out of the jungle for a while. Return to civilization.*

His mind now at peace, he gave his muscles a quick stretch, then set off running again.

Chapter Eight

"As Ja'hal lay in darkness, a prayer came to him from Samala, and summoned the least of angels, Compassion."
--Dersonial 52:15

Zerrick kept his nose to the mossy earth as the main force of the patrol swept by. Through strands of his black hair and the dark ferns surrounding him, he could see the commanding officer of the small force trudging through the swampy terrain by the river. The men wore red Endersian military uniforms which were easy to spot in the jungle, and carried muskets with bayonets. Straining his ears, he could hear the man speak to his subordinates.

"Any signs of them?"

"No sir, the bandits left a trail heading northwest, but it dissolved once it hit the jungle. We'll keep searching."

The commander wiped sweat from his balding forehead. "You'd better. I don't like it when Stonefist gets this close to town. We'll have to double the guard. Take five men and try to see if that trail was false, if they went another way. Catch up with us upriver. And be quiet!" The two men saluted and the party began to break up. Zerrick huddled in tense silence as they moved on, passing within scant feet of him, too engrossed with the tricky mud pits and slippery vegetation to take notice of him.

He waited until all sounds of their passing faded away, then slowly straightened. A few rays of sunlight not blocked by the scattered cypresses fell across his cheek as he scanned the tangled marsh for signs of life.

That one had been a little too close, he thought as he adjusted his belongings. Four days had passed since his escape from the Stonefist Gang, and this was the third patrol from Depin he had encountered. That was good, he had to remind himself. He must be very near the town. The trees upriver and the rising terrain hid any view of the town, but there were signs of a fairly used trail over on the high banks of the river on dryer ground.

Keeping near the trunks of trees, Zerrick made his way over to the trail. He tried not to think of bandits or of anything else as he continued on towards Depin.

The next morning brought view of the walled town of Depin, a fort against the wilderness, bristling with gunposts and watchtowers. Zerrick paused, hiding in the early morning mist, to shave, comb his hair, and attempt to straighten his clothes. He had to look respectable enough to be allowed past the town watchmen, though no amount of washing would ever regain the splendor of his once grand wardrobe. That was just as well--he also didn't want to attract attention, and posing as a workman would hopefully let him pass without notice. He remembered Alden's warning about the Church's power.

The day was unbearably hot and humid, with clouds drifting slowly across the sky, pregnant with their next rainfall. As he neared two armed soldiers at the gate, he saw that the heat was working for him. The men were dull-eyed and listless, leaning against the iron gates which were open to allow farmers to pass outside to their fields. They gave him only a cursory glance.

"State name and business," one drawled, mopping at his upper lip.

They must be used to bandit raids and outlaws out here, Zerrick thought nervously. Aloud, he said, "I'm Turin. I'm an accountant." That should explain the fine clothing, he reckoned.

"Lots of competition. Good luck," the same fellow responded, and handed Zerrick a lead token granting him access.

Zerrick smiled with false confidence and eased past the guards. Once inside, he stared at the busy avenues of shops and cheap living accommodations.

Depin was twice the size of Harrow, and far busier in that it was the main supplier of slaves and gold in the colonies. As he strode down the main street dividing the compact town, he could see lumber merchants, hear the shouts from houses of gambling and prostitution, and found his nose assaulted by smells of the wares of every kind of merchant, from rubber to coconuts. He even saw a line of struggling slaves, pulling a covered cart for a richly dressed soldier.

He stopped and stared a moment, feeling lost among so many people he had never met in a town so different from home. Towards the center of town there were no churches or courthouses or even a lord's manor. Instead it was dominated by an impressive military post which swarmed with activity and energy. He noticed that all the men wore pistols or swords, even smiths and farmers. He hadn't eaten since yesterday, so Zerrick entered one of the calmer taverns and sat down at a table, feeling conspicuous and disorientated. He suppressed the urge to jump away when a serving wench came up and tapped his shoulder.

"You're new. What d'ya want?" Her voice was rough, disinterested, but she leaned in very close, her loose frilly blouse sliding off one shoulder to invite hungry eyes. Zerrick clamped down on that urge and stared at the table.

"Some sliced meats, I think. And ale," he stammered, blushing. She chuckled deep in her throat and brushed him with her sleeve as she sauntered off to fetch his food.

Zerrick sat back, trying to relax now that he was once again among people in a walled town, but he knew he couldn't stay long, at least not without somehow making peace with the law and with himself. He really should go--he didn't belong among civilization. He was a killer, a hated witch, and an outcast. Just the thought of how black his soul must be by now was enough to drive him to tears, but he squeezed his eyes shut and willed away the despair. What a mess he had made of things. He would give much to be able to lie down and rest.

His food came, and he set to eating it, eyes glancing nervously at the other patrons as they sat drinking and talking.

A robed man entered, bearing an armful of papers and an avid look on his face. The marks on his yellow robes revealed him as a pastor of the Church, and Zerrick paused to watch as he nailed a paper to a space of wall by the door with several community notices.

For a moment he had a wild fear, that this must be a wanted notice for his arrest, that he had been found already, but the other men barely glanced at the papers, and returned to drinking. The priest came over to Zerrick, and he was startled by the priest's youth, a youth that seemed quickly fading as the priest noted the disinterest of the other patrons. It was his eyes that drew Zerrick's gaze, despite his fear. They were kind and gentle, a warm earthen brown which made him feel somehow at ease, calmer. The man gave a shy smile as he handed Zerrick a paper, then made his way to the door and out into the daylight.

Zerrick wrenched his eyes away from the door to the paper, half expecting to see a likeness of himself imprinted there. But instead it was an advertisement, asking people to attend tomorrow's service by the old tree on Miller Avenue.

He shook his head in wonder, realizing for the first time just how much power his family had held in Harrow. There the church had been one of the first buildings erected, and everyone was a devoted worshiper. Here, a soft-eyed young priest had to beg people to come pray beneath a tree. And on the heel of that thought, came another. *If they care so little about religion,* he thought, sipping down the last of his water, *then they might also be less interested in the magical crimes of a person like me.*

The idea that he might have actually reached a place where he could live in peace drifted to the core of his heart and ignited a tiny spark of hope there. But even as that thought warmed him, his ears caught a few softly spoken words from a conversation to his left. His eyes flew open. They were discussing witches.

"No, they'll never hang her. She's Terwin's daughter, and he's got enough money to buy half the town. He'll probably pay a small sum, lock her up somewhere, and go on with his business," a man in a soiled apron announced, cradling a mug of ale in his large hands.

A smaller man sat across from him, smoking a pipe. "Too bad. She may be learning hexes from the slaves, but she's a damn fine catch. Think of the dowry!"

The first man let out a choked laugh, gulping at his drink, then set it aside. "Forget it. If Mr. Terwin didn't kill you, one of her brothers would. She ain't a fine looker, anyhow. Not that it matters."

"Yeah, doubt I'd care to wed a witch. Now about those nails I ordered . . ." the conversation turned to other matters and Zerrick got up to pay with the small amount of cash he had managed to hide from the bandits. If he did decide to move on from this town, he would have to sell his sword for supplies. A machete would be far more useful in the wild anyway.

He walked out of the tavern, trying to concentrate on his plans, on the supplies he needed to continue his journey and the path he should take next, but in the back of his mind the two men's conversation played over and over. This wasn't another Vera Smith they were charging, but a wealthy young lady. He wondered if she were indeed guilty, then sighed. Once he would have been certain she was innocent, or at least harmless. Now he couldn't be sure.

Zerrick halted in front of an inn, undecided about where he should go next, and too burdened with guilt to care. He looked at the little paper still clutched between his fingers. He knew he shouldn't press his luck, but the preacher hadn't seemed to recognize him. He had looked kind, of a much gentler religion that what Father had preached. . .

Well, it was worth a try, Zerrick thought. Tomorrow he would go and speak with the man to see if he could somehow be absolved of his guilt, live in peace again. Even if he had to forsake magic. He went through his things, picked out a few things he could sell, and went to find money for a night's stay at the inn.

At sunrise, Zerrick was busy at the fountain by the market square, rushing to wash and dry one of his velvet coats for the service. He had found the "old tree" was a giant ironwood which dominated the square. The shade was nice, but with the humidity left over from the early morning showers and the lack of sunlight on the square, Zerrick knew he'd never get his clothes dry in time.

He donned them wet as a watchman called out the hour, and went to sit with a small group over by the base of the tree, where the young pastor was preparing his sermon. The preacher smiled and welcomed those in the gathering, waiting patiently while a few more arrived. He looked angelic in his pale yellow robes, holding nothing but the Holy Book in one hand and a pair of spectacles in the other. A slight breeze swept through the branches above, making spots of light dance around his feet. A few last stragglers came to the meeting, then he began.

"I'd like to welcome all of you, especially those who are new," he announced, looking at Zerrick, "I am Pastor Tait, here to give you strength and blessings by the word of the Creator, the god Iahmel."

He put on his spectacles and smoothed back his hair. "Before we begin today's lesson, I'd like to express my utter shock that someone in this town is accusing Miss Mira Terwin of the terrible sin of witchcraft. I find such a notion preposterous; Mira has been one of our most faithful patrons here with the Church, as evidenced by her lovely singing in our choir." The pastor waved a hand to a very small group dressed in white, seated on stools to the right of the rest of the assembly.

Zerrick found himself searching for the accused girl, but then he heard Tait continue, "I am grieved to say Mira and her family could not be here today, as the court proceedings are taking place shortly and as she must remain in the holding area until acquitted. Let us all pray for her, that the lies may be uncovered for what they are, and that she may go free."

He led them in a prayer out of the Lost Years by Kazimir, and Zerrick noticed that around him, the people were not as convinced of the girl's innocence, merely mouthing or murmuring the words. He thought about all the faces that had been staring at him and fell silent, unable to speak past the lump in his throat. Could he risk that again?

The prayer ended and the lesson began, while Zerrick sat and pondered his predicament. He found it ironic that today's lesson was on persecution, on the story of Ja'hal's First Coming, "Ja'hal, the seventh son of Emir Nurimar, fair-haired son of the Melian Samala and a true descendent of prophets, was first visited by angels as a ruddy youth of eight. And the Emir, fearing his son's strange prophesies, shut him up, even until manhood. Yet still the angels came, and Ja'hal became wise beyond his years, understanding how to create great works by his Lord Iahmel's majesty."

Zerrick tried to stop the thought, but it came regardless. So what made Ja'hal's miracles any different from other acts of magic? He gave himself a mental slap. Ja'hal had never killed anyone, had refused to even lift his hand against another person.

Tait continued, "But in the east, the Empire of Al'Tuon was growing, ruled by sorceresses led astray by Ainéra's teachings. They swept across the land, coming finally to the Emirate. The first of Nurimar's sons was killed, coaxed into a bog by one of the High Sorceress's creatures. And the second son, Dalnuri, was ensorcelled, and went mad, and rampaged among the men of his squadron. The Emir came to Ja'hal because he knew the youth was aware of all that transpired as well as all the secrets of the enemy's magic."

Zerrick fidgeted . Had the minister glanced at him when he said the word 'magic'? Did he have any idea how personal this sermon was to one listener in particular?

"But Ja'hal would not teach his father the witches' sorcery, not even after the third and fourth of his brothers were killed, for he knew it was against the word of Iahmel. Then the Emir threw him into the dungeons, to force him to submit, but he would not."

And now I finally see why, Zerrick thought, feeling sick inside. If he had known what he was capable of, that he could cause such destruction . . . Zerrick hunched his shoulders trying to hide, but in his mind's eye he still saw Lotus being swallowed alive, the ground reaching up to pull her down. No confession would absolve him, but maybe it would at least end his suffering.

"And when word came that the fifth son was dead, the Emir flew into a rage. It was at that time that a messenger for the Dark Land came. He promised the magic that the Emir craved, in return for Ja'hal. And in his rage, the Emir agreed." This story had given him nightmares as a child, Zerrick thought. But of course, the way his father told it made it sound far worse.

"And when Ja'hal was summoned to the evil messenger, the Emir saw that he had made a terrible mistake, for the messenger was not a man at all, but a dark creature of Angist, the Ravenger. It was too late, however, for upon seizing hold of Ja'hal, the Ravenger took his true form, that of the crow-winged horse, and beat his four dark wings, driving back the Emir and his servants. And the Ravenger carried Ja'hal off to the City of Sin, Margué."

And so the tale went on, telling of how Ja'hal's people prayed for him, and how he was saved by the least of angels, delivered from the deepest pit of sinners. The story, as told by such a young and passionate man as Pastor Tait, stirred hope in Zerrick that he did in fact have a chance here. "Far off, thousands of miles apart, Samala cried out to her son, that she blamed him not for his hard decisions, and prayed to Iahmel to save her son, and deliver him safely back. Iahmel heard. That was the calling of Compassion. Compassion freed Ja'hal, and healed the sinners he was imprisoned with. With Compassion, Ja'hal found the strength to call to Iahmel. And Iahmel heard. Ja'hal was granted the ability to fly, and he returned to help his last brother and his father defeat the evil sorceresses."

Tait went on to explain the lesson, that one must never judge, that they be judged and found wanting, and that with love, even the lowest sinner could be saved. That final part firmed Zerrick's decision. He resolved to speak with Tait immediately after the service.

As the sermon ended and the townspeople left to their own business, Zerrick sat, hands clenched, trying to appear calm though his insides churned with fear. The pastor watched him as he chatted with locals and waved goodbye to everyone. Then the square was deserted. Tait came and sat down beside him.

"You look like something is troubling you," Tait began, keeping his eyes lowered but not before Zerrick caught him staring at his dirty clothes and unkempt hair.

It was folly, but he could not help himself. "I ran away from home--I did some terrible things, but now I'm tired of running. I need to talk to somebody--I feel like I'm losing my mind--"

"Easy there--I'll try to help, of course, but you need to slow down. Where was your home?" Tait forestalled Zerrick, raising a hand and setting it lightly on Zerrick's shoulder.

Zerrick took a deep breath, eyeing the pastor for any sign of deception or cunning. The man's face looked benign. He began to tell his story, of how as a boy a kind witch had befriended him, how he learned magic, never knowing the evils he was playing with. He left out any mention of his father's name or occupation, stating simply that Alden had been discovered by the town pastor, then he himself. He exaggerated the part where the town was determined to execute him.

Tait hissed softly, shaking his head in dismay. "A serious business, what you fell into. But surely the church should have seen your youth, your basic ignorance of that which you did. It was probably best you left. Death seems too harsh a punishment in a case like yours."

Zerrick shifted uncomfortably, glancing around the market square to be sure they weren't attracting undue attention. No one seemed to be paying any mind. "I wasn't too repentant at the time," he confessed to Tait.

"But that has changed, I see. I think I can help you, if you'll trust me. Captain Greynor acts as the lawman in these parts, and thanks to the bandit activity, he has little love of witches. However, I could probably persuade him to give you a light sentence, especially if you could provide help towards catching bandits." Tait paused to press a linen handkerchief to his face and brow. The day's heat was growing, and Zerrick realized he must be cooking inside his ecclesiastical robes.

He considered what else to tell the clergyman. "I did run into a group of bandits on my way here. Their leader's name was Clint Stonefist."

Tait gasped. "The Stonefist Gang? Did you see their hideout?"

Zerrick forced himself to nod, feeling that sickening horror sweeping over him again. *Please don't ask what happened there, he thought.*

"I can see something happened between you and the bandits," Tait mused, rubbing his chin. "But you are here now, and talking to me, so I must assume you evaded them. Well, this is excellent. I'm certain I can ease your sentence. Once you have paid your due, you may live free of the burden of these sins."

Zerrick closed his eyes, feeling for the first time an easing of the forces which seemed to be pulling him apart. Yes, he would make himself forget magic, find a job, maybe even marry. If he settled his affairs here well enough it was even possible the long arm of his father would be unable to touch him.

Tait rose to his feet and offered a hand to help Zerrick. The watchman called out the midday, but Zerrick was too excited to even think of stopping for a bite to eat. He wanted to get this over.

"Can we speak to the Captain today?" he inquired, as Tait gathered up his things.

"Yes, I think today would be best. He is at this very moment handling another witch case, and if we sneak your case in now, there will be less time for talk among the townspeople to spread."

Having gathered his books, Pastor Tait lead the way up narrow streets and alleys, headed for the large fortress at the center of town. As they walked, Tait spoke casually of the way this little military fort had sprung into one of the busiest towns in the Colonies, thanks to the big slave trail which led west to the base of the Jagara Mountains. Mr. Terwin and others utilized those trails to bring through hundreds of slaves.. Zerrick nodded his head in feigned interest, while he took careful note of the streets they took and the way uniformed soldiers became more and more numerous as they neared the fort.

As they entered the walled compound, Tait ended his speech about how prosperous the place was and how much work there was to be done in the name of the Church. The pastor nodded his head to the men on duty, and they in turn ignored him.

"So why all the military here?" Zerrick asked as they went across the courtyard to the command center at the other end.

"Oh, the gold mines also run their business through here. The foothills are just drenched in the ore, and that of course brings crime and gambling--"

"And makes this place important to His Majesty in Endersey," Zerrick finished for him, unwilling to hear another speech on the pastor's unending work. He paused a few feet from the threshold of the command center, staring up at the three story stone and wood building and the iron studded doors which were open and manned by blank-faced guards. From inside could be heard the sound of men arguing.

Tait crossed the threshold and peered inside to the left, ignoring the guards who eyed him critically. "Oh dear. Poor Mira is still having her trial, and it doesn't seem to be going well. I'd hoped to give your case a little room, let the captain have time to rest."

Zerrick peered inside. Before him was a hallway leading into a wide chamber with tables and benches, probably a dining hall for officers. The voices, however, came to the left, from a small office. Zerrick frowned. This was the courtroom of the town? He turned to Tait, feeling less sure of his plan. "We could come back later."

"No, no, we could learn something here, and besides I want to speak on Mira's behalf. Just find yourself a corner, try to blend in. I'm sure everything will be fine."

With that, Pastor Tait passed through the hallway and entered the office, coming to stand next to a middle aged man with a startling shade of red hair, streaked with gray at the temples. The man paced around, waving a hand in the air and speaking in a loud voice. Zerrick stood in the doorway, observing all the room's occupants as he sought a safe place to stand. To his left, along one wall were two women, probably wives of farmers or laborers, a handsome fair-haired gentleman fashionably dressed, and an elderly matron, possibly his mother.

He glanced at them curiously, but the older woman threw him such a haughty glare, he hastily drew away from them, situating himself in the opposite corner next to a painting of an open meadow.

Cautiously, he turned his gaze to the three women crowded along this side of the office: two slaves and a pale-skinned woman with auburn hair so curly it could barely be contained by the simple bun it had been pinned into. There was nothing remarkable about her looks--her skin was lightly freckled, her face pretty enough but not beautiful, but from the anxious look in her warm cocoa eyes, Zerrick knew that this must be the infamous Mira Terwin.

"Mr. Terwin, I will kindly ask you to settle down and let me speak!" the last occupant of the room snarled, and Zerrick saw that the judge of this whole affair was a man not ten years older than himself, with long golden hair slicked back into an impossibly neat military braid. His buttons were shiny and the blue uniform was miraculously wrinkle-free, buttoned all the way up to his neck despite the heat. He stood behind the only piece of furniture in the room, a desk cluttered with papers, many of them sealed with the royal emblem.

Mr. Terwin stopped pacing and came forward to lean against the desk, his hands clenched into fists. "All right. This trial is nothing but one opinion 'gainst another. How do you want to handle it, Captain? Remember, I'm very powerful in not just this town, but in the whole colony."

"Yes, yes," the blond captain said, looking annoyed. "Mr. Cohen, do you wish to add any further statements to your case?"

The well-dressed gentleman remained where he stood and spoke with a thick Old World accent, "I do not believe there is anything more to say. That girl nearly scared my mother to death with her barbaric cures or curses or whatever. And my servants are certainly not the only witnesses who have seen Miss Terwin in strange rituals with the natives. I merely present the case to teach a man like Mr. Terwin that above all, a young lady should be kept strictly among civilized human beings--"

"How dare you speak about my Mira in that snobbish tone!"

"Gentlemen!" The captain knocked the hilt of his sword against the desk. "Pastor, are you here to speak on this case as well? I'd like to conclude this shortly."

Tait came forward, giving those in the room a faint smile. "I merely wish to confirm that in all the years I have known Mira, she has been a faithful church member and a good-hearted girl. In the eyes of the Church, she stands innocent."

The captain gave a weary sigh. "That's lovely, Pastor, but in the end, what do we have? Two gentlemen, both unhappy about the situation." He stepped away from the desk, giving Mira a bored glance, and walked up to Mr. Terwin. "To tell you the truth, I suspect your daughter really has gotten into a little touch of witchcraft. She spends too much time with those slaves of yours. But I don't really care about all that. I think the entire situation could be rectified if you put a few controls on her."

He turned to Mr. Cohen. "Sorry to disappoint your dear loving mother--" he gave the old woman a withering glance and she made a face at him which could have melted iron--" but I do not wish to hold a burning for some wayward girl. We'll settle this by money. Mr. Terwin will pay the fees for this case, and also he'll pay a small sum to compensate you for your troubles. Say, about two thousand in all."

"Ridiculous!" Mr. Terwin bellowed.

"Satisfactory," said Mr. Cohen.

Zerrick shook his head in amazement, wondering how Mira must feel about all this and whether the lack of justice would help or hurt him. While the captain and Mr. Terwin bargained out their price, he turned back to Mira and glanced curiously at the slaves dressed in servant's dresses, their long black hair pinned up into neat little buns. Maids, perhaps? Or a nanny and cook? What bothered him was that these were the only ones here on Mira's behalf. Didn't she have other friends? And what about her mother? Even at his mockery of a trial, Zerrick's mother had been present to show her impression of him in her clothing and attitude. As he thought about it now, no one who had spoken of the Terwins had made any mention of a Mrs. Terwin.

As he stared at her, she slowly turned her eyes from the debate, seemingly disgusted by what she saw there, and allowed her gaze to fall squarely on him. He felt a surge of excitement, quite unexpectedly, and looked away. He expected her to turn away as well, but instead she inched towards him, her olive skirts brushing the floor. He noticed she was eye to eye with him, not that he considered himself tall, but it was somehow daunting. She paused beside him, peering at the paintings along the wall.

In the center of the room, the men were ending their negotiation. The original price seemed to be the best for all parties involved. Zerrick shuddered; it was all too reminiscent of slavery.

"What are you here for?" Mira asked, right at his ear. He jumped, then stared open-mouthed at her. Her voice was low, melodious, and absolutely beautiful. Pastor Tait had said something about her singing in the choir, but no one had mentioned that she might have true talent. If she sang anything like the way she spoke, he shouldn't be surprised if she was the best singer in the colonies.

He tried to speak past the sudden dryness in his mouth, "I--uh-- I'm trying to make a new start, here in Depin."

"Oh? As a soldier?" she asked, indicating the captain. With the low thrum of her voice still in his ears, suddenly her homemade dress and collar did not seem so plain; in fact he saw now that there was an elegance to the simplicity of her looks.

Then he caught what she was saying. "Oh no! I'm here to --well-- to confess a few things I did in the past." He struggled to speak, aware his face must be bright red by now and painfully aware of the sorry condition of his clothes. He saw her eyes widen with alarm and realized just how bad his story sounded. "I was convicted of witchcraft," he finished lamely. He held his breath, and watched for her reaction.

Incredibly, he saw only an increased interest in her eyes. He saw also a naive curiosity which confirmed for him her innocence. She seemed about to inquire further, but an announcement from the captain interrupted her. "All right, then, we have a settlement. Nineteen hundred in fine gold, to be paid immediately to the plaintiff and court, divided seventy-thirty. Miss Terwin must remain here until all accounts are paid, then she is free to go with the solemn promise that she henceforth stay clear of the natives."

"Outrageous," muttered Mira under her breath, but she curtsied and tried to smile. "Thank you, Captain Greynor, for your mercy."

Mr. Terwin hurried over and put a callused hand on Mira's shoulder. His voice was gentle, yet his stance was straight and domineering. "Don't you worry, my darling. I'll take care of everything."

"Of course," Mira answered, but her voice was flat.

He went on, smiling encouragingly. "Just take me a few minutes to fetch the payment, and you'll be home by supper. I'll have Cook make something special. Just set tight." He glanced once in Zerrick's direction. "Don't talk to strangers."

Zerrick flinched and turned away, searching for Tait in the crowded room. He found him over by the captain, and with one last glance at Mira who was calmly reassuring her father that she'd be fine, he crossed over to Tait.

Tait clapped a hand on his shoulder. "Ah, this is the young man right here. As you can see, he's been through a bit, and has come to see the error of his ways. I think he shows great courage and strength of character in coming forward."

"Another damn witch," the captain muttered, and it seemed to Zerrick that all conversation seemed to halt momentarily. He stiffened, but then he heard Mira's pleasant voice bidding her father farewell. Mr. Terwin made the loud announcement that he was off.

"Yes, he told me he was acquainted with the dark arts, but he will renounce them, help you with information regarding the Stonefist Gang, and take his punishment, in the hopes of starting a new life here," Tait went on, and now the silence was definite, as Mr. Cohen nudged his mother and crept away to the door. Mira remained where she was, while her two slaves whispered among themselves.

"I think I understand," Captain Greynor said, smoothing back a few pale strands of his hair and straightening the fabric of his uniform. "Let me consider this a moment."

"Excellent. We'll be at hand if you wish to know further details," Tait offered with confidence, pulling Zerrick back over to Mira's group. He released Zerrick and ran forward to catch Mira in a wide embrace.

Zerrick stood to the side and dared a shy smile at the elder of the two slaves. She smiled back, her teeth especially white next to her reddish-brown skin, in a round face and a wide, flat nose. Her eyes fell to the pouch around his neck, and she gave a little gasp.

"You learn the ways of the Put-na, yes?" she asked, holding her hands together as if in prayer.

"No, but my master did. This was his gift to me," Zerrick answered, feeling a sudden exhilaration. So the people really did exist! And here was someone who might be able to direct him to them. Then he stilled his thoughts. No more magic, no more running away to stranger lands or people. He was going to find his peace here.

She nodded solemnly, as if guessing that the 'master' he spoke of was now gone. "The Put-na are just on the other side of the mountains. You should go to them. Your gifts will not be appreciated here. There, you do much good."

He looked her straight in the eye, uncomfortably aware that Mira and Tait had finished greeting each other. "No, I don't think so. I'm staying here. I don't want anything more to do with magic."

"You think it that easy? All right," the slave said, and threw up her thin brown hands. She bobbed her head in a show of deference to him, the straight shiny strands of her hair reflecting light from the candles along the walls. Then she winked. He could see, this close to her, that for all the civilized clothes she wore and the careful pinning of her hair, she was still very foreign, untamed, with her pierced ears and the small initiation scar beside her nose showing her former life.

Again Mira spoke to him, and again he was entranced by the sound of her voice, "I hope you like it here. I wish I could say I'd be seeing you again, but after all this, I doubt I'll be allowed out much." There was bitterness in her words, and a profound loneliness which shook his heart. "I do hope," she went on, "that you won't be too afraid of my 'Nanna'—my nanny--" she indicated the slave who had spoken to him. "She's wonderful to talk to, and since you both have spent time out in the wilderness, you could perhaps relate experiences. I only wish I were so free to travel." She seemed to think she had said too much and fell silent, suddenly taking great interest in a frayed thread along her sleeve.

Zerrick made a promise to himself that if they allowed him to stay, he would work to change the way certain people treated her. Starting with dear father.

"Pardon me!" That ingratiating voice breaking into their conversation made Zerrick want to snarl some extremely nasty curse, but he fought that urge and turned to the captain. The captain stood imperiously, a few official forms in his hands. He cleared his throat. "I need to ask you a few questions."

Obediently, Zerrick returned to the desk, as Captain Greynor dipped his quill in ink. "Are you of considerable power? A beginner or advanced?"

"A beginner. Still an apprentice," Zerrick answered, trying to sound as benign as possible.

"Ever caused any real destruction with your--mm--witchcraft? Any deaths?"

Faced so directly with the question, Zerrick found he couldn't lie, but he did try to make it sound better. "There was one death--it was inadvertent, really--she was a witch, casting her own spell. My magic caused hers to backfire. She was with the Stonefist Gang, but I never meant--"

A cold gleam of joy flared in the captain's eyes. "You killed one of the bandit witches?!"

"By accident," Zerrick said, grimacing.

"Fantastic! Welcome to Depin, young man. I definitely think we can allow a lesser sentence, seeing as you've already done some of the work for me. Killed a bandit witch! I think we're going to be great friends," the captain said, his manner now open and smiling and far more interested in the matter at hand. He started writing very quickly, then signed his name with a flourish at the bottom.

Great friends, huh. With someone who loves killing witches. I can't wait, Zerrick thought, anything but relieved at this sudden change of heart.

Though he heard Mira whispering excitedly with her nanny, Zerrick kept his eyes on Captain Greynor's desk, not sure whether he should be joyous or embarrassed at this strange success. Some ugly little part of him had never expected this to work. Still, there was a punishment to face.

"All right, I think you'll find this acceptable," the captain said, applying his seal to the document. "Twenty lashings by the switch or whip--your choice--plus a year's servitude in the garrison here, specifically to aid in the capture of any bandits in the area. Only here at the frontier's edge, can you get this kind of leniency. In Endersey you'd be a dead man."

Zerrick nodded, looking the paper over even though he couldn't read most of it. "That's fine--ah, I'd prefer whip to switch, if it's all right."

"Don't like thorns, hmm? Very well. Report here tomorrow morning and we'll get the lashing done with. Then I'll have you look at some maps." Captain Greynor pocketed the court papers, pulling out a pipe and some tobacco. He cracked a smile at Zerrick. "Case closed."

Chapter Nine

"My brothers, I see now thy faces bold with evil, and I know no place to turn."
--II Ja'hal 34: 12

The following day Zerrick waited in Captain Greynor's office, dressed in a new shirt, a tan vest lined with otter fur, and a sturdy new pair of leather breeches. He felt like a human again in the clothes Greynor had given him, clothes hinting that an expedition for the bandits might begin that very evening.

He waited tensely for the captain to return and oversee the lashings, but he hoped this wouldn't be too painful--no worse than a beating by the local boys. Or a reprimand from Father. One thing that puzzled Zerrick was where the lashings would be delivered. He had expected from the captain's casual manner of issuing the verdict that the punishment would be held inside the fort. Instead, according to the note Greynor had left on the desk, they were holding it in one of the market squares, in the western and more affluent part of town.

Something must have changed after he left, Zerrick thought, brows furrowed. Mr. Cohen could have changed the site; he remembered how patiently and quietly the man had waited throughout the proceedings, how he had hidden himself near the doorway while Captain Greynor arranged a time and place for Zerrick to meet with him. Zerrick had wondered at his silence at the time--after all, he had been the chief speaker against the witch activity. He'd felt safe, however. With the captain on his side, there had seemed little to worry about.

As he'd concluded things, Mr. Terwin had arrived, taken Mira's arm, and thrown his sack of gold on the table. Zerrick had only been able to catch a flash of her dark eyes before Mr. Terwin pulled her through the door. He wondered if Mr. Terwin had changed it--to show Mira? That thought was interrupted. The guards outside shouted their salute and the doors swung open. A wave of air heavy with moisture swept through the office, and Zerrick's ears caught the patter of a soft steady rain falling on the steps outside. The captain entered, brushing droplets off his dark blue cloak.

"Are you ready?" the captain asked, leaving his cloak and hood on but wiping his face on a towel offered to him by a young officer. Two guards who had entered with him came forward, and Zerrick was forced to endure his second frisking of the day. When they were satisfied that he had no weapons concealed on him, the four soldiers lead him over to Captain Greynor.

"Let's get this over with," Zerrick said, throwing his shoulders back and trying to sound nonchalant.

"Indeed." Greynor said, all business today in his royal blue uniform which had somehow avoided the wet outside. He waved a gloved hand, motioning that Zerrick should follow, and strode back out into the rain.

Zerrick blinked as he stepped out into the warm drizzling rain, wondering why he hadn't thought to bring a cloak. Well, he'd be shirtless soon enough anyway, he thought.

Their procession went across the grassy courtyard, past the thick log walls of the fort and down the main street to the Jeweler's Market Square. Patrolmen were positioned at intervals along the narrow dirt street, and through the windows and doorways of the shops and townhouses, Zerrick could see faces watching him with a mixture of awe and fear. At least they weren't shouting names or chasing him with firebrands. It was eerily quiet.

Zerrick plodded along through the mud, watching for one particular face. He didn't see Mira, but he did notice that a few of the merchant's daughters smiled and blew kisses at him. He wondered what kind of gossip his coming had produced. He wished he could talk to the captain, but the captain stayed well ahead of him, eyes peering straight ahead, his stride perfectly in time with a silent drum. The rain continued to fall, landing in noisy drops in the puddles and plastering Zerrick's hair to his skull.

They finally came upon the square. Here there mingled a few brave souls out in the rain, bundled up and clustered around a crude wooden block with a pole jutting up through the middle. Sitting on the steps of the block was a man in a black uniform, with a red badge over his left breast and a leather mask hiding his face.

Zerrick tried to fight the cold sliver of fear that settled in his heart, but he couldn't help wondering if this was the town executor as well as discipliner. Or was he more specialized--an interrogator, perhaps? He steered away from that line of thought.

A single egg whizzed by his shoulder as they emerged into the square, and he traced its path to an old woman leaning out her second story window, muttering. The patrolmen ignored her, and as they passed out of range into the center of the square, Zerrick tried to push away his fear in a fierce exhaled breath. He stood face to face with the masked man.

"Remove your shirt and vest," the man said in a rasping voice, pulling from his belt an evil looking cat-o-nine-tails. Zerrick stared at the knotted strands of the whip and reminded himself that he had chosen this. He shrugged out of his vest and set it on the top step, then slowly unlaced his shirt, scanning the small crowd for a familiar face. There were a few slaves dressed in servant's livery, but with their cloaks and hoods, he could not discern any of their faces. One of the guards came forward to help him remove the sodden shirt. He folded that as well and placed it on top of the vest. Zerrick shuddered as the rain ran down his back.

Unsure how to proceed, Zerrick began climbing the steps, then he was pulled along the rest of the way by the man in black, and made to stand in the middle of the platform. Captain Greynor came forward, shoulders thrust back, and announced in a clear voice, "It is by my decree as lawmaker of the town of Depin, that this confessed witch, who has forsaken his arts in order to lend his aid against the marauding bandits, shall now pay his debt to society by enduring a lashing of twenty strokes by the whip. He shall then serve under the patrol units here for one year, providing all possible aid in return for his freedom and good name. Are there any who oppose my decision?"

The old woman began screaming something about death and damnation, but Greynor ignored her. "Proceed," he ordered, then went to stand under the overhang of a nearby building.

Zerrick watched as the masked man pulled out a rope and one of the guards forced Zerrick to wrap his arms around the pole. Obediently, he offered his wrists to be tied. For one instant there, when the captain had asked for any opposing views, he had felt something strange, like a whiff of smoke on a clear day, foretelling trouble, but then the feeling was gone, making him wonder if he had been imagining things. All too real was the sensation of wet wood under his wrists, and the strong grip of the ropes, pinning him in place. He swung his head around to pull the sticky mane of his hair away from his back.

He heard a few gasps from the crowd, and turned his head just enough to see the man he would call his tormentor brandishing the cat, cracking it like a whip, making a show of the punishment for the onlookers. Zerrick winced in anticipation as a strand flicked across the back of his thigh.

At some silent command the tormentor decided the fun was over. Zerrick just caught the sudden blur of his arm, and then his knees buckled as slashes of fire tore into his back.

He lunged away, biting back a cry. Why did the man have to hit so hard? Tears welled up in his eyes as rain ran into the welts, but he tried not to think of that, or of anything. He braced himself for the next blow.

It came with a brittle crack, and this time a small cry did escape his lips.

Blinking tears and rain from his eyes, Zerrick risked a glance to the captain, but the man had turned away. He chatted with a merchant and his wife, unconcerned with the proceedings.

Again, nine talons clawed into his back and he whimpered, trying desperately not to scream as his back grew increasingly raw. He braced himself against the pole, trying to remain upright, but his legs wouldn't hold him. He clung to the pole, fear twisting in his bowels.

Another blow sent him staggering, and instinctively his mind leapt, searching for a living scrap of magic to draw from. He realized what he was doing and tried to stop it, but everywhere now he could sense the traces of magic--in the wood, within weeds on the ground, even as far as a small planted tree on the other side of the square. But he couldn't reach any of it.

Some part of his mind remembered the amber inside Alden's pouch. As the fifth stroke fell, making him dizzy with pain, he felt part of him calling to that magic, conjuring forth visions of fire raining down on his tormentor, or on the callous townspeople so heartless as to think of this as entertainment. But the other half of him shrieked to block that calling, at whatever cost.

"No! Never!" He cried out, struggling to control his powers. The world turned ablaze with light to his inner eyes.

Then he had a waking dream.

He burst through flames, hollering, then he was inside, smoke curling up from burns on his flesh and the smoldering remains of his clothing. He was not safe, not yet; all around him was fire, a wide ring which spared only the ground he stood on. It crackled at his back, cooking the air that he breathed, warning him that he could not stay long in this refuge.

Beyond the fire towered the ring of mountains, and they seemed nearer than ever, the purple heights and cool shadowed passes calling to him. He choked on fumes, gazing at the thick flames which still blazed between him and his goal. The ground was bare within the circle. No magic. If he remained here he would die.

He glanced behind as a lick of flame passed close to him, searching for Alden, his father, or the wolf beast, but none of them were present.

A cool breeze brushed his cheek, parting the waves of heat for a second, and he suddenly realized he was not alone, that there was a woman standing out there, just beyond the ring of fire. She wore a long flowing robe which seemed to reflect several colors at once, from yellow to green to deep russet brown. Her hair fell all the way down to her feet, adorned with bird feathers.

"Do not forsake me," she pleaded, holding pale hands out to coax him on. The flames and the heat hid her face from him but he knew she was beautiful, that to leave her would break his heart.

"Help me!" He shouted, swooning as the fires slowly baked him.

She bowed her head, and he caught a glimpse of her pale ivory cheeks, flushed with emotion. "I am sorry, but I cannot. I too am imprisoned." She glanced up, and he froze as the indescribable weight of her gaze pierced through him, pinning him. "You must come to me."

She released him from her gaze and turned away, slowly making her way back up the foothills to the circle of mountains. A fresh breeze swept at her robes, then fanned the flames around Zerrick, threatening to overwhelm him. As tiny sparks ignited on his clothing, forcing him to plunge forward, he could still hear her voice ringing in his ears.

"Free me!"

With a thunderous crack, pain lanced up his spine and down his arms, shocking him back to reality. He found himself on his knees, draped against the pole like a sack of grain. His jaw ached from being clenched, and he felt a suspicious heaviness in his chest and throat which told him he had been crying. Cursing, he struggled to stand. All too well he could envision the mess they had made of his back. How long had he been dreaming?

"Twenty. That concludes the punishment," the masked man said, breathing hard. He threw down the cat-o-nine-tails and it landed in a pile beside Zerrick. Zerrick watched the rain wash the blood away into tiny red streams which ran along the cracks in the wooden planks. Merciful gods, at least it was over.

He stayed still as the guards came forward and untied him, wondering how he was going to survive the expedition tonight. Remembering all too vividly his strange dream, he glanced around at the people still milling around and at the captain leaning against one of the supports under his dry overhang. Everything was just as he'd left it--apparently he'd at least been successful in stopping his spellcasting. No doubt his vision had been brought on by stress, the strain of torture . . . except he would never forget the feel of those eyes upon him, the irresistible call of her voice. One thing had been made clear to him. Magic was never going to leave him alone.

"All right now, show's over," Captain Greynor said, emerging from his dry spot and stepping out to the platform. "You can all go home now," he said to those hovering near.

Slowly, they began drifting away. A guard pulled Zerrick to his feet and gave him support as he forced himself to stand, hunched over. He concentrated on not embarrassing himself further by fainting. Numbly, he took his shirt and vest as they were handed to him and held them to his chest. The cold wet cloth only made him shiver violently.

He was making his way down the steps when a loud voice cut across the square, halting everyone. "Hold there! Who is to say that this town has jurisdiction over the case of Zerrick Dhur? He is not of this town. Therefore, he is not yours."

"Who says this?" the captain demanded. He stood, chest thrust out in defiance, fists clenched in anger as a cloaked figure emerged from the crowd.

He crossed over to stand before Captain Greynor with a regal arrogance. With long thin hands, he removed his hood. Those black eyes stared out at Zerrick from a face all too familiar. Zerrick shut his eyes in horror. Dellin Dhur had found him.

"My God, no," he whispered, and would have fallen but for the quick-footed guard standing next to him. When he opened his eyes the world was spinning.

"I am the deacon of the Church in Harrow, and grandson of the Curate. Zerrick was already tried by an official court of law in Harrow, found guilty, and sentenced to death by burning. He was born in Harrow, and he committed his crimes there. I'm here to bring him back," Dellin said in a low voice which crackled with exultation. Zerrick could see by the way he clenched his fists and shifted his feet that he was very excited at having ended his search. There was something odd, however, which seemed to tickle at him. Again the sense of something foul brushed him.

Greynor was not cowed by Dellin's attitude. "Regardless of his origins, Zerrick is now here, under military rule. He has information highly prized by the forces of His Majesty's troops, and I do not intend to give him to you until I get that information." Greynor swatted at the water streaming down his cloak, clearly annoyed at having this conversation out here in public, in the rain.

"Witchcraft is a crime of heresy, and therefore handled by the Church," stated Dellin, with a sneer that again evoked that queer itch along Zerrick's spine. Trying to ignore his pain, Zerrick hobbled over to join the discussion.

"I don't care, frankly," Greynor returned, then raised a hand toward the fort. "Shall we take this to my office? I can show you the papers regarding the case." He looked eager to escape the rain.

"No, that won't be necessary. I'm sorry he has knowledge you need, but my mission was to retrieve him at once and deliver him for his execution. If you want, you can fight this in the courts. It might be interesting to see who wins, the military or the Great Church." Again there was that slight sneer as Dellin delivered his ultimatum, and now that Zerrick was closer, the sensation of wrongness felt stronger.

He faced Dellin. "What about your deal with Father?" As he spoke, Zerrick let his eyes wander over the muddy ground around him, seeking a healthy clump of weeds. He had forsworn magic, but something was wrong here. A tiny spell of discovery would be harmless enough.

Dellin glared at him, and replied, "The deal is off. It has not been pleasant chasing after you." He turned back to Greynor, a sudden light in his eyes. "How much money does the Church supply you with each year?"

Greynor paled, and his straight shoulders slumped. "Surely for such a small case, you wouldn't need to trouble the fathers of the Church with the matter of money, would you?"

Dellin drew himself up to his full height. "He is the pastor's son. The Curate's grandson. To ignore this is to weaken the entire structure of the Church."

Zerrick swallowed, hearing far too much of his father in Dellin's words. He stared hard at his brother, and couldn't see any tangible reason for his strange feeling. Dellin looked as he always did, dressed in a deep gray suit of wool, his hair pulled back, wearing the cravat he'd worn for the family portraiture a few years back.

It was in his stance that Zerrick noticed a difference--Dellin usually stood stone still, but today he couldn't seem to keep his feet in one place for long. There was also that sneer, and the very hard anger in his eyes. Dellin was not typically a man who showed his emotions so openly.

"I may protest this, but I cannot jeopardize the well-being of my troops for one man, no matter how useful. If you insist, you may take custody of Zerrick Dhur. I still ask that he be allowed to speak with me on the matter of the bandits. With Zerrick's help, we could put an end to their crimes," Captain Greynor concluded, and raised his eyes to the skies with a relieved smile. The sky was clearing; already the rain had become only a drizzle.

Zerrick watched as townspeople ventured out and began to crowd around, wondering what he could possibly do. He was certainly not just going to stand by and become trapped again. Spurred by the fire of his pain, he rasped out, "How dare you change your mind now! We had a deal!" He wasn't sure which one he was addressing--but it didn't matter. Everyone was turning on him.

"Sorry, brother. But your actions have removed all rights you may have enjoyed. I'm not letting you out of my sight for one moment. We'll leave immediately." Dellin turned to Greynor and gave a slight bow. "I'm sorry, but I dare not let him talk to you--he would only try to escape again. I'd like an escort as far as the gate. Then my men should be able to take over. Thank you for your cooperation--I will of course mention it to my father."

"I'm not going with you. I'm not even fit to travel," Zerrick insisted, wincing as he shifted his weight. With the rain letting up, the blood on his back began to harden. He couldn't tell the extent of his injuries, but he could see that the back of his white stockings were now stained with red.

"You will come, or the guards will kill you right now," Dellin said, then leaned in close. "Trust me. I'm your brother."

This last was spoken with great emotion and conviction, but Zerrick also caught a scent--that of cut leaves. He reached out his hand and plunged it into the pocket of his brother's doublet.

It was filled with freshly plucked weeds.

Zerrick wasted no time but immersed himself in the sweet magic pulsing within the weeds, and pleaded for the ability to see the truth of this situation. There came the thrill, the triumphant flare of the magic passing into him to do his bidding, then he backed away and locked eyes with his brother.

At first nothing happened. Dellin's black eyes challenged him, but suddenly his eyes began to lose color. Within seconds they had faded to pale green, and the face began to lose definition also, falling away like the skin of an onion, revealing an entirely different set of features underneath. An illusion, Zerrick realized with shock.

He recognized the true face of his accuser. And panicked.

Zerrick whirled and dove through the guards, thinking, *Never! I'll never let you get your hands on me again!* Inside his head, he heard mocking laughter, and cursed himself for not recognizing that taint sooner.

You can't run; they'll shoot you down! Give yourself over, and we'll try to make it quick and painless. You have nowhere else to go, you murderer!

The guards were pulling their guns; the first one shot, and a bullet grazed his ear, but Zerrick kept running. He crashed through the stunned crowd, trying to make it to the cover of a narrow alley. *Get out of my mind, Murtis!* He screamed inside, clawing at his ears.

He slipped a patch of mud and fell to his knees, sending blinding pain up his spine. Behind him the townspeople scattered, and Greynor gave the order to bring him down. Still in his mind he could hear that awful laughter of the bandit witch, and he knew only he alone had seen through the magical disguise. To all other eyes, he was running from the respected churchman, Dellin Dhur.

There were no plans in his head, only the need to run and escape Murtis the Crow. He scrambled to his feet and ran down the nearest alley. Hopefully, with all the side streets and shadowed doorways, he could elude his pursuers.

Another bullet flew by. He forced himself to run faster, and heard behind him the guards' boots splashing through the puddles. Ahead of him he could see that the alley ended at the stone wall of one of the larger estates--a slave farm, by the looks of it. He dashed into a side alley, hoping he could somehow circumnavigate the building.

He was about to try one of the doorways along the alley, when a hammering pain in his left thigh drove him forward into the ground. The sound of a shot echoed all around him off the buildings, sounding like a hundred gunshots instead of one. He tried to get up, but his leg refused to hold him, and he crumpled, pain exploding from both his back and leg. He was trapped.

The world was spinning, but he saw two pairs of dark-skinned hands grabbing and pulling at him from an open doorway. Another deafening shot whizzed past and he caught a glimpse of three guards turning the corner, then he was being carried into a dark corridor.

One of the two shadows carrying him stumbled, jamming his leg against something wooden--a cabinet, he realized. He lurched and moaned with the agony, but as quickly as the sound escaped his lips, a hand pressed against his mouth, warning him to be silent.

Blood streamed down his leg and he knew he could not stay conscious much longer, but he strained his eyes as his captors descended stairs into a dimly lit cavern. He caught sight of rows of ceramic bottles lining shelves along the walls, and decided it must be a wine cellar. It felt mercifully cool down here, and by the light of a single candle, he could just make out the forms of his captors. They were large, well-muscled men with short cropped hair and skin so dark they blended in with the earthen walls, one tall, the second short and stocky.

He saw the tall one open the lid of a chest, empty the rack of bottles contained within, and then he was being stuffed inside and covered with blankets.

He would be smothered, he thought dimly, trying to fight back, but the men were too strong. With a horrifying thud, the lid shut, and he was enclosed in darkness.

Mira

Book Two:

The Put-na

Chapter Ten

"The greatest spell is woman's touch."
-- unknown Put-na warrior

Mira poked at the eggs on her plate, watching as her father fastened on his gunpowder horn. "So how long will you be gone this time?" She tried to keep her voice calm, but a note of anger crept in.

He crossed the breakfast niche to stand behind her chair and placed his hands on her shoulders. "You'll only be alone two days; Hastings and Howard should return from Drayen with that contract with the Duke. He wants two hundred slaves to take to Endersey, so of course I've got to go on another hunt."

"I understand," Mira said, sighing. She gave up on her breakfast and set to clearing the dishes.

Her father gave her a puzzled look. "What are you doing?"

She paused, her arms filled with dishes. "What does it look like I'm doing? I'm cleaning."

He removed the wide brimmed hat he wore on his "hunting" trips and ran a hand through his bushy red hair. "Where's Ranu? Why isn't she doing her job? A Terwin shouldn't have to do menial labor. Not any more."

Always trying to escape the old world, Mira thought, and readied her answer. "Ranu's daughter is sick with a fever. I told her to take the morning off." She hoped the lie sounded convincing.

"How inconvenient. I was going to have her accompany you to Hasting's place. It would probably be best for you to stay with his family while I'm gone. Hasting can protect you if there's trouble . . ." his voice trailed off, and Mira felt her cheeks grow hot with the reminder of that embarrassing trial.

"You can trust me. I wouldn't even go near the slave huts; I'll just stay inside the house." Mira thought about her gossiping sister-in-law,

Abigail, and her squalling baby, wrecking her peace. Worst of all, she could imagine how her brother would react once he learned of the trial. He'd probably do one of two things--challenge her accusers to a duel, or lock her up in the attic.

"Sweetie, it's for your own protection. The people are scared, especially after that witch went berserk yesterday. I don't want anything to happen to you." Edmond Terwin came over to take half her load of dishes. "Well, let's get this place cleaned up." He grinned, the lines around his walnut-brown eyes deepening.

Mira smiled also, despite the nervous tingle in her stomach. Two days, that didn't give her much time. And dodging that busybody Abigail would take some doing. Ah well, she thought. There was always a way, if you wanted something badly enough.

By the time they were finished, Nanna had come downstairs with Mira's bags packed and ready. The slave paused by the breakfast table, keeping her dark lashes lowered, but Mira could see the faint sparkle of her eyes.

"Father, can Nanna take me? The servants can get along without her for a while," Mira asked, trying to suppress the excitement which made her hands tremble. He had to say yes, she reasoned; it was either Nanna or one of his slavemasters from the fields. And she knew he didn't trust any man other than her four brothers near her. To her mind, it made no sense. With her curls which she couldn't pin into the fashionable coiffures, her too-long legs, and those awful freckles, she doubted she would tempt any man.

"Nanna? Yes, I suppose that will work," her father said, wiping his hands. He came out of the kitchen and stood before the slave. "Remember, Mira's safety is in your hands. You think I don't know about all your sneaking about with her, letting her stay with your people down in the fields. She can't do that anymore. Take care of her."

"Yes, my lord. She is like my child; I would not let harm come to her. I swear it by the Mother." Nanna spoke gravely, staring up at Mr. Terwin without fear, despite the fact she was half his size.

Mira glanced over to her father, wondering if he really understood this woman he had long ago assigned to be her guardian after the terrible illness took her mother. But he hardly acknowledged the slave.

"Whatever. Just see to it she gets to her brother's." He took his bags and shouldered them. Turning back around, he stared at Nanna, specifically at the lobes of her ears, where she had hung two rings of gold with amber stones embedded within. The slave flushed and put her hands to her ears.

"Take those things off. And no more of your tales of a 'Mother' goddess around my daughter." With that, he stomped off to the stables.

"Daddy, wait!" Mira called, running to the door, but he was already down the steps, walking out of earshot. She turned back to Nanna. "He forgot to say goodbye."

Nanna removed her earrings and stowed them in a pocket on her apron. She came over to Mira and gently hugged her. "He is worried, is all. I think he will remember two miles down the trail, and give himself a kick in the head," she said and grinned, her teeth shining.

Mira couldn't help but smile. Her father was hotheaded, narrow-minded, and as stubborn as the bark of an ironwood tree. But he did love her, of that she had no doubt. Sometimes, though, his love was so stifling! At any rate he was leaving now, and that meant she was free, at least for a little while.

Mira watched the dust settle after her father's men rode off, her ears open to the sounds of slaves singing in the fields as they worked, and wind sweeping through the palm trees lining the porch. All was as it should be; she didn't hear the approach of any of the slavemasters or any of her father's party returning for forgotten items. She and Nanna were alone.

"How long, before Abigail starts to worry?" she asked Nanna.

Nanna's lips curled into a smile. "A good hour. I will say we stopped to shop. We need sugar and flour. I could go get them, and you could stay--since you don't need to leave the grounds, yes?" Nanna's brown eyes gleamed with mischief, and Mira had to suppress a chuckle, as her pulse gave a little jump. No, she would be just fine, right on the grounds. And Abigail wouldn't suspect a thing.

She took a deep breath, expelled it, and smoothed the wrinkles in her skirt. "Ranu is already there?"

Nanna nodded. "Behind the medical potions your father keeps. You go ahead. I shop, come back as soon as possible, and we can then go to your law-sister."

"Sister-in-law," Mira murmured, good-naturedly. Nanna never could understand why there had to be any distinction other than sister for anyone of her race--the Put-na all called each other family. Certainly Nanna considered herself mother to all the slaves on this farm, and she had adopted Mira as well into her people's circle.

The Put-na were an entire language group, broken up into numerous tribes scattered along the Jagara Mountains which all shared a similar world view. From the age of five, Mira had been raised to speak the language, learn their customs and beliefs. That was why she insisted on calling Abigail an in-law. With the time spent with the natives and with Nanna for a guardian, Mira felt she belonged with the Put-na more than with her own people.

She rubbed cheeks with Nanna, positioned her bags at the front porch so they would be easy to grab on the way to her brother's, then retrieved a plate of food and a jug of water. After checking herself in the mirror, she set off for the back of the house.

The storm cellar was a custom that went back to her father's people who came from a country north of Endersey, where there were terrible wind storms, somewhat similar to the tropical storms which occasionally came here. The cellar had been built for these storms and as an emergency stronghold against bandits or natives, but it had not been used in years. Mira doubted her father was even aware she knew of it. As she approached the two wooden doors, two slaves apparently napping in the shade sprang up. They pulled the heavy doors open, muscles bulging on their red-skinned backs, then they stood aside and murmured greetings for her to enter.

"Mother's blessings onto you," she responded in their language, and descended into darkness.

It felt cool and moist, the rich smell of the earth pervading the long narrow room. Stacks of boxes lined the earthen walls and divided the room in half, blocking the rear from prying eyes. The boxes were labeled in the sprawling handwriting of her father: ammunition, bandages, grain alcohol, and even stranger things: ground unicorn horn, snake venom antidote, and bones of a long deceased saint.

How many of these did he use to try to cure Mother's illness? Mira wondered, stepping over a low box.

There was only one light in the narrow room, a small lantern on the floor at the back of the room. Its pale light fell on the form of Ranu, the chambermaid, who sat in a reed chair pulling the seeds off a jungle plant. A quilt had been laid on the ground, falling over Ranu's feet, but the stacks of boxes prevented her from seeing much else. She crept closer.

As she came into the light of the lantern, Ranu rose and put a finger to her lips, cautioning Mira to stay quiet. Good. If he was sleeping, she could take time to get a better look.

She passed the boxes and glanced down at the man lying on the quilt. He was turned on his side, with his bandaged leg away from the floor, and bandages crisscrossed his torso, supporting pads against his shoulders and back. His thick black hair trailed across the makeshift pillows, a few strands falling across his angular face. He was deep asleep, eyelashes fluttering in the midst of some dream. Even in sleep, however, his face remained haggard, drawn in pain. Mira blew out a breath.

She shouldn't have been out there at the lashing, but something about the man had intrigued her. Perhaps it was just that he was young, handsome--even beautiful--but that wasn't what had drawn her to don a hood and creep out in heavy rain clothes. There was something else about him, something frightening and exhilarating. Magic.

She'd told the captain the truth; she was innocent of witchcraft. That was not for lack of interest, however, but merely lack of opportunity. The Put-na protected their priests of magic with utmost devotion--none had ever been captured by white man. She had heard tales of them, though, fantastic tales of wonder while seated at the feet of Nanna and Ranu.

Mira had gone to the lashing to see him escape, throw one last spell and disappear into the jungle. She didn't know who had captured him or why he had been willing to wait for Captain Greynor to pronounce judgment. He was haunted by something, from that terrible look in his eyes. His remarkable, crystalline eyes.

Hovering behind Nanna, she had expected only to catch one last glimpse of him before he disappeared, but to her utter shock and horror, he had let himself be punished. That horrible crack of the cat-o-nine-tails pierced her; she watched open-mouthed as the town executor drove the barbed strands of the cat down into the poor man's naked back.

A cry escaped her, and she averted her eyes, fearful she might become sick. Instead, as the whip fell again and she heard a few murmurs of awe and approval, she found she was far too angry to be sick. She was going to stop this whole wicked affair!

Mira stomped over to the platform, but as she came close enough to see the face of the witch, she halted. A pouch hanging from his neck was glowing a bright yellow, and inscribed on that pouch was a rune, one from the Put-na tribe--a symbol of the Mother. The man's eyes were open, but they stared right through her, seeing some other place, another person. She thought he said something, like "help me" or perhaps "free me," but she was too afraid to move. Never before had she actually seen a person ensorcelled.

And even stranger, as he came out of his stupor and the last blow fell, Mira could have sworn she saw the shadow of a woman, supporting his body and lowering it gently to the ground. Mira retreated back into the circle of onlookers, and drew close to Nanna who always accompanied her on such ventures.

"We need to see him somehow," she told Nanna. She was about to say more, but silenced her tongue at the look on the woman's face.

"We have already made preparations. If it is the Mother's will, he will speak with us again."

Mira hadn't understood, until that incident with the man who claimed to be this man's brother. He had cried out in terror, again seeing something no one else could see, then had run away, straight towards her father's estate.

"Nanna!" she urged.

"Hush, child. Everything will work out," Nanna had said, and she had been right. When the young man was shot--what horror!--Ranu's husband and brother were near to drag him to safety. With the help of other town slaves, they had been able to smuggle the man here, where he had been drugged and treated for his injuries.

Now here she was, beside this remarkable man, able to see him and speak with him without the suffocating presence of her father.

"Is he still drugged?" she whispered, kneeling at his side, her back to the earthen wall. Her fingers hovered over the bandages at his left shoulder.

"No drugs today--Nanna, she come, want speak with him," Ranu labored to explain in the common tongue, undoubtedly so Mira would understand. She was still working on Ranu's Put-na dialect.

Well, that explained the need for quiet. Mira watched the man's slow, even breaths, wondering whether she should wake him before Nanna returned. Just watching him was pleasant enough. She heard a sudden catch in his breathing, and the fingers of his right hand clenched, as if grabbing for something.

"He's dreaming, isn't he?" Mira murmured.

Ranu nodded. "No wake him. Dreams very important."

Trust Ranu to bring up her superstitious beliefs, Mira thought dryly. She saw his eyelids flutter, the dark thin brows furrowing in concern. Maybe she wouldn't have to wake him. The dream seemed to be becoming more violent.

The muscles in his arms bunched and flexed, and Mira scooted back a little, awed by the strength apparent there. He was too thin, but nothing could hide the strong musculature in those arms and shoulders, as if he'd hacked through an entire continent of jungle. Which, Mira thought, could very well be true.

He cried out, waking, and she gasped, flattening herself against the wall as he lurched to a sitting position. For a moment he sat there as his eyes searched the room and found her.

The look in his eyes grew less haunted, gentler as he stared at her, his breathing becoming steady as he realized the danger was past. He seemed more in control now, so Mira cautiously drew away from the wall and attempted to introduce herself, "I don't know if you remember me, but I'm--"

"I remember you," he interrupted. "Mira."

The way he formed the word was almost like a caress. Mira pressed her hands against her cheeks which had suddenly grown warm. The only man who had ever called her 'Mira' was her father; to all others she was 'Miss Terwin' or simply 'Ma'am.'

Her silence seem to make him very uncomfortable. He looked down, seeming to become suddenly very interested in his fingernails. She regained her composure and prompted him. "And you are . . ."

"Zerrick." He spat the name out, like it was a nuisance.

"That's right, I remember now," she said, smiling. That seemed to make him even more nervous.

"Where am I?" he asked.

This she was prepared for. "My father's slaves found you in an alley, when you were shot. They took you here where you could safely mend. You're in the storm cellar of my father's house. Don't worry--he left this morning for an expedition."

"Hunting slaves, right? My grandfather used to do that," he said, with a bitter chuckle. He tried to stretch and grimaced, a hiss escaping his lips.

"It still hurts, doesn't it?" she inquired, motioning for Ranu to fetch the water.

He gave up and lied back down on the pallet. "I think it will always hurt."

146

What? Mira thought, completely mystified. What wound was he talking about? She chose to ignore the comment and rose to take the water from Ranu. She had to set it down almost at once, as she noticed that her hands were trembling.

She considered backing away, to tell Ranu to take over, then scolded herself for her nervousness. He was just a patient. No different than the slaves she cared for, applying salves to their bruises and whip marks after the slavemasters were too harsh.

"If you could lie on your stomach, I could apply some herbs that will lessen your pain and help the healing," she said, taking the seed pods Ranu had been sorting, mashing them into a thick paste. Into this she poured a little of the water, and made sure the consistency was just right.

"Pitchu seeds for sores and open wounds, right?" Zerrick asked, eyeing the mixture.

Mira gaped at him. "How did you know?"

He gave a bleak smile, one that hinted at pain of a different sort than his wounds, and lowered his gaze. "I was trained in herbalism by a well-known woodsman. And witch."

"Really?" Mira said, unsure how to proceed. There was a deep sadness in his voice, a sense of loss. He offered no more, so she dropped the subject, respectful of his privacy. "Just turn over and I'll change the bandages. Unless you prefer Ranu here to do it--she's better than me--in fact, she taught me all I know."

"Whatever you like," he mumbled, obviously embarrassed. Well, he spoke like a gentleman, and gentlemen usually didn't come across ladies so bold as to touch them while they were shirtless--and worse, Mira mused, glancing at where Zerrick's breeches had been slashed to allow access to the bullet wound. Well, she wasn't much of a lady. And she didn't care what he thought.

She directed him to change position, then carefully removed all of the bandages, trying not to look at the angry welts. After dipping her fingers in the cool salve, she gently spread it across the inflamed skin.

He gave a little grunt, squinting his eyes. "How bad . . . is it?" He laid his head down on his arm, taking shallow breaths, then gradually his muscles relaxed as the numbing herb went into effect.

Mira started applying the salve in earnest, making sure it covered every place where the skin was broken, including the hole in the back of his thigh. Nanna had already removed the bullet, so everything should heal now, but it would be days before he could travel.

"You'll soon recover from the lashing. I want to make sure there are no infections, but they'll soon heal enough for you to move around. Your leg, however, will take longer. You shouldn't walk on it for at least a week." She finished and leaned over to blow the salve dry so she could replace the bandages.

When he spoke, his voice sounded strangely husky, almost as if the drugs were still at work on him. "So I'm trapped here for a while."

Mira cocked her head and gave a half smile. "There are worse places to be trapped."

"Indeed there are." Mira found the look he gave her somewhat unsettling. She finished drying the salve and went over to the boxes to fetch clean bandages. From here, she saw that the door was still open, and she could hear Tak and his brother softly talking. She also noticed that Ranu had left. That was a little peculiar; she was now totally alone with Zerrick. But it also seemed hopeful. If Ranu trusted this stranger enough to be alone with Mira, he had passed all her superstitious tests.

She returned and set to reapplying the wrap, trying to remain cool and aloof despite the fact that in order to cover all the wounds, she basically had to circle his body with her arms, passing the strips of cloth from hand to hand. She felt grateful for the fact that he kept his eyes lowered, holding his arms out to make things easier.

"Where is your chaperone?" he asked in a low voice, as she went on to wrap his leg. His head was turned and he was watching her out of the corner of his eye, his chest rising and falling as his breathing deepened.

Still in pain, Mira decided, relieved that the dressing was almost over. It was chilly down here, under the earth, but she could feel a heat radiating from the witch's body. It was beginning to make her sweat.

She finished and inched back. "Outside, with her--" she began, then fell silent at the look in Zerrick's eye. She saw hunger, but also sadness, and a look she recognized only too well. Simple loneliness.

"I'd like to thank you," he whispered, edging closer and reaching out to touch her hands.

"It's no trouble, really," Mira stammered, again flustered by the heat he seemed to sow within her. She glanced at her position, cornered against the back wall, and at his lean body, now curled towards her and was suddenly struck with the vision of a panther, coiled to spring for its prey.

"Oh good, you are awake," the gravelly voice of Nanna cut across the chamber, as the usually agile slave stumbled noisily over the boxes, stirring up a cloud of dust from the earthen floor which sent both Zerrick and Mira to coughing.

Behind her followed Ranu, with a basket of papayas and two sacks. Nanna glanced down at Mira and chuckled, setting herself down on the chair Ranu had occupied earlier, and motioning for Mira to join her. With an anxious glance at Zerrick, Mira rose and went to sit on the floor by her guardian.

Zerrick sat up a little, regarding Nanna with suspicion. "It was you behind this rescue, wasn't it. And you'll probably want something in return."

A shaft of light fell across his face, illuminating one pale eye. Only moments before there had been life stirring within those eyes; now they were shadowy, mirror-like, even haughty as he held his head straight, setting his jaw into a stubborn line Mira knew only too well from her father.

Nanna didn't seem to notice his change of posture. She leaned forward and spoke in a quiet, even tone. "Yes, there is something I would like, but you don't have to give it unless you want to. I want to know who your teacher was. And what you plan to do now."

149

The shoulders slumped, and once again Zerrick became the helpless young man, troubled and lost. "My teacher was known as Alden. He was burned for witchcraft, on the same day I was supposed to burn. I escaped. And I have no idea where I'm going now."

This last was said in despair, reminding Mira of the look the slaves had when they were finished with their 'training,' ready to be shipped off to the Motherland. She also saw now that it wasn't so much his wounds that were trapping him here. It was his spirit.

Nanna sat back again, nodding to herself. "Alden. I don't know if he ever came to my tribe, but he must have joined some tribe to have learned magic with them. I know that from the rune you wear round your neck. It is a *kumalido* pouch with magic crystal and the Mother's sign of protection." She brought out from her pocket the earrings she had been wearing earlier and handed them to Mira. "You are young-- please go and hand these to young master Zerrick. I must sit a while."

Mira did as she asked, wondering how fast Nanna had needed to run to shop at the local farmer's market and return here so quickly. Nothing Nanna did surprised her, however; she was a remarkable woman. Mira wondered sometimes, just who she had been before the slave traders came.

Zerrick took the gold hoops, and stared after Mira as she resumed her place at Nanna's feet. He looked the earrings over, passing them from hand to hand as if they were heavy, or warm, even hot to the touch.

"Don't worry, this is just to make sure you tell the truth. Please, if you would, make the stones glow. I have been told there is magic within these, so it should not be hard." She smiled." For a witch." Nanna folded her bony arms in her lap and lay back in the wicker chair, almost seeming to be asleep, but Mira knew better. She was carefully observing the witch, assessing him.

He laid the earrings in his palm, and it seemed to Mira that he was almost blushing, under the gaze of the three women. He closed his eyes, looking faintly worried, then suddenly a look of sheer ecstasy came over his face, and he opened his eyes as a burst of light emanated from the crystals. Wonder filled Mira--it was real--it was all real, the tales! She wanted to ask him so many questions, but he was frowning. The light faded.

He regarded the stones with longing, but held them out for Nanna to take back. "That should prove everything to you. I don't want to use too much of the power there," he said in explanation. Nanna rose, took the earrings, and considered them for a moment, then put them back into her apron.

"That is good, master Zerrick. And now I see what side you fall on. These earrings were my mother's. She was a follower of *Kumara*, the Mother."

"A Mother goddess?" Zerrick sat up straighter, and Mira saw a light in his eyes. He rubbed his fingers as if they itched. Was this magic so tempting? Addictive? She put the idea aside to consider later.

Nanna nodded. "Yes, Mother goddess, She who created the world and all life on it. You might want to learn more of Her, for it is Her gift you use when you cast your spells. In my tribe She is the highest power."

Zerrick chewed his lip. "Alden wanted me to study with the Putna, but I was caught instead by the Stonefist Gang. They had two witches. Both of them were evil."

Nanna bobbed her head in understanding. "You now fear the power. Yes, my people know badness, we call that one *Kormu*. But while some may use power to blast and destroy like a hurricane wind, in the end they find only misery for themselves. The storm passes, the wind dies, and still Kumara the earth mother is left untouched. Power is not for power's sake."

"And what about power you can't control? I've been having dreams and I'm being pulled somewhere by something and I don't have enough control of my magic to even understand. I keep trying to run away from the power, but it keeps finding me. And using me." As Zerrick spoke, Mira looked in concern to Nanna--power beyond his control? Like what she had seen at the lashing?

Nanna sighed. "I do not know all the answers. I was kidnapped from my village when I was ten--I did not learn my mother's art, and I do not have the gift of understanding dreams, like the dreamtellers of my tribe. I left behind my old self, my old name, and became 'Nanna.' I do know this. My people can answer your questions, they can help you with the magic, and they can ask the spirits what the Mother intends."

Nanna rose from her seat and bent down to squat beside Zerrick, her liquid black eyes looking deeply into his. With her long thin hands, she cupped his cheek and pulled him close.

"Go to the mountains. Go to my people."

Zerrick's eyes were wide with fright. "But how do I get there?"

Nanna chuckled. "Mira can show you."

Chapter Eleven

"Freedom--and slavery--is within a person's mind."
--Nanna

A shocked silence followed Nanna's statement. The pain in his leg restrained Zerrick from leaping to his feet, but his eyes widened and his jaw dropped. "You can't be serious! I would never endanger someone so . . ." He looked helplessly towards Mira. Her eyes were bright with excitement, the pulse in her long slender neck beating rapidly. She looked like an exotic bird, tall and graceful. And fragile. He swallowed. "So innocent," he finished, embarrassed.

"I wonder. I hadn't meant to say that. And yet, it does make sense," Nanna said under her breath. She stared a Mira a moment, and shook her head. "No, you are right. Mira is not yet ready. I have a feeling, though, that she will someday leave. She fits here about as well as you do."

"Me, go out into . . . the jungle?" Mira whispered. Zerrick could see the thoughts whirling inside. He could hardly deny that he would love the company, but no, he couldn't possibly take her into such dangerous territory.

He cut off both women's musings. "I go alone, or I stay and take my chances. I'll not endanger anyone. And believe me, just by staying too close, you both are in danger. My talent is not entirely under control."

Nanna rose. "I will think on this. There may be one on the farm here who is willing to risk an escape with you. I will come back tomorrow. Ranu will care for you in the meantime."

"Ranu," Zerrick murmured, watching as Mira set out food she had brought for him at the foot of his mat. She kept her eyes lowered, hiding any emotions reflected there. The excitement he had seen earlier had died as quickly as it had risen, leaving him uncertain he had really seen it. But he would not forget it.

He touched the hem of her skirt. "Will you be leaving also?" he asked, unable to hold the question inside where it belonged.

He was gratified by the look of concern which crossed her face as she turned to answer. "Oh yes. I'll come back when I'm able." She turned and went over to the boxes, placing distance between herself and Zerrick, and looked shyly at him over her shoulder. Then she hurried out of the room and into the sun.

Nanna stayed a moment longer to gather up her packages. She saw where his attention was focused and squatted down beside him, regarding him thoughtfully. "Don't be disappointed if she doesn't come. Her brothers are returning, and they keep her tightly controlled. I am sorry I suggested her coming, but I do not know how to help her. She is like my daughter. And like me, she is a slave. Goodbye, Master Zerrick."

She stood and bowed, then passed out of sight.

The days were painfully long, as Zerrick attempted to exercise his wounded leg by clinging to boxes and pacing around the narrow room. Nanna was faithful in coming once a day to check his progress, and each time she brought a slave to tell him about tribal customs, trails he might follow to the mountains, and names of relations who might be left to aid him if he stumbled upon their camps. None were ready to attempt escape and follow; already his reputation as a dangerous witch had circulated through the town, both among his people and theirs.

He asked about the whereabouts of the man proclaiming to be his brother and learned 'Dellin' had made a three day search for him, then had left town. Incidentally, bandit activity outside of town had increased. It seemed a segment of the Stonefist Gang was lurking around the town perimeters.

After a week, his back had healed considerably, and he could limp along if he held onto someone for support. He'd eaten almost constantly, and he had to admit this rest was doing him a great deal of good, but he was anxious. Mira hadn't been able to visit him at all-- Nanna said her brother Hastings had locked her in the attic of his town house as punishment for being accused of witchcraft. That sort of news made Zerrick smolder.

If only there were something he could do! But of course there wasn't, and that was what drove him crazy. He wasn't used to inactivity. He'd been running for too long. Back in Harrow, he probably wouldn't have thought twice about a girl in Mira's shoes, but now things were different. He understood in a new light what it meant to be caged.

Zerrick sat on one of the boxes and rubbed an oily substance into his backpack to seal it against water, wrinkling his nose at the bitter smell. Nanna had come yesterday with a few things of his--his possessions had been either thrown out or stolen from his room at the inn, then recovered a piece at a time by her many native friends. Several of his things were probably lost forever, such as his pistol and his velvet coats, but he had regained the backpack, machete, and his sword.

He suppressed a little jump as the lock to the basement shutters gave a loud clank. The doors opened, letting in a stream of light which framed a head crowned with copper hair. Zerrick smiled as Mira descended the steps into the cellar, her arms full of clothing and food. She dumped her armload on a stack of boxes and gave him an awkward curtsy.

"Hello. Sorry I took so long to return," she said.

Zerrick could see by the flush of her cheeks and by her breathing that she had been running. He hurried to set aside the oil then pulled down a crate for her to sit on. "I understand. Won't you sit down and join me? It's been quiet around here." He noticed her eyes straying to the fresh loaf of bread and roasted ham she had brought. "Have you eaten?"

She gave a shy smile. "I haven't eaten, actually. Thank you." She hesitated before sitting down, and Zerrick realized she wasn't sure if she was supposed to serve her guest. He grabbed the bread and ham and a flagon of wine, then set up another box to use as a table. Sitting back on his own crate, he broke the bread and handed her a piece.

"You don't know what a pleasure it is, seeing you. It gets so quiet and dull in here," he commented, pulling out his knife and cutting off a few slices of ham for each of them.

She nodded, engrossed in her food. "At least my prison has windows. Servants too."

Zerrick flinched, remembering her situation. He kept to eating, sneaking glances at her without letting their gazes touch. Then he peered over at the pile of clothing she had brought. They appeared to be rugged men's clothing around his size. He wondered how she had come by them.

She answered his unasked question. "I haven't had much to do, so I've been gathering some of Hasting's less-used clothing and altering them so you could use them. They're suited for the jungle--my brother, like my father, travels the wilderness extensively."

Zerrick swallowed his bite. "Won't he miss these?"

Her face became grim and cold. "I hope he does. It serves him right for locking me up."

This was dangerous territory, but Zerrick had to ask some of the questions which had been burning inside the past week. He kept his voice neutral. "How can your family treat you so?"

She smoothed her hair back and took a deep breath. "I'm the only daughter, living in a rugged town. They fear for my safety." She paused a moment, glancing at Zerrick as if deciding how much she should tell.

He made himself wait patiently. It was strange. Just in the short time he had known her, he himself felt a protectiveness for her. She was kinder than anyone he had ever met, and it was only natural to want to protect someone so innocent. But he wondered, were his feelings of the same kind as her family's?

She decided to continue. "I liked it once--it's a simple way to live, never having to worry about anything." Her eyes suddenly hardened. "But that was when I was young. I don't need quite as much protection now as they think I do. I'm tired of living like a china doll everybody thinks is going to break. That's why I sneak away with Nanna sometimes."

Mira grew quiet and turned away. Zerrick tried to break the uncomfortable silence with the first thing that came to mind. "If you want out of your family's protection, why not marry someone?" He tried to make it sound casual, like a simple debate over the weather or town politics. Still, he couldn't help blushing.

She laughed and shook her head, not seeming to notice his discomfort. "Get married? I doubt it."

Zerrick's eyebrows went up in surprise. "Why not?"

She stood and smoothed back her fiery hair again, and twirled before him in her plain black skirt, "Well, look at me. I'm not beautiful, I'm strange because I talk to slaves, I'm now considered a witch, and finally, my brothers and my father would shoot any man who even tried to talk to me."

"Besides," she added as an afterthought, "I have no interest in marriage just yet. I would like a little freedom, a chance to see the world. A husband would just replace the authority of my father." With that, she picked up the clothing, dropped it on his makeshift bed, and stood by Ranu's empty chair, glancing from Zerrick to the door. "I shouldn't be here without Nanna."

She was going to leave him, perhaps disappear forever, Zerrick thought in panic. He wasn't going to be here that much longer; he had to make the most of whatever time they had. And he certainly didn't want to part like this.

"No, please, I'm sorry I brought the matter up. I just worry sometimes--I mean, you've been kind to me, without knowing anything about me. We can talk about whatever you like. Just don't leave yet." Zerrick drew on all the eloquence which was his family's heritage, escorting her back to her makeshift seat and pushing it in for her. He himself sat down several feet away, trying not to let the flash of pain show on his face.

And they talked. They talked about his town where one could encircle the entire settlement in a little over an hour along the wooden palisade, attend a ball at the old lord's manor, or catch fish down at the old mill. And they talked about her childhood with the slaves, spending days picking coffee beans alongside aborigine children, singing songs in a strange language she now knew almost as well as her own. They avoided any bad memories, any hints of their present predicaments. Zerrick was completely happy.

Then Nanna burst into the room.

"Quick, child, your brother's coming up to the house, and oh, he is angry! You better get to your room; pull out some books or something. I'll help keep him a moment."

A resigned look replaced Mira's smile, and she nodded and clasped Zerrick's hand. Her dark eyes looked deep into his. "Please tell me when you plan to leave. I will come say goodbye."

She let go and headed for the door, then turned and gave him a naughty smile. "Even if I have to put shackles on all of my family!"

It was a week and a half later before Zerrick saw her again, and then she was with Nanna, helping to ready the house for her father's return in a few days. Zerrick's leg was as healed as he had time to allow. Fall was approaching, and while that meant little here in the tropics, it could make a great deal of hardship when he began climbing the Jagara mountains.

Then too, there was the matter of Murtis the Crow and his gang. Two days ago Zerrick had received word from one of the slaves that the Stonefist Gang had supposedly gone east, back towards the coast. Now was his window for escape, before Mr. Terwin returned with all his men.

In his brief contact with Mira, he managed to relate that he planned to leave in two nights. A strange look crossed her face, one of determination and anguish. Then it passed, and with a cheery smile, she promised she'd see him off.

He wondered at her reaction, but shrugged it off; three of her four brothers were in town, and she was constantly being watched and kept busy running errands, watching over households and children, and

Iahmel knew what else. It contrasted so much with his family life, the neglect and lack of feeling. But both neglect and excess seemed to drive one insane.

Zerrick spent his last two days pulling himself up the stacks of blocks using his fingers and arms in preparation for the mountains. He ran and leapt, making sure the scabs on his back and leg wouldn't break under stress. All seemed in order. He stuffed his pack with enough food for a month and both hot and cold weather clothes, and summoned Nanna to organize his escape from town.

"Your face is too well known in town to simply walk out," Nanna mused, pressing her fingers into the hollow of his cheek. She squinted and shook her head. "Your face is angular, and with your color of hair and eyes, a disguise would be very hard. It might be better to hide you completely from sight. Or I could make you a woman."

Zerrick pulled away. "I think a woman traveling alone would cause a stir. What's the security like along the walls? Can I go out some other way than the gates?"

Nanna sat back in the old chair by Zerrick's bedding, her lips pressed together. She gave a shake of her head, her bun bobbing. "Oh no. Bad idea. You are in a military outpost, remember? The watch here is very good." She was silent a moment, then her eyes lit up. "Smuggle--that is the word you use when you hide items and trade them out, yes? We could smuggle you out in a trade caravan. Many of these leave for the coast. Once you were out of the town, you would simply have to escape from a few guards."

Zerrick had another idea. "I could use magic. Make a disguise, like my enemy did."

Nanna's eyes grew wide. "I had forgotten that. Yes, that might work. And I have a perfect person in mind you could leave town as." She grinned. "Mira's brother, Hastings."

Zerrick's heart leapt. "But I've never even seen him!"

"Mira has some talent at drawing. With the three of us, we should be able to transform you. Then you'll be able to simply walk out of town."

The choice seemed obvious. "Let's get started," Zerrick said.

The choice seemed obvious, Mira thought, stitching the hem of a woolen cloak. She paused, listening to the hum of voices as Hastings and his wife passed by her door, ready to spring to action if she heard the sound of a key in the lock. But the sounds grew fainter, until all was quiet once more in her prison. She hurried to finish the garment.

She believed in Iahmel, she believed in family and one's duty to one's father, but she couldn't mold herself to fit within the meek and obedient role of daughter any longer. And as she was so fond of telling herself, the rules didn't really apply to her because she had been raised half native. Therefore she must do as a native would, and fight to escape, when escape was possible. Fly to the wilderness.

What better chance would she get than now? How many kind and good hearted men came into her life who would be able to help her on a dangerous trek into the unknown? It wasn't as if she would be a burden; he would be slow while he mended and he would probably need her expertise for the full recovery of his leg. What Nanna had spoken had been a divinely sent message. Go with Zerrick.

And how convenient that they needed her help to complete his escape! She packed away the cloak into the lightweight pack she had patched up from Hasting's previous excursion, took out the breeches she had hidden under the mattress to give them a last inspection, then put them on underneath her dress, making sure the boyhood clothing of her youngest brother Eddy would fit. Satisfied, she brought out the drawing she had made of her brother Hastings and folded it into a small knap sack, along with a few special items she had picked up for Zerrick.

With a quick glance at the deepening sunset outside, she set to braiding her hair and planning her own escape from the house.

As the half-moon rose, Zerrick sat on the porch of the main house, turning Nanna's earrings over in his hands and watching the shadows for signs of the slave or of Mira. The night was cool and clear--a rare treat in the tropics. His insides were wound tight at the thought of what he was about to attempt.

He stood as two figures emerged from the shadows of the estate's gated entrance and watched as Nanna and Mira stepped up to the porch. Mira was shrouded in a cloak that could have been either dark green or blue, but looked black in the pale moonlight. Zerrick looked curiously to see what she wore beneath the cloak, but gave up as she looked up and gave him a charming smile. She drew out a small pack.

"I have the drawings here. We'd better get started," she said, excitement humming in her voice.

There was something a little odd about the way she kept her front to him, as if hiding something under her voluminous cloak. Zerrick looked to Nanna, but her face was indiscernible. Her bun gave a bob as she nodded. "Go ahead. We must hurry--curfew is past and we don't want to make them too suspicious."

"Why the cloak?" Zerrick asked Mira, trying to remember Mira's brother from the glance or two he'd stolen while in hiding. A Mr. Terwin look-alike, minus the beard, and about twenty years younger, he recalled. Hastings had a darker shade of red than either Mira or her father and was tall and muscular, but not as broad shouldered as Mr. Terwin, which was fortunate. The hair and eyes should not be difficult to produce, but a larger body frame was something else. Well, he'd be a little shorter and leaner. Hopefully it wouldn't matter.

He returned his attention to Mira as she replied, "I thought it best to be as unseen as possible. It hides my hair--hopefully less will remember seeing me, so I won't get into too much trouble afterwards." She adjusted her cloak, shifting her weight. He could see now she wore full skirts, which only made it even more difficult to see if she was carrying anything other than the small pack.

Zerrick shrugged, satisfied with her answer, and began to picture every dimple and pore, every strand of hair, glancing occasionally at

Mira to take note of the pale hue of her skin, her eyes . . . colors he would have to duplicate. Luckily it was night, so only a fair semblance would be needed.

In addition he asked questions of how Hastings walked, what his voice sounded like, and his habits. He found Mira was an intelligent observer. She demonstrated the swagger that her brother used and noted that he tended to scratch at his ears when thinking and chewed his fingernails when nervous. That last would be no problem--Zerrick's nails were down to the quick with the last two weeks of hiding. He thanked her and retreated into a dark corner surrounded by high shrubbery. Time to work the magic.

He felt nervous at first, wondering if he had forgotten everything, unsure if the sweet power in the stones would answer again, but he need not have feared. As he closed his eyes to look for the energy, he found it was right there leaping up in his face, bright and excited and eager for his instructions. He concentrated very hard; the mistake with the candle hadn't hurt anyone, but now he had to immerse his whole body in magic. Any wrong thoughts could do him great harm.

He treated the energy as if it were intelligent, picturing a thin layer of seeming enveloping him, making his features appear as he wished. He hadn't learned illusions on people, though Alden had taught him to make images on things like tables and chairs, but upon seeing Murtis's illusion, the way to alter a person's appearance had suddenly become clear. It was a mask of magic on the surface of the person, coloring the hair, the eyes, and the skin just so. This magic within the earrings needed no extra coaching. As he pictured how he wanted to look to others it fairly danced up from his hands up his arms, along his torso and down his legs, finally stealing over around his head, giving him pleasant chills down the spine. Then all physical sensation passed as it seeped into his skin and seemed to disappear--but he could see in his mind's eye, that it had done its work.

He opened his eyes and looked for the changes, but evidently he was immune. Other than a barely discernible glow over his skin which would be apparent only to other witches, there were no visible signs of the illusion. Pocketing the earrings, he went to test the illusion.

He crossed to the porch, practicing his swagger, and felt a glow of success when both Mira and Nanna gasped, staring at him nervously. Nanna relaxed first, then Mira.

"Oh, now I see it's you. At first you really did look like Hastings!" Mira said, coming forward with a hand raised, as if debating whether or not to touch him. Shyly, she reached out and touched his cheek. "Strange--it doesn't work for touch. I see Hasting's beard, but I can't feel it."

Zerrick wasn't sure how to react. "But you mean to say you can see through it?" *Oh please let it not be another mistake,* he thought, insides wrenching.

She drew back, pursing her lips. "Well, I expected to see you look like Hastings. At first the image looked complete, but while my eyes saw red hair and a red beard, my mind kept telling me that it was really you, that your hair really should be black, your face fair. I'm seeing kind of a half-illusion. It seems layered and fades in and out."

"It is because we know the truth. I think the guards will be fooled, however," Nanna assured him, and completely surprised him by throwing her arms around him and embracing him. "Keep the earrings, Master Zerrick. I cannot use them, but perhaps you can to do great good."

Zerrick nodded, suddenly torn between his friendship with this strange woman and his need to leave. "Thank you for all the help you've given me," he said in a voice heavy with emotion. "I won't forget you." He hugged her back, then looked to Mira.

She smiled. "I can say a proper goodbye at the gate. I always kiss my brothers goodbye when they're leaving on a long journey."

He tried to keep from blushing. "Oh, well, that's good," he stammered, then began putting on his packs. "Even with the illusion, I'd prefer to keep out of sight as much as possible. And we'd better hurry. I don't know how long my spell will last. I seem to be gaining in power, but by how much, I don't know."

"Let's go then," Mira exclaimed, helping to adjust the strap on Zerrick's backpack. He tested his packs for balance and nodded, satisfied. Mira blew out the candle, then the three of them descended into the shadows.

Nanna led the way down dark side streets, past slave quarters, moving with an easy grace. Zerrick immediately gave up trying to see where he was, instead letting his hearing and his touch be his guides, following the soft patter of Nanna's feet and the jangle of something inside Mira's small pack. They disrupted a few rats and an irritable monkey, but few people were about these parts of town. He caught sight only of a lone slave on some errand and a cloaked gentleman sneaking into an apartment, perhaps for nightly pleasures or gambling.

They reached the wooden palisade wall, curving around like a great toothy grin. Beyond the wall, Zerrick could hear the cackle of night birds, the sounds of the jungle. He looked at the wall and at the guards pacing along the narrow rampart, glad he hadn't tried to scale those impressive heights.

He noticed Mira was also regarding the walls with fear. He walked a little closer to speak with her. "Do the guards worry you?" he whispered, nodding his head towards the wall. They continued along the road following the wall, nearing the western gate.

She laughed nervously. "Well, it's not so much the guards; it's the wall itself. Do you think they built it to keep animals out, or to keep people in?"

She and I think alike, Zerrick thought with surprise. Sagely, he answered, "The walls keep the two worlds apart--civilized and uncivilized."

"What does that make you, and the others who cross them?"

He stared ahead and sighed. "I don't know."

No more words were spoken as they approached the western gate, stopping as the guardsman came down from his lookout post. He eyed them. "Rather late to be leaving the city. We generally try to keep a curfew, 'specially with the bandits. Not too safe, traveling in the darkness."

This reaction had been planned for. Mira threw back her hood, doing her best to look hurried and annoyed. "Markus, you should know better than to give my brother that speech. A last minute order just came in with Eddy from Quentin. They need slaves fast, and Father is still out hunting. Hastings must get word to him; see if he can get his hands on a few more."

Now Zerrick stepped forward. He allowed the light of the torches to fall on him and spoke in a gruff voice as close to Mr. Terwin as he could manage. "Five's the usual amount for your trouble, right?" He brought out a handful of silver coins, letting the coins clink together to show he meant business.

The guard brightened at seeing Zerrick's altered face. "Hastings! By the day, you've lost weight. Didn't recognize you at first. Sure, five's fine."

Zerrick paid him the silver, then swaggered over and put his hand on Mira's shoulder. "Did you want to see me through the gate? Or say goodbye here?"

"Through the gate. I have a surprise for you to take to Papa."

"Really?" Zerrick did not have to feign his surprise. He had expected to leave her here, but evidently she wanted a few words alone with him. He wondered if she were lying about the surprise. Then again, he'd been suspicious that she carried more than that little pack all along.

They waited while the guard unbolted and opened the smaller gate used for scouts while leaving the larger gate locked shut. Zerrick went first, careful not to let the guard get too close a look at him. He was lucky the gate itself was in shadow. On the other side was a wide moonlit clearing, then tall thick jungle and the trail, wide enough to allow cart travel. The Slave Trail to the Jagara Mountains.

He strode over to the clearing until they were out of earshot and more importantly where his disguise would still appear real. He turned and watched as Mira whispered something to Nanna inside the gate. Nanna nodded and Mira continued through while she stayed behind, watching.

Mira strode up to him and pulled from her pack a shiny new flintlock pistol and an ivory gunpowder horn. "Here, Hastings. I think this should come in handy in the brush."

Zerrick didn't know what to say--it was a fine surprise, and much needed since he'd lost his pistol. He took the weapon and horn and fastened them to his belt, stammering thanks in what he hoped was an appropriate way.

Mira surprised him further by pulling him close in an embrace, then she whispered in his ear, "Now that you are properly outfitted, I can give you the other surprise. Nanna's a slave--they won't allow her to step beyond the city walls for any reason. Just as I planned. Now there is no one to stop me from joining you."

Zerrick sputtered and tried to pull back, but Mira's strong arms clasped him tight. He whispered back into her ear, "You can't come with me! You don't have the proper supplies, you'll be in constant danger--this is not a pleasure trip, it's a flight for survival!"

"I've got three packs on beneath this cloak with everything I need, and I'm well aware this won't be easy, but someone has to be able to communicate with the Put-na. What Nanna said was true. I don't belong in Depin. Besides, you still need mending on that leg. And two can climb a mountain better than one."

Her reasoning was sound, but Zerrick didn't want to hear any of it. He wanted nothing more than to haul her back over to the guards and tell her to--what? Lock herself up again? But he couldn't be responsible for her safety as well as his own. And gods help him, he couldn't get her entangled in the road his magic was leading him on.

"I can't let you come. You don't understand what the jungle is like. What it does to people." *Like me*, Zerrick added to himself.

She gave him a kiss on the cheek and drew back a little but stayed near enough to let him hear her murmured threat. "If you don't let me come, I'll tell the guards who you really are. Your illusion's starting to fade right now."

Not surprising, considering the emotions he was experiencing. "Please let me go," he pleaded, glancing first towards the jungle then back towards the guards. The guards had heard nothing of their conversation, but any more dawdling would appear suspicious. He was not up to another chase.

Mira crossed her arms with a determined look on her face, one Zerrick had seen before only in short flashes. "Oh, I'll let you go, but I'll be following. That you cannot stop. And wouldn't I be safer with you than alone? I am determined not to remain a prisoner any longer. The jungle calls me just as it does you."

He eyed Nanna watching through the gate. "Does she know?"

Mira shook her head. "She's innocent, I think. In any case, she won't try to stop me. Especially if I'm with you."

"The guards are sure to give chase."

She grinned and winked at him, then stepped back, raising a hand to her ear. "Hastings, do you hear that?" she asked in a loud voice, "I hear horses! It must be Father returning early!" With a girlish laugh, she waved for him to follow and ran off towards the trail, disappearing into the shadows.

"Mira!" He shouted after her, aghast. He heard snickers from the guard post and realized Mira's crazy idea was working. They probably thought she was a silly girl who couldn't be controlled by her protective brother. He smiled abashedly. "I'll be right back."

He strode off after her, not caring if his walk was right any more as the magic of his illusion began to fizzle uncertainly along his skin like pinpricks. He reached the shadows and ducked beneath the foliage just in time, as the magic dissipated into a burst of sparks. No matter. By the time the guards found out that this wasn't a game, he and Mira would be long gone.

Crazy though it seemed, he found himself much more excited now at the journey ahead. He scanned the brush along the mouth of the trail for her and walked quickly, ignoring the pain. "Mira!" he called out again, adding just a little indignation to his voice for the sake of those still waiting for them.

The floor of the trail was bare but for a few trailing vines and roots, and he hurried down it, expecting any second to see Mira waiting for him, but she was nowhere to be seen. He rounded the first curve, and then called her name again, this time a little more afraid for her. He was rapidly drawing away from the town, but he couldn't go much further without knowing where she was. Had he passed her already? "Come on now, this isn't a game! I really will let you come, but you have to show yourself first," he called in a soft voice. He noticed a rustling in the trees.

"Psst! I'm under here!" came Mira's gleeful whisper. He saw her hiding behind a low hanging curtain of vines and crawled over the marking stones of the trail to join her.

"The jungle's dangerous enough without wandering alone off beaten trails," he growled, unsure how to deal with her and her new adventurousness.

"It really worked, didn't it! We're out of reach from everyone now." Mira was grinning, her eyes alive with excitement. "You can't imagine how wonderful it feels to be free."

Zerrick felt all his anger melt away. The joy in her voice and in her eyes was catching; he soon found himself grinning as well. Gently he took hold of her arm and led her back towards the trail, "Yes, we're free, but to remain so, we have to keep moving. Watch out for snakes and leeches, and don't touch any plant you don't recognize as safe."

"I know my plants as well as you," she retorted, but she did take greater care in where she stepped.

They hurried on, and after several more minutes, they heard a woman's voice echo out through the trees, calling Mira's name longingly. "That would be Nanna," Mira said in a subdued voice. "I never even said goodbye--I just couldn't, because I thought I might lose my nerve. I hope she forgives me some day."

"The guards won't let her out to search for you," Zerrick said uneasily, "but you can bet your brothers will soon know. We'll stay close to the trail, but I think we'd better keep out of sight. We need to move as quickly and as quietly as possible."

With that, they crept into the dense brush lining the trail, crossing over into the clearer area under the canopy, then winding their way around trunks covered with thick vines and moss. Over an hour of silence passed, but as they climbed a small ridge to relocate the trail, there came the sound of horses, riding hard towards them from the town. Zerrick snatched Mira's arm and pulled her down into a patch of low plants.

They waited as the sounds grew louder and louder, thundering in their ears, and Mira cringed as they heard two men's voices, calling frantically for her. The two of them froze as horses rode past at a fast gallop, then the men rounded the corner, the sounds echoing off into the distance until there was silence once again. Zerrick stood. "Let's move. We have a few moments before they decide to double back."

They began walking again, and Mira stayed close to Zerrick, worriedly eyeing the moonlit ribbon of trail. "You would have had a much easier escape without me."

Zerrick was busy crawling through a dense stand of young ironwood, but he answered, "Too late to worry about that. Don't worry; I've gotten very good at hide and escape. I'm looking for a good place to conceal ourselves for the night, then we'll stop. Your brothers can ride around all night, but they won't find us, not where I'm planning to go. He reached the edge of the stand and peered up into the dark canopy above them. "There," he said, pointing ahead of them.

"What is it?" Mira asked, trying to break past the trees which seemed to have caught hold of her skirts.

Zerrick came back and carefully freed her. "I saw a big kapok tree up ahead. We can sleep up in its branches and remain hidden. Now all we need are a few ferns to take as extra cover. Follow me."

They went over to the edge of the trail. Very carefully Zerrick pulled out a few large plants and strung them to his belt. They hurried back away, just as the sound of horses reached their ears.

"Hurry! They may see where I uprooted these," Zerrick hissed, and charged off deeper into the jungle. Mira scrambled to keep up with him, holding her skirts high.

They reached the kapok tree by the edge of a wide pond. As the sounds of horses became unbearably loud. Zerrick pulled rope from his pack and fastened it around his chest. "Tie the other end around yourself and step where I step," he instructed, handing her the rope.

She made a series of knots in case one didn't hold, and watched as Zerrick climbed up with ease, using vines attached to the trunk as handholds and footholds. Up higher in the tree, it became clear what he was making for--a nest of some sort where the branches came together, forming a hollow screened from view with dense foliage and shadow. Hesitantly, Mira followed, boots scraping against the slick bark. Zerrick hoped she didn't slip.

He was halfway up when she did slip, but the rope caught on one of the knobby vines and held; Zerrick grunted at the rope's extra weight and pulled her back up to a thick vine. "Just a little more, Mira. You can do it," he whispered, continuing up. There was no sound of horses now; all had grown terribly still. Mira pulled herself up to the next vine.

"They're searching the trail to see where we left it," Zerrick said quietly, pulling himself up to a branch just before the nest. He peered into the sanctuary. Whatever creature who had lived here was apparently gone. A curtain of vines and a latticework of moss covered twigs shielding most of the nest from view. It looked perfect, if Mira could just reach it in time.

"Zerrick, I can't make it," Mira whispered fiercely as she struggled to reach a high thin branch. Any moment Zerrick expected to hear footsteps below him and the accusing voices of her brothers.

Zerrick crawled into the nest and reached down to haul her up by the rope, using a broken-off stump as leverage. Last time he had slept near a tree this huge, the magic had sung to him so loudly it was deafening. It was the same this time--but he could also feel the magic extending down into the roots of the tree extending far out into the jungle, almost feel the tree's awareness that someone was approaching. With a last heave, he pulled Mira up to the nest.

"Cover yourself," he urged, throwing his cloak over himself and covering the two of them with the ferns as he strove to wedge himself as far into the shadows as possible. Mira pulled her own cloak over her pale skin and huddled against the hanging vines. Zerrick put a finger to his lips. He could hear footsteps below.

"The trail ends here, at the water's edge," a man who could only be Hastings announced, as Zerrick crouched low to peer down. In the darkness he could make out about five men dressed in travel gear. They circled the tree, peering around in the bushes and hollows of tree trunks. The tree tops received hardly a glance.

"Could've crossed the pond to cover the tracks. Or maybe this is a false trail. Who knows what kind of man spirited her off?" a shorter man commented, poking a stick into a hole between two fallen trees. Zerrick glanced over at Mira to see if she recognized this second voice. She was huddled into the farthest corner, her eyes shut tight as if that would make her invisible. "He had to be the witch--who else could steal your face?" the short one continued.

Hastings nodded. "If I find him, I'll tear his guts out. Come on, they may have run to the other side. If not, we'll need more men and a decent lantern--there are thousands of places to hide." He smacked his hand against the tree in frustration and stalked off, followed closely by the other men. Zerrick listened as they remounted, slowly riding until they were out of earshot. Zerrick waited out a few moments of silence, then turned to Mira.

"We'll camp here until the search dies down and leave before dawn. Try to get some sleep." He shifted himself into a comfortable position, laying his head on his arm.

He heard Mira do the same, then the sound of her voice, timid and subdued. "I can't go back to that, I just can't."

He reached out a hand to pat her knee. "Don't worry, you won't have to. Just rest, Mira. Everything will be fine."

He wished he could believe that were true.

Chapter Twelve

"The way to cross a raging river is to leap straight across."
--Put-na warrior saying

As the sun peeked over the treetops behind them, Zerrick and Mira paused in their running long enough to take a swallow of water and a bite of fruit. They had started an hour or so before first light, and Zerrick felt confident they had put a few good leagues between them and the searchers. Later they could rest again, but he wouldn't feel comfortable until they were several days gone from Depin.

Mira had proved to have remarkable endurance--she had not complained once, running beside him, long hair flowing free. They'd burned her dress to ashes, and she now wore breeches and a shirt. Every time Zerrick looked at her, his breath caught in his throat. She was beautiful.

As the sun rose into a cloud-flecked sky, they kept to the side of the trail, ready to leap off in case of trouble. There was no need however; all was peaceful, the only sounds the cries of birds and animals undisturbed by man. They kept a steady pace through the day, walking quickly but carefully as the trail grew somewhat narrower, now only wide enough for two horses to ride abroad. They paused occasionally, listening for pursuit and to allow Zerrick time to rest off his wounded leg, but they neither heard nor saw signs of anyone. The day became cooler and foggy, which helped them cover their escape. Mid-afternoon, it rained.

The heavy waters ran like a river down the path during the downpour, leaving a muddy mess. They only hoped some of their tracks and most of their scent had been washed away from whatever might be tracking them.

By late afternoon they reached a rise in the land. In the distance behind them could be seen the towers of the fort peeking above the green of the forest. Zerrick's leg was throbbing--he didn't think he could go much further without rest. He stumbled and nearly fell, and Mira ordered him over to a rocky knoll to sit.

"All right--drop the breeches and let's take a look. If you've torn it open we'll have to find somewhere to hide a few days," her voice took on some of Nanna's authoritativeness, and though there was a blush to her cheeks, she did not hesitate to inspect the wound when he turned around. He hissed when her fingers passed over the area. The skin felt swollen and hot, and there were signs of stress along the scabbing, but no blood.

Mira dug into one of her pouches and brought out a clay jar. "I thought we'd be needing this--crushed Pitchu seeds with some mashed hopbrush for pain, and a touch of brandy to stop infection." Her fingers scooped out a little of the dark green paste, and she made a poultice, laying fresh leaves across the wound to hold it in place.

"That should work for a while. Pity it couldn't have healed a bit more before we left. Do you want to go on? Or find a place to hide for the night?"

Zerrick grimaced as the herbs went to work, making his leg sting then tingle, but as the pain-nulling effect started to cool the area, he breathed easier. "We can't stop--at least not until there's more distance between us and your brothers. And while I'd like to travel by night as well, I'm not familiar with this area. It would be too dangerous in the dark--there are probably jungle cats out in these parts. We'll walk until the sun sets, and find another tree to sleep in."

"Lead on then," she said, and helped him to stand.

They climbed the rise and descended into a valley choked with tangles of vine so thick and strong they made passage beyond the hewn trail impossible. If any rider had come upon them then, they would have been caught, for even with their machetes, they never could have gone far--the vines were covered with sharp thorns. After they left behind the choking vines, they rested again, watching as the sun began to sink into the Jagara mountains.

"Thank goodness we're out of that!" Zerrick exclaimed, trying to stretch the muscles in his leg "Now if we can just find a good tree, we'll be set for the night. I'm afraid I can't go further. You're right. I should have waited another week!" He closed his eyes; the pain was making him sick and dizzy.

Mira picked out a few strands of vine which had caught in her hair. "Don't worry, we'll find something soon. Do you want to lean on me?"

Zerrick nodded. "Any time now I expect to run into your father--this is the only trail and he should be on his way home right now--very close, in fact, if he's going to return by the time he said he would. I'm surprised we haven't run into him yet."

Mira went white. "I'd forgotten about that. Then we have to hurry! Come on, put your arm on my shoulder."

They left the trail and searched for a place to rest, but the trees were either too tall to climb or too fragile to support them. They settled for an outcropping of rock surrounded by palms and some kind of flowering shrub with smooth twisting branches. Exhausted, they spread their blankets on the soft mossy ground and lay down to sleep.

Zerrick was asleep almost instantly, but Mira lay awake for a while, staring up at the dense canopy far overhead and the endless chatter of unknown creatures. A light mist began to fall, and she reached over a hand to pull the spare blanket over Zerrick. No dreams troubled him tonight. His face looked angelic in the twilight, peaceful and serene, as if this were his own safe bed.

He belongs out here, she thought, amazed. She was unsure now whether she regretted her decision. He had been partially right--she had been thinking this would be a fun little adventure. She'd never dreamed what it would actually feel like to lie out in the jungle at night, miles from home or friends. Or from help, should they need it. She had not wanted to be protected any longer, though. Her father had succeeded in protecting her from life itself, from experiencing anything. This was life, pure and wild! *If only I weren't so afraid,* she thought.

Mira froze as something scampered past their camp, then relaxed when she saw it was only a monkey. She settled back into the blanket, turning her head to watch Zerrick. He snored softly, his damp hair falling into his eyes.

And what did she feel about him? She liked him, certainly. He made her feel safe, but at the same time free to speak her mind, and he expected her to pull her own weight. That was heartening. And the way he sometimes stared at her--but she didn't want to think about that. Not yet anyway. It would only complicate things.

Still, he was so odd sometimes. There was much he was hiding from her. What really had made him run? There was a great fear in him, but of what she didn't know. Magic was a part of it, but there was something else. Something terrible must have happened, to give him the haunted look in his eyes.

He's certainly hard to fathom, Mira thought, chuckling. *But I always did like a challenge.* Well, mysteries would hardly disappear overnight, and she was exhausted. Best to sleep when she had the chance. With that thought, she closed her eyes.

It was still dark when she was gently shaken awake, a darkness so profound it made her gasp in fear. She started to ask what was wrong when he laid a hand across her lips. Zerrick's voice was barely a whisper. "There's someone prowling about."

She heard it, a slight rustle in the bushes near them, the barest whisper of feet. She gripped Zerrick's arm in fright.

He caressed her fingers in the darkness, then pressed the butt of the flintlock pistol into her hand. "In case something happens to me," he whispered. She heard the soft hiss as he drew his sword, then he was gone. She readied the trigger and held the gun out from her body, ears straining.

Zerrick paused beneath the bough of a strangler fig, staring into a thicket of low sprawling vines where he could hear the sounds of footsteps. It could be a beast, perhaps another wild pig, but he didn't think so. Every now and then he heard the scrape of fabric against leaf and bark, and the sloshing of water in a bag. There was a man out there. He gripped his sword tightly.

Cautiously he crept forward, listening for the footsteps. Only a few weak beams of moonlight broke through the canopy to shed their light on the forest floor. Zerrick thought he heard something to his right, nearer now, and turned, ready to fight or flee at the first sign of trouble. But he never got the chance. Out of the shadows a figure came flying, knocking him into the soft earth and sending his sword spiraling into the brush. Hands fastened on his throat, pinning him down. A face as dark as the night hovered over him and whispered words which seemed familiar, but somehow escaped his understanding. He realized he was being held by a native.

Feebly he struggled to loosen the choke hold just enough to gasp, *"Miborgi! Ngai miborgi!* I'm a friend!" He hoped what little Put-na he knew would convince the fellow he meant no harm.

His words brought an immediate response, but not the one he had expected. The man spat in his face and jerked him to a kneeling position, wrapping an arm around his neck to form a head lock, and hissed in his ear, *"Ba'landa Kuno'ora! Borderima ngai inyamina maring wariji!"* He laughed low in his throat and drew out a long knife.

Zerrick gulped. He couldn't understand all the words, but the meaning was clear enough: kill the white man. Fear turned his blood to ice, freezing his muscles as the native pulled his head back, baring his throat.

In his fear, however, he heard the call of magic. Like a siren's song, it suddenly filled his senses, beckoning from every side around him. Several small plants were touching his skin--all he had to do was draw it to him--he closed his eyes, swaying as power surged through him, and imagined strength flowing through his arms and legs, strength and agility enough to throw off his attacker.

The magic heard and obeyed. The rush of power to his limbs was so overwhelming, he was hardly conscious of tearing the native's hands from his throat, grabbing his arms and pinning him to the earth. He heard a buzzing in his ears and felt so much power he could hardly contain himself--he threw back his head and roared with the joy of it. Then he grinned down at his prisoner who was staring at him with growing horror and amazement.

"*Kumalido!*" the native murmured in awe, letting the knife drop from his fingers. By his short beard and still fresh initiation scar, Zerrick saw he was little older than himself, and his body was painted red and black. Hunting colors.

The power raged in Zerrick; it would be so easy to stamp out this man's life, just let the magic take his hand and smash it into the fellow's windpipe. He had to shut his eyes and clench his fists to restrain himself. The magic had worked too well; he was strong now, but also violent. He realized his breath was coming out in gasps. He felt if he did not make some action, he would explode.

"Zerrick! What's happening?" Mira stumbled into view, still holding the pistol out with one hand and clutching a candle in the other. She froze upon seeing them, her hand with the candle shaking, making the circle of light around her dance.

Zerrick crouched over his prisoner like a beast over a kill, loathe to let her see what was occurring here. He raised his eyes slowly to meet hers. She gasped and took a step back.

"Your eyes are glowing," she said in a trembling voice.

"Get away, Mira! This man tried to kill me--I used magic, and now I'm dangerous. Just go back to the camp," Zerrick said in a rush, inching away from her. Where before there had been a terrible urge to kill and smash things, now there was an even stronger urge to suddenly throw her down to the forest bed and make love to her.

He let go of the native and grabbed onto a tree root, as if by anchoring himself he could keep himself from springing either towards her or back to kill the native. Sucking in gulps of air, he tried to still the lustful trembling of his body.

As soon as the native was free, he sprang up and fled a little ways, then hesitated and turned back. "*Ngai wo nagandidda Kumalido ngainma poko,*" he said, bowing to Zerrick. He turned to leave but Mira stopped him.

"Wait!" she called, then added something Zerrick couldn't understand, especially in his present state. All he had to do was pounce, then rip off her clothing . . . he shook his head to dispel the urge, then savagely drove his hand into a tree stump. He used the pain to shut out the crazy impulses.

"Zerrick? Zerrick, snap out of it! This man says there is a camp of white men just over the hill to the west--a camp bringing slaves captured from his tribe. Do you think it could be Father?" Mira said after conversing with the native. She stayed out of reach of him, but he could see the smooth contours of her legs in the corner of his eye.

He lurched to his feet and hurried to put a little more distance between himself and her. Gripping the truck of a thick rough-skinned palm, he dared to look up and answer, "It must be him. And we've been making too much noise here. We'll have to move on as quickly as possible." Inside he was glad for the need to run. It would allow him to expend this awful strength and concentrate on something besides her. Gods, she looked so vulnerable, standing there with her shirt half out, the pistol held out away from her body as if it were a live thing which might decide to fire on its own. She could not know what she was doing to him, standing like that . . . he shut his eyes and pressed his cheek against the bark of the tree.

"No, you don't understand. He says most of the slaves are from his tribe! He means to attack the camp tonight and free them. He's asking for your help, since you wield the magic. And mine, since I speak his tongue." Zerrick heard the concern in her voice; she sounded torn. He could imagine why. Help a slave, against her father? It had to be a difficult choice. As his choice between magic and his family had been.

Of course he wasn't sure she should trust his help right now. When he glanced at her, though, he could feel the power flash through him, seeming to make everything flare red--or was that just his eyes? With his eyes closed, Zerrick was a little better to think, though the delicious sound of her voice still made him ache with desire. He heard in that voice a need to intervene, to stop this inhuman practice of taking slaves. He also saw an opportunity to rid himself of the power, even though in any other state of mind he would have thought it folly.

"Yes, I'll help. I'll not kill anyone, but I can keep the men busy while you free the slaves. Does this native here have a plan? Or was he just going to go in and start fighting?" Zerrick glanced at the young warrior who had crept forward to reclaim his knife. They stared warily at each other before turning to Mira.

She related Zerrick's answer to the native and listened while he replied, his hands making figures in the air. Zerrick pushed down another surge of violence, assuring the power that it would soon be used. After all, helping the natives might gain them an ally or two, and he could hardly make a greater enemy of Mira's father. He had already stolen that man's greatest possession.

The slave finished speaking and Mira laid out the plans for Zerrick, "Tamur--that's this man's name--says he was going to sneak in and kill one of the guards, dress himself as a Boderima--a white colonist--and go break the chains that hold his people together. He doesn't seem to think his actions would wake anyone, and I don't think he's taken my father's gunmen into account. He did count them. Thirty prisoners, ten men 'with sticks'--that would be the men carrying muskets--my father, his tracker, a slave master, and two guards with swords and pistols. That does sound about right."

"Muskets. That will be the main problem. We'll need to distract them, then somehow deal with the guards. The chains will not be a problem. I could break them with my bare hands right now. But guns now, there must be something I can do about those . . ." Zerrick paced around his tree, unable to stand still a moment longer. His muscles were whispering to him of strangling each and every slaver. He clamped down on that urge. He would not allow the violence to overcome him. He would not kill. That meant he would have to pull magic again, and attempt some other spell. Did he dare? Alden had been right; he was drawing more and more power now, with shaky control at best.

He didn't dare any magic which directly affected men--this spell on himself showed that clearly. Illusions, however, should be safe--the muskets could only be fired once before needing to be reloaded. What would men shoot at immediately? It had to be something he had seen, and could visualize accurately. He smiled grimly.

"Mira, what would be your father's reaction to being attacked by the Stonefist Gang? Would he recognize who they were?"

Mira looked quizzically at him. "He'd defend his prizes and he'd shoot to kill. Captain Greynor has a hefty bounty for bandits, dead or alive, and there are drawings of the most famous ones. Why?"

"I'm going to attempt an illusion. It's not going to be easy, but I'll only allow them swift glimpses of attackers, and I know what the leader looks like well enough. Hopefully they'll use up their shots on shadows. It won't last long, though. I hope they all fire at once." That it would not be easy was a gross understatement. He had never before attempted such a large-scale illusion. With the power singing in him, however, he felt he could do it.

She considered it a moment, then spoke with the native. They seemed to be arguing, at one point, then the native finally shrugged and nodded. He went to retrieve his knife and Zerrick's sword and handed the sword back with deference, hilt first. Zerrick accepted it with a nod.

"Tell him to lead the way," Zerrick said, strapping the sword to his waist before he could be tempted by any thoughts to wield it. He felt like a smoldering volcano, quiet for the moment, but filled with pressure that would eventually make him explode.

They stopped back at the camp long enough to pack up and stow their things where they could be easily picked up on the run. Then they crept down through the jungle to the slaver camp. Zerrick soon learned that it was impossible to be completely silent-- patches of mud sloshed and squelched around his boots no matter how carefully he tread, but as they neared the camp, he realized he needn't have worried. The slavers were celebrating.

Raucous laughter could be heard from the main tent where even the two guards standing watch outside were toasting each other and taking long gulps from their wineskins. Only a few were not joining in the merriment: the head slave master, a hard looking man with a shaven head and a long whip, and a lone tracker sitting atop a crate of supplies. He kept his musket across one knee and watched the jungle warily, a pipe dangling from his lips.

Zerrick urged everyone further back under cover, flinching when his hand brushed Mira's. *Concentrate, concentrate,* he urged himself, shoving down another series of lustful thoughts. "Only four to really watch out for. If the native can handle the two guards--and I mean handle them quietly--then I'll take out the slavemaster."

"What about the other fellow? I remember him. He's quite famous for his marksmanship."

Zerrick tried to think, but the magic was becoming too strong for him. He had to act, and soon. "I'll take him too," he muttered, rubbing his temples with one hand. He noticed his other hand gripping the hilt of his sword.

Mira took note of his struggle. "Leave him to me. As I said, I know him. He won't fire at me, and I can distract him from taking a shot at you."

She didn't allow him any time to contemplate or object to her joining the effort; instead she ran straight out into the camp, breaking into noisy tears and flinging herself at the famous marksman. She clutched at him, appearing to be faint with relief, "Thank Iahmel! I am saved!" she cried.

Zerrick's body propelled him forward to complete his own tasks, but even as he crept through the shadows towards the slaves, he plucked out a young vine and greedily sucked out the magic, formulating in his mind the images he wanted all else in the camp to see. Murtis's face would be clear from that tree over by the main tent, he thought, and Clint's further back, and so forth. He urged the magic to do its work and was gratified when one of the drunken guards gave a shout. The guard began firing off his pistols into the forest, insisting they were being set upon by bandits. The other guard fired of his musket, then shouts of fear and cries of warning were ringing out all over the camp.

Zerrick took a deep breath, taking stock of the situation before he let the magic take over. The native had vanished, but suddenly a guard fell down and did not get up again. Mira kept the attention of the tracker to herself and her harrowing tale. It was time to free the slaves.

The magic swept over him like a tide, power flowing to his veins to do its work. He uttered a low growl and set his eyes on the hulking figure of the slavemaster, could smell the man's nervous sweat as he drove the slaves into a circle to deter them from thoughts of escape during the excitement. Zerrick's eyes narrowed. Blood pounded in his ears. Silently, he lunged.

Mira saw the faces of strange men peeking out from the trees and noticed they were glowing slightly--Zerrick's illusions, she hoped. She was practically wrapped around the tracker, trying to keep him distracted until Zerrick could bring help in the form of freed slaves. At least she hoped he would come back to help. She'd tricked him not once but twice now, and in his present state, he might decide to leave her with her father.

"Lady, will you get off me! How can I defend you with you holding onto my gun arm?!" He finally succeeded in throwing her off, and she bowed her head and forced tears to her eyes, weeping pathetically, a meek mild poor lost girl with a mean-hearted brute. Her pitiful sobs got the desired effect.

"Oh lady, don't do that--look I'm sorry. Just hold on a bit." He fumbled for words, and only then brought his musket up, searching the surrounding jungle. There had been a flurry of shots as the faces first appeared, but now the guards were busy reloading, and the faces had disappeared. Mira hoped she had bought Tamur and Zerrick enough time.

Zerrick's world spun as he fought to gain some kind of hold on the struggling slavemaster. They rolled on the ground, equal in strength, and Zerrick let the magic guide him to block the larger man's punches, kicking fiercely even as he twisted round to pull the man's arm behind him. A fiery surge of power blinded him momentarily, and he felt his fist connect with soft flesh. He heard the man's groan from somewhere far away, and was faintly aware of grabbing hold of his stunned opponent and smashing his head into the hard ground.

Then sensation returned with a rush, and he saw that the slavemaster was out cold, sprawled out beneath him. The scents of the jungle assailed his nostrils, and the sounds of shouting just beyond the ring of tents rang in his ears. He tasted blood on his tongue.

Kill, break, destroy, his thoughts hammered about inside his skull, but he made himself turn away from the unconscious slave master. The slaves cowered before him, and he knew his eyes must still be glowing, for they seemed clearly defined, even in the dim moonlight. He spotted the chains binding them together. Something to break!

He ran his hands along the chain, feeling for the weak link. With a snarl, he pulled the link apart, and the chain broke. He didn't stop there but began breaking the chain in other places, until all the slaves were free. They fled in various directions, not willing to find out if he was a friend or foe.

When the chains and manacles lay in ruin about him, Zerrick struggled to remember what he was supposed to do next. From far off, beyond the pounding of his heart, he recalled a name: Mira. An image flashed--that of her running towards the tracker, flinging her arms around him to distract him.

Jealousy flared.

Must get Mira, he thought sluggishly, struggling to keep the magic at bay. He realized dimly that if the magic did not leave soon, he might very well become another Madame Lotus, a beast with no vestige of his former self.

He shook his head to clear it, then slunk back into the shadows, letting the magic guide him one last time to prowl soundlessly in the brush, a panther after its prey.

Mira wanted to cheer as the first of the slaves ran past her and into the jungle, but she was kept busy making sure the tracker didn't manage to shoot any down.

"How can you fire at them; they're people!" she cried, planting herself in his way once again.

"Lady, if you do that one more time--oh good here comes the Master. Sir, this here lady--"

Mira turned in alarm, watching as her father strode right towards her, all the fires of damnation in his eyes as he glared at her in mixed surprise and fury.

"What in God's name are you doing out here! Get into that tent this instant, young lady! There are bandits and worse afoot!" He stood before her, bristling with anger, and reached out a hand to snatch her from the tracker.

"I, I . . ." she stammered. This had not been part of the plan. Around her she could see total chaos, as her father's men tried to chase down escaping slaves, ducking and cursing about phantom bandits. Where was Zerrick? she wondered.

"She was telling me about how she'd been kidnapped by bandits," the tracker answered for her, packing the gunpowder into his musket and recocking the trigger.

"And how did that happen? You were supposed to be staying at Hasting's place, and last I heard, these bandits were outside the city walls!" Her father's face was red with outrage as he tried to keep hold of her and keep track of his men's hunt for the escaped slaves at the same time.

She could try to lie, but what was the point? She was sick of obeying, sick of feeling trapped and powerless. With a sudden jerk, she tore her arm free of his grasp and said, "I left the city and I wasn't captured; I chose to run away with that witch who was in Captain Greynor's office the day of my trial. I left, because I don't belong, and I have no future, thanks to the way you and my brothers have kept me locked away. I'm sick of that life! And I refuse to return to it."

She was ready to fight her father then, but at that moment Zerrick appeared, looking a little more sane, the glowing of his eyes now just a faint glimmer. He rose up out of the brush right before her, holding a pistol to the tracker's back, a deadly look on his face.

"Time to go, Mira. Take his musket, and we'll just back out slowly," he said in a low voice. She could see his shirt was ripped and matted with grass and leaves, and his hands were raw and bleeding, but he seemed not to notice. She was glad she hadn't been there to see him give in to whatever spell he had cast on himself.

Mira inched forward to take the musket from the tracker, aware that the camp was recovering from its shock and that reinforcements would soon be there. As she reached for the tracker's gun, however, he swung it around in a last attempt to stop Zerrick. The shot exploded in her ears, then she was thrown back as a strange figure leapt out of the shadows to knock down the tracker.

She recognized Tamur as he wrestled down the tracker, then she was being pulled away by Zerrick who had somehow managed to dodge the bullet. Her eyes strayed to where her father was staring open-mouthed. She read the hurt there, and the bewilderment. "I'm sorry," she gasped, unable to hear his response past the ringing in her ears. Then she was running, Zerrick beside her, tearing through brush to where their things lay hidden.

Zerrick stumbled once, and she saw that the last glimmer had left his eyes.

"It's gone now. I used the last of it to escape the bullet," he panted, slowing to a loping trot, his chest heaving with exhaustion.

"Just a little further. How's your leg doing?"

They slowed to a walk, listening to the shouts and shots of slavers fighting freed slaves. There was no way her father would be able to organize a search for her for some time. Still, they had to keep moving. Now she was just as much an outlaw as Zerrick.

"All right, actually," Zerrick answered at length. "I think all that magic may have actually done it some good."

"You look exhausted." That was an understatement. With the glimmer of magic gone from him, his face was pale and shiny with sweat, and despite his assurances, he was limping heavily. In short, he looked spent.

"It's all right. If we can just keep to a slow pace, I'll be able to keep going. Alden did warn me that after a powerful spell, it's common to feel depleted. I'll rest once we're a safe distance away." He began walking straighter, and smiled encouragingly at her. He might be trying to assure her, but in truth he looked positively waxen, as if his blood had been drained from him, instead of, as he said, the magic.

"We'll move slowly." Mira tried to figure the time by the faint gleam of moonlight, now slanting through the trees behind them. By her reckoning, they should still have a few hours of darkness. They'd leave the trail here and head straight towards the mountains, to throw off any pursuit.

She took Zerrick's arm, helping him up the hill to the tree where they'd left their packs. At least he wasn't avoiding her touch any longer. "Thank you for coming to get me. I seem to keep pulling surprises on you, and you've been very good about it. And thank you for traveling with me. I don't know what I would have done otherwise."

"Don't mention it," Zerrick mumbled, absently rubbing his arm where her fingers had rested. He hefted his pack over his shoulders, grunting. "Your idea back there was a good one, and it was probably best you acted on your own. I wasn't in any shape to discuss things rationally." He readjusted his packs, and took a long swig from his waterskin, and Mira stretched, promising her tired legs they would get rest--later.

"Shall we go?" she asked.

They crept off into the shadow of the jungle once more.

Chapter Thirteen

"A fledgling knows not that it can fly until it spreads its wings."
--Put-na mother

Zerrick climbed the last rocky ridge and stood panting on the sun-filled plateau, turning around to let the dazzle of the morning rays fall upon his cheek. Behind him, Mira also struggled up and immediately collapsed onto a large boulder, sucking in gulps of air.

"And to think this is only the beginning!" she gasped, gazing towards the mountain range before them.

Zerrick turned away from the sun and peered at the lush valley below them to the impossibly high peaks of the Jagara mountains, outlined into brilliant color by the rising sun and seemingly close enough that he felt he could reach out and touch them.

"We're through most of the foothills. I think it's time we decide a path through those mountains. Did Nanna ever mention how her people cross them?"

Mira thought a moment, while Zerrick sat watching pink parrot-like birds flapping from tree to tree down in the valley. Up here, the jungle was broken by the bones of the earth--huge slabs of black stone on which only grasses and molds grew. Mira stood to peer down at the valley of green before them, and sighed. "No. Nanna was taken from her village too young. She remembered that there were trails, but not where those trails could be found."

"And she only told me how to get to the mountains, not how to cross them. Well at least my leg isn't a problem any longer," Zerrick said, rubbing at his leg where through the fabric of his breeches, he could feel the hard scar tissue beneath. Somehow, during that night in the thrall of magic, his leg had been healed. Mira had postulated that the magic which had been sending strength to his limbs had also sped up his body's rate of recovery. Whatever the reason, he wasn't complaining.

"I still think we should have tried to find Tamur. He could have helped us, I just know it," Mira said, not looking at Zerrick.

Zerrick stifled a retort. After their escape from her father, she had suggested they double back to check on Tamur and his freed people, but he had insisted they take no chances. Sure the fellow was a potential ally, but Zerrick could not bring himself to trust the warrior-- after all, Tamur had tried to kill him. And besides, he reasoned, they didn't even know if he escaped alive. Best just to look out for themselves.

"Well, we're not getting any closer standing here," he said when the silence became too much. He took a swallow from his waterskin and secured it at his belt, then went to stand at the edge of the plateau, surveying the land to determine the easiest path. Mira came up to stand beside him.

"You weren't jealous of him, were you?"

That was unexpected. "No," he said immediately, a little harsher than he meant to. "Why should I be?" To forestall any answer, he crouched down and lowered himself off the rock, raising a hand to help her down as well.

As they made their way back down into the thick of the jungle, he found his gaze straying to Mira who was chopping away at constricting foliage. Ever since the slave rescue there had been a tension between them. Perhaps the spell over him had made him a little crazy, but he couldn't forget the feelings he had experienced that night--he felt them again and again, each and every time he looked at her or when they touched hands or he happened to catch a glimpse of her sleeping when he awoke with the first light of dawn. Perhaps it wasn't as urgent as it had been under the magic, but it was definitely there. He didn't know what to do about it.

As for her, she had remained carefully casual about his odd behavior. *I must seem like a lunatic to her*, he thought grimly. First he'd been wounded, then the fleeing outcast, then a half-mad sorcerer. And now he was acting the consummate oaf, directing her to follow his lead and keep her opinions to herself, despite the fact he had no idea where they were headed. He deserved to be smacked.

They walked for about an hour, deeper into the valley, and then Mira suddenly stopped. "Zerrick, this way isn't going to work. The ground is getting damp--I think there may be a bog up ahead." Mira adjusted the scarf keeping her unruly curls away from her face, and winced, rubbing at a blister on her heel.

"We're in a valley--of course it's going to be damp." Zerrick groaned inwardly even as he said the words, but he was worried. The next mountain they were to climb had looked impossibly high back on that rock. He had noticed a great waterfall towards its base, which meant there was either a river or a lake down in this valley, but of course the trees had hidden any view of such things. If it had been only himself, he would have gone on, uncaring if he made mistakes because there was no one to judge him.

Now there was Mira, and not only did he care about her judgment of him, there was also her safety to consider. And her discomfort. She was going through what he had on his first week away from Harrow, suffering sore muscles, insect bites, and the unending toil of facing the jungle day after day. He longed to take those poor delicate hands and soothe away the red blisters. But he dared not.

They went on a little further, then suddenly the ground seemed to become liquid under their feet, sucking greedily at their boots. Climbing on top of a rotting tree trunk, Zerrick finally acknowledged the truth. "This isn't going to work. Any suggestions?"

Mira joined him on the log, readjusting the light scarf she wore to keep the sun off her already tender skin. "All I can think of is to skirt along the edge of this and try to find a firmer way to cross it. I don't much fancy wading through it. Who knows what creatures may lurk in that sludge?"

"I had quite an experience with leeches myself. I think I'd like to spare you that if possible." Zerrick pulled at a few branches of the log, hoping to find a pole they could use to test the ground, but the wood was too wet to break off.

"Thank you, I think." Mira stepped off the log and plodded over to dryer ground where she managed to find a sturdy stick. She waited as Zerrick joined her, his gaze carefully averted, and they began walking, poking at the ground when it became suspicious-looking.

She'd given up trying to figure him out. One moment he was brooding and secretive, lost in some dim place where she was only a nuisance, then the next moment he would say something like that and gallantly try to aid her every step. She wasn't used to such mercurial behavior--Father and the boys were overbearing and obnoxious, but that was a given constant. And she didn't know what she felt for him, but she was aware of one thing. His coldness was beginning to hurt.

In the next hour, they managed to make headway against the boggy terrain. The mountain before them loomed promisingly closer as they moved from "island" to island of firmer sod in the soggy marsh.

Then they came upon a lake.

It stretched out before them, a sudden expanse of water dotted with tall cypresses, leading all the way up to the rocky face of the mountain. Mira could just see in the distance the source of the water; a magnificent, but deadly waterfall cascading down some three hundred feet or so from the dark red rocks of a jagged peak.

"Oh no. How do we cross that?" she murmured. The water looked deep. And murky. She felt a touch of fear in her breast, trying to imagine herself wading in there, with gods knew what else. "Maybe we should go around," she suggested, looking beseechingly at Zerrick.

He frowned, looking at the distant shore. "I have a feeling this may be at least one, if not the only source of the Divenin River. That means we won't be able to go around it very easily. Best to cross here. It doesn't look too far--we can use a piece of wood to keep us afloat and swim to the other side."

"But I can't swim!"

Zerrick paused at the note of terror in her voice and looked at her. She could see sudden warmth flood his pale eyes, and slowly he came toward her, gently taking her hands which had been clutched at her cloak, ever so gently cupping them.

"You don't have to swim--all you'll have to do is hold onto the wood while I push us across. The wood will float, and as long as you hold on, you cannot sink. You just have to be calm and keep your head up."

"I can't! I hate water!"

His warm hands were slowly calming her fingers, but the rest of her was still shivering with fear. He moved to embrace her protectively then pulled back, wavering. That was just as well; if he began comforting her in earnest, she would surely fall apart.

"You can do this. I know you can. You've done incredibly well this past week. You never complain, you carry your own weight, and you're not afraid to argue with me when I'm wrong. I can't think of another woman--hell, even another man--who could stay out here in the jungle like you have. I can't believe you're going to let a little water scare you now." Zerrick's eyes were earnest on her, crystal blue almost seeming to burn through her as he spoke.

Mira gave a nervous laugh. "That's not a little water. That's a lot of water."

"It's not my first choice of routes, but I don't think we have much choice. If we try to follow the edge, we'll be back in that boggy area. And believe me, that is much worse than water. We might not be able to cross it at all. This I know we can cross. But I'm not going to make the decision this time. What do you want to do?"

Mira eyed the water, then the spans of jungle they had just crossed, and was forced to agree. It would not be as easy as he made it sound, but it would be better than walking into a mud pit or quicksand. There was also her pride to consider. She had invited herself on this trip; she would prove herself competent if it killed her.

Hopefully it just wouldn't come this way.

"So where do we find a good log? I want to get this over with quickly."

Zerrick smiled at her flippant consent. He was all business however, when he showed her the log they would use--a fallen tree with a knobby trunk. They hacked away to clear the dead twigs and branches from the log, then he directed her to don extra stockings and wrap cloth around her arms, hands, and ankles, closing off any access to her skin from the parasites lurking in the waters. She didn't mind the attention as he gently checked the back of her arms and legs for places missed. Then the fun was over. The lake before them beckoned.

Mira grimaced as she set foot in the water, shivering at the cold clammy dampness seeping into her boots and up her stockings. She secured her arms around the log, gripping one of the stubs where they'd removed a branch, then slowly she and Zerrick waded deeper, until the water was at their waistlines.

"Are you ready?" Zerrick asked, moving his feet around in the muck which threatened to swallow their feet. He breathed deeply, moving his arms, preparing to swim.

"God, I hate this," Mira groaned, flinching as she brushed past a long submerged tree trunk. She prayed that any slimy things would stay well clear of her.

"It won't be long, I promise," Zerrick assured her, and wrapped his arms around his end of the log. He kicked his feet clear of the mud and propelled them forward. "Hold on!"

Mira wrapped her arm tighter, pressing her cheek against the cold mossy wood as the ground gave way beneath her feet. She tried not to panic as she kicked down and felt nothing but water, praying that the wood would hold her up, that she wouldn't lose her composure completely and let go. She squeezed her eyes shut, then opened them again. Best to see what was around her, rather than let her imagination take control.

After a few moments of keeping fearful vigilance on the waters around them, Mira calmed somewhat. She lifted her head to gaze at the shore falling away behind them. Zerrick's breathing was sharp and steady, as he diligently propelled them forward stroke by stroke, his eyes a mirror of the murky waters.

"Not so bad," she said between breaths, afraid to break his concentration.

"Of course not. Only be a few minutes," Zerrick said, puffing. The wood definitely helped, but Mira suspected they would both be better off if they made camp right after reaching the far side--these were different muscles they were using, and they'd probably both be exhausted by the time they were across. She knew it must be hard for him to talk and paddle at the same time, but the soft lapping of water all around them seemed menacingly quiet, and she felt exposed out in the middle of this lake, half of her body not even in sight. She found herself babbling.

"My, look how far we've come already. Amazing that we can just float across. You don't suppose there are actually fish in here--I mean, little ones, maybe, but nothing large, surely--" she broke off as something made a soft plop in the water off to her right, forming an ever widened circle. She gulped, peering at the spot where the sound had come from.

"Uh, Zerrick, you don't suppose . . . Is there anything dangerous here?" she asked, feeling out of breath, her eyes scanning the water for any other signs of activity.

Zerrick sounded exasperated. "Mira, I really don't know. All I know is that the sooner we're across, the safer we'll be. Stay quiet and hopefully we'll be left alone."

Mira said no more after that.

They progressed slowly across the lake, Zerrick resting every now and then to catch his breath, and as they drew closer to the far shore, Mira was struck with the beauty of the hillside. It seemed almost a vertical wall of jungle, rising up out of the misty lake and towering into the heavens. Flocks of parrots and other birds darted in and away from the tree-topped peak, a wild show of pink, yellow and red. The waterfall was close enough to be heard now, thundering into the lake to send up a spray of white mist.

She turned back to Zerrick to comment on the view, when she saw, perhaps a hundred fifty feet off, another large plop in the water and the hump of something dark, green and snake-like, making a little trail as it swam towards them.

"Zerrick," she said with a gulp, "Zerrick, there's something coming towards us."

He paused in his swimming and looked over a where she was staring. Calm water, she noted; no hump or long green body to be seen, but the ripples were still there, moving across the water towards them.

"What did you see?" he asked, searching the water.

"I don't know. A snake, maybe," she answered. She didn't add that it had seemed awfully large. Maybe she had just imagined it.

"I hate snakes," Zerrick muttered, and began slowly swimming again, glancing back at where the ripples had come from. "Hopefully it will just leave us alone."

Just as he said that, Mira heard another soft splash, and a hump again surfaced, lined with a thin flapping fin, and then a long tail surfaced behind, making a sweeping curve in the water before the whole thing again submerged.

"That's not a snake; that's a serpent!" Zerrick cried, and began with renewed efforts to steer them away, kicking frantically to produce more speed.

"Oh God, it knows we're here," Mira said in a half-strangled voice. To be attacked here in all this water. To be pulled down under the surface, trapped in those slimy coils--she kicked at the water in panic, willing them to move more quickly towards the shore. Her kicking was chaotic and untimed; soon Zerrick was expending energy just to combat her wild movements. They slowed to a crawl.

"Stop--just let me do this! And get out my sword!" he ordered, his face red with exertion. A third set of ripples told her the serpent was now only fifty feet away.

She dug her hand into the packs, pulling at the ropes they had used to secure them, and felt cold steel. She tried to pull it free, but the leverage was all wrong; she'd have to let go of the log and use both her hands. That would mean swimming.

"I can't get it free," she whispered, tugging with all her might.

Zerrick swam over to help her. The shore was still several hundred feet away--as much as he'd like to have firm ground to stand on, not to mention all that green life there for his magic, there was no way they would reach it before the lake serpent was upon them. He berated himself for forgetting to bring some fronds for just such an emergency. How many times had Alden told him never to be without some fresh plants, some kind of source of magic? Some witch he was turning out to be.

Together they managed to get the sword free. Zerrick told Mira to work on getting the pistol free next--it had been deeply wrapped to protect it from the wet. He hooked his left arm to the log and faced out to where the serpent would probably emerge.

He was not disappointed. With a great splash and an eerie high-pitched wail, the serpent reared out of the water, the long crest along its back extended, the mouth open wide to reveal two dagger-like fangs.

Its face was reptilian but also had a disturbingly human aspect: a broad forehead and high cheekbones, which made the gaping mouth all the more grotesque. Its underside and face were a light tan and lined with fine sharp scales, while the crest and along the length of its body, it was a dark muddy green slashed with black stripes.

All this Zerrick quickly took in before the serpent struck. The wide mouth filled Zerrick's vision, and he only just managed to swing the sword, the metal ringing as it bounced of one long fang and sliced across the creature's nose.

The serpent reared back in pain and surprise, its glassy eyes measuring first Zerrick and his sword, then Mira, who was still digging in the packs for the pistol. It opened its mouth to strike again.

It lashed this time at Mira, but again Zerrick parried its attack, this time the blade scraping across the sharp scales over one eye. The creature pulled back quickly, before Zerrick could draw blood, and hovered over him, apparently trying to decide how best to breach his defenses. Sunlight caught in its eyes, making them seem to glow red as it glared at him.

"Zerrick, use Nanna's crystals! Make yourself strong again, anything!"

Zerrick carefully inched towards where he could better defend two at once. "The crystals are in my pouch--if I let go of either the sword or this log, I'm sure that thing will attack," he answered.

He could leave her here and make an attempt to dive down and strike the creature, but he had the feeling that letting go of the log could be a fatal mistake. He wasn't a strong enough swimmer, and he knew those coils were for more than swimming. The serpent, meanwhile, made another cautious attempt at biting Mira; he quickly put an end to that thought, jabbing his sword at its nose again. It backed off a little more, then suddenly submerged.

"I've got it! Now where's the creature?" Mira said, triumphantly holding up the pistol and turning away from the pack to stare at the place where the creature had been.

For an answer, Zerrick pointed down.

"Oh, no," she moaned, looking down through the murky waters. She seemed to suddenly have trouble breathing, her face losing all color.

"Climb onto the log; here, I'll help. If you see it, shoot it," Zerrick said, swimming over and lifting her so that she could throw a leg over the log. It tilted and bobbed, threatening to spill their packs, but Mira managed to get one leg hooked to where she could, with effort, pull herself up.

Zerrick kicked hard to give her added boost. She was just balancing herself on the log, when Zerrick suddenly felt something slimy brush up his leg. He gave a cry as a green coil whipped around his waist. Then the snake pulled him under.

Zerrick's world was turned inside out; he couldn't tell which way was the surface in the dark waters as he thrashed with the serpent, his lungs burning from lack of air and from the powerful coils tightening around him from chest to mid-thigh, trying to crush the life out of him.

He had managed to get his left arm free before the coils pinned him, but his right arm was hopelessly trapped. He was simply grateful he hadn't dropped the sword.

Fighting the blackness creeping over his eyes and the fire in his lungs, he transferred the sword from his right to his left, just in time to hold it out as a dark mass suddenly came into his vision--the head, he assumed.

He took an awkward swing and at the same time tried to kick free, but the creature would have none of that. It began turning in the water, rolling him over and over just below the surface, dizzying him with flashes of sunlight and black depths. For an instant he broke surface. He gulped for air just before being pulled under again.

"Zerrick!" Mira screamed, fumbling to set the trigger and bring the gun around to the spot where he'd been. She didn't dare shoot; the water was too cloudy, and all she could see was a large black shape moving beneath the surface. She bit back tears that were threatening to spill, and readied herself to shoot if so much as a scale emerged from the water.

For a few agonizing seconds, nothing happened, then she saw a mass emerge--a seething tangle of dark green serpent against human flesh. She tried to find a target to aim for, but the serpent had drawn itself into a tight ball around Zerrick.

Just as the serpent began to submerge the head came up, eyes flashing as it grinned at her, lips pulled taut over the deadly fangs. Not satisfied with the catch it had already made, it made a strike at her leg.

She shot it between the eyes.

For a moment it didn't seem to realize it was dying. It missed her leg by inches and sank its teeth into the log, chewing at it as if it were flesh. Then the death spasms began, and it pulled its fangs free, thrashing madly in the water, snapping at everything, including itself. Mira abandoned her position on top of the log as the snapping jaws just barely missed her, a trail of green frothy venom burning a trail down her arm. Even in its death throes it refused to let Zerrick go--she saw him stabbing repeatedly at the coils and gasping for air whenever he surfaced. Then, as suddenly as the thrashing had begun, it ended. With a groan, the creature's head fell back into the water. The whole mass began to sink.

"Mira!" Zerrick managed to gasp before he was pulled under again, his sword extended to her in a last plea for help.

She never thought twice about it. With a few strong kicks, she pulled the log over to him, grabbed the blade of the sword, and heedless of the damage to her hand, pulled with all her might.

The fact she had wrapped her hands and arms to protect against leeches helped; the blade did not bite as deeply as it might have. Still, she winced as the blade cut into her, fighting against the creature's weight dragging Zerrick down. A moment passed where neither side was winning, where she wondered if the log would be pulled under as well. Then something jerked at the sword. Zerrick's other hand emerged and grabbed hold of her shoulder.

The sudden weight of him, as he used her shoulder as leverage to pull himself up, pushed her under, but only for a moment. Once he had broken surface to breathe in a great gulp of air, he realized what he was doing and transferred his weight to the log, pulling her back up, sputtering and choking. Zerrick looked almost guilty, she thought, as if he expected her to blame him for this entire situation. That hardly mattered to her, though. She felt so happy to see him alive, she threw an arm around him and hugged him.

"Thank Iahmel! I was afraid you were lost to that horrible thing! I thought that when you kill something, it is supposed to go limp, but that serpent refused to let go of you even after I shot it!" Mira said, firmly affixing Zerrick's arms to the log and again stowing the sword. He just hung there, panting for breath and coughing up some water he had inhaled in the fight. The meaning of her words seemed to slowly sink in. He gaped at her.

"You shot the creature? I heard it, but I didn't think it had hit. Figured it was just tired of my struggling and was going deeper to finish the job" Zerrick found breath enough to say, hugging the log, looking a little green. He coughed up a last bit of water, closing his eyes and resting his head on the log.

Mira grinned. "I got him right between the eyes. I'm a good shot when I have to be."

"That's . . . that's . . ." Zerrick stammered, still looking disbelieving. "That's great," he finally said, looking at Mira in wonder. "Thanks for saving my life."

"Well, I," she stammered, blushing. "You were doing pretty well there. I think you could have beaten it if you'd used magic." It was amusing almost, his sudden discovery that she had some skills with a weapon after all.

"Magic takes concentration. And a source--there are green things living in the waters, but they slip past you; there's nothing to lock onto. You saved me. And I'll remember it," Zerrick said. They fell silent a moment, staring at each other as the water gently lapped around them. Zerrick's pupils were huge, staring at her eyes; she couldn't imagine he could find anything so fascinating. Then he noticed the blood running down her hand.

"You're hurt," he gasped reaching over to take her hand and inspect it. A clean slash crossed her palm from index finger to mid-palm. He pressed the cloth wrappings to the wound, to stop the blood.

Mira winced a little, but she didn't pull away. His touch felt nice. "I can take care of it once we reach shore. I think we should get moving again. Just in case that thing decides it's not dead after all."

Zerrick let her go and appeared to be attempting to muster his strength, but it was no use. He was obviously exhausted, and looked depleted as well. He held onto the log limply, scarcely able to keep himself afloat.

"I'm afraid I can't, Mira. If I try to swim, I think I may black out."

Mira looked at him. His face had turned deathly pale, and his eyes looked sunken and colorless. Certainly the fight would have tired him, but this was an almost unnatural pallor. An idea struck her. Could he have been bitten? She had to get him to land to check.

"Tell me how to swim, and I'll get us there," she said.

Zerrick nodded, too tired to even offer an alternative. "Pretend you are climbing a mountain--push down and away with your legs and keep them rotating. You have to push at the water to move forward. Or you can do the breast stroke--have you ever seen a frog swim?"

"No," Mira said, experimenting with a few different movements to see what felt best.

"Don't worry about it. We can't be more than a couple hundred feet away. Just lean on the log and kick away. And don't be afraid to rest if you have to. I'll hang on for a bit anyway."

Mira wasn't so sure, but there was no point in arguing. She began kicking, and soon found that the water hindered some movements while encouraging others. She found a cutting motion seemed to work best and set to work, pushing the log and simply hoping they were making headway. Her head was much closer to the water this way, and she couldn't entirely depend on the wood for support, but the kicking seemed to counteract that. After a mouthful of muddy water, she kept her lips firmly shut and breathed through her nose.

For a while it seemed she was pushing and getting nowhere, but when she stopped to rest and check Zerrick, she saw the shore was much closer now. Zerrick's eyes were closed, his breathing labored. When she tried to check for any wounds on his arms and upper torso, he merely opened one eye to look at her, then closed it again.

More worried now than ever that there some bite or wound hidden where she could not see, she went back to swimming, not caring how tired she was or how much her legs begged her to stop. They were going to make it to dry land, even if it was only to die.

When she didn't think she could kick another time, when the whole idea seemed ludicrous and she was ready to just give up and let go, her foot finally brushed solid ground. Gasping with relief, she gave a few more kicks, and could now feel the tops of rocks. She pushed against these with renewed vigor as Zerrick's arms started to lose their grip and his head slumped down into the water.

She let go of the log to grab him as he slid into the water and waited to sink herself, but instead her feet found firm footing, and while she was immersed up to her chin, she could walk with difficulty towards the shore, carrying Zerrick with his head over her shoulder and guiding the log along with her other arm. They reached the shore and she dragged Zerrick to a broad sunlit rock to dry off, then pulled the log far enough ashore to remove the packs. That accomplished, she collapsed next to Zerrick.

She only rested a moment, then crawled over to him and tried to rouse him. His breath sounded shallow and uneven, and now she could feel a fever in him, as he shivered from the dampness of his clothing and the cool breezes descending on them from the shadow of the mountain. She managed at last to wake him; he coughed a few times and stared hard at her, as if his eyes could not focus properly.

"What's happening? The world feels gray, somehow. Am I dying?" He rasped, trying to rise and succeeding only in rolling over. He closed his eyes, swaying.

"Did the serpent bite you? Are you in any way wounded?" Mira asked, swiftly removing his wet shirt and stockings and laying them on the rock to dry. Not a mark could be seen on him anywhere, though she had to remove a few leeches.

"Did you swallow the water? Are you ill?" she continued to ask him, pulling out her herbs and their blankets from the packs. She wrapped him tightly and gently chaffed his shoulders, trying to stop the shaking but it did little good. His skin looked frightfully pale, and the fever was growing worse.

"I don't know," he managed at last, wondering why the world seemed so dim and washed out. He felt the chills and fever distantly, as if was happening to someone else. Tiny pins seemed to be pricking his skin all along his extremities, and his blood seemed sluggish, crawling through his veins at a snail's pace. He felt . . . drained.

"The serpent," he croaked, suddenly locking onto an idea. "Had to be magical to be that size. It had me. Why didn't it bite me? Why didn't it start to eat me?"

"You're asking the wrong person. I know little about these magical beasts," Mira answered. She had a number of herbal remedies spread out before her, and was sorting through them frantically.

"The damn thing drained me! That has to be it," Zerrick cried, fumbling at his neck pouch for the crystal there. He found it, but it was empty, all the magic sucked out. He felt around for his things. "Nanna's earrings, quick!"

Mira found the earrings in his pouches--she weighed each in her hand, as if by weight she would be able to tell which had more magic. She ended up bringing both to him, looking puzzled and uncertain.

He grabbed them in her hand like a man dying of thirst and without even letting go of her, starting pulling the sweet magic into his body, seeking strength, health, rejuvenation. Another wave of dizziness swept over him, but this time it was the euphoria of magic; he moaned as the power filled his veins and swirled within him, driving away the fever and chills and the sense of being disconnected. Again he could sense the world around him, the bright ocean of magic radiating from each and every living thing.

There was still some power left in one of the earrings, but he was filled again, and he let the remainder stay there. With his inner eyes there seemed to be a golden glow all about him, and an indescribable feeling of peace and happiness. And beside him, he became aware of Mira's presence, similarly glowing; a second radiant pool of gold.

He opened his eyes in alarm, and realized he was still holding her hand.

Her eyes were closed, her mouth slack as she sat resting her weight on one arm, the afternoon sun making a halo of orange about her head. The tip of her tongue brushed her lips, which Zerrick suddenly noticed were no longer chapped. Similarly, the sunburn was gone from her skin and in his hand, her palm felt smooth, free of the slicing cut. He felt a shudder pass through her; she slowly opened her eyes and the sun illuminated speckles of amber within them as she raised her eyes to look at him.

"Oh . . . my," she breathed, licking her lips once more as she tried to catch her breath. He could feel her heart pounding, and there was a warmth in her which went beyond the heat from either the rocks or the sun. Both their clothes were miraculously dry. "What just happened?"

"I--" Zerrick said, sitting up. The weakness was gone as if it had never existed. He felt ready to climb a mountain. "I think I just healed us."

"A miracle," Mira exclaimed. She breathed in deep and sighed. "If that's what it feels like to use magic, I'm surprised you hold back at all," she added, the glow about her now manifesting itself in an ear to ear grin. "Truly, as Nanna says, magic must be a gift of the Goddess."

"I don't know about that. It does prove useful, sometimes. I apologize for involving you in that spell. I didn't mean to," said Zerrick. He meant to release her now that the effects were fading. Instead he found himself pulling her closer.

Mira wobbled as she lost her balance and reached out her other hand to Zerrick's shoulder to steady herself. "Don't apologize. It was wonderful."

Zerrick could not stop what came next. It was almost as if there was a force propelling him forward as he pulled her close and melded his lips to hers. For a second she resisted, but the press of his lips coaxed hers into responding as he felt her resolve weakening, until she was leaning into the kiss, matching his pressure with her own. The kiss lasted only a moment or so before Zerrick broke it off abruptly. He sat staring at her, waiting for the slap that would surely come.

Instead she withdrew as if nothing had happened, and set to gathering his clothes from the rocks. She did not glance at him when she returned his things, but he could see a flush in her cheeks and throat. She did not seem angry. "We'd better set up camp," she said, standing a little ways off. She seemed preoccupied with rubbing the hand he had been holding.

Still a mystery, he thought with a mental shrug. He pulled on his shirt and followed her over to the packs. So they would pretend it had never happened, simply forget it and move on. An excellent plan as far as he was concerned.

Except he would never forget.

Chapter Fourteen

*"Pass beneath the shadow of the mountain, and break through to the other side--
this is the passage of a man's life."*
--Put-na elder

The ring of mountains stood before him, a circle of jagged teeth and claws thrust up from the sands of the desert to the wide lonely skies above. Before, those peaks had looked cool and inviting, but now he could see they were not--the rock was black and edged like knives, piled one atop another in sharp peaks, broken crockery from a celestial tantrum. They absorbed the rays of the sun to burn the skin even as they cut the flesh. He was near the base, yet the heat of the peaks before him felt like a wall of fire.

The vast desert stretched out behind him, broken only by an occasional shrub. In the hazy distance he thought he could see the towers of a beautiful city which gleamed white and gold, but the image wavered and danced in the heat rising off the desert, making him wonder if it were real or merely a mirage.

"Zerrick," a woman--the woman within the circle of mountain--called to him, and he returned his attention to the climb, desperate to see that awesome figure again, learn more about her.

"Who are you?" he called, trying to pull himself up to a ledge which might offer a view into the valley he knew was beyond. Before he could go forward however, the rock he was holding onto gave and suddenly broke off, leaving him scrambling for a new hold, the rocks scratching his hands and arms.

He finally succeeded in reaching the ledge, but it offered only a view of a higher, even rockier rise. Still, he could feel her--the incredible pull which would make him labor on to reach her, regardless of the damage to himself. When she spoke, he had no choice but to listen with all his being.

"You must not delay. It is vital that you come to me, that you free me. I have stayed in one place too long. The power is too concentrated," the voice, so regal, was imploring him, and the desperation in that voice nearly made him weep aloud as he sought a path up the next rise.

"I'm coming as fast as I can, but I'm only human!" He answered, desperately trying to find a path up that would not be deadly. "But please tell me why! Why are you calling me, of all people, and who are you? What are you?"

He could feel her searching for an answer, the pull wavering a moment while she thought, and in that moment he could suddenly hear another voice, a much softer, but still insistent voice of another woman also calling his name. He looked behind him and out of the blurred image of the city Mira walked towards him, dressed as a native in a leather tunic and leggings, calling for him frantically.

"Zerrick, please! You don't have to do this, you don't have to go! I've found a place, where we can both be happy." She spotted him and ran up, but the black rocks daunted her. She stood at the base, arms reaching up to him.

"Do not be distracted," the woman again implored, and he was torn, feeling the irresistible pull, but unwilling to leave Mira.

"Mira, you don't want to be a part of this. Stay back!" He called, but she refused to be warned off. She began climbing, and he could see the rocks cutting into her pale soft skin, see droplets of blood fall to the white sands of the desert below her.

"Do not forget," the other voice called to him once more, but it was much weaker, the sound bouncing off the high rocks of the mountains and losing intensity. Zerrick heard a clatter of rocks falling and turned in time to see Mira falter, clinging to a ledge jutting out over a long drop.

"Zerrick!" Mira cried, and he watched, horrified as she slipped and fell onto a rocky spire. The sharp rock stabbed deep into her chest. Blood spilled in a rush down her tunic, and her head lolled back, the red of her hair blending into the red, red blood.

He scrambled to reach her, his feet slipping on the treacherous rocks, then he too was falling, hurtling down towards the bottom to join her. . .

"Zerrick, wake up--it's only a dream!"

He woke to find Mira's arms around him, his head cradled against the soft curve of her throat, her beautiful voice calling his name. He groaned, and very nearly found himself reaching to complete the embrace, wanting to pull her lips down to meet his. Instead, he pulled away, coming fully awake. How were they supposed to keep things safe and platonic if these temptations kept assailing him?

He gently removed her hand from his shoulder and sat up, silently repeating to himself that he was not going to reach over and tussle her hair, falling loosely down her shoulders, or do any one of the hundred other things that were springing to mind.

"I'm awake," he said rather needlessly.

Her chuckle sounded relieved. "So I see. Another one of those dreams?"

He nodded, unwilling to discuss the events of this particular dream with her.

She didn't press him, but said, "Ranu believes dreams are messages sent by the gods. From what I've seen of yours, I think your gods must be particularly unfriendly. I had to wake you or risk being kicked to death!" Her joking manner belied the concern in her eyes.

Zerrick flushed, wondering if any of his kicks had connected. Then the meaning of her words sunk deeper, and the muscles of his stomach clenched in fear. Dreams, sent by gods. And before, the one about the wolf creature had come true, at least in that he had met such a creature. What did this mean, that she was in the dream now, and that she had fallen, perhaps to her death . . . covered in blood . . .

He would not let her out of his sight.

He glanced at the overhang of rock they had chosen last night for shelter, and at the pink dawn light filtering through the trees, then pulled on a light cloak against the morning chill. "I suppose we might as well get moving."

"I suppose," Mira responded, obviously hoping for more from him, but she stood and set to folding the blankets. Cool morning mist hugged the land, an eerie fog trapped beneath the canopy which shifted and swirled in the mountain breezes, giving rise to wraith-like shapes that danced and merged with darker shadows of foliage.

They were well into the mountains now, having climbed that first awesome peak by the lake some eight days ago. There had been little talk between them since then--the climbs were difficult and made even more treacherous by the nightly thunderstorms and drenching rain. On the sheer cliffs of some of these mountains, there was time only for quick instructions and warnings. Concentration took precedence over companionship.

The vegetation here was just as dense as it had been in the lowlands, the trees somehow even taller on the rugged slopes, and with the high canopy and dense underbrush, they had seen little of what might lie beyond the mountains, or indeed how far the mountains stretched and whether they were crossing them or merely traveling along the range.

There had also been only a few signs of the tribes so often spoken of as inhabiting this region. A few spear points, a broken stone knife; these were all they had found of the elusive Put-na, and despite Nanna's teachings and Mira's own friendship with the slaves, they had not been able to recognize any clear signs of trails which might lead to a habitation. They spent the first part of each day foraging for fruits and berries to supplement their dwindling food supply, then they continued the weary climb up further into the mountains. In clearings, they could see the tip of a great peak in the distance growing closer day by day, barren and rocky at this time, but probably topped with snow in the cooler months.

The days were beginning to grow shorter.

They made short work of gathering some roots, tera bush seeds, and a few ripe bananas, then set off down the mountain, heading for that tallest peak in the hopes of getting some sight of the flat lands Nanna said stretched out beyond the mountains. At first they went down single file through the tangled brush, but as they came upon a much clearer area where the dense canopy above blocked out the light and held back the ground foliage, Mira quickened her pace to stride side by side with Zerrick.

The look on her face was one of determination.

"Zerrick, we need to talk," she announced, holding a branch for him to pass under.

He kept his eyes averted. "Certainly. Whatever you like, Mira."

She kept a steady pace next to him and appeared to ponder her next words carefully. "What is the matter with you lately? You weren't this closed-mouthed when you were staying in my father's cellar. There we could talk about anything, it seemed. But now we've been traveling together two weeks and instead of knowing you better, I feel I know you less and less! Why are you shutting me out? I know you didn't want me to come. Are you still punishing me?"

"Of course not!" Zerrick exclaimed, shocked that she should think him so cruel. Then, embarrassed at his outburst, he said in a low voice, "I've just been preoccupied lately."

Mira stepped into his path and fixed her gaze on him. "Then why don't you ever really talk to me? Why do you flinch when I touch you, or avoid looking at me when I'm speaking like you're doing right now?"

Zerrick forced himself to meet her gaze, searching for a possible explanation, one she could accept without coming too near to the truth. "I'm trying to protect you," he began weakly, then said in a firm voice, "I told you back in Depin that my powers were not under control. I've brought nothing but trouble to everyone around me, and I'd like to avoid getting you any further involved. Believe me, the less you know about me, the better."

Mira sighed. "Too late, Zerrick. I'm already involved up to my neck, if that encounter with the serpent was any sign. So stop trying to protect me. Tell me what it is that you're so afraid of."

What am I afraid of? Zerrick wondered, watching as Mira slapped a mosquito away from her freckled skin. Would it really be so terrible to confide in her, to trust someone? He had always been surrounded by people circling him like hawks, waiting for just one wrong move or word to swoop down and attack. Mother had been especially good at it; she would feign sweetness and understanding, and when he opened up and told her something of his feelings or thoughts, she'd chastised him for being such a fool. "Only a stupid child would think that!"

Mira was different. There was no denying that. But would she really understand the struggle he was having with magic, the terrible lust? That seemed to be asking more of her than he felt was fair.

"Well?" Mira's gentle reminder pulled him out of his thoughts.

Fine then. If she was asking for it, he'd give it to her.

He stopped by a sunlit pile of moss-covered rocks and faced her, arms crossed. "You want to know what scares me? Everything. I'm afraid this magic will take over my mind and cause me to do something terrible, I'm afraid I'll never find this tribe, never understand the crazy dreams I'm having, never find safety. Most of all, I'm afraid that you'll be dragged down with me and be hurt, or even killed."

He uncrossed his arms and ran a hand through his sweat-damp hair. "I'm not going to pretend any longer. This is not a wise, all-knowing woodsman before you--I know little of the area we're now in, little of what we will run into beyond those peaks. I don't even know what kind of creatures live there. And last of all, I'm only guessing the way. I think we may already be hopelessly lost."

With that, he sat on the rocks, head bowed. "So there you have it. You're lost in an uncharted wilderness with a half-trained witch who's afraid of his own shadow. Is that enough for you?" He waited for the fiery retort from her, for that loud, highly emotional fight they'd been skirting for days now.

Instead, she laughed.

"Oh Zerrick," she sighed, shaking her head. She looked at him, a sad knowing in her eyes. "It really is hard for you, isn't it? Letting out everything that's bottled inside, sharing it. Someone did you wrong--you're always on the defense, waiting for an attack."

His laugh was without mirth. "If you knew my family--"

"I don't," Mira said, eyes flashing, "Although I wish I could meet them. I'd have a few things to say. You think too little of yourself. We have come farther than any white man ever recorded has come, yet you say with embarrassment that you know nothing of these woods." Mira paced as she spoke, unconsciously copying her father's movements at the trial, her hands punctuating each word, spots of sunlight dancing in her hair. Zerrick swallowed, suddenly frightened. With her incredible voice and her passion, she spoke almost as well as Father.

She came up close, lowering her voice. "I didn't choose to go with you because you were all knowing, or a witch. I simply liked you, and I knew you would try to protect me, without stifling me. You don't have to know everything, and it's all right to admit that you don't. The wise are the ones who know there is much to learn. Just don't overdo it. You're not stupid, and you are not as much of a curse as you seem to think you are."

This was back into dangerous territory. He was being enthralled by her voice again, and she was standing too near. At this rate, he could almost imagine falling in love with her, and that he couldn't allow to happen. If he loved her, she was doomed, right alongside him.

"We are still lost," he reminded her, moving off down the slope, out into a small clearing. The face of the mountain up ahead stared down at them like a gnarled old man, challenging them.

"Of course we're lost. We're off the end of the maps! I think even Nanna would be uncertain of the way here, except she might have a better feel for what kind of signs her people would leave." She squinted at the sun, just seen through the treetops, making its way over the peak behind them.

She continued, "We know west. All we have to do is reach the top of that tallest peak, and we'll know where we are in this range, and how best to proceed. I predict by tomorrow evening, we'll know our way to the savanna, and perhaps even spot a settlement. Should we be moving on?" She raised an arm towards the peak before them, all the former frustration gone, a pleasant smile playing on her lips.

"That sounds like a good idea. And I'm sorry I've been acting so strange, but can you do just one thing for me?"

One auburn eyebrow went up. "What is that?"

Zerrick tried to keep his voice cheerful, but his worry somehow seeped through. "Be careful during the climb."

The rest of the day they spoke little, as they descended the last mountain before the peak they were aiming for, but they were forced to wait a little to begin their ascent the next morning; without warning, a downpour drenched the mountain, making the ground slick with mud and hundreds of tiny gurgling streams. Then, as the small river suddenly transformed into a rushing torrent, they were forced up a tree until it dwindled just as quickly to a trickling stream once the rain had passed. The jungle glistened with fine droplets, and the birds were happily soaking themselves in the newly made puddles. When the sky above cleared and they could no longer hear the sound of water running down the hillside, they set off again. They were climbing the base of the mountain they decided to call Lookout Peak, that high mountain they had seen from far off with the bald spot.

At first the going was easy. The base wasn't too steep, and tangled roots of trees helped them avoid the wet and muddy areas by providing handholds and footholds. Soon, however, the ground rose sharply, and the vines and roots gave way to palms. Palm fronds littered the floor of the forest, and Zerrick soon learned how treacherous the footing could be on partially rotten, thoroughly soaked fronds. Midday, they stopped for a quick lunch before starting the climb again. A short shower made the already slippery terrain worse.

"This is crazy!" Mira said, after skidding for what seemed the hundredth time and nearly falling into a bed of mushrooms.

"It will get better the higher we go. I'd like to get above the tree line before we rest for the evening," Zerrick said, tightening the strap on his packs to make sure they would stay secure if he took a little tumble. The two of them were already covered in mud.

"We might be better off stopping now and continuing the climb in the morning," Mira said, scrambling to catch up with him.

Zerrick shrugged. "It rained last night, it rained today, and it will probably rain again tomorrow. We're going to run into the same problem whether we wait or not. I'd rather get to where I can actually see around a little." He pulled her up over a rotten log blossoming with toadstools. "I think it starts to get pretty steep just ahead. You go first, and I'll follow."

Mira wrinkled her nose at him. "What, so you can catch me if I fall?" she taunted.

Zerrick saw she was only playing with him. He countered, "No, so I don't fall on top of you if I fall."

She chuckled, and gave him a pinch on the arm. "Yes, you're so fat!"

This time he did not smile. "You're looking thinner too, I think."

She shrugged, glancing at where the trousers had been gathered in to fit a suddenly narrower waistline. "Unavoidable part of the journey, I suppose. I must say, however, that I've never felt better."

"Lead on, then," Zerrick said, reassured. He couldn't help but admire her firm buttocks as she climbed up the next rise. Small rations had a few rewards, after all, he mused.

After the treacherous palm forest came the hardier ironwood trees, giant cedar, and a scattering of tall thin trees neither had seen before, with prickly needles and almost no branches. The air was growing decidedly cooler, and in clearings there were no more ferns or vines, only grass and wildflowers, or the dark red rock now peeping up here and there in the steeper passes. They were nearing the tree line, the ground becoming steeply slanted, making their knees ache as they pushed themselves to reach clear slopes.

A few wandering clouds had passed over the sinking sun, but no more rain threatened for now, which was fortunate. The footing was becoming increasingly difficult.

"My knees are about ready to give out--why don't we camp here and leave the view to tomorrow's climb? I'm sure it will still be there in the morning," Mira said, panting. They had filled their skins in a stream a few hundred yards back in preparation for the dry rocky heights, and it weighed heavily at their belts.

"We've just about made it--just a little bit further," Zerrick said in gasps, "Just think how great it will be to be able to see how far we've come." He said this with a cheerful smile, but he could not help the fact his arms were trembling with exhaustion or that both of them were walking stooped. Still, hope beckoned, that he'd be able to see a way beyond this treacherous peak. He had to reach the summit.

"All right--just to the area where the trees become sparse enough to see a little. And that's all," she answered, adjusting her packs and shaking her head amusedly.

They came around a tight bend to the first truly treeless part of the mountain: a rocky expanse falling to a sheer drop, bare except for a few tussock grass plants. The land was too steep here to camp, but they could see a little meadow just beyond, sparsely wooded by dwarf trees and protected from the elements by an overhang. Eager to remove their packs, they set off across the rocky face.

Zerrick stepped on a dark patch he thought was moss-covered rock, but suddenly his foot sank through, causing him to nearly lose his balance as his boot descended over a foot into mud and slime. He carefully pulled it out, grimacing.

"Step where I step," he directed Mira.

"I don't think I'll follow that particular step," Mira teased, but her voice was tense.

They inched across the deceptively smooth surface of the slope, eyes fixed on the treacherous footing. The problem Zerrick had encountered soon became clear--with the nearly continuous rains, mud from the higher slope had settled into cracks and crevices here, held in place only by a thin layer of moss.

Mira stepped across one such cavity and slid on a patch of mud; Zerrick reached out a hand, but she steadied herself immediately. "Don't worry about me. Keep finding a path," she said.

Zerrick returned to his slow progress, keeping Mira close enough to touch, but not letting her see the concern in his movements. The image from his dream was still clear in his mind.

He returned his attention back to the slope just in time to see his own peril. A rock which had looked sturdy was in fact embedded in more mud, and as he stepped on it, the rock and then a whole section of ground gave way. Zerrick found himself sliding towards the edge of the cliff, and every effort he made to pull himself up only loosened more of the mud, covering him in a slimy coat and making him slide faster and faster. He caught hold of a sharp rock right at the edge and held on for dear life, his right leg slipping over the edge of a hundred foot drop.

"Hang on! I'm coming!" Mira called from above, and before he could yell for her to stay put, she clambered down the slope, reckless in her speed as she sought to reach him.

His heart hammered in his throat until she reached a butte fifteen feet up and stopped, unable to descend any further without entering his mud trap. She pulled off her packs and rummaged around.

"Where's the rope?" she asked in panic, her things scattered across the rock.

"I have it," he gasped. He would have laughed, if the situation had not been so dire. And here he had worried about her making a misstep. She moved like a mountain goat.

"Here, I'll use the blanket," she said, sliding along her belly down the butte to the edge of the mudslide. With a flick of her wrist, she snapped the blanket at him. The far corner settled into the mud a few feet from his head.

Zerrick hesitated in reaching for it, despite the ache in his hands that warned him he would soon lose his grip. "Are you secure there?"

Mira glared at him and growled, "Grab the blanket, Zerrick!"

He wasn't going to argue with that tone of voice. Praying to Iahmel to protect at least her, if not his tainted soul, he grabbed for the corner and held on as his other foot slid towards the edge.

Mira struggled to sit up, pulling as she did so, but even with her recent increase in strength, she could pull him no more than a few feet. She began to slide herself, towards the mud-slick rock.

"Let go--maybe the blanket will give me enough purchase to get to you," Zerrick ordered, unwilling to take the chance that she would lose what hold she had on the slope. A bird cried out, far below them.

Mira started to object, then fell silent, looking at where his foot was slipping. She let go, and he scrambled up the blanket as it began to slide down, trying to get up to drier ground. He succeeded in getting to a small depression which at least stopped the downward slide, but he was still just out of reach of Mira's outstretched hand.

"Mira, don't worry about it--just get back up the slope. I can get up from here," Zerrick urged, wondering now that he had his hands free whether he should use magic.

Mira refused to budge however, but rather began stretching towards him, extending out over the mud. Grimacing, he reached for her--to get out of this as quickly as possible, and to keep her from extending too far.

Too late. As she stretched herself to the limit and grasped his hand, her other hand slid into the mud, and she lost her grip. With a cry, she went tumbling into the depression with him, and then her momentum sent both of them skidding back towards the brink.

Zerrick pressed his cheek against the cool slimy rock and dug in the fingers of his free hand into a crevice, holding onto Mira with the other hand. Now, their positions were reversed; her legs were dangling off the edge.

"Merciful gods!" she breathed, eyes wide with terror.

"Hold on!" Zerrick said with a grunt, trying to get a firm enough foothold to let go of the crevice and fetch his rope.

It was no use--he was too covered in mud, and the footholds were too tiny to do him any good. There was nothing his could do now, but search, driven by desperation and a terrible sense of guilt, for the magic which had to be buried somewhere around here.

Fungus, dead leaves, and old roots . . . Zerrick saw each little glimmer of magic, weak magic, deeply buried traces of past life energy. Those tiny traces could not help him.

He could feel his fingers straining on the rock, heard from far off Mira's frightened pleas for him to wake up. He pushed all that away and dug deeper, searching for enough power to solidify this mud, pull Mira up to safety, and create a safe path to the other side.

Straining his Othersenses, he went deeper into trance, aware of the magic of the trees below him. There was an entire mountain beneath him, and yet it was out of reach . . .

When he thought he could not strain his senses any further, he suddenly ran into a veil, on which the other side held vast amounts of power, power so pure and so all-encompassing he wondered if he was against the gates of Heaven itself. Or Hell. He tried to break the seemingly delicate veil separating him, but it eluded him, as fine as silk and as strong as armor. Suddenly he felt the world falling away behind him and realized he had located too much power, that it was pulling at him through the veil. It would either absorb him, or burn him away completely. He struggled to return to himself, to pull back, but it was like trying to pull away from the mountain itself.

Inexorably, he was drawn closer and closer.

"Not yet, my pupil. You are not ready to venture into that sea of magic," a kind but firm female voice--the voice from his dreams--admonished, and suddenly with a wrench that seemed to go through his very soul, the veil was gone, the power again hidden from his senses.

He opened his eyes. And gasped.

The mountainside was dry, the mud hardened and lined with cracks, as if it hadn't rained in weeks. Even the mud on their clothing and skin had dried, flaking off into small bits of dust. With solid ground beneath him, he stood and pulled Mira up beside him.

"Wow, what a spell!" Mira exclaimed, dusting herself off, her hands shaking. She edged away from the drop.

"Let's get out of here," Zerrick replied.

Once they were settled in the woodland area beyond the bald spot, Zerrick tried to reconstruct what had happened. That power hadn't been connected to any source in nature that he could discern. And never before had he encountered power hidden--protected--by any kind of shield, or whatever that veil had been. In such magnitude, it was like comparing a campfire to the glory of the sun. Magic power came from life, so what kind of life produced that? A whole mountain? The Goddess Herself? Things were getting stranger, and he wasn't sure he liked these waking dreams, or being called the Lady's 'pupil'.

"Come and see the view!" Mira's voice brought him out of the troubles he'd just as soon let lie. With a sigh he joined her on a ridge, where she was huddled in their one remaining blanket against the onset of night.

He sat down beside her and she offered a corner of blanket which he gladly accepted. As grimy as they both were, he couldn't think much about the romance of their setting, but he could definitely appreciate a little shared warmth. He shivered and leaned forward to take in the view she'd pointed out.

It was an awesome sight. Peak upon peak of majestic splendor, spanning out in every direction, the tallest mountains alongside their own vantage point, to the north and south in a rugged line. Looking towards where they had come, Zerrick could just see beyond the mountains a tiny sparkle of the lake where the serpent had attacked them, then the flat jungle stretching out into twilight. Somewhere in that green expanse lay the towns of Depin and Harrow. And beyond that, the ocean, which could bear one all the way back to Endersey, far to the east and north. It was a dizzying sight, taken in its entirety. Focusing only on the lands immediately below, Zerrick could see they had taken a diagonal pathway across the mountains--not the shortest path, but by no means the longest either. They were making progress.

"Tomorrow we'll cross to the other side of this peak and see where this range ends," Mira spoke aloud both their thoughts, her face a pale beacon in the deepening gloom of night.

Zerrick drew close to wrap one arm around her, for assurance, he told himself. "The sooner we get to a tribe, the better I'll feel." The cold mountain breezes stirred around them, making them huddle closer. In the east, all the land was now one with the night, as overhead the stars began to shine.

She nodded emphatically. "Your spells seem to be growing in strength. I'll never figure out how you did that thing on the mountainside. We didn't even have any plants around."

He looked at her solemnly. "I didn't do it."

In the gloom he could see her eyes widen. "Then who. . . "

His shiver had nothing to do with the cold. "That's what we have to find out."

Chapter Fifteen

"Step light; speak soft; Somebody is watching."
--Put-na Dreamteller

Zerrick expected another visitation in his dreams, especially after his second daytime experience, but his sleep was undisturbed. In fact, he slept like the dead, waking only when Mira tore the blanket from him and splashed water on his face.

He opened his eyes blearily. "Morning already?"

Mira smiled. "Some time ago, actually. While you were dozing, I went for a little exploration."

Zerrick sat straight up, instantly awake. "After what happened yesterday, you went off alone?"

She remained unperturbed. "You were the one who slipped. Anyways, I went exploring, and discovered something. I want you to see it and tell me what it is," she said, handing him his ration of food and the waterskin. He eyed the cold salted pork with distaste.

"Come on. I have to show you this!" she urged, and reluctantly he rose to his feet.

After forcing himself to eat the rations, he followed her through a sunlit meadow dotted with thin kauri pine and up another rocky face, up around a bend to a patch of woodland--the last thick patch of trees this side of the mountain. She led him up to a small cluster of trees he had never seen before. They were glowing.

He approached with caution, remembering the glowing beetles he had encountered in the lowlands, but this glow seemed to be coming from the trees themselves, a faint hazy glow of russet and green and gold. He put his hand just inches away from the smooth reddish bark but did not touch the wood. Magic stirred to life under his fingertips, in concentrations normally found only in the most ancient of trees.

"They're focus plants," he murmured in wonder, drawing away his hand to retrieve the amber from Alden's pouch and Nanna's earrings. He knew focus plants could be used to store and transfer energies--he had seen Alden transfer it to crystals many times. But could he do it? Should he?

"Ah, so that's what they are. But that's not all. Come look over here," Mira said, pulling him from what could have been a very risky venture, over to the other side of the stand of trees. He gave an exclamation of joy.

A trail, clearly marked, ran from the grove up the other side of the mountain in a steeply climbing curve.

"Finally," Zerrick breathed, knowing now why Mira had rushed to wake him. He glanced once more at the grove, wishing he knew how to transfer the energy there without actually using it up in a spell. Unfortunately, he didn't. Dismissing the idea as too risky, he urged Mira to return to camp, and together they packed up and set off to follow the trail.

They were fortunate Mira had found it, for the ground here became very rocky and steep, and without the clear markings, they could have spent hours looking for a way up the slope. The trail wound around the mountain in an ever upward spiral, marked clearly with a gouge running down the left hand side--probably to be used as a drainage system during the rains, Zerrick realized.

The work had to have been done by magic--it would have taken years for men to chip away at the hard granite in order to create such a system. And the fact it was here at all suggested this was a well used trail, providing easy access to the mountaintop.

But for what purpose? Zerrick wondered, glancing back at the way they had come. A trail which began with a stand of magic trees didn't sound like a normal passage for hundreds of people traveling between their seasonal homes on either side of the mountains. They were probably walking on holy ground.

"Do you think it's a good idea to be following this?" Mira asked, mirroring his thoughts.

He was about to make a reply when the two of them rounded a sharp bend. Suddenly below them stretched the view they had been waiting for, the back side of the mountain, and the full view of the Jagara range.

There were no more mountains this side of the range, only foothills gently leading to flat savanna, stretching on for as far as the eye could see. The elevation of the land was higher here, and much drier, covered with grasses and brush, broken here and there by small stands of trees. He could see a thin winding river reaching out into the distance, widening into a sizable lake just on the horizon. And on the shore of that lake, he could just see it--a thin trail of smoke, twisting up to touch the morning clouds.

"There it is," he breathed, hardly able to contain his joy, "There's the summer camp."

Mira shared his enthusiasm, "Zerrick, can you see those moving shapes--I think that's a herd of akiya, that Nanna used to describe!"

She turned to him to explain. "In the rainy season, the tribes stay on this side of the mountains where it's drier, and hunt for akiya . They then travel to the jungle for the mild winter and spring." She paused. "Of course, over the past ten years they have ventured less to the jungle side, in order to avoid the slave hunters. Nanna says eventually they will all stay away permanently."

Alden had spoken of akiya once or twice. Supposedly they were similar to Old World deer but with long twisting horns. Not that Zerrick had seen more than a picture of either. Well, no matter. He only hoped they could learn how to hunt those creatures. A freshly cooked steak would be nice about now.

They stood for a moment, trying to see if the trail they were standing on wound its way down or merely led to the top and ended there. Despite the fact the woodland here was sparser, the brush was still thick enough to hide any signs of the trail. They continued up the trail, walking faster now, hearts lightened with the knowledge that the climb was near its end. The trail also seemed to hurry along, becoming steeper and narrower, with rough steps carved out of the mountainside.

Zerrick started to ask Mira what she knew about the Put-na and their stoneworking skills when they came upon a new section of trail. Here the steps were not merely rough carved bedrock; they were of some foreign stone, ornately carved, curving up to a high plateau above. As Zerrick neared the first step, a stone embedded in the center began to glow faintly. He inched back, and it became dull and lifeless once again.

"That was not done by the Put-na I know," Mira said nervously, eyeing the scrollwork on the sides of the steps.

"This was done by magic. By a very powerful witch," Zerrick agreed, noting how each step had its own stone--and each stone would have needed its own magic stored within to be able to glow like that. This was far beyond his skills. Or Alden's.

Mira eyed him dubiously. "Do you think it's wise to go up those?"

"Do we have a choice?" Zerrick muttered. He got the distinct impression that something or someone had led them here. "Let me go first. If anything's going to happen, it will happen to me." It would be just his luck. Like being struck by lightning, or hurled back by some unseen force. Or another of those visions. But when he gingerly placed his foot on the first step, nothing happened. The stone on the step he stood on lit up, as well as the one on the next step. That was all.

A guidelight to lead one at night, he realized. An incredible endeavor in magic just for a simple convenience. Was the witch who created this so powerful that this was simply a parlor trick? A frightening prospect.

"It's safe, Mira; come on, it's not far to the top," Zerrick urged.

They climbed perhaps three or four flights of stairs before coming to a plateau which extended out level for thirty feet before rising gently up to one final stairway to the mountaintop. That stairway was once again rough-hewn rock--the plateau seemed to be the final focus of the strange path.

The focus was clear. On the flat space of the plateau, just before the edge, was a dais of polished red stone, on which stood a pedestal of white quartz with a matching basin filled with water. The white quartz gleamed in the sun, looking pristine and inviting. Too inviting.

The whole plateau sung with magic, a grand symphony to Zerrick's senses, singing to him in like a siren. He drew near the dais, giddy with power that seemed to grow stronger the closer he came. In his mind's eye he could picture the veil again, that thin divider over incredible power; only here the veil was gossamer thin. Part of him knew he was in danger, but the pull was irresistible.

Mira found herself standing small and hunched, as if there was a great weight in the air, bearing down on her. The sun might be shining, but here it shed no warmth. She glanced at Zerrick and saw he squinted his eyes, one hand raised as if to protect himself from the glare. It wasn't that bright, she mused. He had that look on his face again, the one he had worn when he used Nanna's crystals for the first time. That did not bode well.

"Zerrick, leave it alone and let's hurry past this place. I'm getting a bad feeling about this. It almost seems as if somebody is watching us." She tried to explain the impression she was getting, of a great eye centered above them, surveying the area.

She pulled at his arm, but Zerrick was beyond her pleas. He swayed, fingering the pouch at his neck as if it itched.

"Who in the world do you think built this? And for what purpose?" he murmured dreamily, not looking at her at all, completely engrossed with the pedestal and basin.

"Who knows? Who cares?" Mira said in a hushed tone, glancing around nervously. As far as she could see they were alone, but never had she felt more surrounded, and the worst watcher seemed right at her shoulder. Watching, waiting, not focused on the two of them yet, but merely guarding the entire area. She wanted to move through as quickly as possible, and not draw that attention to themselves.

Leave it to Zerrick to have other plans.

"Zerrick, now is not the time to have one of your spells overtake you. There's something evil here, I can feel it. Leave it alone!" she said in a fierce whisper, circling round to block his way. What she saw in his face told her the effort was useless. His eyes were glazed and he was oblivious to her presence.

"Zerrick, come back to me! Zerrick!" She grabbed his chin and turned his face so that he was looking at her.

"Huh?" he said in a half daze, blinking slowly. "Mira, what's the matter?"

"This whole place is the matter. Wake up for a moment and look what it's doing to you. And there's something else. Something evil. Let's come away, Zerrick," she said, looking straight into his eyes which were half closed, almost drugged-looking.

He gently removed her hands. "S'all right," he said in a slur, patting her hand, "She says s'all right." He turned back to the dais and stepped around her, his eyes again losing focus, seeing a world beyond hers.

Zerrick saw Mira only as he would see a fly--an insignificant fleck in the corner of his eye. The magic was a net, entrapping him and reeling him in.

It was more than the power calling him; he could sense that this place was here to answer questions, and he had a multitude to ask. He had heard stories about ancient mages using crystal balls or pools of water to see distant places, past and future, and asking questions of spirits good and evil.

He thought that must be the purpose of this place. The basin was filled with water, and here at the edge of the dais he could see images flashing across its bright surface. He felt close to the higher beings up here on this mountaintop. And there was one woman in particular he wanted to talk to.

He stepped on the dais, and there was an audible hum under his feet--the stone recognizing a user of magic. From far off he could hear Mira mutter about drawing attention, and then suddenly he could feel it, a presence hovering nearby, like a black cloud blocking out the sun. He paused, shivering.

With effort he closed his eyes to the glamour of magic, and could now feel two things at once--the pull of magic, and of curiosity, but also a counter pull, trying to force him away, make him flee this place. He stood still, caught between the conflicting urges, his heart pounding in his chest. Before he had been too engrossed with the magic to take note of his surroundings, but now he could see the view this vantage point offered. The land seemed to stretch on forever at his feet, flat and dry and almost treeless beyond the lake with the settlement. His gaze was pulled further west, into the bright horizon. Some part of him knew that going west, the land became drier and drier, until it became a vast desert. The desert of his dreams. And beyond that desert, the ring of mountains, and Her.

With that thought, he felt a renewal of the tug pulling him away, then an overwhelming urge, pulling him back to the dais. What was happening? Toward, away, toward--it seemed two powers battling within him, and he was caught in the middle. He took a step away, thinking once he was away from this place, he could think clearly, decide whether this was really a good idea or not, but as soon as he did, something gave within him. The tug away vanished, leaving only the pull of magic, singing him back into a stupor. He fought against it, not entirely sure if it was Her will that led him, or another's, but he simply wasn't trained well enough to resist. As the magic washed over him, he closed his eyes and let it pull him to the basin.

Mira watched as Zerrick stepped on the dais, staring out into the distance, silent and thoughtful as if struggling with something. She tried to go to him, but at the edge of the dais she found she could not take another step. It felt as if a great hand was pushing at her, preventing her from going further, pushing back the air in her lungs so that she could hardly breathe. She watched in anguish as Zerrick suddenly swayed. His eyelids closed, and in a kind of sleepwalk, he approached the pedestal and stood, placing his hands on the sides of the basin.

His back was to her so she couldn't see his face, but the tendons in his hands strained as if trying to pull away from the white stone. He moaned a low despairing note, shaking his head, and she noticed that the stone had begun to glow. The chords of his neck grew taut, but he leaned in closer as the glow of the basin surrounded him.

Then all of hell broke loose.

The whole mountaintop went dark, as if a great shadow had fallen over them. A blast of wind knocked Mira off of her feet, sending her into a sprawl several paces back. She held her head, dazed, as wind howled around her, eyes shut against swirling dust.

As abruptly as it had begun, the wind ceased, and the shadow passed over. After the screaming wind, the silence that now surrounded her seemed all the more ominous; not a bird sang, not a bush rustled. The sense of being watched withdrew and slowly faded away. She dared to open her eyes.

She tried to stand but she was too dizzy; for minutes she simply sat hunched over, shaking with fear. That blast had been icy cold, a cold which penetrated more than the skin, cutting all the way to the heart. And for a moment, she thought she had heard laughter--an evil man's laugh, and whispered words in the deepest voice she had ever heard. The dizziness passed, and she stood up. Everything appeared normal now, except for the absence of bird calls and the unusual quiet. That, and the fact Zerrick lay unconscious at the edge of the dais.

With a cry, Mira ran to him, propping his head in her lap and trying to rouse him. His skin felt cold and clammy. She rubbed his arms to bring warmth to them, but to no avail. Finally she simply gathered him up in her arms and held him. A moment passed, terribly quiet and unending, where she could hear nothing but the sound of his ragged breathing, as he grew warmer. He started shivering violently, and she hugged him to calm him down. One particularly intense convulsion ran through his body, and Mira suspected it was because of this that he woke, blinking slowly, dazed.

He stared blankly at the sky for a moment as the shivers slowly subsided, making her wonder if permanent damage had been done to him, then suddenly he gave a cry as if waking from a nightmare; his arms jerked, and he surged up, trying to break free of her embrace. She resolutely held him down, and was gratified to see sense return to his eyes.

"Where am I?" he whispered, his voice choked with fear, his eyes locked on hers as if terrified to see what was around him. He looked like a lost and confused little boy.

She responded with a motherly attitude. "Shh, it's all right, you're safe now. We're still on the mountaintop. And as soon as you can walk, we'll get off this mountaintop and away from here." She gently rocked him, marveling at how nice it felt, how natural.

Amazingly, he didn't pull away. Instead, he clung to her, burying his head against her neck and shaking with what sounded suspiciously like sobs.

That was more than she was prepared for. "Zerrick, what happened? What did you see?" She ran a hand down his cheek and found it wet with tears.

He raised his head, struggling to sit upright. "I don't know. Something terrible. I saw--" He closed his eyes and quivered. Too many images. Images of his future, images which filled him with horror.

There had been an intelligence there, warning him that if he continued on the path he was on, it would lead to great pain, suffering, and eventually his destruction and Mira's as well. That intelligence had first enthralled him through the magic, led him to the basin, and then forced him to see the images. Then that intelligence had revealed itself. That was what had made him black out, what was making him cry like a child now.

Before, he had been one half-trained witch wandering in the wilderness beyond anyone's knowledge--just a simple fool too weak for anyone to care about. Not anymore.

The God of Evil, Angist, knew of Zerrick Dhur now.

At the basin, he had tried to contact the Goddess, but the magic had long ago been corrupted, and it had led him straight to Angist. He'd seen the god, in all his indescribably horrid splendor.

Pain twisted through his muscles, as if he'd been wrung out, emptied. Angist had looked into his soul, and seen everything. Then he'd laughed, exulting in Zerrick's defeat, in his inevitable downfall. The laugh had been enough to shake Zerrick to his core, but then came visions of his future--what would happen if he continued on the path of magic, if he became trained and powerful. He had been promised swift retaliation for any power he received from the Goddess.

Mira looked at him in concern and Zerrick realized he hadn't answered He struggled to relate his experience. "I saw too much too fast to understand anything--I saw a city of white towers on the edge of a desert, you with a spear in your hand, a funny little creature with amber eyes, a dragon killing a native . . ." He didn't tell her all the images, like the one of her fighting a horrible winged demon, both of them being wounded by a variety of terrible monsters in a barrage of visions, or of himself lying prone before that most terrible of creatures, the Ravenger.

It felt like a hundred different futures had tried to fill his sight at once. He couldn't tell which were true or if any of them were. He hoped it all had been a hallucination.

Mira dashed his hopes of that. "I've been having dreams lately of a city like that--with white towers and dark skinned people writing on parchment. I also had a dream once that I was a warrior with the Putna. What do you think it means?"

He shook his head. "I don't know. One more thing to ask the dreamtellers, if we find them." He thought about telling her about Angist having noticed them, then decided it would be best to keep that a secret--Mira looked anxious enough. In fact she looked disheveled, as if she had been in a fight. He looked hard at her. "Did something happen to you as well?"

She brushed back her hair, trying to smooth it. "No, I think I just got the backlash of what happened to you. A blast of cold air and some sounds I'd just as soon not discuss. Shall we get moving? I don't think we should linger."

They would discuss this later. He should alert her to the danger, if only for her own sake. For himself, he wasn't sure there was any choice. He just wondered how far back it went. Had Alden known about any of this? Just how deep had his worship of Ainéra been? Had his whole life been planned long ago? The call of magic, the price of magic--perhaps Father had been right. And yet that mountaintop, yesterday--the sheer bliss of that other realm he'd so briefly encountered . . . so many questions. He was a moth caught in the flame. Poor Mira, doomed now to pay for his folly.

She looked so worried that he felt he had to say something. "Thanks. I've never been held by a woman in quite that way."

He was surprised when she flushed bright red. But she didn't let her embarrassment slow her response, "If you can keep out of trouble next time we encounter magic, maybe--just maybe, it can happen again."

She took off down the trail before he could think of a reply.

The way down the mountain was much easier than the way up had been, especially after they found the little trail they had been following joined a much wider trail which cut down through the valley. It showed ample signs of use, from broken spear points to campfire sites. They followed this into the foothills until it split into several smaller trails, which dwindled into nothing over the next few days before they reached the wide, flat brush lands.

The plants and animals here were strange to Mira. They tried seeds of one plant, but decided against that after they spent a night fevered and delirious. Wild game was plentiful, and once they had an idea of which beasts were magical and therefore dangerous, they were able to hunt for their food among the non-magical hares and herd beasts. She found Zerrick's favorite was the meat of a gigantic running bird with dull brown feathers.

The first few days after their encounter on the mountaintop, they concentrated on food, for their supplies were nearly depleted. Neither of them mentioned the incident on the mountain, but Mira knew it was on both their minds.

At least she assumed it was on Zerrick's mind. He seemed happier than he had been before their climb down Lookout Peak ten days ago, but he hadn't used magic once since those visions, hadn't even talked about spells, or dreams, or even the lovely essence of magic he was always noticing in nature. That last worried her a little. She had enjoyed hearing him try to describe the magic buried within trees and plants and even, so he said, in the rocks and soil. Either he was really trying for another embrace, or something was wrong.

Mira wiped the perspiration from her brow, squinting up at the blazing sun. It might be early fall, but the days were very hot, and there was little shade to protect them. She could not understand how such a heat could disappear so quickly at night; the evenings were downright cold. In all, a very strange land.

She followed Zerrick down a small dip in the land into a valley dotted with trees--oaks, she realized with a start--or at least something similar to oaks, she amended, seeing the slight differences in the leaves and branches. At least it was shade.

A few paces ahead of her, Zerrick clambered down a rocky bank into a ravine choked with weeds and spiny shrubs. He cursed as one caught at his pack.

She chuckled in spite of herself. "Zerrick, why do you always choose the most difficult path?"

He grinned. "My nature, I suppose. But I have a good reason this time. I can hear water running. I think there's a stream down in this gully."

Mira nodded, "That would explain the trees." She hurried down a small embankment to join Zerrick, avoiding the prickly bushes. "I hope it's more than a trickle--I'd like to take a bath." It would also be nice to stop for a moment and talk. It was impossible to speak with Zerrick while stumbling over groundhog burrows and skirting around herds of wild akiya through the tall grass.

To her surprise, he pulled off his shirt and started walking faster. "You're not the only one craving a bath. Just ahead there, I can see it. Looks like that river we saw from the mountaintop. Come on!" He wove his way through the weeds, creating a zigzagging trail for her to follow. She followed as quickly as possible.

They had been aiming for the river, hoping once they reached it they could use it to lead them to the settlement. If this truly was the main river and not one of its offshoots, they were closer to their goal than they had imagined. She caught up with Zerrick on the bank of a wide quiet river a good hundred feet across, winding slowly through the low hills into the plains. He was busy pulling off his shoes and stockings and making a pile of clothes to launder. Mira noted he left his breeches on.

"I never thought I'd be so happy to see water," Mira said, pulling out her own things to wash and wondering just how much she dared take off. She settled for stockings and shoes.

"Yeah, after all the jungle rains I thought I'd had enough of water, but I suppose not. Just keep watch for animals when you go in. The water's shallow, but it's best to be safe. I'm going to get these shirts clean before they wander off by themselves. You'll never believe it, but I used to be called a prig, I was so finicky about cleanliness," Zerrick said, bringing out the soap from its leather pouch and working up a lather.

Mira watched the vigor with which he set to scrubbing the clothes and decided she believed. For herself, she set to unbraiding her hair and combing it out, grimacing at the mass of tangles her curls had become.

Working the brush slowly through her hair, she went over and sat above where Zerrick was soaking their laundry.

"So how much magic can you find in water?" she drawled, watching Zerrick out of the corner of her eye. It was time to learn a bit more about him.

233

If he was surprised at her sudden change of subject, he did not show it. "There's no magic in water, actually--it's too changeable. Magic can only be found in solid material, and usually only living material at that."

"Then how can soil or rock hold it?"

He glanced at her, and Mira could see the curiosity in his eyes, wondering what she was up to. "Soil is composed of that which used to be living, so it has a little energy, but it's hard to reach. Rock--now that's a different matter. No one is really sure how or why, but pure rock forms like crystals can hold huge amounts of energy. Other types of rocks can hold a little, but it's buried even deeper than in soil. Alden had a theory--" He paused, frowning. "Just why do you want to know all of this?"

Mira answered carefully, "Well, I wanted to understand about the magic, because it's so important to you. Lately you haven't used magic at all, or spoken of it. Were the visions really that bad?"

Zerrick shrugged, looking uncomfortable. "I thought it might be best to stay clear of magic until we reach the tribe. I need to be trained."

"Is that all?" Mira asked. He wasn't looking at her again, and she was learning that meant he was hiding something. "That shouldn't stop you from talking about it." A thought occurred to her. "You still haven't explained to me what happened on that mudslide."

Zerrick rose and picked up an armload of clothing, then waded out into the river to rinse them. Mira also stood and went to join him, taking her share to rinse in the cool water. She gazed into his eyes and could see the struggle there.

"I--" he started to say, then grimaced. He began again, "I'm not entirely sure myself what happened there, but I have a suspicion. Alden taught me that once Ainéra entered the world, She became the patron of magic. She existed with that first Chaotic Energy before the world; She may even have existed before the magic. In any case, one who studies magic is studying Her realm. And now it seems She has taken to studying us. I think that was Her doing on the mountain."

Mira didn't know how to respond. It was one thing to sing hymns to some unseen god on high, but this sounded all too . . . solid. Real. And apparently, very very close. No wonder Zerrick was so ill at ease. As she stood there, trying to assimilate the situation, she was shocked out of her worries with a splash of cold water. Gasping, she turned to see Zerrick smothering a smile.

"You splashed me!" she cried.

"Did not!" He grinned.

"You most certainly did!"

He was trying to distract her from worrying, she realized. And it was working. When she turned her back a moment to hang a few shirts on a high tree branch, another cold splash hit her backside. She whirled.

"Now I know you did that one. I'll get you for that!" She waded over to where he had fled, still clutching his bundle of clothes.

She allowed him to hang out his clothes before she smacked him with a wave of water.

It then became an all out war, with both of them madly splashing each other, Zerrick even going so far as to grabbing the soap and rubbing it in her hair.

"I'll tame that wild mane of yours!" he said, laughing.

Mira squealed as soap nearly ran into her eyes and flailed, trying to get free of his arms which had left shampooing her hair and were now working their way down her neck and shoulders, inching their way under her sodden linen shirt. She managed to grab the soap from him and gave back a little of her own treatment, until the two of them seemed to be immersed in a mountain of bubbles. They were both laughing so hard they could barely stand.

"Why, you fiend!" Mira cried when she had the breath, dipping down to wash away the bubbles.

"I think I missed a few places," Zerrick said with a wicked grin, reaching over for the soap. She snatched it away.

"I don't think so. You just keep those hands to yourself. You're still looking a bit dirty to me," Mira retorted, feeling heat spreading across her cheeks and down her throat.

"I'll be right back," he said with an all too mischievous look in his eyes, and swam off downstream to a more covered spot by the bank. Mira glanced down and grimaced. He had taken the soap out of her hand.

She scrubbed herself as best as she could with the soap already on her and a handful of sand, and finally after a few rinses, she felt much more herself.

She contemplated what to do with the wet clothing she was wearing. The linen shirt clung to her breasts in an unseemly manner, and the wet leather breeches seemed to have shrunk. There was little she could do--it would be impossible to pull them off now, and everything else she owned was now hanging out to dry.

She settled for tucking in her shirt from where it had been pulled loose in all the splashing, and arranged her hair to hide the vital areas. She waded over to where Zerrick was dunking his head to rinse off the suds. He flipped his hair back and sighed contentedly, his back to her.

"Human again!" he announced, chuckling.

Mira had been about to ask him more about their predicament, but the words died on her lips. He looked . . . very nice, now that he was clean. All that black hair, trailing down his bare back . . . she could feel herself blushing again, and turned to leave before he could see.

He turned before she could take a step. "Oh no you don't--we have unfinished business!" he said in a low voice, and swiftly overtook her. Before she could utter a protest, he was behind her, his arm around her, grabbing her and lifting her right off her feet, pulling her against his body as he reached with his other arm to scoop up a handful of water.

She struggled to get her feet back on the ground. "No wait--I'm clean now, truly!" She managed to find ground again, but he didn't release her, holding her tight against his chest. Both of them should have been chilled in the cool water, but Mira felt warmth through her wet shirt from his bare chest, and that seemed to be stirring a fire within her as well.

They stood there while time seemed to stand still, and neither made a move to break the hold, as the water lapped softly at their thighs. Mira's heart pounded; it seemed she felt an echo of that frantic pace from Zerrick. She gulped back a shuddering breath.

"Are you going to let go of me?" Mira asked after a moment, timidly.

He spoke right at her ear, which set a shiver dancing down her spine. "I've been behaving myself lately . . ." His voice trailed off, as if he feared to go on.

She really shouldn't let him tempt her like this, she knew, but it all felt so nice, those arms around her, his breath falling lightly on her neck--she shouldn't feel these things, it wasn't proper. But she did.

"Mm, what are you thinking about, Mira?" his voice hummed in her ear, sending down another shiver.

So what was she afraid of? Nanna and her family were far away-- there was no one here to judge her, except Zerrick. She doubted he would mind.

She turned around in his arms so that she was facing him. "I was thinking I'd like to try . . . this," she said.

She kissed him hard on the lips.

As those soft lips met his, Zerrick bit back a groan of longing. Was this really happening--her firm body melded against his, her arms wrapped around his neck, cradling his head--she wanted him!

There was no fighting the surge of emotion which rose up in him, making his heart pound and his head swim. He eagerly returned the kiss, pressing one hand into the small of her back while he ran the other one through her rich damp hair.

Too many nights of sleeping beside her, having to ignore the press of her against him as they huddled for warmth . . . he wasn't letting her get away this time.

Mira's lips left his for a second as she paused to take a breath, and he took that opportunity to kiss the rest of her face, behind her ear, down her throat. To the home of that most beautiful voice.

Her head fell back, pressing her small firm breasts into him. He reached up a hand to cup one, bending his head to kiss her lips once more . . .

A man's chuckle stopped him cold.

Mira's head came up swiftly, her eyes wide as she clutched at Zerrick. He scanned the trees lining the river. All along the bank there emerged Put-na hunters, dressed in leather loincloths and holding spears. An older fellow with gray in his beard pointed at them and shouted something.

"Don't move," Mira whispered.

The Put-na had found them.

Chapter Sixteen

"We are on the Path of Spirit, walking single file . . ."
--Put-na worship song

Zerrick and Mira tried to keep up with the natives, walking single file through the woodland near the river. Zerrick was careful not to stumble as he'd be unable to get back up--his hands were tied behind his back, as were Mira's who walked ahead of him. He winced, feeling the sharp point of a spear jabbing him as he fell behind.

"Pikkaii!" The native behind him ordered.

Mira spoke to translate, "He said--"

"I know what he said. He said go faster," Zerrick growled, then felt immediately sorry. This wasn't her fault. He tried to apologize, and was again poked in the back. Sighing, he quickened his steps.

When the natives had found them, Mira had tried to speak with them, but these particular natives seemed to have a hatred for white men--they barely let her get a word out before dragging them both out of the river. They were forced to pack as quickly as possible; the natives wouldn't so much as touch one of their "evil" garments. Then they were tied and led down a narrow animal trail to the trail they now followed. At least they were headed in the right direction, toward the lake settlement. Zerrick did not think they were in immediate danger. He had plants on him, which he'd carefully packed against his skin when they weren't looking, and the Put-na were not supposed to be violent. He hoped that was still the case.

They walked all afternoon, then into dusk, stopping only once for a water break. As the light began to fade around them, Zerrick decided they'd simply keep walking until they reached the settlement. Hopefully, that meant it was close. Some of the natives in front of them started talking in low voices. This time when Mira translated, the natives did not bother with them.

"Huh. So that short one is saying they never saw such a sight as the two of us. They think we're both crazy, standing in the middle of a river in daylight, kissing--um--and such. They could hear us a ways off," Mira whispered, lifting her foot over a mound of dirt. In the gloom Zerrick could barely make out things, but the natives didn't seem to mind. In fact they seemed to recognize the terrain, for they started moving even faster.

"I think we're almost there," he whispered back, then he was hushed by the native behind.

They came into a clearing and the natives gathered around them in a tight circle. Zerrick couldn't tell if it was to protect them or if they were afraid Mira and he would try to escape. In the dark it was hard to tell, but Zerrick thought he saw huts up ahead. He was about to comment on it to Mira, when one of the natives, the leader it seemed, let out a loud cry like a bird. He gave the call four times, then was silent.

The natives all paused, listening. Zerrick found himself listening also, breathing as quietly as possible. The temperature was dropping rapidly. He tried not to think too much about that--there was no telling if they'd be sleeping indoors or outside. A long trailing call greeted them from the vicinity of the huts, and the hunters made ready to move on but then, the leader took aside another of the party and whispered to him.

"Uh-oh. Doesn't sound good," muttered Mira.

"What do you--" Zerrick began, and then was jabbed in the side. He glared at his harasser, a boy not older than sixteen.

The men in front were continuing their discussion, and Mira was becoming more distressed. She finally burst out, *"Ngaiya miborgia Put-na! Ngaiya bialilla miborgia Moiabu, biallá Kalurna, kumalida!"*

"Moiabu?" Zerrick murmured. She was telling them she knew the daughter of a *kumalido*, Moiabu.

"Nanna," whispered Mira. "Her tribal name--it means 'sheltering one'." She turned back to hear the native's reply.

What they said apparently didn't satisfy her, for she forced her way over to the leader and continued her pleas, *"Nginya miborgi Tamur? Tamur ainji? Ngaiya mibu muniyana anka!"*

"Tamur?" The leader looked puzzled. He conferred with two others, too quietly for Zerrick to hear, and then nodded.

"What's going on?" Zerrick asked Mira.

"Remember that scout Tamur, when we rescued the slaves from my father? I think he may be from here--that fellow there has the same initiation scar. We need someone who will speak for us."

"Why?"

She looked at him solemnly. "Their policy against strangers has changed. They were talking about killing us!"

Zerrick felt his jaw drop and tried to remain calm. "Alden always said the Put-na were peaceful."

She nodded. "They are, but I guess you can be pushed only so far. There are three different tribes in this settlement. All three of them have lost people to the slavers." She paused, listening as another hunter joined the discussion over with the leader. "Don't worry; killing is too new to them. If we give them a good excuse, they'll drop that plan."

"So give them an excuse!" Zerrick urged, turning Mira back to the discussion.

He needn't have bothered; at that same instant the leader approached Mira, and asked her to come with him. The hunters parted for them, then took their places around Zerrick, keeping him guarded. He watched as she disappeared into the darkness, towards the huts. Some of the natives around him sat back on their haunches to wait, and as tired as he was, Zerrick gladly followed their example. It was several minutes before he could see Mira returning, followed by the leader, a short hunter, and two elderly figures in cloaks.

The hunters around him leapt to their feet and he followed more slowly, staring hard at the short hunter as he came closer. He'd recognize that insolent face anywhere. It was Tamur.

Zerrick felt the hackles on his neck rise. Brave Tamur, oh-so-wise Tamur, had a hand on Mira's arm and was talking excitedly with her, his body language looking far too friendly for comfort. Mira responded, her speech a bit slower, but also excited, and welcoming.

He fought against the grimace that threatened to spread across his face and schooled his features into what he hoped was a winsome smile. Then he strode over and laid a hand on Mira's free arm. "Well, what do you know, if it isn't Tamur. *Kumaran Ngandidda!* Mother's Blessings," he greeted Tamur, grinning wolfishly.

Tamur eyed him, then said something to Mira. Zerrick only caught the last part of it, something about weasels. Nice to know that he was loved in return. But he didn't want to come across as too threatening-- he needed the tribe to trust him enough to teach him.

Swallowing his dislike for the young man, he struggled to let him know he wasn't a danger anymore. "*Ngai koyda kumalida.* I'm not using any magic now."

Mira seemed to approve of his attempt. "I've explained to him that you have been refraining from using magic because you recognize you need training, and that you come here seeking their aid. He doesn't much trust you, but he is willing to speak for you since you helped free the members of his tribe."

She stood by Zerrick, holding his arm anxiously as Tamur went over to the two elders and the leader of the hunting party. They spoke too fast for Zerrick to understand, so he watched Mira, hoping to get an idea of what was going on from her expressions.

At first she looked unsure, and at one point seemed ready to join in the discussion, then Tamur went into a long speech and she relaxed. The two elderly men nodded as Tamur talked, their faces neutral, then they spoke together.

Mira let out a breath, leaning against Zerrick's arm, and he knew a positive decision had been reached. The group finished their talk and she murmured to Zerrick, "It's a lucky thing we were able to help Tamur free those slaves. That convinced them. I didn't realize how much things had changed since Nanna was taken. They've become very suspicious of us. Colonists, I mean."

"I hardly blame them," Zerrick whispered back, then fell silent as Tamur approached them with the two elders. He introduced them as Jerapo and Burkis, chiefs of the tribes Kutjali and Karu, respectively. The third tribe's leader was in a dream fast, and could not be disturbed.

Once introductions had been made, it was agreed that since Tamur knew them, he was responsible for setting them up in the village and watching over them. The hunting party broke up to take to their beds. Tamur led them to the smallest of the villages, apparently newly set up from the trek across the mountains.

They learned that as a young scout, Tamur did not have a hut of his own, but slept outside by the fire. That suited Zerrick fine--he could keep an eye on both Tamur and Mira, and there would be an opening in case they needed to make a quick departure.

He set down his pallet and watched as scouts and hunters around them raised their heads to stare at them, not saying anything, just staring. Sighing, he lied down on the pallet and pulled his cloak over him. In all, a very strange introduction to the Put-na.

Mira woke early, as always. She looked at the huts and the cold fire pit around which she could see the sleeping figures of scouts from last night. Grass huts, just like Nanna had described. It was surreal to know she was really here, in a Put-na village. From the direction of the river, she heard the sound of women talking and children playing. She rose without waking Zerrick and went in the direction of the sounds.

On a rocky bank overlooking a wide clear lake, she found what she'd been seeking: the village women preparing the daily meal. It was her first time seeing women of the tribe in their natural garb, without having been "civilized" by her people, and she had to repress the surprise on her face at seeing how little they wore--only a leather wrap-around clasped at the shoulder by carved bone pins. They paused upon seeing her, eyeing her with mixed suspicion and fear. A few of the younger children, playing naked in the shallow banks of the river, hurried out and hid behind their mothers.

Well, she could stop those looks quickly enough. "Mother's Blessing on all of you. Do you need help here?" she asked in her best Put-na, bowing slightly in case any of these women happened to be the elder's wife or a Dreamteller.

That surprised them; Mira could see one of the girls nearly dropped her basket of fruit.

Another woman was not surprised, however. She stood, her black eyes boring down on Mira, and humphed. She was thin, even bony, but somehow gave the impression of being much larger, towering over the group. "Who are you, pale spotted girl with blood in her hair? You think because you speak the tongue you can just sit with us as a sister? I know that hair. I lost a son to a slaver with that hair!"

Mira opened her mouth, but nothing came out. She felt herself flush to the roots, staring helplessly at the other women who seemed as shocked as she.

She was rescued by an extremely elderly woman in the corner of the group. Her eyes, set in a maze of wrinkles were sharp and bright, and her voice, though reedy, carried well, "Did this child take your son, Ghuldini? By her very hand? I think not."

"But my father," Mira said, then gulped. She had forgotten that Tamur's tribe knew her father, in his worst guise, as a slavehunter. He must have taken Ghuldini's child. The name made her cringe. Ghuldini in Put-na meant 'Fist of Stone.'

"Are you your father?" the wizened old woman asked her softly. Mira felt eyes all around, weighing her. Shame burned in her face; she knew she must be a sight, standing there mute before them. She had to speak, but she had to choose her words carefully. She prayed Nanna had taught her the dialects well.

"I have--" she didn't know the word for shame, so she chose the closest thing--"sorrow, that my father and brothers were hunters of men. I did not know the evil of what they did when I was little, but I do now. I have sorrow for the evil of my people. I come here, because I do not belong with them."

Her grasp of Put-na was not enough to go any further into it than that. She wanted to say the practice horrified her, that she was sorry their two people had such different views, that her people were so domineering. There was little she could do to pay back these people. They would certainly be justified if they did not accept her. She hung her head, unable to look into Ghuldini's eyes.

Silence stretched on for a moment as Ghuldini eyed first the old woman then Mira, and nobody moved or spoke to come between them. Then Ghuldini sighed, and sat down. She made a movement for Mira to sit down as well. Mira did so, hesitantly.

"Tamur has spoken of the rescue and how you helped him. It does not excuse you from the blame of your people's crimes. But it earns you a second chance," Ghuldini stated, staring straight ahead as if unwilling to lay her eyes on Mira. Mira nodded in understanding.

"Thank you," she said.

Someone handed Mira a basket of seed pods to crack open. The old woman smiled, and came out of her corner to sit beside Mira, the sun lighting up the wispy white strands of what was left of her hair. "An excellent answer, Ghuldini. May she prove herself worthy." The old woman stared deep into Mira's eyes as she spoke. Mira shivered at the intense gaze. "I am Darya, and I've been expecting both you and your friend the *kumalido*." She smiled, showing that most of her teeth were still good. "I am a Dreamteller."

Zerrick woke to find Mira gone, but he could see Tamur was right where he'd camped last night, sitting up and talking with a large group of old and middle-aged men, all of whom wore necklaces of straw with wooden beads, all different. Other than the necklaces, they wore only a leather loincloth and fur cloaks decorated with feathers. From the way they occasionally glanced in his direction, Zerrick knew he was the subject of yet another discussion. He sighed. Well, he was here, and he might as well see what could be done. He donned one of the shirts he had cleaned yesterday, the leather vest from Captain Greynor, and a sturdy pair of woolen leggings. He tightened his belt against the growling of his stomach and went to join Tamur.

"Where is Mira?" he asked--he could manage that much Put-na at least.

"Fire head? She with . . ." Here Tamur went into a series of long words, only one of which Zerrick understood--women.

Tamur then led Zerrick to the others, and one deeply tanned and leathery faced old man strode up and took hold of his neck pouch, studying it intently.

"Alden," he whispered, feeling the markings there.

Zerrick's heart leapt. "Yes! I mean *owei,*" he amended in Put-na, staring hard at the man. Could it be possible that Alden's tribe was here also? The odds were certainly against it.

The old fellow nodded, rubbing at his ears which stuck out at odd angles, and grinned. "You knew Alden, I am right? I am Mok, of the Besprii tribe. That tribe is no more, but Mok is still here!" he said in perfect Endersian, without even an accent. He cackled, and then his laughter turned into a coughing fit.

"Mok! I remember!" Zerrick gasped, thinking back to that last conversation with Alden, "there is a tribe of the Put-na, called Besprii, which has some knowledge of magic, enough to help you gain the control you need. There is one in the tribe, Mok, who speaks our language."

"Where is the wily dog?" Mok asked when he'd gained his breath.

Zerrick felt the old familiar ache. "He's gone. The colonists--I tried to save him--" he couldn't finish and had to turn away to mask the pain from his face.

Mok gripped him by the shoulder in understanding. "My tribe, also, is no more. It is a heavy loss, but we must be survivors, yes?"

Zerrick nodded, pushing back the knot of emotion. He turned back and smiled. "I'm honored to meet you, Mok. Were you Alden's teacher?"

Mok started laughing again, waving his hand in the air. "No, no. I am just an old scout. I meet Alden on his travels and we spent much time together, years ago. But I have no talent for the magic."

Zerrick frowned. "And I do? I thought anyone could learn. Alden never mentioned anything about talent, merely the will to learn." Had Alden seen his ability as a young child? Had he arranged for him to witness him using magic? Again he wondered, has my entire life been set up for this?

Mok patted him reassuringly. "I am sure you must, since you are here. But I know little of this. Here is the one you need to speak to."

One of the men in the gathering stepped forward. He was a very large man with a redder tint to his skin than most, long loose hair, and a braided beard. He looked like a bear out of the Old World, and he thrust forward a meaty hand to give Zerrick a bone crushing handshake.

"This is Hirkumos, our most powerful *kumalido*," Mok announced.

Hirkumos commented something in Put-na, fingering Zerrick's neck pouch. Zerrick backed up a few paces, adjusting the pouch so that it was covered by his shirt. All this attention was beginning to annoy him.

Mok listened, then translated. "He says you've learned how to drain the crystal in there. He wonders if you also know how to fill it."

Zerrick gave a weak smile. "No, not yet. That's why I'm here. Alden warned me that I was pulling more and more power, but my control is weak." He watched the witch's face carefully. If they were going to refuse him help, it would probably be now.

Hirkumos's face appeared grave as he listened, and he stared hard at Zerrick, measuring him. He must have liked what he saw; he finally gave a shrug and responded.

Mok grinned. "He says he thinks he can handle you. You look like girl, wearing no beard. In any case he'll teach you."

There was nothing he could say to a comment like that, so he simply nodded and tried not to look too embarrassed. Was that why everyone stared at him so? He remembered from Alden, his grandfather, and from Nanna that all Put-na men wore beards. His clean shaven face must make him seem either a youth, or as Hirkumos said, a girl. Hirkumos set the time for his first training session the next morning, then Zerrick followed Mok to his hut to work on his grasp of the Put-na language.

On his way, he passed by a group of women cutting fruit and grinding seeds. He caught a glimpse of Mira, seated beside an ancient woman with wispy white hair. The woman glanced up, and he felt the impact of her dark eyes.

"Who is . . ." he started to ask Mok, but the man was too far ahead, urging him to keep up. He glanced back, but the woman had turned back to Mira, directing her on the seed grinding. A shiver ran through him. Never had he seen a gaze more . . . penetrating.

Zerrick spent the next few hours learning vocabulary from Mok, as well as general customs he must adhere to among the Put-na. Mira had acted correctly when she went to join the women. Men and women were assigned different tasks, and were generally kept apart except for the midday meal and in the evenings. He asked if it was common here for women to hunt like men with spears, and received a dubious look.

"Strange rumors you hear. Women do not fight except to protect their young, and never with spears but with knives."

Well, this wasn't the source of those visions then.

They broke from their studies as women called that the midday meal was ready, and Zerrick hurried to grab a woven grass mat, upon which he piled fruits, a strange sort of flat cake, and meat boiled with thick orange roots which were sweet to the taste. Harvest season had arrived, and there seemed to be a feeling of celebration among the natives as they told jokes and tales, piling their mats high with food.

Zerrick watched for Mira and found her with a group of younger women, serving the men of the hunting party. Tamur was with the hunters, and as Zerrick watched, he smiled up at Mira and said something which Zerrick could not hear over the talking of those seated near him. He found himself crushing a handful of berries, and hastily released them, wiping the juice on the mat. Too bad Tamur hadn't seen that kiss on the riverbank--he might stay a little more clear of Mira. He shook his head, wondering why he was even having such thoughts. Mira wasn't his. The last thing she needed was yet another protector.

Mok sat beside him jabbering about various people seated near them, indicating a tall thin man who was a tanner of hides, another who was the best dancer, and so forth. Zerrick pretended to listen while watching Mira, who was working her way over towards him.

Quickly choking down a bite of meat, he rose and offered her a seat. "I've met the head witch here and started to learn the customs. How was your day?" he asked, giving her some meat and taking a few flatcakes from her basket. She handed the basket to another woman and sat down beside him.

She scarfed down one of her flatcakes before responding, "My morning went well--barely. They know of my father, and almost rejected me because of my hair!"

Zerrick humphed, reaching up to touch a fiery curl. "At least they didn't call you a girl because you have no beard."

She chuckled, coloring slightly. "Oh my, that's true! They would think that." She blinked in surprise as Mok leaned over and waved a hand in her face.

Zerrick rescued her by placing her hand in Mok's. "Mira, this is an old friend of my teacher Alden. His name is Mok."

"Of the tribe Bespirii," Mok added, surprising Mira as well with his grasp of their language. She glanced at Zerrick.

"Looks like you don't need my teaching any longer," she commented, her voice sounding a little strange. Zerrick could almost hear regret in it, or perhaps anger, but her face remained bright and cheerful.

One of the elders who were sitting near Tamur interrupted Zerrick before he could reply. He thought it was Jerapo. The man spoke slowly, which helped Zerrick to understand, "It looks like you both will be staying with us. Will you need a hut?"

Zerrick and Mira looked at each other, then turned to Mok. The old scout grinned. "He's asking if you will be sharing a hut. If you two are married."

The two of them immediately reacted, but while Zerrick responded yes, looking towards where Tamur sat, Mira emphatically shook her head and said no.

Jerapo laughed and said something as Zerrick and Mira both flushed crimson. "Courting then," Mok translated for them.

The elder then made arrangements--Zerrick would sleep in Hirkumos's tent, while Mira would stay with Darya for the time being. Zerrick got the impression that they didn't expect her to remain single long. Most of the Put-na married young, at age fifteen or sixteen, making Mira at eighteen more than eligible. He felt disappointed and a little hurt that she hadn't said yes. There would have been less trouble then, but he supposed he couldn't blame her. After all, she had come for her freedom. He couldn't deny her that, whatever his wishes.

That settled, the natives turned to discussing other things, allowing Zerrick and Mira a moment of peace. They sat for a moment, not daring to look at each other while they ate, until Mira lifted her head and smirked at him. He paused, with a piece of meat in his hand, and shyly met her gaze.

"So are you courting me, Zerrick?" she asked coyly.

"No!" Zerrick blurted out before he had a chance to think. He knew his mistake immediately; saw her suddenly close up, the light in her eyes dying.

He apologized, but she turned away and went back to eating, ignoring him entirely. Defeated, he returned to his own meal, even though he had now lost his appetite. It was all so confusing. Should he have said yes? And if he'd said yes, would he have meant it?

He was woefully inexperienced when it came to women. Not that he was a complete innocent; he'd been with a girl when he was fifteen. He remembered that all too well, for afterwards her brothers had found out, and beat him within an inch or two of his life. His mother had been in hysterics over the whole thing of course, and his father had preached to him about morals. In all, he'd spent nearly a week abed. He'd been lucky no bones had been broken. He didn't think he could have survived a longer stay under his mother's care.

After that, he had little to do with women. There had been Alden, and magic, and his studies to become a clerk. Then when he was a little older, around seventeen, Mother and Grandmother had both started pushing for him to go courting. By then, he was sick of their power games and all their posturing and determined to do the opposite of whatever they wanted. So he'd taken little time towards thoughts of marriage. In truth, he'd never thought about it because he'd never been in love.

But now . . .

He sat, deep in thought throughout the meal, then gave a half-hearted farewell to Mira as she went back to join the women. Mok summoned him to join the scouts. He spent the rest of the afternoon learning how to carve a hunting spear, something every Put-na boy could do by age six, but which took him fifteen tries before he carved one straight enough to hunt with. While they chided him on his inexperience, they certainly didn't seem to mind when he conjured a warm breeze to sweep through the camp against the evening chill--he trusted his control for that simple a spell at least, and in fact they seemed more curious of him than anything else, now that the village elders had accepted him, asking where he was from and what he had seen on his travels.

All the while, he thought about Mira.

He'd never had such an attraction to any other woman in all his life, or such feelings of protection--or jealousy. And he did enjoy her company; they'd just spent a month in the wilderness with no one but each other for company.

But marriage?

He would have to think on it. Surely Mira wouldn't choose one of the natives anytime soon. She was probably enjoying her single status. She would still be free for yet a while.

And yet . . .

He remembered the days following the encounter with her father's slavers and how she'd gone on and on about Tamur, and how nice it would be to have a scout's skills. He also remembered Captain Greynors comments, "You spend too much time with the natives . . ." Mira had spent her whole life with this culture. Maybe she would find one of them to her liking.

Zerrick paused in his carving to bring out the whet stone and sharpen his machete--he'd been offered one of the stone knives the other men used, but he wasn't going to tackle this skill with both no experience and an odd knife. He whisked the blade across the stone in a swift downward stroke which imitated his state of mind.

Maybe he should talk to her tomorrow, tell her yes, that he was courting. She'd probably like that, plus it would make any other suitors think twice. Why he would care about that, he didn't know. Perhaps his feelings were a little muddled where she was concerned, perhaps he wasn't sure if what he felt was . . . no. It couldn't possibly be. Not love.

But she was certainly attractive, and kind, and smart . . . and tender . . . courageous . . .

Zerrick shook his head. This was foolishness. He'd apologize to Mira, tell her he was courting, just to make her happy, and get to his studies. He had enough to worry about without adding her. And if she stayed angry with him, too bad. He couldn't let things like that affect him.

His mind resolved, Zerrick took his stack of spears and set off to learn how to throw. *Wait until Mira sees that I can be a hunter-scout too, he thought, taking aim at his first target.*

Chapter Seventeen

"I am the flame; I am the water; I am the space where dreams do dwell."
--Kumalido mantra

Zerrick tried to get Mira alone to talk, but for the next four days both of them were kept busy. Darya had discovered Mira's herbal training and sent her off daily with the gatherers to collect food and medicinal herbs, which probably saved her from slaving over the hot cooking fires every day, but which also kept her out of reach. Meanwhile Zerrick was being drilled on his Put-na, while learning the basic tasks necessary for any male member of the tribe. When he wasn't learning to hunt or chopping wood or stretching hides, Hirkumos kept him busy with the hardest magical task he'd ever tried to perform.

Hirkumos sat Zerrick down on the floor of his hut, placing a sprig of kaisha bush in his hand and drew a circle with powdered chalk around Zerrick. Zerrick felt a charge in the air, then saw the other man's magic surround him in a protective shield.

Shields, that was one new thing he'd seen here, but it was beyond his mastery. Alden had known shielding but seldom used it, because a shield was only effective against magic, and Zerrick had been the only witch around, and very weak at that time. Hirkumos promised that once he completed today's task, he would learn shielding.

Once the shield was complete, Hirkumos sat down, and Zerrick looked down at the sprig, suppressing a sigh. He was back to working with the tiniest amounts of magic. Of course it was a good idea; he hardly wanted to create the kind of havoc here that he had in the wilderness, but after perceiving so much power on the mountaintop, well, it was like comparing a drop of water to the ocean. He'd grown used to working with more power.

And the task? It was close to impossible--he'd told Hirkumos that three days ago when he'd first attempted it, and he still felt the same way. He was supposed to draw out the magic, hold it, and tell it to do . . . nothing.

"Can this be done?" he asked, fumbling at his Put-na.

As always, the large man sat perfectly still, serene and unreadable. "I do not ask you to do the impossible. This is needed for you to control your powers. You must be able to kill a spell if it becomes necessary." All this he spoke while Mok translated, sitting over in the corner and lazily smoking a pipe. He had picked up other things in his travels besides the colonists' language.

That was more than Hirkumos had said the dozen or so other times Zerrick had attempted this. He breathed deeply and tried to relax, letting his mind go blank, staring at the sprig in his hand. The kaisha bush was very common here. It was olive green, with two rows of leaves down the branch, and had a faintly acrid smell. Strangely enough, the tiny spark of magic it held also had a sharp "feel" to it.

Do nothing . . . nothing . . . He thought like a mantra, closing his eyes, trying to lose himself in the blackness behind his eyelids. He pushed away his worries about the future, of Mira, of gods watching men's actions, and tried to put all his concentration on . . . nothing.

He reached for the magic. Finding it was easy, but holding it was not. It kept jumping about within him, wanting an action to perform. He tried to tell it to stay, just stay, and not do a thing. For a few seconds, he had it, but just as he rejoiced in that small accomplishment, it slipped. His mind wandered just a little, an image of what he was doing flashed in his mind--holding magic, like water in a bucket. With a pop, the magic burst free to complete its task, and Zerrick found himself sitting in a small puddle of water.

Sighing, he moved away from the puddle before it could soak his leggings. The magic shield surrounding him dissipated with a fizzle, and Hirkumos rose to hand him another sprig. Zerrick glared at the sprig, his insides knotting up with frustration.

He turned to Mok. "I had it there for a moment. How long does he want me to be able to do this?"

Hirkumos explained at length while Mok listened. Mok translated to Zerrick, "Hirkumos says he doesn't want you to hold it. It is good that you can do so--that is the right way to prepare magic before transferring it to a focus plant or crystal. But you jump ahead. He wants you to release it, but not let it do anything. He wants it to vanish. Dissipate. Scatter to the four winds, I don't know the exact equal in your language. But that is what he is asking of you."

Zerrick bit back a groan. The hut felt small and hot, pressing in on him on all sides. Gritting his teeth, he sat back down, away from the drying puddle. He breathed deeply several times to dispel his anger--after all this was important. He should be able to do this.

The shields closed over him again, and Zerrick tried to concentrate, but a question nagged at the back of his mind. "Hirkumos, why didn't Alden teach me this, if it is so important?"

The witch sat for a moment, softly stroking his beard. He answered carefully, choosing words Zerrick could understand, "Your teaching with Alden was in the first steps. To learn magic, first you must be able to see magic, then pull it and make it do something. Only after that does one pull and make it do nothing. This is the control you need."

Zerrick ran his hand along the stem of the sprig, sensing the magic there. Just touching it, not pulling or doing anything else with it was somehow soothing. "Wouldn't it be better to control the way I make things happen? Magic always seems to do some of what I want, but not exactly what I'm asking of it."

Hirkumos nodded. "From what you tell me, it is because you pull more power than the spell needs. This is the first step to control that too. If you can stop magic from acting, you can put back the extra magic pulled and control the power of the spell. Please, now you must continue."

Zerrick nodded, encouraged enough to go on. Working magic as often as he had in these lessons was hard--it took concentration and mental focus, all of which took energy. And somehow his insides where he held the magic were beginning to feel raw. Nevertheless, he would repeat this until he got it right. No more excuses for his lack of control.

He cleared his mind, trying to achieve a calm state where nothing mattered, and everything was at peace. His breathing slowed and his body felt far away, like it had when he had found the veil--a phenomenon which was still as yet unexplained. When he'd mentioned it to Hirkumos, the man had looked bemused. Unlike that time, however, now he wasn't searching, only drifting. The tiny flame of power was in his hand. He pulled it, and set those calming feelings to it--not images, just feelings. It still vibrated within him, wanting a release, but it felt somehow more restrained, more in his grasp, so to speak.

Now the hard part.

He told it to release with just a flash of light. He'd seen Alden do it that way, and that seemed a harmless way to disperse it. It obeyed with a burst of sparkles, nothing more.

He regarded Hirkumos hopefully.

"No. Try again."

He closed his eyes, fighting off a wave of despair, and reached up to be handed another sprig. This time Hirkumos didn't even bother to lower the shield, merely reaching through it. That would weaken it, but with the amount of magic Zerrick was working with, he could do little damage.

Again he tried.

This time he made mistakes right away, and quickly turned the magic to something harmless before he lost it. White rose petals fell from his hands.

"Again."

And again he tried. And again. Every time something happened, from a swirl of cold air which sent him shivering, to a sphere of negative space which sucked up the air around Zerrick before popping out of existence. Hirkumos berated him on that one--he said when he wanted nothing, that meant no effects, not nothingness, which was very dangerous as it always tried to fill itself with something.

Finally Zerrick threw up his hands in defeat. "I give up! I just can't do this. How do you tell magic to do nothing?!"

A smile touched the lips of his teacher, and he came forward to stand before Zerrick, holding out another sprig. "Where does the magic come from, Zerrick? Where do you pull it from?"

Zerrick suspected it was a deeper question than it appeared, but he couldn't make himself care. "From the plant," he answered, knowing that was only the beginning of the answer.

Hirkumos surprised him. "Right. Where can you put magic when you cast a spell?"

Huh? "Well, you can put it in a focus plant, or a crystal--"

"Or in a person, if you are ensorcelling them? Or in the air around them, to create an illusion, yes?" Hirkumos answered for him, and Zerrick wondered what he was getting at.

"Yes, I suppose that's true," he conceded, needing Mok to step in and translate their conversation. He needed to understand every word Hirkumos was saying--the answer was close to being revealed.

"So." Hirkumos handed him the sprig, and backed away. "To cancel a spell, what you must do is keep the magic in its original state, and set it free to the winds as magic. Nothing more. This magic then settles in the rock. Did you never wonder how rocks can contain energy? That is how. Airborne magic."

Zerrick's eyes widened. "That's it? That's all I have to do? Why didn't you tell me that sooner?"

Hirkumos's calmness was becoming irritating. "You didn't ask." He smiled and gave a chuckle at his joke, then as Zerrick continued to stare at him with growing impatience, he became serious. "I wanted to see how dedicated you are to learning, test your control and your knowledge. While you have been trying different things to solve this task, your control has improved. That last spell, the nothingness, had to be perfectly in control even to be conjured. You should congratulate yourself. Now, complete the task. Release magic."

Now that his task was clear, Zerrick wasted no time. He dove into his othersenses, and felt the magic in the sprig. Then he paused. This was no longer impossible, but it was still very difficult. He had never tried to keep magic in its original state before--it was, after all, the most changeable and unsteady of energies. He immersed himself in it, trying to understand its nature, not directing it, but simply asking it about itself.

And therein was the answer.

When he asked the magic, it answered--in volumes. Most of it he couldn't understand, as it tried to tell him the entire span of its existence, but he suddenly had understanding of it--enough to complete the task. Gently, more gently than he had ever pulled before, Zerrick coaxed the living magic out. The plant, this time, did not fall away to dust or shrivel up, but stayed as it was before, living and healthy.

The magic was somehow calmer within him, as he ever so delicately released it, careful not to disturb it in its primal state. It took incredible concentration, but he felt it first yearning for an action, then suddenly that yearning ceased, and it leapt forth from him.

And did nothing.

The magic was still there; Zerrick could "see" it with his inner eye, but it was suspended in the air like tiny droplets of mist, softly drifting to the earth. Harmless to anyone.

As soon as the shield was dispelled, Zerrick leapt up, exhausted but unable to contain his joy, and ran out to first hug Mok, then give Hirkumos a respectful handshake. He couldn't help but grin.

Mira cursed as a thorn pricked her finger and carefully plucked out another handful of the astringent Elise berries. Some of the women digging tubers around her glanced up at her outburst, then turned back to their work. Apparently, they'd grown accustomed to her swearing.

She had thought her search for happiness would end once she found the Put-na. She had thought she belonged with them. Now she was learning differently. Mira didn't know if it had been the time she had spent with Zerrick, free in the wilderness, or if she had simply been blind to it back on her father's estate, but she now saw that the Put-na were not as enlightened as she had thought. They were not equal in their treatment of men and women, though they were still better than her own people. Perhaps as a white woman she had been treated differently in Depin, or perhaps because of Nanna's influence. Here she was just another girl and expected to hold to the same restrictions as other women.

That meant sweeping huts in the morning, preparing the midday meal, tending the village garden, gathering food, making pottery, fetching water, and minding the children. And because she was young, strange-looking, and a newcomer, they also gave her the nastier jobs such as beating dust from the grass mats used for sleeping. Then on top of that, she was ignored for most of the time and not spoken to, except in command.

Darya was the one exception. The old woman had taken Mira under her tutelage, impressed with her herbal knowledge and hopeful that she might have a talent for dreams herself. So far, she hadn't shown an ounce of talent, but that didn't seem to bother Darya. God bless her, she was the only one who had kept Mira from simply stomping back off into the wilderness.

Her problem was just loneliness--even with Darya and with the occasional odd word with Tamur, she was always alone, even though she was surrounded by other women. Ghuldini was partly to thank for that; the woman resumed her iciness towards Mira the moment Darya was elsewhere, and many other women had taken up the practice as well. As the daughter of one of the village elders, Ghuldini was respected among the women.

Then there was Zerrick, and his oh-so-haughty attitude. After all they'd been through, now he was casting her off on his high and mighty search for magic. Three days, and no sign of him, but from the gossip of other women, she knew he'd been spending his time in Hirkumos's tent, learning magic while she scratched her hands on stubborn bushes. It was enough to make her cry, his sudden dismissal of her. No matter how much her emotions were bruised, however, she was not going to let him see that.

The worst thing was that she missed Zerrick, despite his change of heart. She missed their times together. So he didn't want to court her after all, even after the kisses they had shared, everything they had been through. She shouldn't have been bothered. After all, he was completely beautiful, and she . . . well, she wasn't. Still, she had thought he shared the same feelings for her that she did for him. Apparently not.

Well, she had been alone before this, and so what if she still was? It didn't matter. She would simply refuse to let it matter. A tear splashed on her hand. She hastily wiped it away, grimacing at the sting of salt on the scratches. Resolutely, she stuck her hand into the prickly bush for another handful of berries, before a sob and more tears could join the first.

A shout from the direction of the village forced Mira to swallow her tears and turn around. She'd recognize that passionate voice anywhere. She stood clutching her basket, trying to still the drumming of her heart.

"Mira, guess what happened today!" Zerrick called, running up and dusting off what looked like dried and withered kaisha fronds. He was grinning like a fool, and his trousers and shirt were damp.

She, however, was not in the mood for his games. "You got into a fight with a kaisha bush."

"Ha, ha, very funny," he said with a laugh, not to be deterred from his good mood. "No, I controlled my power! I dispelled magic! Sent it harmlessly into the air. That means I'll soon be able to cancel out other's spells, create shields, store my own power in crystals-- Hirkumos told me I'm coming along quickly. Isn't that great?"

"It's fabulous." Mira tried to put enthusiasm into her voice, but it came out flat.

Zerrick was instantly sober. "What's wrong? I heard they've been keeping you busy. Are they working you too hard?"

Mira put down her basket, hoping Zerrick wouldn't see the scratches on her hands or the wetness on her cheek. She worked up a smile and kept her face lowered. "Nothing's wrong. Darya had been wonderful to me--she's even tried to teach me a little of her dreamteller skills."

Zerrick's eyebrows rose. "And? Are you learning about dreams?"

Mira shrugged. "About interpreting them--a little. But the other thing Dreamtellers can do is have prophetic dreams about themselves or other people. I don't seem to have any reliable talent in that--just the one dream I had with the white city. So I guess other than my herbal lore, I'm just a normal, unremarkable girl."

Zerrick gazed steadily at her. "I would never say that about you."

For a moment, hope flared, and she thought he might come closer, maybe even kiss her again. Then he seemed to become aware that they were not alone, that in fact there were several of the village women watching them.

He backed away a little and peered up at the sky. "Lovely weather today," he said in Put-na. Glancing down at her, he gave a shake of his head for her to follow him.

Mira did so, ignoring the tittering of the women behind her, and together they retreated to a little grove of trees which could provide some cover and privacy. Once they were alone, Zerrick spoke. "I want to apologize for the way I reacted when we first arrived. I thought it might be best if everyone thought we were married so they would leave you alone."

Mira had been thinking the same thing since then, especially since the women had more respect--and thus less work--for a married woman. But she bristled at the patronizing tone in Zerrick's voice. So was that the only reason he'd said yes? "It was nice you were thinking to protect me, but I assure you, I can take care of myself," she said cautiously, trying to see where he was going with this.

He was quick to answer, "Oh, I know you can, but wouldn't it be easier if you didn't have to? I can help with that, if you like. Only if you like, of course."

Her patience was running thin. "Zerrick, what are you saying?"

He struck a pose which had to come from his minister father, hand held high in entreaty, and said, "I'd like to court you. If you want me to. I would, of course, never do it if you didn't want me to."

Mira wasn't sure how to react. Yes, she wanted him to, but what were his reasons for offering? To protect her? Or something deeper? "Why?" she asked, keeping her voice neutral, "Why would you want to do that?"

"Oh--I--" he fumbled, "For your freedom--so you'll be left alone--so the women are nicer to you--and it might be fun, you know." He blushed and picked at his nails. "It was only an idea."

But for all the wrong reasons, Mira thought, wilting. So it was just a friendly favor, with no real emotion attached to it. Well, if he thought he could play with her heart that way . . .

She replied in a clipped, professional voice. "Thank you, Zerrick, but you need not trouble yourself. You might have forgotten, but the village already thinks you're courting me, and they'll probably go on thinking that whatever you do."

"Oh, but it wouldn't be any trouble for me--"

She cut him off, her pain now turning to anger at his ignorance of her feelings, "No thank you. You needn't concern yourself with me. I am sure you are quite busy already with your magic lessons. And I did come here to be free, allowed to speak with others without a suffocating, protective brother at my shoulder. So perhaps I don't want to be left alone by others. Except by you, unless you have a better reason for courting me." Perhaps she was being a little hard on him--after all he was just being nice, but she had to know the truth, and she was in no mood to go gently searching for it. She didn't care if she hurt him. Her chest hurt, the scratches on her hands stung, and all she wanted now was to be away from him.

Zerrick stood for a moment, his mouth working with no sound, then he swallowed and turned his face. "Sorry. I was just--I didn't mean for you--" He backed away several steps. "Never mind. Sorry to have bothered you--just forget about it," he said in a rush. With that, he turned and fled, leaving her feeling stupid and more alone than ever.

Zerrick tried to avoid Mira after that, which wasn't easy, since the Dreamteller had decided that now was a good time for him to discuss his dreams with her. Mira was often with her, and he couldn't explain his dreams with Mira right there, so he usually made an excuse to delay the meeting, saying there was a hunting party he was supposed to go with, or a magic lesson, or chores.

That worked for about two weeks, then Darya seemed to figure out why he was delaying, and scheduled a time when Mira would be out gathering with the women.

The weather had suddenly grown colder, so before they began, Zerrick cut up some firewood and made a small fire on the floor of the hut to warm the two of them. The Put-na huts were not really built to have fires, but if the fire got out of hand, he could douse it with conjured water. Another trick he had learned from Hirkumos.

Darya seated herself on a bed of straw and furs, her two apprentices hovering nearby to serve herbal tea and fluff the straw for her. She was obviously feeling her age today, her small frame looking hunched and frail. Her eyes, however, were as bright as ever. "So," she began, speaking slowly so he could understand. "Mira has told me some of what she dreamed, and what you saw in visions. You saw her in a city of white towers with a spear in her hand. She says you dream of a woman calling to you and she says you think the Mother is watching you."

Zerrick nodded, accepting a cup of herb tea from one of the apprentices. He added, "That's not all." Glancing at the two young girls, he raised his eyes at Darya. "This will not be easy to listen to."

Darya humphed. "These girls have seen darker dreams. And if you fear of them talking, do not. If I tell them to stay quiet, they will."

"Good," Zerrick said, hoping he had not offended anyone. He launched into a full description of his dreams, how they had come both awake and asleep, and how they had included Mira. He told her about the mudslide, about the veil and the voice and mud drying. He even told her about the shadow on the mountaintop, and the visions he had seen. He described in brief Angist's warning not to become stronger.

The two girls paled at the mention of this last part, and even Darya looked grim, rubbing her hands as if they pained her. He finished his tale and waited for her reaction.

"Mm. Interesting. Young man, did you tell Mira all of this?" Darya's face was inscrutable, but Zerrick had the feeling he had better answer carefully, or risk her wrath.

"I told her most--except for her being wounded or fighting monsters, and the voice in the shadow during the visions. I knew it would frighten her." He saw the fire flare in her eyes and hurried to explain, "I didn't want her involved in my troubles. And now that she's here, and safe, there is no need. She's made it clear she wants to go her own way now."

Darya nodded. "Let me think on this a moment."

The apprentices offered Zerrick food and drink and he munched a flatcake while Darya began mumbling to herself, falling into a trance. Minutes passed, while he finished the flatcake and threw another log on the fire, waiting for a sign from her. She remained perfectly still, hardly breathing, until he feared she had reached the end of her long years. Just as he thought that, however, she opened her eyes and came out. She motioned for him to sit close, and when she spoke she sounded winded, as if she had just completed a long journey.

"I see shadows covering the truth. Powers beyond my own are involved, and in such a case it is difficult, if not impossible, to get a clear reading. Your own feelings about your visions are probably correct, that they are warnings. Possible futures, but not certain. Since you are seeing possible futures, it is dangerous for me to advise you, as every word I say may influence your actions, and the outcomes. However, there are some things I must tell you."

Darya paused for breath, watching him, seeming to weigh her words. "First, you are not the first who has had dreams of a woman calling for freedom. Many of those able to use magic have had similar dreams. Hirkumos himself had these dreams when he was younger."

Zerrick was stunned. "It isn't just me? I'm not alone?" He wasn't sure how to react. It meant he wasn't mad, but it also meant that he was involved in something larger than he had ever dreamed.

"No, others have shared dreams of calling, but without the warnings of the future you saw in the basin. I and my sister Dreamtellers discussed it long and hard. But this was twenty years ago. No one has these dreams any longer."

"Why not?" Twenty years--about the time of his birth. It had to be a coincidence, right?

Darya answered, "The dream asks that you travel to Her, to the one who seems to be the Mother Goddess. It foretells hardship, passing through a great desert, fighting evil beasts. A few listened to the dreams and left. They have not been heard of since. We assumed that they had succeeded and stayed to dwell with the Mother, or, more likely, that it was a false calling, that it was *Kormu*, leading our most important brethren, the *kumalido*, to their death."

She took a sip of tea, her face pale with exhaustion. "Hirkumos and the other ones still here who had the dream resisted it. The dreams eventually stopped. You are the first one who has had these dreams in years."

Zerrick whistled under his breath, feeling a chill go through him. Maybe he was cursed after all. "So what does this mean?"

Darya gazed down at her hands, silent for a moment, then raised her head to look at Zerrick. "While I was searching the Dreamworld for answers, I came upon an old memory of mine, long forgotten. There was in my childhood a popular tale in my village, which is no longer told now. Why this tale vanished I do not know. Perhaps *Kormu* had a hand in that too. You must make up your own mind what you think of it."

Taking a deep breath, she began, "Long ago, it was said that the Put-na had no winter home, but traveled year round, innocent like children, without *kumalido*, without the wisdom of dreams, worshiping only sun and earth. The Mother Goddess came then, and began to teach the Put-na, taught them magic, dreams, farming, pottery, many many things. She never stayed long, also wandering on Her own, visiting each tribe, a nomad. During that time She was near there was always peace and happiness, and plenty of food and game. The years passed, many generations. Over time, the Mother visited less and less. Evil creatures began to roam the land, like the *Ashwa-grippa*--"

Zerrick shuddered.

"--the dragon, the serpent, and many others came to prey upon the Put-na. Finally the Mother came no more, and the Put-na were fearful that they had offended Her. They sent a party of scouts deep into the land to search for Her. Across wide plains, down a distant range of mountains, they found a city of white stone with giants possessing great magic and art. The Mother was there, and the city was being attacked, by *Kormu*."

She made a protective gesture over her heart. "It is said that he defeated Her. I, for one, cannot believe that. If She was defeated, the Great Earth and all her mysteries would be lost. But after that, She came no more to visit and teach the Put-na. Perhaps the battle took something from Her so that She could no longer travel, or perhaps She is angry that we Put-na did not send help. But that is how the story goes. The scouts returned and told their tale. Many have since tried to search for the Mother or for the white city, but both have eluded us. The Put-na did not give up, however. It is supposedly because of this that Put-na began to have a summer and winter home, coming across the Jagara Mountains each year to the plains, in hopes that the Mother would come down from Her white city and teach us once more."

Darya fell silent while Zerrick digested the story, his half-eaten flatcake all but forgotten. The room was quite warm, with the softly crackling fire and the cozy fur rugs, yet he found himself chilled. It sounded like a very old tale, and it could have come right out of the Holy Book. But he had the feeling this had not happened all that long ago--three or four hundred years, perhaps, when his own people had been beginning to build great cities, recovering from the Lost Ages, several hundred years after Ja'hal's Second Coming.

And from the things the woman had said in his dreams, like "I have been in one place too long," and "You must free me," he had no doubt that the tale was in fact true.

Ainéra had fought Angist, and lost. She was imprisoned somewhere across a vast desert, in a circle of mountains made of black obsidian. And She was the Patron of Magic.

So where did that put him and his talent?

If She had been fighting the god of evil, that was good--it meant She was his enemy, not friend, as many in his father's religion said. But that She was weak enough to be overtaken, that did not bode well for Zerrick. If magic could so easily fall into the hands of evil . . .

"Let me get this straight," he said, fighting down another shiver, "There is an old story about the Mother Goddess fighting the Dark One then disappearing. Then, twenty years ago, all the magically gifted get a message to come rescue a woman who could be the Mother. Why didn't anyone think of this tale before, and how could any have refused such a calling?"

"As to why no one remembered--that was my fault, I fear, for only I and a very few others are old enough to have heard it. Or perhaps--" she began, then grimaced. "Who can say? None know what powers the Dark One possesses. But as to the calling, that I can tell you. Fear and doubt have kept back many from leaving."

She leaned forward and looked hard at him. "I still have my doubts about the dreams. Why would the Mother of Earth need a human's help? How could a human help? It makes more sense to believe *Kormu* is the creator of the dreams, that it is merely a clever trick to lure kumalido out to be destroyed. That shrine you found on the mountaintop--that was once used by my people, but for the last few generations it has become evil, luring *kumalido* to see visions then hurl themselves from the cliffs. It might have been good once, but it is broken now. So you see, there are many reasons to mistrust these dreams. Remembering the story, however, I cannot say what is true. Perhaps in my old age I am losing some of my talent."

There was that sinking feeling again. And the old question--was magic a force which could lead one to good? Or only to evil? If even the Dreamtellers could not agree, there must be a thinner line between the two than he had imagined, Zerrick thought.

"But if the calling itself is evil, what then of the warning on the mountaintop on the pedestal? Or that mud which dried up, saving Mira and me from falling?" He persisted, hoping, wishing for an answer.

Darya shook her head, eyes closed in consternation. "I do not know. There are dark shadows surrounding you--this has also been true of the others with the dream. That makes me believe the Dark One is involved. I caution you against following the call, but I cannot forbid you. These are matters beyond my sight. I simply do not know the truth of it."

Of course. It was foolish to think a mere mortal could interpret dreams sent by gods. Still, he wished he could learn whether he should fear and loathe his powers, now that he was finally gaining control of them. Zerrick rose and thanked Darya for her time, then stepped out the door, dreading his next magic lesson but determined to go on with it. His thoughts were so drawn inwards that he did not see Mira creep out of the shadows by the side of the hut.

Mira quietly snuck in the *akiya*-skin door flap and sat at Darya's feet. "So now we know," she said in a low voice.

Darya nodded. "You were right--he hid things from you, but do not be angry . I spoke true when I said there were shadows gathering around him. Heavy shadows. You may want to reconsider following after him."

Mira shivered, wishing Darya were not so blunt. The apprentices were readying the dreamteller for a nap. The old woman was looking decidedly weary, but Mira had a few more questions to ask.

"Are you sure about your visions? Will he really be forced to leave?"

Darya chuckled to herself, rubbing at her temples. "You young people. Always so full of questions. I saw what I saw. Flames. Magic. And Zerrick facing the village elders, being forced to leave, traveling to the white city, perhaps alone, perhaps with a group, you included. You heard him yourself--the calling is strong. I think he will be one of those who has no choice but to follow it."

Mira tried not to show her misery. Darya had continued trying to teach her the dreamteller skills, but she simply had no powers, which frustrated her, and seemed to surprise Darya. She wanted to follow Zerrick wherever he was going, she needed to. But she felt useless. Worse, if she could not defend herself, she would be a danger to him.

"I wonder if he'll let me follow him now. He must hate me for what I said," she mumbled, more to herself than anyone else, but Darya heard.

"You torment yourself, child. Talk to him, and he will forgive."

Mira shook her head. "What am I doing here, Darya? I'm completely useless, I have no magic, no visions, and my only skill is in herbal cures. And your people hate me. I'm beginning to think I should just go home." Her eyes started to tear and she wiped at them hastily.

Darya's voice suddenly became sharp, startling Mira. "What is this I hear?! Young Firehead, giving up? Why must you have magic to accompany your love? Most people have only their hands and their minds to work with and do perfectly well."

Mira's tone was sarcastic. "Most people don't love a witch with a supernatural calling."

"This is true. But as I've told you before, I think you do have a power, one which simply hasn't revealed itself yet. After all, my dreamtelling did not appear until after I had my second child."

Mira leaned back on her hands, sweating in the warm hut but somehow not really feeling it. "I can't wait that long."

Darya rose with the help of her apprentices and moved over to the straw pallet which had been covered in soft rabbit fur. "I don't know that you'll have to. As I said, I see no signs of the Dreamteller skill or of magic in you. But I've dreamt of you. That means something." She thought a moment, brow furrowed. "These powers are both of the sphere of the Mother. Perhaps there are powers beyond that sphere."

Darya's dark eyes fixed onto Mira's. "You believe in and follow the Mother, but you have told me you were also a follower of the Sky God you call Iahmel. We know little of that one--if He exists, He does not deal with us. But your people do. You do, when you sing your songs of worship. It may be that you have powers I cannot see or understand, because they flow not from the Mother, but from Him."

She lowered herself onto her pallet, feebly shooing away the apprentices when they tried to help. Her breath wheezed in her throat, but she didn't seem to notice, keeping her sharp gaze on Mira. "You must make a decision. If you feel in your heart that you belong with Zerrick, you will have to find a way to follow him, whether or not any power within you decides to show itself. You will need to learn how to protect yourself, how to be a strength to him, not a weakness. Talk to Tamur. He can help you in this."

Exhausted, Darya leaned back, closing her eyes and drawing in great wheezing breaths. The oldest of her apprentices, Anali, took Mira by the hand and lead her away, whispering, "Please, let her sleep; she is very tired. You come later for your chores," and with that, gently put her out the door into the cool autumn air.

By the sun there was a still a few hours before mealtime, and Zerrick would be at his magic lesson. Mira had avoided her morning chores, but if she hung around too long in one spot they'd find her and set her to some horrible task.

There was only one way to go.

Covering her red hair with a scarf, Mira set off to find Tamur and his spears.

Mok

Book Three:

The Fight against Angist

Chapter Eighteen

"Keep your head low when the vultures circle."
--Put-na hunter

Zerrick studied the shield of the witch across from him, looking for weaknesses in the small woman's complex shell of power. The cold autumn air sent leaves dancing around their feet, and for the first time ever, Zerrick could see his breath. He was bundled in his thick cloak from the trek across the mountains, as well as a new tunic of goat hair which itched but kept him warm. The Put-na wore more as the days grew colder, including leather tunics lined with rabbit fur.

They stood in a wide clearing of dug up earth kept carefully clear of inflammable debris. Hirkumos stood to one side monitoring them, resplendent in a long cloak adorned with parrot feathers.

The other witch, Irulen of the tribe Kuri, raised her hands and with a simple gesture, released two tiny bolts of lightning to test Zerrick's shields. He urged the magic surrounding him to become resistant, like opposing poles of a magnet, and her lightning bounced off the iridescent sphere to come hurtling back to her. She absorbed it harmlessly, then lowered her shield. He did the same, disposing of the dried remains of the plants in the bag he carried, and went to join her and Hirkumos at the edge of the clearing.

Hirkumos nodded to them. "Well done, Zerrick, Irulen. Controlled energy, and a good strategy there, using your shield to return the energy."

That seemed to be one of his stronger defenses--it came almost instinctively, which had surprised Hirkumos, until Zerrick told him of Lotus, and how he had defended himself against her.

"Lessons learned under stress are the deepest learned," was all he'd said after hearing Zerrick's tale.

It had been a month since his talk with Darya, a month full of learning new skills and control in his magic. A month full of hard work and concentration. Also a lonely month; he had scarcely seen Mira, but when he did see her, she was with that wretch Tamur, dressed in a boy's hunting leggings and tunic, carrying of all things, a spear. At the look of happiness on her face, Zerrick had bitten half his fingernails to the quick.

He was going insane with jealousy, but there was little he could do. Mira was making her preferences clear, and he had blown his chance. There was only one thing he could do to comfort himself: immerse himself in magic, working every day at it until exhausted. That also helped to ward off his dreams. They, like his nerves, were growing increasingly worse.

"Am I ready to work with the other *kumalido?*" Zerrick asked after Hirkumos had evaluated them both.

He stamped his feet against the morning chill, needing to be active both for his warmth and because he felt uptight. Last night's dream had been particularly gruesome, but he only remembered a few horrible details--a Put-na hunter running, his clothes on fire, black claws disemboweling Mira--it was one of those visions from the mountaintop, elongated and in more detail than he'd ever wanted to see. As on the dais, he'd been pulled in two directions. First he'd have a frantic calling for help from Her, then a nightmarish vision of what he'd have to pass through to answer that call, often both in the same night. He had considered seeing Darya again, but what was the use? He had tried resisting, hoping that would lessen their intensity, but it only seemed to make them worse.

Hirkumos thought a moment. "I think you have sufficient control now not to be a danger. The others are starting shields practice by the lake. I'd like you to join."

Zerrick tried to suppress a surge of joy. For the past week, he'd been allowed only to watch the other *kumalido*. This was a great step in Hirkumos's trust in him.

They walked through the tall yellow grass, skirting around the small gardens the Put-na had planted. Normally all the tribes left by this late in the season, but these three tribes had decided to stay through the winter, unwilling to lose any more of their children to slavers.

His people were causing many changes for the Put-na, Zerrick thought, watching women pick out some kind of grain the tribe called *manéa*. From a totally nomadic to semi-nomadic tribe, and now they were preparing to become wholly sedentary. Already they were hard at work weaving cloaks, tunics and dresses for the oncoming of winter, mild though it would be. Zerrick heard Mira was becoming renowned for her sewing skills.

They passed through a stand of Argessan oaks, kaisha brush, and palm trees, which looked very much out of place out here in the brushlands. After passing down a steep rocky slope, they came upon the wide beach of the *Tar-non* lake, the "too deep" lake, so named because no Put-na had been able to dive to the very bottom.

On the beach were the other *kumalido* of the three tribes. The oldest was Mavra, weak in power but skilled in creative tactics which made her a dangerous foe despite her grey hair. Then there was Ablor, the second eldest and a quiet man in his fifties. Youngest were the two apprentices, Svak and Durnan. Zerrick went to stand these two— they'd recently become friends. Svak was of medium build and barely old enough to grow a beard, while Durnan was tall, thin, and blessed with long flowing hair.

"What, still no feathers in your hair, Zerrick? Do you hide at mealtimes so no girl can find you?" Svak chided while they waited for the master *kumalido* to gather plants of proper strengths for their students. Svak was referring to a number of girls who had recently started noticing him, thanks to his growing proficiency in magic. It was a custom for girls to lace parrot feathers in the hair or beards of the men they favored. For luck, and also as an invitation to be courted.

Durnan, of a more serious strain than Svak, defended Zerrick, "He has no time for such silliness!" Then he smiled "Besides, Zerrick's eyes are still for the fiery-haired one."

Zerrick growled under his breath, silencing both men. Swallowing, he murmured an apology for his outburst, but he couldn't keep the slight growl from his voice. Burn that Tamur!

Further talk halted as their masters came over with the necessary energy for today's practice: fronds for Svak and Mavra, branches for Durnan and Irulen, and to Zerrick's surprise, a large sack with focus plants brimming with power for him to use. He glanced up at Hirkumos as he took the bag.

"I'm testing your pull and control," Hirkumos said. He clapped Zerrick on the shoulder, smiling, then went about twenty paces out, securing a position by the water's edge while Irulen moved closer to the rocky embankment and Mavra chose a position mid-beach. Zerrick separated himself a little from Svak and Durnan, enough so that the crossfire of offensive magic wouldn't endanger anyone. He readied a large plant with the power of a sapling tree, and watched the others for directions.

Hirkumos, as most powerful, lead them in building up a spherical shield thick enough that it made a bright shimmer in the air around him which was probably visible even to non-witches. The other kumalido's shields were transparent, except for Zerrick's. That caused a murmur or two from the others--only today had Hirkumos let him pull enough energy to create such a shield. The first of the plants was spent.

Once everyone was ready, Mavra fired off the first shot, a strong wind which would try to blow dust into Hirkumos's eyes, rendering his own power useless. The shield stopped the magical wind but not the unmagical dirt it stirred, and soon Hirkumos was coughing and rubbing at his eyes. One successful strike for Mavra.

Next Hirkumos set Svak against Irulen, and at the same time threw a spell testing Zerrick's shields for flaws. Zerrick grunted as a force like a massive hammer battered against him, and hurried to make his shield hard and prickly. Prickly, to break up the force Hirkumos was using against him into little harmless bits. Svak was equally unsuccessful with a dazzling display of light, meant to break Irulen's concentration. She held firm, squinting her eyes against the glare.

And so it went on, strike and counter strike, offense and defense. One by one they used up their supply of plants, until only Zerrick remained with one good-sized shrub, worth a small tree. Across from him, only Mavra still had a functioning shield.

"Go gently with her, Zerrick," Hirkumos warned as Zerrick decided on his attack.

Mavra humphed. "Do your worst, boy," she taunted him, wagging a wrinkled finger. Hirkumos rolled his eyes.

Zerrick decided he would try something Hirkumos had recently taught him--a "hand" of force, which could punch or grapple an opponent to stun them. The best defense would be for Mavra to dodge the magic, as magic wasn't smart enough to track her down once fired. But if he sent it fast enough, she might not be able to dodge it. He would direct its force only at her shield so that it wouldn't harm her if it did connect.

He rocked back on his heels, trying to look nonchalant as he prepared the spell. He had no shield himself to worry about. Hirkumos had knocked that out earlier with a blast of fire. Therefore, he could put all his concentration on the offensive magic.

Setting in his mind the task he wanted performed, Zerrick drew the magic out of the last remaining shrub, filling with the power, building, building . . . building . . .

He released the magic with a rush, and sent it speeding towards Mavra, so fast it was only a blur to his senses, fast enough she had time only to gasp in surprise before it was upon her.

The shield, made by her lesser amount of magic, was knocked out almost instantly, but the force of the magic didn't end there. With a smack, it hit Mavra herself, knocking her to the ground. Even then it did not dissipate, continuing along the shore with a great rustling of leaves, until it finally merged with the magic within the plant life on the embankment.

Zerrick gasped and dropped his bag. "Mavra, are you all right?"

He didn't wait for an answer, but sprinted over to her side where he was joined by Hirkumos and Ablor. Hirkumos knelt to help Mavra to a sitting position while Ablor checked her. Zerrick felt relieved to see she was conscious and apparently unhurt.

"You just stunned me, boy," she finally answered, rubbing her temple and peering up at him.

He knelt beside her and hung his head. "I used too much power. I didn't really expect it to hit you; you usually dodge them."

Mavra chuckled then winced in pain. "Must be getting old."

Zerrick chose not to respond to that. Mavra was young compared to Darya, but her hair was grey. His insides shook. That blast could have killed her.

Mavra patted him on the shoulder and smiled. "It's all right. I'll just take a moment to catch my breath. I guess you're just a little more powerful than any of us expected."

Zerrick stood, uncertain of what he should do. Svak and Durnan were staring at him with fear in their eyes. He swallowed, looking with apprehension to Hirkumos. "I don't want to be powerful." The visions from the dais filled his head.

Hirkumos looked troubled, but he wrapped a meaty arm around Zerrick's shoulder. "Do not worry. This is my fault--I wanted to test the limits of your control. Your control seemed perfect. Never have I seen such a fast attack. I'm very proud of you. You're not even winded, or dizzy." He paused, and a flash of uncertainty crossed his face, then it passed and he smiled.

"I'd like for you to tell Mavra's apprentices to ready her some tea. I think she is getting one of her headaches."

That was a dismissal if ever he'd heard one. Dejectedly, Zerrick walked off to complete Hirkumos's request.

In his head he could almost hear Angist's laughter.

Mira sat with her spear across her lap, watching as Tamur carved a funny little device the Put-na called a *gretzal,* which was attached to the end of a spear to allow a hunter to throw it extra long distances. The shape of the gretzal had so far eluded Mira's carving skills, so Tamur was talking her through it, step by step.

In the weeks they had gotten to know each other, Mira had to admit that Tamur was not nearly as interesting as she had first thought him. Nice, certainly, and always willing to help. But he was also impatient and a little dull-witted when it came to matters outside his experience. Unlike Zerrick, she had Tamur pretty much figured out now, and all in all he was, she had to admit, a little boring.

He had been the only one willing to teach her how to fight and hunt, however. He was taken with her, always telling her how he adored her unusual hair, how she was so much more beautiful than the girls of his village. His praises and his attentions were a little annoying but it was the price she had to pay to become proficient with the spear. If she hoped to be ready when Zerrick moved on, she had to work fast. Darya had told her last week that his time here was almost at its end.

"So you see, Mira, you carve the hook right here, below the handle," Tamur was saying; Mira forced her attention from where she had been staring at the entrance of the village, trying to take note of what he was teaching.

"Oh, I see. And you make the hook large so you can adjust it to different sized spears," she commented, taking the half-finished gretzal from him and turning it over in her hands.

Tamur went on to explain the variations and intricacies of gretzals far beyond what Mira would ever need or want to know, while she found her attention wandering back to the entrance of the village, where the hunters would return from their excursion.

Zerrick had left this morning with Mok, a couple of his *kumalido* friends, and a party of hunters, in search for big game which was migrating through the brushlands less than a day's march from here. He had looked depressed and she'd tried to go talk to him, but he'd dodged out of sight with a skill that made her certain he'd been learning a few scout tricks of his own. It figured--just as she'd finally gotten enough courage to speak to him, he had lost his.

Mira had heard about the mishap yesterday, how Zerrick had nearly killed one of the elder *kumalido* during practice because his magic was too strong. Poor Zerrick. It seemed he was destined never to find peace until he found someone his equal in magic. Hirkumos had seemed to be that equal, but from the gossip she had been hearing, it was said he might not be able to handle Zerrick's power. Darya had foreseen correctly. It would only be a matter of time before the village decided Zerrick was too dangerous to teach and told him to move on.

Tamur finished his instructions and took back the *gretzal*, informing Mira that it was time for him to start his watch.

"Thank you, Tamur, you've been very kind to teach me all this. I'm very appreciative," Mira told him as he rose to leave.

He paused in the gathering of his carving tools. "So does this mean I can court you? Will you be finding a feather for me?"

Obviously she had been a little too nice. "I didn't mean that, Tamur. You know I am only interested in Zerrick."

"But you hardly speak to him. I do not see any gifts from you that he wears," Tamur retorted, his dark brows drawing together.

Mira was ready for that one. "You know the stone thrower he has?" she said, referring to Zerrick's pistol, "I gave him that. That was my gift for him to wear."

"Ohhh," Tamur said, nodding vigorously. Mira knew he had been impressed when the colonists had started firing their 'sticks', wounding a few people in his tribe during the escape. While she could see questions arising in his eyes that he must be dying to ask, he only said goodbye and made a hasty retreat, telling her he'd sit by her at mealtime.

Mira let out the breath she'd been holding. Another close escape. Ah, well, he could keep asking her until he grew red in the face, and she would keep making excuses. At least he was still helping her. With the women snubbing her for her skin color and the men avoiding her because she carried a spear, it was a wonder that he didn't abandon her. Honorable Tamur, however, never forgot a debt. He thought he owed his life to her, first for keeping Zerrick from killing him, and second for giving the rescue of his people some much needed assistance.. Without her, the rescue would have failed.

Mira quivered. She was glad to be away from all that. No matter what her troubles were here, at least she was no longer a part of her father's slave business.

She stood and gathered her carving tools and a few new spears she had finished securing tips to, and glanced around. She had been seated on a fallen tree near the front of the village, right by where she and Zerrick had spent their first night sleeping with the scouts.

Nobody was here now. The men were all off hunting or keeping watch, their grass mats containing their things the only testament to their places here, all rolled up around the fire pit which the village kept at a continual low burn with the cold weather creeping in. One of her duties today was to stoke the fire and occasionally add wood. She added a log to it, avoiding the cloud of sparks which flew up as it fell with a crunch into the embers, and sat down to continue her watch for Zerrick. Then something caught her ear.

Four *kumalido* walked past her, murmuring amongst themselves. Hirkumos was with them, and he looked troubled. She caught a few words one elderly woman was saying--it was about Zerrick. Mira ducked behind her log, then watched as the group passed out of sight, heading towards the Dreamteller's huts. They were probably going to talk with Darya, she thought, even more curious now. Had Darya spoken to them of her visions?

This was important for her to know, Mira decided, so she crept off towards the group, keeping close to the huts and out of sight. She saw them enter Darya's hut and tiptoed over to listen through the akiya hide covering the doorway.

"Welcome, followers of *Kumara*. It must indeed be grave questions which bring all three of the master *kumalido* to my hut," Darya greeted them, as her apprentices offered seats and tea, both of which were politely refused by Hirkumos and his companions.

Mira felt surprised when it was the elder woman, not Hirkumos, who spoke next, "I think you know who we've come here to discuss.

We are concerned about the strangers who are staying here, in particular Zerrick. I'm sure you heard about the accident yesterday."

Darya's voice sounded reverent, but unconcerned. "I heard about it. It is common, I have heard, for apprentices to make the occasional mistake, especially in gauging the strength of their spells."

The other woman humphed. "One may make the occasional error, but not with the amounts of power he is pulling. A focus bush, Darya. Similar to a sapling tree. And he wasn't even dizzy after pulling it."

"So you haven't found his limit yet. But strength alone would not cause enough concern for you to talk to me. What exactly is bothering you?" Darya's crisp voice cut right to the heart of the matter and Mira had to smile, imagining the *kumalido* reddening like chastised children. Darya did not talk around subjects.

"What bothers me, Dreamteller," the elder woman said, her voice stiff with formality, "is that not only is he powerful and still in training even at his age, but also he seems to be troubled by nightmares. Hirkumos told me he has them just about every night, dreams violent enough to wake him in the middle of the night crying out. I have heard that he came to see you about these dreams. I wish to know what you learned of them."

There was silence a moment, and Mira could feel the tension between the two women thick in the autumn air. She knew Darya had to be affronted being asked about a person's private dreams, but her voice was steady and calm. "He's having the dream. You all know the one, all of you except Irulen who is too young to remember. The one with the desert and the jagged black circle of mountains. And Her. He's also having the other, darker dream. About *Kormu*."

She heard an intake of breath which sounded like Hirkumos and a groan from the other male *kumalido,* an older man Mira hadn't seen before.

"But that ended years ago! Surely one of those who left before was successful," Hirkumos said loudly, and Mira could almost see him bristling. He fell silent, but Mira could hear him breathing, hard and fast. That was puzzling; she'd heard he was such a calm man.

"I suppose not," Darya murmured.

The elder woman cut in, "That dream was not a true summoning; it was a lure from Him. And now we see the heart of the trouble with our new apprentice. If he cannot defeat the dream, he will have to leave."

Mira felt the urge to jump into the tent and speak her mind with, but she heard Darya respond first. "You are the eldest *kumalido* of the tribes here. You have the authority to do with an apprentice as you like. The decision in your heart has already been made. I will tell you this. I've had dreams which I cannot discuss yet, as it may affect events here, but I think you should wait a day or two. The answer will be presented. And do not feel guilty. The Mother guides her own, trust in that."

In a day or so, the answer will be presented, thought Mira with a shudder. So soon. She had to speak to Zerrick tonight, to warn him. Darya hadn't spoken of her vision to anyone, not even her apprentices, but from the look that crossed her face whenever she mentioned it, Mira knew it must have been bad.

The *kumalido* were preparing to leave, so Mira snuck back the way she had come. The fire needed another log, but there was no sign any of the hunters had returned.

She sat down and prepared for a long, anxious wait.

Zerrick crouched low in the brush, watching Mok's hands as he made scout signals, *Wait . . . wait . . . Now!*

As one the hunters stood. Zerrick combined his strength with Durnan and Svak to cast a blinding spell on the herd of *akiya*, while the hunters ran down into the valley to cast their spears at the leaping herd, sent into a confused mass by the sudden flash of magic in their eyes. Zerrick dispelled the rest of his magic when he saw it would not be needed; felling six animals before the akyia found a pathway out of the falley away from the hunters. A very successful ambush.

Zerrick completed the ritual for the hunt by cutting out the eyes of one of the animals even as Svak and Durnan also did so, and together they buried them in a small pit along with the withered remains of the plants they had pulled magic from. This was done as a tribute to the Mother in thanks for the gift, and also as a protection against spirits seeing the magic through the lifeless eyes of their kill.

Afterwards they tied the carcasses to spear poles and prepared for the long walk home, two men to an animal, carrying it on the poles over their shoulders.

Zerrick shared carrying a kill with Mok, and the party started off down through the valley in which they had caught the herd, moving through the tall yellow grass dotted with short desert trees which were still green. A wind had picked up from the east, which sent the grasses dancing in long streams. It was so different out here, under open skies. He was still trying to learn how to move through the thick grass. It was somehow eerie, not having a towering canopy over his head.

Zerrick mentioned his thoughts to Mok, who laughed. "You fair-skinned wanderers. First your people come from across the ocean and complain about the closed treetops like your friend Alden used to, then you decide you like the trees covering you and don't like the sky. We Put-na, now, we have grown accustomed to both. With trees you are kept cool from Sun's bright rays, but out here, the wind keeps you cooled and you can see for miles, both prey and predator."

The scout tilted his head and sniffed the wind. "Speaking of predators, it might be wise for us to get to the trees. These kills could attract something," he said in a half-joking manner, quickening his pace a little.

As Zerrick was about to make an equally witty reply, he noticed shadows flitting across the sunlit grass, dancing along them like the sun and the wind. They were moving quite fast. "Looks like the vultures have already arrived."

Mok glanced at the shadow, which now appeared to be one shape rather than a flock, sweeping across the gold wispy tops of the grass.

He frowned. "Too large for a vulture." He turned around and squinted up into the sun, searching for the source of the shadow.

There was a screech of some mighty creature high above them, and Zerrick could just see a black spot against the sun, flying in a tight circle far far above.

All of the hunters now turned their attention skywards, and suddenly they were dropping their kills and running frantically towards the trees.

"Run, Zerrick--it's a dragon!" Mok said in a strangled shout, dropping his end of the pole, his eyes wide with fright.

"No, don't run! The tree cover is too far away. Stand with us, and we can combine our strength to defeat it, " Durnan argued, but Zerrick could see he too was ready to flee, tossing away the young buck he'd been carrying and quickly tearing weeds out of the earth to provide power.

"The trees will give us an advantage. Come on!" Mok shouted to Durnan, and as the spot in the sky gave another screech and began its dive towards them, Zerrick followed Mok's advice and tore off for the woodland.

The dragon was eerily silent as it plummeted towards them, and as it came closer, Zerrick learned why. With a great wheezing breath it sent a stream of flame into the grass behind them, flapping its wings hard to fan the fire, which quickly began to race towards them, threatening to overtake them as it leapt from patch to patch of dry grass and brush.

Zerrick kept running, panting against the searing heat trying to surround them. Out of the corner of his eye he saw Durnan stop, clutching at the weeds he'd grabbed earlier, his eyes closed in concentration. "Don't stop! I'll take care of the flames," Durnan shouted.

Zerrick continued on even as he felt the air rush around him from the dragon coming to land, positioning itself between Durnan and the rest of the group fleeing with Zerrick, Mok, and Svak. They climbed a steep hillside and reached a small stand of Argessan oak and dogwood, hopefully tall and sturdy enough to provide them some cover against the dragon's attacks.

The hunters pulled out their spears and armed themselves with the *gretzal,* a few climbing into the treetops for a better shot, while Zerrick ducked under a low branch of one of the largest trees, keeping under its shelter as he peered back to see if Durnan had succeeded in dousing the flames and avoiding the dragon. Svak and Mok joined him to scan the valley below.

Thick smoke prevented them from seeing much, but the flames seemed to have been quenched. The dragon had taken to the air again, circling in a deadly slow spiral upwards, searching the land. Now that he wasn't fleeing for his life, Zerrick could see the dragon in better detail. He had heard dragons were enormous reptiles with scales and impenetrable armor. This one looked much more avian, with sleek black skin and a crest of feathers along its neck and spine, webbed wings, and an incredibly long neck and tail. Also like a bird it had just one pair of legs, held up against its slim body as it flew.

Its head was small with a long beak-like snout which opened wide as it gave off another horrible screech. Then suddenly it paused in its flight, curving its long sinuous neck down as it spotted something in the valley. Zerrick found his gaze pulled down to a lone figure backing slowly towards one tree that had escaped the blaze. It was Durnan.

"We've got to help him!" Zerrick cried, grabbing a handful of small plants from the area around the base of the tree which were still green against the coming of winter. He prepared his mind to spellcast, but Mok put a hand on his shoulder, pulling him back.

"No we can't. We must protect the hunters and we won't do that by giving away our spot. Durnan made the decision to stand alone. Let his sacrifice be worth it." Mok's other hand was on Svak's shoulder, and while Svak was obviously distraught over his friend's predicament, he seemed to agree with Mok.

"Svak, we should be able to cast a simple illusion at it without it knowing where we are, don't you think? We can't just let him die!" Zerrick implored. Svak and Durnan had been best friends since childhood. Surely he wouldn't hide here like a complete coward, Zerrick thought.

"We can't. Magical creatures can see magic! It would track us," Svak said, his voice cracking.

Zerrick glanced at the men he had hunted with many times now. They had been fearless against all of the creatures they had encountered, from wild bison to oversized kicking birds and galundren--the flying rabbit creature--and never had he seen them frightened.

Now they were all terrified.

Zerrick looked towards where the dragon circled over Durnan, surveying the area before its attack, and was filled with an urge to do something. Maybe it was because of his fighting other monsters, like the witch Lotus and the lake serpent, or maybe it was because of all of his terrible visions and nightmares, but somehow this creature failed to stir fear within him. He felt more angry than afraid.

Before he could come to a decision, the dragon struck. With another ear-splitting shriek, it dove, its small but deadly-sharp talons extended. Durnan shot several bolts of energy which struck the creature's belly and tail, but it hardly seemed to notice. With a sickening crunch, it struck Durnan, toppling the tree he had been using for cover and crushing him. The dragon spread its dark wings over its kill and extended its neck down to feed. Svak whimpered and turned his face.

"Die, evil beast!" Zerrick shouted, unable to remain still a second longer. He sent a force blast like the one which had knocked Mavra down hurtling into the dragon.

The magic hit the dragon full on, making it take a couple steps back to regain its balance, as the force pummeled its slick hide, but Zerrick could see it had not been enough. The dragon arched its head up, following the pathway the spell had taken right up to Zerrick's hiding place. Its tiny gleaming eyes fixed directly onto him.

"You! I recognize you, little man! The Master wants you," it spoke into Zerrick's mind, stunning him. By Svak's gasp and Mok's eyes bulging, he realized they too could hear the dragon's silent speech.

Zerrick felt the blood drain out of his face, as he suddenly recalled the dream he'd had the other night--he had watched dragons attacking the Put-na village in an effort to reach him, turning the grass huts into flaming infernos, descending upon man, woman and child. In the dream, he had seen Mira fight only to be caught in the claws of one, the elders leading villagers away only to be sent flying by a lashing tail, and afterwards he had witnessed himself being flown off to meet the Dark One.

He shook his head, trying to make the awful images go away. He couldn't let fear of what might never be cloud his ability to act now. Right now, he was being attacked.

The dragon took wing, quickly covering the ground between the fallen body of Durnan to the cluster of trees where Zerrick stood. Svak backed away, while Mok swallowed hard, watching the dragon with unblinking eyes as the dragon came to a skidding halt on the hillside and rushed over to the trees. It inhaled to breathe, then seemed to think twice about that. With a snort of black smoke, it eyed the trees keeping it from its prey.

"It wants you alive for *Kormu!*" Svak said in a hiss, shaking with either fear or fury. "You shouldn't have thrown that spell. You led it right to us!" He seemed torn between fleeing and fighting, but Mok recovered from his shock and roughly pulled him over to Zerrick.

"To late to worry about that," Mok said, watching as the dragon sniffed around the bases of the trees. It was rewarded by a spear thrust at its tender nostrils by one of the hunters. With a flash of fangs, it snapped at the hunter, but the fellow quickly ducked behind the tree. The blow rang off the bark, sending a shower of brown leaves cascading down, but fortunately the tree stood firm. The dragon was left wondering how to get at them through its tangled branches.

"You will have to work together if we are to live through this. If you can disable the dragon a moment, I'll organize the hunters to try to kill it." Mok looked doubtful, but determined.

Svak started to protest, "But spears won't--"

Mok cut him off. "Get to work, *kumalido*. Or we all die."

290

Zerrick had not been idle during Svak's outburst. Every branch with green leaves still left on it, every living weed or sapling, these he gathered and laid at his feet to be easily drawn from, as the dragon continued to goad him within his mind, *"Come out, little men, and fight me. I killed your friend. Will you let that be? I liked killing him. Just as I will enjoy killing all of you."*

His gut roiled. As Svak and Mok ended their dispute and Svak came to join him, Zerrick handed him a plant to draw from. Svak snatched it from him, glowering.

"We attack with ice," Svak instructed him, and immediately began a spell.

Zerrick had to rush to match his energy with Svak's directions, using a rudimentary form of sensing the man's thoughts to tell his magic to join Svak's and take the form he directed.

Both pulled hard, and the gathered greenery suddenly withered into dust, as a cloud of ice formed out the air in front of them and began to swirl faster and faster, bits of ice creating a white spiral. As Zerrick felt the mental cue from Svak, he pointed at the dragon and released his share even as Svak did so.

"For killing Durnan, filthy creature!" Svak shouted.

The icy wind seemed to unwind from the cloud, lashing out at the dragon in a long line of snow and ice. The dragon hardly blinked at it, however. With a powerful exhale, it sent a stream of flame at Zerrick and Svak, canceling out their ice storm and setting the grass around them on fire. Before his magic was totally consumed, Zerrick directed some of his ice to douse the flames. With a rush of wind, the fire fizzled out, leaving him standing in a ring of singed brush. Zerrick found himself trembling. That had been close.

Svak seemed to have lost his earlier fear, but what Zerrick saw in his face did not hearten him. He was enraged. "I will kill you!" he shouted, running forward to the last tree in the stand protecting them. He saw nothing green left nearby--it had all been either plucked by Zerrick or destroyed by the dragon. Svak put his hand to the oak and Zerrick saw the magic flood into him in a violent rush. With or without leaves the tree held an enormous pool of power, and it all poured forth, bathing Svak in a red glow as it sought to overcome him.

"No, Svak, that's beyond your ability!" Zerrick cried, but he was too late.

He could see some of the magic falling away as Svak tried to dispel that which he could not safely hold, doubling over in pain, but the stream was too fast for him to control.

The dragon charged forward, its mouth agape, but the magic was quicker. There was very little control in the power, but Svak's killing rage was all it needed to find a task. It swept out of him even faster than it had entered, in what must have been agony, Zerrick knew, from his experiences with Murtis the Crow and his own near brush with disaster.

Svak screamed as the magic left him, the magic surrounding the dragon in a choking cloud. The dragon thrashed and flapped its wings in an attempt to escape or disperse the deadly cloud while Mok hurried to gather the hunters and they began throwing spears at the dragon, but spear after spear bounced off the seemingly impenetrable hide. The magic began to lose its focus, as the tenuous control Svak had over it broke. Dispelled by the dragon, the cloud dissipated, and the dragon rushed forward, drawing breath in a great whoosh and exhaling it in a burst of flame.

Svak collapsed, leftover magic still glowing in him, and the flames that had been aimed at him hit the tree instead, quickly lighting the now dry, dead wood. Zerrick and Mok ran forward to grab Svak's arms and dragged him back further into the stand. The entire group retreated away from the fire threatening to turn their sanctuary into a death trap.

As the flames consumed the first tree and began to spread to nearby trees and bushes, the dragon came forward, and with a mighty swipe of its tail, it toppled the flaming oak into a shower of sparks and smoke. It stepped forward through the flames, its neck extended, searching for them.

"You will all die, little men. I will feed on your flesh, I will crush your bones under my feet and I will fly your souls to my Master." The dragon again taunted them, and by the looks on the hunters' faces, Zerrick was certain each and every one of them heard it.

Flames were spreading everywhere. The dragon seemed in no hurry now, for they were near the end of the stand and beyond the last dogwood tree there was only the hillside and a long open stretch to the wooded area by the river.

Zerrick's back pressed up against the last tree. He coughed as a plume of smoke swirled around them and glanced at Mok and his burden. Svak showed no signs of recovery, but from the look of pain on his face and the heaving of his chest it was clear he was still alive.

"What do we do now?" Zerrick asked.

"Dragons are tough, but not invincible. Not very smart, though they try to make you think that they are. Your force spell is fast. Surprise it, and you may pin it. Then I can hit its one vulnerable place." Mok looked hard at Zerrick, and he could see sweat beaded over his forehead from the rising heat. "Make sure you pin the entire creature. Especially the head."

To immobilize a creature that size . . . Zerrick thought with a twinge of doubt. The dragon was thirty feet long if it was an inch.

The hunters were becoming restless as the flame claimed another tree and the entire glade began to flare up. One man, a more seasoned warrior from the third village, charged the dragon, and was immediately set flying by a flap of its wings into a blazing bush. His screams were cut off when the dragon swung its head around and bit into the man's throat.

"Zerrick!" He couldn't mistake the urgency in Mok's voice. He handed over Svak's inert form to two of the younger hunters and set to readying himself, his spear in one hand, a stone hunting knife in the other.

"You think I don't know what you two are planning? I will hurt you, but I won't kill you today, Zerrick. I will take you instead to Angist." The dragon was upon them now, its body keeping the worst of the flames and heat

from them, but that would change the instant it opened its mouth to breathe.

Zerrick looked around to find a source of power, and realized the only source great enough was the tree at his back. He was stronger than Svak, but he didn't know what the surge would do to him, if he could master control as Svak had. He didn't know what damage Svak had taken, whether he still had his senses, or his wits. Still, he couldn't let anyone else die, and he wouldn't give in, though it seemed the visions were starting to show that they might very well come true.

The dragon blew smoke at them, making a noise that sounded like a chuckle, then inhaled deeply, turning to Mok and the hunters. Zerrick prepared his mind before he began to pull, knowing once the magic rushed through him it would be too late to think up an attack.

Lotus had defeated an older, flightless dragon with a conjured water creature. That wouldn't work here; Zerrick didn't know how to conjure anything that large, and this dragon could simply take to the air to escape such a threat. Ice hadn't worked, physical blows were useless, and it obviously had a liking for fire. Mok was right; the only thing that had shown an effect had been his force blow. But he needed something more exact now, a great hand, to knock it back and then hold it on every side. A giant hand of the Goddess's magic.

Please, Ainéra, let this work. Let magic be truly under Your domain, and not the Evil One's.

He pulled.

The force of magic surging into him was incredible. It filled him to bursting, a screaming cacophony of sound within his head, a violent shuddering mass of energy in his gut. It was everything, and nothing. With a shock that almost seemed to belong to someone else, he realized he had pulled it all and hadn't exploded or lost control, though that would change at any second. His head was spinning crazily. The image of the dragon's head swam in his vision.

He envisioned a great hand blasting forward, pummeling like a fist then spreading out to push down every inch of the creature into the earth. The magic heard, and tore out of him with a roar like a howling wind, nearly deafening his senses. It was agony as the magic left, all of it, leaving him empty and pitiful, a mere mortal once more. He groaned and fell on his face as his knees gave out.

A hunter helped him sit up to see the effect of his spell, and he realized he must have blacked out for a second, for he didn't remember sights or sounds of the kind of destruction which was before him. The force had knocked the dragon onto its back with such incredible power, it had actually driven branches through the tough membrane of its wings. That impact had uprooted two other trees which had fallen onto the dragon, pinning its neck and tail. The magic was still there, a great glowing hand pressing the creature into the earth as it screamed in fury and pain.

With a fierce battle cry, Mok ran forward towards the head. He climbed over a bush whose flames had been smothered by Zerrick's magic, and with a viscous thrust, stuck his spear into the creature's eye into its brain. The entire form shook in a series of seizures, then was still.

Zerrick had the presence of mind to instruct the magic, which had not used up even close to all of its strength, into smothering the rest of the flames. He then dispersed the rest of it, as pain began to creep behind his eye sockets into what he knew would become the worst of all headaches. Actually his whole entire body ached, and he felt dizzy and nauseous.

Before he could let go of his tenuous hold on consciousness and sink into blissful nothingness, he saw the sky overhead darken beyond the haze already caused by smoke, and felt the air suddenly turn icy cold.

"You were warned. You could have remained weak. I would have left you alone. Now your will suffer. Wherever you go, I will find you. You will suffer, and all those around will suffer. There is nowhere you can hide. I will track you through the magic."

Zerrick couldn't get away from the painfully loud voice echoing within his skull, each word punctuated by a wave of pain. He crawled on hands and knees, body acting in a futile attempt to escape, and threw up what little breakfast he'd had that morning. Again that awful feeling of being watched, of an incredibly evil presence was all around, making the hunters cower and pray to the Mother for protection. Slowly, the feeling passed, and the sky cleared. Coughing at the taste of bile, Zerrick risked another lance of pain to raise his head and look around.

The hunters were hovering near, looking safe, though frightened. Mok was returning with the dragon's head, and Zerrick took one last look at the awesome creature lying dead in the burned out glade.

He blacked out.

Chapter Nineteen

"Do not shrink from evil; stand, and it will shrink."
--II Ja'hal 23:22

At first there were only sounds: water dripping into a pot, the rub of fabric on fabric, and the soft whisper of breath close by. Then slowly smells and sensation could be felt: a wet cloth over his forehead, air on bare skin over his torso, a scent of herbs and of sweat--his own, most likely. Zerrick tried to open his eyes only to find a cloth draped over them and someone's hand pressing it firmly down. He reached to remove the hand, and heard a delicious chuckle. His heart clenched as the sound danced down his spine. Mira.

"Where am I?" he said, or rather croaked. His throat felt raw. All of him felt raw, in fact, from his toes to the roots of his hair. His hands were wrapped in bandages, he realized.

"Darya's hut. She's with the village elders, discussing what happened," Mira said, and while she did not say it aloud, Zerrick knew he was the focus of that discussion, once again.

"What happened? I remember Mok killing the dragon, then . . ." he trembled with the memory of that evil voice. A new fear pierced him. Had Mira heard about it? About Angist watching him?

"The men brought you back after you lost consciousness. I was on duty watching the fire, and Darya called me with my herbs to tend you and the other *kumalido* Svak," Mira explained, pressing her fingertips around his temples. Her touch felt cool on skin which could somehow still feel the heat of those flames in the glade.

Apparently he had something of a fever. "I'm going to redip this cloth. Keep your eyes closed, Zerrick." She removed the cloth, and he heard her drenching it in what smelled like herbal water, squeezing the excess back into the pot.

He tried to open one eye, just to see the look on Mira's face, see whether she was still angry with him, whether there was any emotion whatsoever for him in her eyes. He caught a split second of light and color. Dizziness assailed him. He groaned and shut his eyes tightly.

"Told you to keep them shut," Mira said, but she did not sound angry. In fact she sounded worried. How much damage had the magic done to him? And what of Svak?

"How bad is it? Svak and me. And the others, of course," he asked, fumbling with the words. Why could he never speak a coherent sentence around her? She was sitting too close, he decided.

"You're going to be fine. You were a little burned by the fire, and the spell you cast--well, Hirkumos says it is to be expected for you to feel like this after a spell of that that magnitude. You need peace and sleep, and by tomorrow morning you should be up and about. Svak, however, is not doing so well." She spoke low and hushed, and he could hear the stress in the tone of her words. She was worried, he realized. But she didn't understand what was at stake.

"I can't rest, Mira, I need to talk to Hirkumos and the village elders. And maybe I can help with Svak. It's my fault, really, for what happened to him." Zerrick thought about the vision of the dragon attack and the fact Angist knew exactly where he was now. He'd already caused damage here. He didn't want to bring more.

"You're not going anywhere. Now drink this," Mira said, pressing something cool to his lips. It was either drink or be drenched, so he drank and was surprised at the sweet citrus flavor. With an aftertaste of blackroot.

"Mira, what are you doing?" he asked. He could already feel the root beginning to take effect, numbing his lips and making him feel drowsy. Blackroot was a powerful sedative.

"See you in the morning, Zerrick. Then we'll get everything straightened out. Until then, rest and recover."

He felt Mira pull up a light fur over him and replace the cloth over his eyes. Then drowsiness overcame him.

Mira waited until his breathing rhythm changed and she was sure he was asleep before letting out the sob she had been holding back. Why hadn't Darya told her? Something would happen to make it impossible for Zerrick to stay here, that she understood, but a dragon?! Attacking Zerrick when he was alone, away from her? He could have been killed! It was lucky she was in here rather than at that meeting. She'd have a few things to say to that Dreamteller. What was the use of prophetic dreams if you didn't use them to protect people?

Her emotions threatened to overwhelm her, as they had when they'd first brought Zerrick into the village, sprawled out on a makeshift litter. All of the men had suffered burns from the intense heat, though few had actually had contact with the flames. She'd been unable to help at first, however, bursting into tears over Zerrick who'd looked a step away from death.

His skin had been shiny with fever, his dark hair damp against his scalp, and his hands had actually been glowing with leftover magic. Hirkumos had directed her how to deal with that while he began treatment on Svak.

Svak--the poor man. Hirkumos had told her Zerrick would recover quickly. From what Mok had described, he'd had complete control over his large spell, and should be back to normal after a good night's rest. But Svak was dying.

Zerrick was resting comfortably, so Mira rose and went to the other makeshift pallet which had been set up in the hut, and the still form upon it.

They had tried bundling him in furs, they had tried bathing him in cool lake water. Neither seemed to have any sort of effect on his terrible fever. He was being consumed, it seemed, from the inside by this unrelenting energy. And he had not regained consciousness once, since the time the magic overcame him.

She raised the fellow's head to force water down his throat--at the rate his body's water was being sweated away, he would dehydrate quickly without her ministrations.

Hirkumos had been torn away to speak at the meeting raging on right now, but he had told Mira before he left her in charge that it was beyond his skill. It looked hopeless.

After she finished giving Svak water, Mira changed the wet cloths wrapping his extremities. Not only was he burning on the inside, Svak had sustained the worst of external burns as well. Most of his skin on his arms and face were blistered and she knew if he were awake, he'd be in agony. Once the cloths had been moistened with herb water and replaced, Mira left Svak and returned to sit by Zerrick, hugging herself to keep warm against the chill in the air and in her heart. Over and over again the thoughts came, It could have been Zerrick, dying over there with the wraps. It could have been Zerrick.

He was deep in sleep, his chest rising and falling in smooth rhythm. Mira checked his temple and found the fever had lessened. It would break soon, just as Hirkumos had told her. She removed the cloth and looked at him. His long lashes lay gently against his cheek, and his thin brows were not furrowed in either pain or worry. In fact, his entire expression was serene, for once completely free of foreboding dreams.

Mira smoothed back a damp curl that had fallen across his lip. He, who was usually such a light sleeper, did not stir at all. She chuckled. This was probably the first decent night's sleep he'd had. She should make him drink her potions more often.

Knowing the blackroot would not wear off for several more hours and that her time alone with Zerrick was now all too rare, Mira leaned forward and lightly brushed his forehead with her lips.

"I love you," she whispered at his ear.

She left him to return to her other charges.

Zerrick woke to a cloudy day and a great deal of hustle and bustle in the small hut.

Irulen and one of Darya's apprentices had taken over care of Svak, one waiting at his head, while the other consulted with two extremely elderly gentlemen at Svak's feet. Darya herself was resting on her pallet, and beside her, on the floor fast asleep, was Mira. Hirkumos, the last occupant of the hut, stood impatiently over Zerrick.

"We need to hear from you. As soon as possible," Hirkumos stated, handing Zerrick his shirt.

Zerrick took the shirt and pulled it over his head, marveling at how much better he felt from last night. No fever, no headache or dizziness, only a slight itch over his chest and hands, which were still bandaged.

"Here--you won't be needing those any longer," Hirkumos said, and removed the bandages. His hands looked a little raw, but that was all. Zerrick looked up at Hirkumos.

"Do you know what happened? That I pulled from an ancient dogwood tree? And controlled it?" Zerrick followed as Hirkumos began walking out the door, handing Zerrick a wet cloth to wipe his face with. Zerrick tried to ignore the itch of his unkempt hair and unshaven face. Apparently this was too important to wait for his white man's morning absolutions.

He tucked in his shirt as they passed through the village. With his state of dishevelment and the way Hirkumos was rushing him forward, Zerrick suddenly had the image of himself being led to his trial back in Harrow. To add to his fear, the wind was whipping up around them, throwing his hair in his face one moment, then trying to lift his shirt from him the next.

In all, not a hopeful way to begin the day.

They reached the main village firepit. There was a large group gathered there, including the elders of all three tribes, Mavra, Mok, Ablor, Tamur, the hunters from yesterday's incident, and a fair number of women and men he knew or vaguely recognized. It seemed the only ones not there were the scouts on watch.

Mavra was first to speak. "Well young man, you've caused a bit of trouble. And some mystery as well, since none of the men with you really understood all of what took place. Come sit by me, and tell us what happened yesterday on the hunt."

Gingerly, Zerrick took his place next to her on the log bench, aware that the people were listening to his every word. He carefully told the entire story of yesterday's events, from when Mok first spotted the dragon, to the attack on Durnan, his own retaliation, and the attack on their hiding place in the grove. He knew Hirkumos or the dreamtellers would be able to tell if he was lying, so he kept strictly to the truth, but he did not mention the dragon speaking within his thoughts or of Angist. There was a chance that Mok and the other hunters hadn't heard enough to make any sense of it, and there was no point in condemning himself at the very start, that he was both at fault for yesterday's tragedy as well as a future danger to them all. He had to talk alone with Hirkumos and Darya first, then decide what he should do next.

"So you pulled from the old dogwood tree--after seeing what the same power had done to Svak? Did you know you would be able to control it? Mavra asked, her eyes intent on him. Svak and Durnan had been her apprentices.

"I wasn't sure if I could, but I had no choice. That was the only power source nearby, and the dragon was attacking," he answered, bristling under her intense stare. She looked like she hadn't slept all night, and her eyes were red and swollen.

"And why did you attack the dragon in the first place? Wasn't Durnan's death enough? Why did you have to endanger the rest of the men there?" Mavra demanded, and Zerrick could see she was on the verge of tears.

Zerrick swallowed back a sudden rush of emotion. Until now, he had been in no shape to really feel the effects of what had happened. Now, looking at Mavra, he knew the awful truth. Durnan was dead. Another hunter--Jert, had also died. And Svak was dying.

But even as grief washed over him, anger arose alongside, that he was being blamed for everything here. With a toss of his head he addressed the crowd, "Am I on trial here?"

Mavra blinked at him. "What is 'on trial'?"

Oh yes, he'd forgotten. The Put-na had no notion of courts, or trials. He tried to clarify himself, standing to confront Mavra. "Why do you want to know the details of yesterday? Am I being blamed for the fact a dragon attacked us?"

Mavra became livid, unable to speak, so Hirkumos answered, "We must know if there was a reason for the attack other than for food. Tell me, did the dragon speak with you?"

Zerrick groaned inwardly. So they knew something, and didn't want to discuss it privately. He glanced at Mok, but the old scout's head was turned away, on purpose Zerrick was sure. He had no supporters, it seemed. Wearily he related to Hirkumos the rest of the tale, about what the dragon had said, and Angist. When he described the darkening of the sky and the evil voice in his head, the other hunters nodded vigorously, and whispered to those around them that yes, that was what they had experienced. Zerrick was shaken. That voice had not been some vision or dream then. All had witnessed the occurrence.

"So what now?" he asked Hirkumos, his voice barely a whisper. So many faces around him, many of them familiar. He'd come to think of himself as a part of the tribe, or at least a friend here. Now, by the looks of fear and suspicion, he was suddenly unsure of his place. Would this be a second scene like that of Harrow, a mob of angry people chasing him out of town?

Hirkumos, however, did not look angry or condemning but merely worried. "I do not know yet. Tell me, when you pulled all that power, were you dizzy? Did you have complete control, or was it merely responding to your state of mind, your feelings?"

Zerrick noted the avid look on Mavra's face, as she recovered from her tears and glanced over. "Yes, I was dizzy, but I had control. I may have blacked out for a second, but when I opened my eyes I saw the magic in the hand-of-force attack. I know that spell needed complete control to maintain its shape."

"But you were at your limit. Well, at least we know your strength now. And that you need a more powerful teacher than I," Hirkumos said, his hand pulling at his long beard. He was obviously distressed to be showing such outward signs.

Mavra nodded to herself, and stopped Hirkumos's pacing with a touch. "It must be done. He cannot stay here."

Jerapo, who had sat quietly through the discussion, suddenly stood. "Darya should be here to advise the young man. I allowed him to stay under my protection as he helped Tamur and my people from the slavers. I will not send him away empty-handed. He has done nothing wrong."

"But you heard him. He cannot stay," Mavra said, and now she looked with compassion on Zerrick.

Zerrick glanced from her to the look of distress on Hirkumos's face and the sorrow on Jerapo's. So they would send him away. But not in hatred, it seemed. It was not the same as the townspeople of Harrow, and yet it was a rejection, just the same.

"Sit, young man, while I go to wake Darya," Jerapo said, indicating a place next to him, on the other side of Mok who fidgeted as if struggling with something. Zerrick went over and sat down, and Mok grabbed his hands with bony, wrinkled fingers.

"You were very brave yesterday. We owe our lives to you," he whispered. Zerrick found himself unable to respond for the sudden tightening in his breast. Such emotion he had never heard in the old scout's voice, a voice usually so full of cheer. Nodding, he gripped his friend's hand and watched Jerapo make his way to Darya's tent.

Mira woke when someone's foot brushed her arm, and blearily opened her eyes to see Jerapo shaking Darya awake. By the light outside and by the hunger pangs of her stomach, she realized it must be mid-morning.

At once she looked to where she had tended Zerrick, but the pallet was empty. Hovering above her, Jerapo spoke in a low tone to Darya.

"He's told us everything that happened, and the *kumalido* were right. *Kormu's* after the boy. He has to go, or he will be our destruction.

We need you out there to advise him. I won't let Mavra simply chase him off no matter how deep her grief." He glanced over at Mira and sighed. "She may want to be there also."

Already they were demanding he leave? Just after he had recovered from what was killing another witch?

"I'm coming," Mira said, standing and quickly tying her hair up in a kerchief. She was still in the clothes she'd worn last night, and the smell of herbs clung heavily to her. "Do you need help, Dreamteller?" she asked Darya, who struggled to rise.

"I'm getting up, I'm getting up. Mira, get my cloak; it's freezing in here, people all in and out everywhere," she muttered, slowly straightening. Mira quickly fetched her cloak and an apprentice came forward to attend to Darya's other needs. After delivering the cloak, Mira waited in the doorway until Darya was ready, then together with Jerapo they went to the gathering.

Zerrick was seated beside Mok, looking guilty and dejected despite the fact those around him seemed to be trying to console him. Mira saw that Tamur was among those.

Darya came forward, unaffected by the number of people watching her, and smoothly took a seat by Mavra. "All right, you've dragged me out of bed. Go ahead and make your announcement, Mavra."

Mavra pressed her lips together in irritation and looked to Zerrick. Zerrick was avoiding everyone's attention, keeping his head lowered, his black hair falling into his face. His face was unshaven, casting his entire face into shadow. Mira sighed. He looked the very picture of guilt.

Mavra stood to speak. "Zerrick, we thought this over very hard, and though we like and have enjoyed teaching you, you are too powerful to stay here, and you need more training than we can give. You need to seek a more powerful teacher."

Zerrick snorted, shaking his head, "Now you think you'll soften the blow casting me out with a few nice words."

Mira glared at him. She could see him withdrawing into his shell, ready to lash out at anyone. That was not the way to receive help or companionship on his journey. She sent a look at Darya, pleading for help.

Mavra did not take his reaction well. "We did not have to teach you at all!" She seemed about to say more, but Darya rose and silenced her with a gentle nudge.

"I foresaw this day, and perhaps for that you will argue that I should have spoken earlier, that I could have stopped this from happening. No. I had my reasons for staying silent, some of which were to protect people of these villages from what could have been a much worse incident if you had not been there yesterday. What's more, however, I foresaw a path for you to take to a greater teacher. I can give you a rough idea of how to reach the white city of your dreams, should you decide to travel that way. You knew you could not stay here forever, Zerrick."

This last was said with more tenderness than Mira had ever heard in Darya's voice. Zerrick looked up in surprise, noticing it as well. He looked around, and Mira could see the concern of those he knew well in the village finally seemed to register with him. He swallowed, looking suddenly unsure of himself.

"So I have to leave, but you can at least give me a direction. I need a moment or two to think about what I want to do," Zerrick said. There was a crease between his brows which told Mira his mind was working furiously, evaluating his options. *He thinks he's leaving alone*, she thought, the butterflies racing in her stomach. It was almost time for her to speak up. But not just yet--she had to play this carefully, or he would want her to stay here, just as he'd wanted to in Depin.

Darya would help, she was sure. Even as she thought that, the old Dreamteller stood, gaining the attention of all onlookers. "There is no reason for you to travel alone. Much could be answered for the Put-na if one from our village could go with him and see if old legends are true. Does anyone want to accompany him?"

"I will," Mok said immediately, standing. "This is the apprentice of my long time friend. I will travel with him wherever he wants to go. There are still a few good years left for me, and if there is a chance to see something new, that would be much better than sitting around waiting to get older. Besides, he needs a good tracker." He grinned, the creases around his eyes making long tracks down his cheeks.

Zerrick smiled, and nodded. "Thanks, Mok. I do need a good tracker."

Mira stood. "I would also like to go." She saw Zerrick start to argue and rushed to say, "I have been training hard with the spear--my aim now is as good as any hunter's. Ask them." She pointed at the hunter friends of Tamur, who had watched her practice. They had laughed at her at first, until she pierced the eye of the straw target at seventy feet.

Zerrick turned to look at the hunters, and they nodded, murmuring a few compliments of her skills. From the women gathered nearby there was a low buzz of agreement that Mira would indeed be a good candidate to leave with Zerrick. Mira had expected that as well, from Ghuldini's dislike of her. She looked at Zerrick's face with all the desire in her heart that she be included in this.

She saw he was warring with himself. Then he nodded. "She can come ... I ..." he seemed to debate his words, " ... I would welcome her help." He blushed and turned away.

"I would also like to go." Everyone turned to look as Tamur stood, peering all too intensely at Mira. She stifled a groan.

"Yes, that would be good if you had a couple hunter-scouts," Darya said. Her comment broke off the protests others including Zerrick had started to make. He looked hard at Darya, and Mira could guess his thoughts because she was having the very same ones--had Darya seen something? It was too late now for anyone to object. Mok heartily welcomed the young scout into the party, and women gave him tearful goodbyes. No others were standing to volunteer.

When the noise quieted and the volunteers sat down again, Hirkumos rose, looking worriedly back to Darya's hut. "I wish there was some way you could bring Svak. His ailment is beyond our skill to heal here, but perhaps out there dwell the great *kumalido* . . ."

"But he's unconscious. I don't think it would be possible to take him. The way is long and difficult," Mavra interjected, and Mira could hear the despair in her voice. Apparently, so did Zerrick.

"What exactly is wrong with him? Is there anything I can do?" Either the press of people or the weight of what lay ahead was pressing down on him, Mira thought; he seemed to wilt, sitting stooped like an old man.

Mavra and Hirkumos looked at each other for a moment, their eyes silently communicating. Mavra murmured as if in answer to Hirkumos's questioning look, "He is more powerful than either of us. It might make a difference."

Hirkumos nodded once, then went over to Zerrick. "Perhaps you can help. Come, let's take a look at Svak," he said, offering Zerrick a hand up. Mavra walked on the other side of Hirkumos, following as they made their way over to Darya's hut. Of course, Mira also followed.

When she managed to squeeze through the narrow opening, she could see Zerrick and Hirkumos leaning over the still form of Svak. Listening hard, she could hear their words, spoken just above a whisper.

"The magic is still within him, burning him up. It cannot leave because he is not awake to tell it to. It must be pulled out by overcoming the will he originally sent into it. You said he was in a rage when he pulled it; therefore removing it may be impossible with that strength of will to overcome."

"Let me try. It's my fault this happened in the first place," Zerrick responded, searching his person for something--probably one of his crystals, Mira thought. Hirkumos handed him one of his.

"Go ahead and try, but do not blame yourself. He chose to pull more than was safe. That was his decision." Hirkumos said, standing behind Zerrick with a hand on his shoulder.

"He should have known better," Mavra muttered.

Zerrick closed his eyes, his fist closed tight around Hirkumos's crystal--a much larger one than Nanna's little earrings, Mira thought. They hardly took note of her. There was still the *kumalido* woman Irulen asleep in the corner, one of Darya's apprentices in Zerrick's bed, and Darya herself had slipped into the hut as well, standing quietly at the doorway. Mira moved further into the room as Zerrick fought to pull the magic from Svak, his face turning red with exertion. The crystal glowed a deep crimson, perhaps in echo of the fury of the magic he fought in Svak's body. After a moment Zerrick opened his eyes, panting. Hirkumos caught him as he wobbled on his feet.

"It's too much. I can't get past his anger," he said between gasps, groping for a place to sit down. He handed back the crystal, looking crestfallen at his defeat. Mira shook her head in sympathy.

"You tried," Mavra said with unexpected tenderness, sitting down beside him. Hirkumos remained standing at Svak's side, tugging softly at his beard.

Silence stretched, as everyone contemplated the still form of Svak on the bed, and Mira could feel the silence, a heavy tingling in the air . . . no, a tingling in her head, she realized. A pressure, way at the back of her skull, reminding her of--she struggled to think--of the mountaintop when that dark presence that she now knew was Angist, had appeared.

As that thought struck her, the air in the hut, always kept warm for Darya, suddenly became chill, colder than even the mountain had been. Zerrick leapt to his feet, sending a look of sheer terror at Mira who understood it immediately.

"Get out, Mira!" he cried, crossing over in front of Mavra, perhaps to protect her and Hirkumos. He didn't seem to see what she could--a sort of shadow crossing the room, headed not for them, but for Svak. It touched the young man's arm, then seemed to sink in, vanishing.

Svak opened his eyes.

Zerrick and the other *kumalido* had time only to blink in surprise as Svak sat up, looking fully recovered, then bolts of energy were flying from his fingertips, striking all the kumalido in the hut. Hirkumos staggered, Irulen reared up from her pallet only to by knocked back unconscious by the blast of energy, and Mavra fell like an uprooted tree, but Zerrick only grimaced, absorbing the blow harmlessly. He must have had enough warning to build a shield, Mira thought. He motioned for her to get out, but that pressure in the back of her head wouldn't let her. In any case she wasn't leaving him to whatever that shadow wanted. She stepped forward past Darya, glancing quickly at her.

Darya had a strange look of fascination on her face.

"It's *Kormu*--he's entered through the magic and the rage," Hirkumos said, sending off a glowing sphere to surround Svak. Svak broke out of it without twitching an eye. "We need to get outdoors near stronger sources!"

"He can do that?!" Possess someone? How do you fight it?" Zerrick asked in panic.

"I don't know. I've only heard of this--never actually seen it. I suggest we run!" Hirkumos responded, panting. He held his side where he'd been hit.

Time slowed to a crawl to Mira. Hirkumos and Zerrick tried to dodge away from Svak, headed for the door, but just as they began to move, Svak, seeming now to possess an unlimited supply of magic, caught both of them in a blinding flash which felled both like a hammer. They were both conscious, but lying prone on the ground, writhing in shock and pain.

Some inner force propelled Mira forward just as Zerrick yelled for her to flee. The pressure in her mind was growing unbearably heavy and she could almost smell the foul taint of evil as she approached Svak. Somehow she knew just what to say. "Angist, you shall have no power over this village or this person. I forbid it. By the name of Iahmel, return now to your shadows!"

Her voice had never sounded so firm and resounding--it almost seemed there was someone else speaking through her. Her thoughts went back to what Darya had told her, *"It may be, that you have powers I cannot see or understand, because they flow not from the Mother, but from Him."* Could this be a power she possessed? From Iahmel?

Taking no chances just in case Iahmel was listening, she prayed with all her heart to Him, to know what she should do next, how to handle this . . . demon.

Almost instantly and with a rush of elation, she knew.

Svak came forward, hissing at her, surprised that she should confront him. He seemed to consider which spell to use on her, but she didn't allow him the chance. She placed her hand on his chest, and let the pressure within her do the rest.

It was pain, but also an exquisite release. Mira screamed as the force of it went through her and staggered, but then the pressure was gone, fading back into the recesses of her skull. She saw the shadow, now fleeing through a crack in the hut. Svak blinked his eyes and he looked normal once more, no strange malice in his eyes or evil glow around him. He immediately fainted.

Mira felt suddenly tired and went to sit on the pallet where Zerrick had lain, resting with her eyes half open until she realized all the *kumalido* were still sprawled out on the floor. She rushed over to check them.

Zerrick struggled to sit up even as she reached him. "How--how did you do that?" he asked, staring amazedly at her. He seemed fine, just a little sore. Hirkumos was likewise recovering, helping Irulen up from where she had fallen off the pallet. Mavra was a little worse off. She was groggy and in pain, having another of her headaches. But even she nodded and pushed away Mira's helping hand. Darya stood at the doorway, looking like an old owl, nodding sagely.

"Very interesting, Mira. I wish I had more time to learn about this new power. We'll have to be satisfied with a long talk before you leave." She chuckled, her eyes glinting. "Very interesting indeed."

"I guess I've found my power," Mira told the circle of amazed onlookers.

He still couldn't believe it.

How could Mira suddenly have powers over . . . over whatever evil thing that had possessed Svak's body yesterday? She hadn't done anything, at least not that he could see. She hadn't used magic, that was for certain.

So what exactly had happened?

Zerrick stood before a large gathering of the three tribes in the early dawn light, waiting patiently as women and men made their goodbyes to Tamur and Mok. They were all burdened with generous offerings of food and supplies for the journey ahead, and each of them wore new cloaks given to them last night by the elders. There had even been a great feast made for them, to bring luck and good future for the tribe after its hardships.

After the hatred and fear of his people in Harrow and the indifference in Depin, it felt strange to have such a warm farewell party, even if they were once again pushing him onwards, away.

Mira had been overwhelmed by the feast as well, but for different reasons. Apparently before she had been an oddity--stared and perhaps snickered at, but basically left alone, Zerrick had found out. Now, however, she was famous. They didn't quite know what she was, only that she had performed a feat never before witnessed. A miracle.

As he looked on, she was surrounded by a throng of tribesmen as they prepared to start their journey. Every wise person, *kumalido*, and elder interrogated her, trying to determine just what she had done and how.

Darya seemed to have explained it best. All in the room with magical talent could sense that something evil had overtaken Svak's body. The magic he had cast had felt more tainted than even Murtis's or Madame Lotus's spells. Darya too could see the evil and possible outcomes of its actions, but no one had been able to do anything to fight it, much less expel it from Svak's body. Nonetheless, Mira had simply walked up and told it to leave, and it had.

Darya said the power must come from Iahmel, for no power of this kind had ever been observed in any of the Goddess's followers. That brought to mind the Holy Book, and all the tales of Ja'hal's miracles and the miracles of the prophets, which had included casting out demons. All Zerrick could say for certain was that it definitely had not been magic. To his sight Mira had simply walked up and touched Svak.

Svak was still confined to a bed, weak with the aftereffects of his experiences, but he was awake and alert, and seemed likely to recover now.

And Mira was confused like everyone else, but also ecstatic. The first thing she had done after she had 'cast out the demon' as people were calling it, was look to Zerrick with that same glowing expression she'd had when Nanna first suggested she come with Zerrick so long ago, and say, "Now you really do need me to come. I'll be your protection against *him.*"

He could hardly stop her now. The day dawned bright and clear, with just a slight trace of frost, and everything was prepared. They would even have a tent of sorts, bundled into a ball with other important supplies like spearhead tips and water, supported by a basket-like contraption of woven reed and cane grass. It would be carried by Tamur and Mok the same way kills from the hunt were carried, with two spears through the basket supported on their shoulders, one carrying in front and one in back of the basket. A very simple and efficient way to travel, without pack animals or carts.

Zerrick jumped as Hirkumos came up behind him and tapped him on the shoulder. Darya was with him. "Ready, my student?"

Zerrick nodded, ignoring the flutter in his stomach. "I believe so. Have we packed enough food?"

Hirkumos nodded. "You have the basics to last you a month. Flatcakes, salted akiya, dates and other dried fruits. We are used to this, you know. You will simply need to hunt every so often for fresh meat. Mok is an expert in that."

"Then we are ready." The words felt so final, so hard, like a wall, cutting him off from what had been his friends and more for over two months.

Hirkumos cut through that feeling by reaching out to touch the pouch Zerrick always wore, Alden's sign of protection, which Hirkumos had taught him was a sign of the Mother. "Your amber there is full, but you have grown beyond its strength. I want to give you my own crystal. Together, they should give you enough energy to fight with all your training. Here." He reached to his breast and pulled out a long well-formed crystal of amethyst.

Zerrick was shocked--such a crystal was very hard to find, especially here away from the mountains. Hirkumos would not soon replace its like. "No, I can't--"

"You must. Or I won't be able to sleep at night, having sent you unprepared. I only hope I have taught you enough. At least I am sure you have the basic control now, that you will not pull too much or lose control like Svak did." Hirkumos sighed.

"Thank you, Hirkumos. For everything." Zerrick found he could say no more, his heart somehow feeling lodged in his throat, so both fell silent, simply acknowledging each other. Then Hirkumos came quickly forward to wrap Zerrick in a huge bear hug. He pulled back just as quickly, holding Zerrick's shoulders, and gave a satisfied grunt. Then he stepped back to let Darya speak.

"Well, boy, it looks like you're finally on your way. First of all, take care of Mira or I'll come haunt your dreams. Second, I have for you a rough map, based on my dreams and visions, on where you are to go to find the white city." She rolled out a rough charcoal sketch on bottlebrush tree bark showing the lake with the village, a series of mountains not to the east but south, and three rivers running out of the mountains.

"In my dreams I saw you walking due south, the sun crossing your path, until you reach the foothills of a mountain range where another tribe, the Rundra live. Do not talk to any of that tribe. They are robbers and thieves and hate the white men. Do not cross the mountains, for beyond them lies the southern coastline. Instead, follow the range west."

Rundra, Rundra, yes, Zerrick had heard Alden mention them once. The colonization had been halted on the south shore because of warfare with them. The only white men now using that shore were privateers and pirates.

Darya continued. "In another dream, I see you heading west, with the mountains to your left, crossing a great river by night. I have seen also two rivers further west, and I believe you must cross these as well, but I had no specific dreams about them. Beyond the third river the range of my sight fails and I can see no more. From there you will have to use your skills of tracking and magic."

Zerrick nodded. "I think if we make it that far, I'll have my own dreams to guide us. I know it stands on the edge of a vast desert."

Darya smiled. "I know you will do just fine. In fact, I wouldn't be surprised if we should see you again someday, once you are a true master *kumalido.*"

"I would like to return someday," Zerrick said, and realized he truly meant it. He had been so close to being accepted here. If only it hasn't been for Angist's hunting of him . . . which brought to mind another question.

"Have you seen everything that is going to happen to me? Was this all destiny? I feel like something has been pushing me since . . . well for a very long time."

Darya shook her head. "I can't see everything, and no, I don't think everything is destined to be. What I see is what will happen if things continue as they are from this day. But you are right, a certain amount of what is happening to you was unchangeable, from the day you approached that dais on the mountaintop."

She looked him hard in the eye. "You will not find peace now until you are strong enough to give *Kormu* such a challenge that he is afraid of attacking you, until you have allies that are too strong a force to oppose, or until . . . well until that which eventually happens to us all happens to you."

Death. "Or until I am taken over, like Svak was," he added gloomily. Back to Father's rantings against magic.

Darya snorted. "Mira won't let that happen to you. She loves you, you know. But she won't tell you herself. She's afraid you'll reject her."

Zerrick felt a surge of joy, but he stomped it out immediately. "Mira loves Tamur," he said, indicating where they were standing together saying their goodbyes to the hunters.

Darya threw her hands up. "All right! Whatever. I am not a matchmaker. Fare you well then, Zerrick. And face your fears. That is the only way they will disappear." She rubbed cheeks with him and went to speak to Mira.

Zerrick went to pay his final respects to the hunters, then girls who had been trying to give him feathers, then Mavra, Irulen and Svak who were resting together in Mavra's hut.

After that he returned, and the four donned their packs, drank a toast with the elders, and lined up to depart. Zerrick and Mira walked in front, then Mok and Tamur carrying the basket with the tent. Mira carried two spears for herself as well as a spear for Mok and Tamur, and Zerrick carried one spear, his machete, with his pistol and sword strapped to his waist.

With the Put-na villagers waving a hearty goodbye, the four of them began walking out into the brushlands, south, to the Rundran mountains.

Chapter Twenty

"I knew that my magic was too sweet a prize for the evil-minded. So I withdrew."
--Ainéra's Book, Alorian

"Aaiiee!" Mira's battle shriek pierced the evening air as she hurled her spear towards the wild goat. The goat bleated once in terror, trying to flee, but Mira's aim was true, pinning the animal as it tried to leap away, killing it instantly.

"Excellent, Mira," Mok said, climbing over the ridge where the group had been hiding. "But next time try not to scream before you throw. That one almost got away."

Mira followed the old scout to the kill and pulled out her spear, wincing at the gruesome sight. "I'm sorry, Mok, I just got excited. That was the first time I tried a kill all by myself."

"What, Tamur never let you lead before on the hunts?" Zerrick asked, trying to keep the ire from his voice and failing. It was the twelfth day into the journey, and just as he had feared, everything was Tamur this and Tamur does it like that. And of course Tamur hadn't left Mira's side once, but even more annoying was that now Mok had taken over training her as well, and the three of them were having a merry old time.

Not so for him. From the day they had set off, he had felt Angist searching for him. He had stopped all spell casting, remembering all too well the warning that had followed the death of the dragon: "I will track you through the magic!"

Of course the dreams were still there, only now instead of dreaming of future possibilities, he was having a recurring dream of himself before a torture table as a man with dozens of snakes for eyes prodded him with a red-hot brand, demanding over and over, "Tell me where you are!" With such pleasant company for dreams, he could hardly help staying in a dark mood.

"He took me hunting and I observed and acted as a backup spearsman. The other hunters didn't let me lead, but if it had been up to Tamur I would have," Mira replied hotly, standing feet apart with her spear in one hand.

It was a warrior's stance, Zerrick noted, taken unconsciously though it would have been unknown to her when they'd first met. He wished his feelings for her could change as well, but they were just as intense as when she'd first spoken to him.

He had nothing more to say to her, so he turned away and readied a couple of spears to tie the goat to. He then brought them over to the kill where Mok and Tamur were gutting the animal and preparing it for transport. They took the goat while Zerrick and Mira took the extra spears over to where earlier they had selected a campsite among some large boulders on a small rise in the land.

They were within sight of the mountains Darya had described, and while they kept close watch for the infamous Rudra tribe, they hadn't seen any intelligent life out here so far, which was just fine as Zerrick saw it. So far, his whereabouts were still unknown to Angist.

Strangely, it was becoming cooler as they went south. Zerrick had always heard how cold it was far to the north in Endersey, but apparently they were truly on the other side of the world, for on the south slopes he saw a faint blanket of snow. He hoped it would not be too long a journey to the white city; he had never encountered snow, but Alden and his father's description of it hadn't sounded promising.

Zerrick set to raising the tent while Mira gathered firewood and Mok and Tamur prepared the goat for roasting. Thank goodness it was Mok's turn in the tent tonight. The tent only fit two with a third sleeping at the opening and the fourth keeping watch outside. Naturally Mok and Tamur insisted Mira sleep inside every night, and he had to agree. He did not like the thought of her sleeping near Tamur, but it was better than her being on watch all alone, open to attack.

Sleeping next to Mira had become hell. To want her so badly--well, he preferred the nights when he had first watch and slept outside. Burn her, but she was making him crazy. He finished the tent in short order and went off to gather his share of kindling, trying to keep within sight of Mira but not close enough that she would decide to speak with him. Unfortunately, his plan failed.

"There's much better brush over here, Zerrick. Come over, I want to talk to you," Mira called, waving at him. In the twilight the first stars were starting to appear over them, but there was still enough of a glow from the west to clearly see the look on her face. Determination, again.

Zerrick cringed inwardly but went, remembering to keep a smile on his face and to look her in the eye. If she thought she knew all of his tricks in concealing his feelings, she was wrong. They gathered in silence a moment, then Mira said, "I'm worried about you Zerrick. You've been so quiet lately."

Zerrick gave a harsh laugh. "Haven't I always been quiet?"

She shook her head. "Not like this. You don't even talk to Mok, and even he says you are acting strangely, not like you were with him in the village."

"Well, he hasn't traveled with me before. I am very focused on the march, you've seen that. Plus I want to make sure he doesn't find us. Or have you forgotten why we're traveling?" Zerrick answered, gesturing west towards the sunset to indicate Angist.

She placed a hand on his arm. He successfully resisted the urge to pull away, but he could do nothing about the flood of heat to his face. "The dreams still torment you?" she asked in a soft voice.

He had to get away. He couldn't trust his responses if she kept touching him and using that voice of hers on him. "Yes, I still have the dreams. What did you expect?" he said with a snarl, and backed away, trying to grab a handful of thornbrush, mindless of the dry hooks sinking into his skin.

"Oh Zerrick, don't pick those, they throw off too many sparks," she said in an undertone, then more strongly she exclaimed, "Well if you are still having the dreams, why didn't you tell me? Now that it's been discovered that I have some power against evil, perhaps I could help. Maybe I can ward them off, or at least lessen their intensity."

"Thank you, but I'm fine," he retorted, more gently this time. He could imagine how she would try to help, by sleeping by his side, or worse yet, sitting watch over him. It might keep the dreams away, but it would also keep sleep away. The soft sound of her breath, just the knowledge of her presence, so close and yet . . . It would be torture. He wouldn't be able to take night after night of that.

"I'm not so sure. You should see your face. There's been a scowl on it since we left, and worry lines are making a deep cut between your brows. Not to mention the rings under your eyes. I'm concerned about you, Zerrick. I don't want something to happen to you like it did to Svak." She came closer as she spoke, and Zerrick found himself backed up against more thornbrush, this patch too thick to dodge through. There was only one way to escape.

He glared at her. "Why have you decided to care now? There's nothing between us now--we're not courting or anything. You should be concerning yourself with your new man, Tamur. I think it would be best if we leave it like that. I'll take care of myself and you take care of yourself."

The look on her face told him he'd stunned her, so he took the opportunity to brush past her and hurry to the other side of the camp, ignoring the questioning looks of Mok and Tamur. From behind him he heard an indignant "Oh!" from Mira.

"Zerrick come back here! I'm not finished!" Mira shouted when she'd recovered her power of speech, but Zerrick was already on the other side of camp, fast disappearing into the shadows of dusk and the abundant brush. Damn the man!

She'd done it; she'd finally gotten up the courage to speak to him and . . . well she had completely botched it, that was what. He hated her so much he couldn't stand to be near her, and all because of that stupid conversation when she'd been depressed and overwhelmed and had turned down his offer to court. Gods above had she been stupid!

She knew better than anyone how prone to self defeat he was, how the tiniest hint of criticism could mean utter failure to him. And now on top of it all he thought she loved Tamur!

She stomped back to camp and flounced down onto a flat rock beside the newly started fire, setting down her kindling and muttering under her breath.

"Something wrong?" Mok asked in a quiet voice.

He had to have heard them--an army a day's march away would have probably heard them. Trying not to direct her anger at him, she answered in her own tongue so Tamur wouldn't hear, "It's Zerrick. Just when I get him alone to talk, he starts snapping at me and trying to escape. I want to tell him I love him, but he's decided I'm already spoken for by Tamur. Tamur is just a friend!"

Mok nodded solemnly, thinking a moment before he replied. "Zerrick has many problems. Through the magic he feels *Kormu* searching for him, and he feels vulnerable. He does not have great confidence in himself. He cannot love you if he does not first love himself. This will change; it is changing already, but slowly. You must be patient."

"I have been patient!" Mira retorted, this time in Put-na. Tamur jumped and gaped at her. "Sorry," she said to both of them. She put her head in her hands and scowled at the ground while Tamur came over to sit beside her. She ignored the brush of his hand across her cheek.

"What is wrong, Firehead? Has your suitor abandoned you? You know I would never do such a thing," he said in a soothing voice.

"Now don't start that!" She snapped, moving away. Then an idea struck her. "Perhaps you could fix this, Tamur. It's Zerrick. He thinks I've rejected him *which I have not,*" she emphasized, to be sure he understood her feelings.

"Now," she continued, "You and I have been together a lot the past few weeks, which has given him the wrong idea. I'd like you to do is go to him and explain that we are just friends. You will do this if you want to keep your friendship with me." She stared hard at him. So often he had said he found her temper attractive; she hoped he would find it so now as well, and help her.

Tamur stammered and Tamur objected, but in the end, Tamur agreed.

Zerrick sat down on a boulder, the hammering in his skull so intense it was nearly blinding. He was furious! The anger was burning him up inside, turning his stomach into knots and beading his brow with sweat. He didn't even know who he was angry at, whether it was Mira or Tamur or himself. All he knew was that he felt like he was about to explode. The power of his rage was frightening--it almost seemed to be a thing outside himself, though that couldn't be possible, not unless Angist knew where he was. He didn't even want to think about that.

He rose and stumbled over to a small brook to splash water over his flushed cheeks and try to somehow get a hold of his emotions. Mira had wanted him once, hadn't she? Or had it been him pushing at her, until she allowed him that kiss at the river? She could have been deceiving him. Had she pretended affection so that he would protect her and help her to the new life she was now free to lead? And Tamur--but he had always hated Tamur. And Mok, he had thought Mok was his friend, but he had betrayed him to stand with Mira.

That's right, Zerrick, hate them. Hate them all, a voice sounded at his ear. He whirled, but there was no one near.

"Who's there?" Zerrick called out, his rage turning to fear. All was silent around him, just the soft singing of crickets and the rustling of the brush. He turned back to the brook to trail his feet in the water and wallow in his misery, and again the voice came, seemingly just at his ear, *Forget them. You deserve much better companions. More powerful companions. Come with me.*

"Who are you?" Zerrick cried, but he already knew the answer. That voice had a singularly evil quality to it that no other could match; it fairly dripped with it. He hadn't used magic, so how had Angist found him? There wasn't a foul feeling in the air, but the night was growing particularly dark. Should he run and warn the others?

I will have you, one way or the other. Wouldn't it be better if you simply joined me now? No more fear, no more running. I could give peace to you, and power, and freedom to do whatever your heart desires. Just think of it! The words coaxed at him, and he felt his emotions stirring even as he tried to shut the voice out. How had he been found? Was there no place to hide?

He was going crazy, that was it. Or he was being taken over by Angist. If he was smart, he should cast a spell right now to destroy himself. Wouldn't that be better for all concerned anyways? With the voice at his ear he couldn't tell anything--what was real or unreal, whether he was enraged or in despair. He crouched in the stream bed holding his hands over his ears and bit back a sob.

"I have looked everywhere. I cannot find him," Tamur announced, stepping into the circle of light from the fire. Mok handed him a leg of goat which had been cooked through and he sat down, sighing.

Mira poked at her own dinner. "Well, go back and keep searching! I know he has to be out there somewhere!" *Please let him be out there, and all right,* she added silently to herself.

Mok gripped her arm, shaking his head. "Let Tamur rest. Zerrick is hiding, and if I know him, he won't be found until he's good and ready. He's brooding." Mok's appetite, unlike Mira's, had suffered no harm from the evening's events. He had finished off a good quarter of the goat all by himself. Mira wondered how he remained so skinny.

She knew he was right, but she couldn't help worrying. There was something wrong out there; she could just feel it. The night was black beyond their little fire, and Zerrick could be lost, or hurt . . . or possessed. The signs were there. She had seen them. With her strange power, she had seen the shadows Darya had described, surrounding him. Not touching him, not just yet, but so terribly close. He was in danger.

She explained her concerns to Mok and Tamur, setting aside her dinner. Tamur shrugged, looking doubtful, but Mok looked hard at her, chewing thoughtfully.

"Darya thought something of you, something enough for her to take you under her study. And you did cure Svak of *Kormu's* influence. Yes, I think we should heed your instincts. I myself heard *Kormu's* voice taunting him when the dragon was killed. Still I think we would be wasting our time to go look for him. What we should do is coax him back here." He put away his meal and rubbed his hands together, humming softly. Then he chuckled. "I know what would get his attention." He winked at Mira.

"Please, share any ideas you have. I'm about at wit's end," Mira pleaded, cringing as she heard a wolf howling far off in the distance.

"Well," Mok said with a grin, "He once let slip that he didn't know why you never joined in singing with the women at the village, that he thought he might like to hear you sing. Singing might lift his mood, and in addition we could try to combat the evil you sense, with a little homage to either the Mother or your sky god."

Mira brightened. Her power had seemed to work better when she'd prayed, and what song would Zerrick know better than one from church? And if she could chase a few demons away as well as coax him back, well, all the better. It sounded like a fine idea.

"I'll sing, but I'd really appreciate it if you would sing as well--I'm used to singing with a group--we call it a choir." Mira didn't know why she felt nervous. After all, it was only an attempt to get Zerrick's attention. Maybe that was it, actually. Her brothers had never liked her voice--it was too low, they said, too promiscuous-sounding. Supposedly it gave men all the wrong ideas.

"I do not know many of your songs. I'll sing one of my people's songs, then you sing one of yours. I am interested in hearing the difference. While I knew a few borderima, they were not singers and I never ventured into your villages to see your ways--slavery does not suit me," he said, standing and going over to his pack. He pulled out a bone rattle he had used praying before their last hunt and returned to sit by Mira, softly tapping the rattle against his knee, thinking.

After a moment, he began:

Ah Kumara, wo ta ngainma moibu,
Ngai taktata ngeinyima kuri'io poru
Ainji ningri! Ainji ning'ri!
Jamenenu mapo--rlio, dipupo greuntari,
Wo ngainma kumalida tjik'ru,
Wo ngainma kumilida tjik'ru,
Kumara.

The song roughly translated as a cry to the Mother for help, for a sign to the hunter in the grasslands, her flying eagle scout. Mok sang with an eerie high-pitched voice, each beat punctuated by his bone rattle. At the second verse Tamur joined in and Mira tried harmonizing, humming just below Mok's tenor voice.

Once the song was complete, Mira felt bold enough to sing on her own:

Sheltering sheltering arms around
Your people's mind and heart,
The joyous People Thou hast found
Need never be apart.

With gratitude and love we sing,
To Iahmel the One,
And let the sound o'er Great Erde ring,
Make Angist's foul work undone!

O'er mountain, hill and deepest vale,
Our voices chant the Calling,
Deliver brethren strong and hale
Safe from darkest Falling.

Divine Hand which leads us straight
Through life's eternal flow,
We pray to Thee, uphold our fate,
Defeat our earthly foe!

And summon souls to fly to Thee,
To kneel beneath the throne,
And taste the truth at last to see
Our Father's Heavenly Home.

As she sang, she felt the gloom lift, or at least her heart was lightened somewhat. Memories of Pastor Tait gently coaxing her to sing in the choir sprang to mind. She wondered how everyone back home was doing, especially her father and Nanna. If Nanna could see her now. Would she be pleased?

At least she would be proud of how she had handled herself with the Put-na, Mira thought, looking at Mok who smiled back at her, still keeping time with his rattle. Tamur was staring at her in adoration. Well, perhaps not everything was well, but if Zerrick would only listen . . .

The voice had stopped, but the pounding in his head was unbelievable. Zerrick was going to smash a rock to his forehead if the pressure did not lessen soon. Violent thoughts were tearing through his skull, like they had the night he had rescued Tamur's tribe. Damn that Tamur, damn him!! He would settle it right now. He would challenge Tamur to a duel over Mira, see if the fellow was really worth her attentions, and if he wasn't, well then he would kill him. By magic, if necessary.

Zerrick stood up, ripped a few scraggly weeds from the sides of the ravine, and tried to see through the thickness of the night to where the campsite should be. He'd wandered quite a ways off, he thought dully. The pressure in his head was still nagging at him, but with his new purpose in mind, it did not pain him as much. Everything was becoming clearer about him, the features of the rocks standing out in sharp contrast to the tangled brush. Above him the cold distant stars shone in a moonless sky. The cold cut at him, making him breathe in sharp gasps. Oh, what he would do to Tamur!

Something caught his ear: a high, oddly pitched caterwaul. Mok was singing, he realized, recognizing a few of the words from the fellow's favorite scout-prayer-song. But there were other voices singing as well--a man's voice, and very softly now, a woman's. Tamur and Mira, he thought, rage and jealousy again surging through him. He would kill him, he would absolutely kill the bastard, singing with her!

He staggered through the brush towards the sound, but either because of the singing or the awful pressure in his head, he couldn't seem to keep his balance. Zerrick fell to his knees on the cold rocky ground, and his vision seemed to gray out. He found himself sprawled face down.

Then he heard a new song begin--one he could not help but recognize, a song out of the Lost Years of Kazimir. It was a tribute to the song Kazimir's people had sung when they began losing members of their True Followers, the Melians, to Angist's lies on their great migration from the southern deserts to the northern hilly country on the western borders of what was now Endersey. Men had started to believe the lies Angist told, that they should worship beasts rather than the Creator, Iahmel. Some were lost forever and became the Bear worshipers of the Northern Tundra, or barbarians without any religion, but many more were brought back to the fold by the sound of Kazimir's singing.

The correlation to his own predicament was too perfect to be coincidental. Mira must know about the voice in his head, the pressure, the struggle he was having with his emotions.

And her voice! Low, rich like the earth, powerful and majestic, yet utterly soft and womanly. Finally hearing that voice on its own, singing those words of gratitude, opened up a floodgate within him. He felt such longing and love as he had never known before. Yes, love--he could not deny to himself any longer. He absolutely with every particle of his being loved her, and it was killing him inside to have to share her with anyone. Such possessiveness would be abhorrent to her, he knew, but he could not help the intensity of his emotions. Worst of all he did not deserve her, and probably would never be worthy of her.

The pressure was receding; already the rage and his notion to kill anyone seemed like a bad nightmare, fading into nothingness even as he sat up. With sudden clarity, Zerrick realized her knew his position in relation to the camp. It should be just over the rise he remembered climbing on his way out here, over to the left . . . he rose and began walking, and in moments he had reached the top of the rise. There down below was the welcoming sight of the campfire and the tent.

With a clear view of the camp, Mira's voice seemed to become even purer in pitch and tenor, each haunting note of the hymn striking him to the heart. He could just see the dark shape of her figure, outlined by the fire, swaying gently as she sang. She raised her head up to sing the final high note, and he saw in glorious detail the profile of her face and the contour of her throat. The note extended into what seemed like an eternity, bringing tears to his eyes, then slowly faded into silence.

Beside her, staring up with completely adoring eyes, sat Tamur.

The pain was a fist around Zerrick's heart, squeezing the life out of him, the hope. She looked happy with her two Put-na friends, without him. Maybe he should leave them here, continue on alone. With Mok's skills they could surely make it back to the villages.
Of course, that would mean leaving her, never to see her again. . . he shut his eyes to shut out the image of her, so he could think clearly, but he could not shut out the feelings. Alone without anyone, not even Mira, he thought, the back of his throat burning with anguish. He opened his eyes but now tears blurred his vision, turning the campsite info a red ball of misty light. At least the singing was over. If she sang any more, he would surely die of grief.

Unsure now whether he should return or not, Zerrick sat on the ground, shivering in the cold. If he was going to sneak away, he would need his packs. Trying to retrieve his things from a camp guarded by those three, well, it was impossible. He'd never been able to trick Mira very well, and of course the last time he'd tried to sneak up on Tamur the man had nearly killed him. He doubted Mok was any easier. In short, if he wanted to leave he'd have to do so as he was, without anything. He'd be dead within a week that way. Clearly, he was trapped to go on with the group.

I am defeated no matter which way I turn, he thought, holding his head with both hands. Tears slid down his cheeks, but he hardly cared about that. Thwarted at everything he wanted--first thrown out of the village when he had just started to fit in, stalked by evil, rejected by her. Gods, what a failure he was. He bit back a sob, hiccupping.

In the camp he could hear them talking softly and moving about. He scrubbed at his face with his sleeve and tried to swallow the rest of his tears. It was late. They might decide to go searching for him, and here he was, sobbing like an infant. That would never do. He'd better get up, march back over there and reassure them. Maybe Mok could take first watch tonight. He could use a good sleep. At least he wasn't confused about his feelings towards Mira any longer.

Resolutely, he rose to his feet, took a few deep breaths, and went back to camp. It they noticed anything strange about the way he looked they did not mention it, but welcomed him back as if nothing had happened, offering him dinner. Mira looked like she wanted to speak to him, but in the end she simply gave him a friendly hug, saying she was sorry they had fought and they could talk about it later. She looked fatigued, and Zerrick wondered if she had somehow been responsible for that terrible pressure leaving him alone. He would have to talk to her. Tomorrow. For tonight, he was exhausted.

He bribed Mok to take the first watch by promising to return the favor, and crawled into the tent. Mira was already there, but he didn't care.

He was asleep before his head hit the mat.

Mira waited until Zerrick was asleep, keeping watch to make sure the shadows stayed away from him. When she was sure he was sleeping peacefully without any dreams, she left the tent, stepping over the sleeping form of Tamur to join Mok at the watch.

"It succeeded. The shadows have drawn away--for now," she told him, trying to keep her voice calm. That had been too close. When he had not appeared during her singing, but had waited so long . . . she'd been sure she'd lost him. He'd looked like hell, coming into camp with dirt on his face and clothes, his eyes red, but he'd been himself, thankfully. She was going to find excuses to be near him all the time from now on. No demon Lord of Evil was going to take him over.

"I don't want to leave him alone too long, but I wanted to thank you for the idea, and I thought your song was wonderful. You are a very special friend, Mok. I'm proud to know you," she said, shaking his dry wrinkled hand.

Mok grinned. "Didn't get to see too many colonist ladies with Alden, but I must say you're a nice girl, Mira. I hope Zerrick comes to his senses and chases after you again. Don't you worry about him. He's stronger than he looks. I don't think old *Kormu* will get a hold of him."

"If I have anything to do about it, he won't," Mira affirmed. She didn't know why, but the words sent a chill down her spine.

Chapter Twenty-One

"Let Purity be your armor, let Hope be your shield, and let Faith be your sword;
with these three things no evil can defeat you."
--II Ja'hal 12:123

The group reached the foot of the mountains two days after Zerrick's skirmish with evil, just in time to see the first snowfall dust the ground. It was gone before morning, but it reminded them how little time they had to reach the fabled city before winter. No one mentioned his fight with Mira, but she spent most her time with him now. Even though her behavior was a little stifling, Zerrick wasn't going to send her away. It was nice to have more of her to himself,. If her attention was on him it was away from Tamur.

As a matter of fact, she seemed a little upset with Tamur. When she thought Zerrick wasn't looking, she sent little hand signals at Tamur, frowning at him. Zerrick wasn't sure what it all meant. When he tried to ask Mok about it, the man shrugged and said it was all too complicated for him to follow.

Once they had reached the foothills, they made camp in a narrow canyon between two bluffs, both for protection against the cold night wind and to hide themselves from the notorious Rundras. As of yet they hadn't seen any of this elusive tribe, but last night they had seen a line of torches moving along one of the mountaintops. Zerrick wondered if they had their own scrying basin up there like the one from Lookout Peak.

Whatever they were up to, he hoped they stayed well away. He'd been careful not to use any magic or dwell on any negative emotions to attract anything. From now on, he wouldn't even say the Dark One's name in hopes that it could keep trouble from finding them. Since that struggle in the darkness, he'd developed a new focus--get Mira to safety within the city. Camp was made without a fire. Zerrick saw Mira take

Tamur aside and they seemed to be arguing about something, but just as he went over to investigate, he heard Mira say in a fierce whisper, "Do it!" Then she stalked off, shaking dirt from the blankets they would be using that evening.

Tamur looked at her retreating back, then at Zerrick. He scowled at no one in particular. Then he sighed. He strode up to Zerrick, bringing along several small cages of twig and reed.

"You want to help set a few traps for tomorrow's meal? I need to talk to you. It will only take a minute," he said in a gruff voice, clearly unhappy about what he had to say but determined to go through with it. Hope stirred in Zerrick's breast. Was Mira displeased with him? Enough so that he had to ask Zerrick for advice? He liked the thought of that. They went off together a ways and worked together to set the traps, neither saying much. Only on the walk back did Tamur begin to speak.

"I know we have never really seen things the same, and I will never fully trust you, *borderima,* but I do admire how you've left behind the people and customs of your kind to live with the Put-na and learn our ways. I am thankful for your help against the slave hunters. It must have been hard to fight against your own people to help us," he began, drawing lines in the dirt with a stick as they slowly meandered back. The words were spoken as if well practiced, hinting that this was something he'd wanted to say for quite some time.

He responded carefully, "You are welcome. And it wasn't too difficult fighting against slavers. I have never agreed with their ways."

The two of them were silent a moment, and Zerrick saw Tamur was walking slower and slower, trying to delay their return. He obliged by stopping altogether. "Is there anything else you want to talk about?"

"Yes, yes there is," Tamur said, scratching his head. He shifted his feet, glanced up at Zerrick, then down to the ground, then back up again. Finally he spoke. "I don't care if you hate me for it, but I am also thankful you brought Mira to live with the Put-na. I won't deny anything--I love her, and I want her to marry me. But she doesn't want to."

Here it comes, Zerrick thought, his insides clenching. Tamur was going to ask for his help, and he was probably going to wring the little fellow's neck.

Tamur continued, "Mira threatened to stop being friends if I didn't talk to you. She wanted me to tell you she and I are just friends. We are not courting. Why I should be telling this to you I don't know-- you are cruel to her and spurn her gifts. To think she wasted a good stone thrower on you!"

Apparently finished with what he had to say, Tamur stalked back off to the camp, leaving Zerrick standing alone, dumbfounded.

Now what was all that supposed to mean? Zerrick stared after Tamur's retreating back. Spurn her gifts? A stone thrower? And she had sent him to tell him they weren't courting. did that mean what he thought it did? Or that she didn't want either of them--Tamur because of some unknown reason and he because he was cruel? He was more confused than ever! Much as he hated to, he would have to talk to Mira. She might break his heart but at least she would be straight with him.

Resolved, Zerrick strode back to camp.

"So did you talk to him?" Mira asked the minute Tamur returned. She had finished cleaning the blankets and mats and laying them inside the tent, and was in the process of gathering up the spears to be stacked near the entrance--just in case of trouble.

Tamur nodded, looking decidedly unhappy. "I told him everything you said for me to tell him. I even thanked him for his help freeing my people. And I still say I think you are crazy if you love him. I'm going to go make my watch now." He stomped to where two boulders made a narrow exit to the hillside, protecting the campsite. He climbed on top of the taller boulder and sat cross-legged, his back to her.

Mira almost went to him to find out what had him so angry, when Zerrick came back into camp. The look on his face was troubled confusion; at least he didn't look like he was going to fight Tamur any second, but this did not look right. What exactly had Tamur said?

"Uh Mira, could I talk to you a moment?" Zerrick asked with uncertainty. The expression on his face was different than any he had worn before: humble, apologetic, and most of all confused. There was something else there as well, a look of sorrow, and of shame. If only she knew what thoughts were running through that thick skull!

"Of course," she responded, leading him to a small gathering of bushes where they could talk in private and she could keep an eye on Tamur as well. He was still sitting on top of his rock, staring out towards the mountains, not really seeming to see anything. Mok was off gathering tubers. She hoped he would be back soon; the light was beginning to fade.

"Mira I'd like to know once and for all," Zerrick began, then paused. He sniffed the air. "Do you smell something funny? I smell something odd--something I've smelled before . . ."

He stepped away from her and peered around, wrinkling his nose. Mystified, Mira followed him, pulling out her flint Put-na knife. She started to ask what he thought he smelled, but the instant she uttered a word he clapped a hand over her mouth and pulled her against him. He pointed up to the butte above them in explanation.

She saw a four-legged shape creep out from the shadow of the boulders over the butte and out of sight. As it slunk away she saw its tail, and the tail was like a serpent, twisting down the animal's hindquarters. She looked to Zerrick. His face was grim.

"*Ashwa-grippa,*" he whispered.

Death-of-Two-Evils. The creature Nanna had frightened her with to behave when she was little, and that Ranu had taught her prayer-songs against. It was headed towards Tamur; it had to see him from it's vantage point and his attention was turned the other way.

"We've got to help him!" she hissed, wishing she'd brought one of her spears. It wasn't far to the tent and the spears, but they had only seconds before the thing decided to strike. She could smell it now herself, a heavy musk scent in the air, growing stronger. A thought pierced her--was that the only one? Or were there more about stalking them?

Zerrick seemed to be thinking along similar lines. "We'll grab the spears first--if there's more than one, we may be a target, and we'll need the extra spears. I wonder if Mok is all right."

Mira gulped. She'd forgotten about him. But there was no time to worry about him now. She hurried to the tent and Zerrick followed close after, each watching the rocks around them for signs of attack. They reached the spears and loaded up as many as they could carry, four for Mira and two for Zerrick as well as his pistol and sword. Then they heard Tamur scream.

"Hurry!" Mira cried, running back to Tamur's position, hoping Zerrick was close behind. When she reached the spot she had been before, she skidded to a halt. Before her was Tamur sprawled out on the ground from where he had apparently fallen from his rock. On top of him was the nightmarish *Ashwa-grippa*.

The creature's jaws were locked onto Tamur's right arm as he desperately tried to keep it at bay. He struck at it with a knife in his free hand as it shook its head back and forth, tearing the flesh of his arm.

Mira never thought what would happen if she missed. She only thought of what would occur if the *Ashwa-grippa* managed to get around Tamur's arm to his throat. With a cry of defiance she hurled a spear at the creature, and felt a surge of relief when the spear struck true. The creature staggered, the spear sticking out from its side.

Tamur scrambled away as the viper tail lashed out at him, apparently unaffected by the wound. "Hit it again!" he cried, staggering down off the rock towards them. Zerrick handed him a spear which he took in his left hand, holding his wounded arm to his side. He was right-handed, but any good scout learned to throw with both arms.

This time Zerrick responded, charging forward and driving another spear into the creature's back with one hand, then firing his pistol at it. The bullet struck one foot, the report of it echoing off the boulders around them and the creature toppled over, howling in agony, writhing in the dust.

"The noise!" Mira cried, glancing around expectantly, readying herself for attack.

"They can speak--I'm sure this one's already told his friends about us," Zerrick retorted, stuffing the spent pistol into his breeches and drawing his sword.

"So you know of us, little man?" the Ashwa-grippa said, with a gaunt grin. Blood poured from its wounds but even as Zerrick came nearer, it returned to its feet, apparently not ready to die just yet.

"I met one of your kind in the jungle east of here," Zerrick replied, keeping the creature at bay as it slowly approached him.

Its reply was drowned out by the sounds of barking and howling behind them, towards the camp and the other side of the crevice. Mok ran up, carrying a broken stick, covered to his knees in blood.

"Mok, are you hurt?" Mira asked, rushing over and pulling out her shirt from her breeches, ready to tear a strip from it if he needed immediate bandaging.

"No, I'm fine. The *Ashwa-grippa*, however, they did not fare as well," Mok said, panting and grinning. He threw away the stick in exchange for one of her spears and kept his eyes focused on the space behind him towards the camp.

Following his gaze, Mira saw why. Along the boulders overhanging them, several dark shapes paced in the deepening gloom, serpent tails raised in agitation, red eyes gleaming with malice. A wicked chuckle brought her attention back to the beast before Zerrick. Behind him, more of his friends had joined him, slinking out from the rocks, lining the high crag above them.

"We're trapped!" Mira whispered, her eyes locked on the creatures in alarm, a spear in each hand ready to throw.

"Use magic, Zerrick, it's the only way," Mok said, feinting with his spear at one creature ready to leap at him. It backed up, muttering a curse at him in Put-na.

"Yes, Zerrick, call our Master with your magic! Let him know exactly where you are!" one of the *Ashwa-grippa* called at them, sneering. It disappeared under a ridge before anyone could throw a spear at it.

"Don't listen to them. They will say anything to break your will. Your magic is the only way to fight all of them. It may give away our location, by it cannot summon the Dark One himself," Mok hurried to point out as he hesitated. Two more beasts had joined the first wounded one across from Zerrick, and on Mok's side they looked ready to strike.

"Just try it and we'll bring the dragons!" the wounded one said, snarling. Its evil eyes were planted on Zerrick, as if trying to mesmerize him with those glowing red depths.

Zerrick had heard enough of their threats. The magic wanted him to use it, and he was sick of hiding and denying it its wish, denying himself the warmth and elation of guiding it. He'd give them a show they'd not soon forget. Let them tell that to their master.

He was wearing the crystal Hirkumos had given him, so it was easy to draw magic to him, shape it with his desires, and release it. Nothing happened at first. He had asked for that so the *Ashwa-grippa* would be confused, sensing his release of magic with no discernible effect. They growled in confusion and paced around, serpents waving in agitation. Behind him, Mira, Tamur and Mok were each defending a side, their hands gripping their spears tightly. Worriedly Mira's eyes left their vigilance to glance at him. At that second he told the magic to act.

Fire began raining down from the sky, blanketing their foes in an almost liquid stream of heat and flame. The flames did not fall on the four of them however, and also did not seem to have any effect on the natural vegetation, only the creature's living flesh. A beast who had been snooping around the tent cried out in surprise as flames covered it but left the tent alone. It fled to roll in the dust, howling in indignation.

The others were reacting similarly, and as they rolled to extinguish the flames, Zerrick ran forward to stab them. The rest of his group took his cue and ran to attack with their spears, Mira staying near Mok and Tamur, taking only the most wounded ones. The beasts were nearly impossible to kill, but after being stabbed several times, their cowardly nature shined through. They fled, whining and barking, serpent-tails curled up against their backs.

Zerrick and his companions stood panting as the stars began to peek through the darkening sky, watching the fleeing creatures and making sure their threats had no truth to them, that no dragons were lurking the skies above. After a long wait, it appeared they were safe.

"I don't think we should stay here. They've fled for now, but they'll be back, with friends," Mok said uneasily, wiping at the blood drying on his legs as if it burned him.

Zerrick was also troubled. He could feel that dark attention on him once again, and he knew pursuit would be swift and deadly, if it caught up to him.

"We'll march through the night, and sleep through the day tomorrow," he said in a low voice.

He prayed they would make it to the city soon.

Somehow, by luck or by Mira's mysterious power, they managed to avoid any encounters that night, and by Mok and Tamur's scouting skills, they hid during the next day to continue on in stealth through the following night. They were only forced to halt their desperate drive southward when they came upon the first of the three rivers Darya had described. It was very wide, and very turbulent, and it was being watched by the infamous Rudras tribe.

They couldn't use magic to conceal themselves, both for fear of drawing Angist's attention and because these natives had their own *kumalido* trained to detect and deal with such tactics. Instead they would have to rely on their scouting skills and Mok's expertise in escaping detection. "Watch what I do and follow exactly," Mok instructed, handing Zerrick and Mira a grass mat into which had been stuffed brush and twigs to create a sort of camouflaging cover. Zerrick threw the mat over his head, trying not to sneeze at the dust and grass tickling at his nose.

Inch by agonizing inch, they crawled down from their hiding spot behind a butte down to the river. They had waited until sunset to do this so that hopefully there would be enough light to see dangerous rocks and eddies yet dim enough to keep them hidden.

Zerrick glanced to Mira, crawling along on her belly, her hair tightly braided against her skull, her white skin hidden under a coat of mud. She glanced at him, her dark eyes confident. He reached over and squeezed her hand. Then he was forced to put all his concentration back to the task at hand, avoiding detection through the softly rustling brush.

If that river had been difficult to cross, the second one was nearly impossible. Between dragons patrolling the skies and lounging in the shallows of the deep wide river, *Ashwa-grippa* in the brush and several Rundras encampments along the river's edge, the four of them decided not to even try to cross the second river but instead to follow it north, into uncharted territory which was becoming more and more like the desert of Zerrick's dreams.

They kept the river just within sight, traveling by dusk and night until they were away from the watch guards of Angist. Zerrick kept religiously away from magic, and Mira and Mok sang softly their prayer-songs every night. At least Zerrick could see they were making progress.

Their plan was a simple one. Mok figured that a city would need water, so the city of white towers would likely be off of a river, probably the third river seen by Darya in her dream-visions. Since it was also supposedly on the edge of a desert, with no mountains looming above according to Zerrick, Mira and Darya, Mok believed it must be north, away from the Rundras Range. And since the mountain range seemed to hold greater than normal concentrations of Angist's evil servants, north again seemed the best direction, into the flat featureless plains. They would follow the second river until it was shallow and easy to cross. Then they would head due west. Hopefully, if Mok was correct, they would hit the third river and the fabled city just beyond.

After about ten days they reached a part of the river which was easily crossable. The water here reached only their knees, and to follow it further upstream would be to risk losing it altogether into its tributaries. The plantlife along the river was lush despite the cold, but beyond that the plains were only sparsely covered with dead grass and isolated bushes. No trees lived beyond the riverbanks.

"Wait a moment there, Zerrick," Mok called as Zerrick climbed up the riverbank up to the other side. He waited for Mok to finish crossing the river, watching Mira as she made her slow progress across, Tamur at her side, aiding her.

"We're not going to camp here, are we?" Zerrick asked. Mok came up and put his hand to a tree, leaning close to sniff at the wood, frowning at the tree. Zerrick raised an eyebrow, as Mok pulled back.

"No, we'll keep moving. Come here for a moment, I want you to test something," Mok said in a low voice. He seemed unusually subdued. Zerrick wondered what was wrong; very few things distressed the old scout. He hurried over.

"Use your ability--sense the magic in this tree. Does it seem at all peculiar to you?" Mok asked, stepping away from the stunted desert tree.

It looked perfectly normal, with rough brown bark and tiny thorny leaves, but when Zerrick touched it, it felt like the focus trees on Lookout Peak--a huge amount of magic was concentrated in one place. Unlike the trees on Lookout peak, however, this did not feel like a focus plant. It felt perfectly normal, unaltered in any way.

"What?" Zerrick muttered, looking at Mok.

Mok shrugged. "I've always told you I cannot sense the magic at all, and that is true. But somehow, around here I am sensing something strange, a heat or a tingling in the air which seems to come from the trees and plantlife. And not just this tree either. I started noting it a few days ago but it wasn't strong enough for me to say anything. Tamur has also noticed it."

Zerrick ran over to another tree and checked the magic. It too was several times the strength it should be. "Do you think it's because we're entering a desert? That all life energy is more concentrated?"

"Or because we are closer to the Mother?" Mok offered.

That was true. But would it affect the intensity of magic? So many questions, still so many questions, Zerrick thought. To be sure he wasn't somehow being deceived, he tested a few others plants, large and small. All were overly abundant in magic.

Well, he couldn't worry about it now, but he hoped the people of the white city could shed some light on this. Meanwhile, Tamur and Mira had crossed the river. It was time to move on.

Zerrick lost track of the days as they traveled ever westwards across the flat featureless plains. Here and there strange new plants began to show up, including small squat things covered with sharp needles but blessedly full of water which was now growing scarce. His machete found a new use chopping up blocks of that strange plant to carry water with them. Before cutting it however, Zerrick again checked the magic. There was no doubt. The further west they went, the stronger and more concentrated the magic was becoming.

There was hardly any animal life out here, but what life there was elusive and hungry. Dust-colored foxes would trail behind them by day and try to steal their food by night, and yellow and black flying lizards would fly at them if they carried their water plant out in the open, trying to snatch it out of their hands.

They also had to keep watch for other terrors of the air--namely dragons--but in this the smaller creatures helped them, suddenly disappearing from sight and calling out warnings to each other. Then Mok would pull out the mats they had used crossing the first river, and they would all huddle, appearing to those high above like nothing but a clump of brush. On clear days they could still see the mountains to the south of them with tiny dots ever circling the cloud tops above the range. They were fortunate to have left that vigilantly patrolled area.

After many days they caught sight of their goal, the third river, a surprisingly deep and wide river with streams and washes coming into it on each side. There was a cluster of little hills just beyond one of these washes, then the scene Zerrick remembered so well: the vast desert stretching into the horizon, broken by steep plateaus and small mountain ranges, sandy brown earth only sparsely dotted with life. Like many taloned fingers, the streams and estuaries of the river branched out from the distant ranges, flowing now, but undoubtedly dry come summer.

There was no sign of a city.

The four of them walked up to the lazily swirling brown water of the river, branching around a sandbar into a modest sized pond before continuing on. Zerrick bent to touch a clump of weeds fighting to stay green against the oncoming of winter. He was hoping to talk to the magic there, see if it knew anything that could help him locate the city. After all, if there was a large number of powerful *kumalido* living nearby, wouldn't the nearby magic in the plants know? But the magic was strangely silent, almost as if reluctant to communicate with him. No help there.

He was about to ask Mok if he should risk actually using magic to find a direction for them, when the sound of fighting pricked his ears. It was coming from the far side of the first hill. Mok raised his head to the sounds as well.

"*Megrez!* I know the cry of those slime anywhere. Fighting against humans, I'd say," Mok announced in a hushed whisper, head tilted as he listened. He noted both Mira's and Zerrick's raised eyebrows.

"Demons," he said by way of explanation. "Hairy monsters who stand upright but have minds lower than animals. They are servants of *Kormu*," he added, looking at Zerrick. "Use magic to kill them."

"But the dragons," Zerrick stammered, glancing back at the distant mountains and the specks flying above. It was a long way off, but at flying speeds, they could probably reach here all too soon.

"There are humans there. Fighting demons. They may be able to guide us to our destination," Mok said.

Well certainly that changed things. If they could only get to the city before reinforcements arrived . . .

"Let's go help them," he agreed, pulling out his sword and making sure Hirkumos's crystal was secure against his skin under his shirt. The magic there felt sweet and inviting, calling to him. He clenched his teeth to stop the yearning to pull it immediately. Slowly, the urge passed. His abstinence from using magic had been a true test of willpower. Hopefully it would soon be at an end.

While he readied his weapon, Mok pulled out his best spear from the packs and strapped his hunting knife to his waist. Tamur did likewise, while Mira readied several spears to throw from a distance-- Zerrick and Tamur had told her if there was fighting, her job would be to stay out of the thick of it and provide assistance from afar. That would help all the men fight better, knowing she was safe.

The group hurried across the river, using the sandbar to keep to the shallower parts. At the deepest part the three men helped Mira to paddle through. On the other side of the river the sounds of fighting grew clearer and more distinct. They could hear a man and at least one woman's voice, and apparently things were not going especially well. One other thing Zerrick noticed was that their language was neither Put-na nor the garblings of the Rundra tribe.

"Hurry, they're in trouble!" Mira said, changing course now to sprint up the hill for its superior throwing position. The three men charged around the hill, the wind of their speed quickly drying their clothes as the sound of battle rang closer and closer.

They came upon the source soon enough. Two women and three men were fighting a dozen or so short hairy beasts. Just as Mok had said, the beasts ran and fought on two legs, but there the resemblance to humans ended. Their fur was long and matted, sticking out at odd angles, and they were naked, although it was difficult to tell with all the fur. With abnormally long arms they held a simple leather shield in one hand and a long stone axe in the other. A few were weaponless; these simply used their claws and their superior reach to fight. Most frightening of all was their faces--they seemed all teeth, with gigantic maws topped by a tiny upturned nose and slitted black eyes. They spoke to each other in growls and barks.

The humans on the other hand were well equipped, but outnumbered and wounded. The women wore a sort of skirt-trouser which flowed like a skirt but was divided in the leg to allow easy movement. Two of the men wore long loose robes, much like the desert people in the Motherland, Zerrick thought with surprise. The third was dressed with an uncanny similarity to Zerrick himself--linen shirt, leather boots and akiya skin leggings lined with wool. All the men had wide curving swords--real metal swords!-and metal shields as well. The women were throwing spells.

A second passed where those fighting noticed the newcomers, and there was a pause in the melee as they quickly assimilated each other. Then a few of the *megrez* standing nearest sniffed the air, looking specifically at Zerrick. They charged him.

It was only his shield practice with Hirkumos that saved Zerrick. The *megrez* were faster than anything he had every encountered; they were upon him in the blink of an eye.

He threw a simple flash of light into their eyes and parried a blow to his side with his sword, the metal ringing with the force of the attack. He could not dodge a pair of claws swinging for his throat, but the magic worked well enough to make the creature miss its target; instead of his throat being torn out, the claws struck his chest, cutting through the thick woolen cloak to leave bloody scratches down his front. A third one missed altogether. Tamur rushed forward to run it through with his spear. It died, but even as it did, it flailed and screamed in a loud wail, nearly deafening those nearby. One of the flailing claws caught Tamur's calf and he nearly went down on top of it to be shredded alive. Mok managed to grab the hem of his fur cloak and pull him back.

It then became total chaos, with the *megrez* dividing their group to engage the newcomers as well as their original targets, two ganging up against each of the magic using humans. Defending themselves as best as possible from the barrage of blows, Zerrick's party maneuvered themselves towards the other group, in order to build up a defensive circle which would help Mira when and if she decided to begin her strike from above.

After a few exchanges of blows, Zerrick found himself standing beside one of the women, her shield a rosy glow surrounding her, fighting with two ghostlike scythes cutting through the air around her. She was dark of hair and skin, but of a lighter, more olive tone then Tamur or Mok--it was almost as if there was a mixture of Put-na and Zerrick's own people mingled in her. Zerrick was struck by the beauty of her features, but it was a cold beauty, clinical and focused as was her gaze as she cut down one of the *megrez*.

Zerrick was forced to turn away from the woman and back to the foray as a second *megrez* nearly disemboweled him. A spear from above caught the creature in mid-strike, knocking it back and pinning it to the earth. Mira had apparently arrived at her position on the hill.

Around him the fighting intensified. Mok stood facing two demons as the man he'd been teamed up with went down with an injury to his calf. Tamur struggled to hold his own against a sword wielding demon who had already chopped one of his spears to bits. The women looked drained, throwing mostly defensive spells. They needed a larger spell to take out all of the *megrez*. Only he seemed in the position to do it.

But what would defeat them? The force blows and energy bolts and scythe-like blades of power the woman had used were not enough--the demons were that fast. He wanted a spell that could take out as many as possible, despite the fact they were all fighting in close proximity. He would have to direct the magic specifically.

"Can you defend me for a moment?" he said to the woman beside him, putting a little magic into his voice so that hopefully she would understand. Apparently it worked, for she nodded and expanded her shields.

The fact they were fighting magic creatures meant the shields could partially block their attacks, but only partially. Hopefully it would be enough to allow him to concentrate.

He wasted no more time, pulling a large amount of power from Hirkumos's crystal. He suddenly remembered Svak's spell, the noxious cloud which had nearly succeeded in killing the dragon. A vapor that could be guided, concentrated in some areas and thinned to almost nothing in others, yes, that might be just the thing.

A hairy claw swung close to his face, but he could not divert his attention now; luckily another spear came out of the sky, missing the creature but sending it back a bit.

He remembered how the vapor had looked-green, poisonous, almost alive in the way it clung to the face and mouth. He envisioned its suffocating power. He released the magic.

The magic obeyed beautifully, and soon the *megrez* were bending over holding their throats, choking to death. He had forgotten, however, the amazing final attacks of the dying *megrez*. All the demons began to go berserk as death gripped them, and in their fury no one escaped unhurt, though he himself managed to take only a glancing blow to the cheek before everyone circled round to shield him, knowing he must guide the magic to the very end when it was certain each and every demon was dead.

Finally the last *megrez* stopped twitching, and Zerrick was able to let go his hold and dissipate the remaining magic. Mira ran down the hillside to join them, as the five strangers regarded them warily.

Mok tended to his and Tamur's wounds; he smiled at the strangers as he worked, then began trying greetings in several different dialects of Put-na and Zerrick's own tongue. When he tried sort of a pidgin form of Put-na mixed with Endersian--rather like what the slaves spoke when learning their master's languages--the strangers responded. Their language was a curious mix of Put-na and very old, out-dated Endersian. It was odd to listen to at first, but as he got used to the strange accent, Zerrick found he could understand.

"Are you saying you come all the way from the East Range and the jungles? And that these pale-faced two come from the Old World? Such a thing cannot be, not without the help of the Goddess," The man dressed like Zerrick was saying to Mok, who nodded earnestly in understanding.

"A people from a land far to the north of here, across the wide ocean, reached our eastern shore, and they have made towns there, and raised families. These two are born of Argessa, but of foreign parents," Mok explained, raising a hand to Zerrick and Mira. Mira did not seem to be listening; she had a peculiar look on her face and was watching the two women, most particularly the one Zerrick had been fighting alongside.

That woman now spoke. "And possessing magic of the Goddess, trained in Put-na fashion. But very strong," she said, her eyes appraising Zerrick. He looked away uncomfortably.

A far off cry brought everyone's attention to the distant mountains. A cluster of dots had left the swarms over the peaks, and was flying towards them.

"The dragons," Zerrick said in a low voice, "They must have sensed my magic use." Again the women both stared at him, calculatingly.

Mok finished his ministrations. "Please, honored people, we request protection. We have been searching for a city near here, a city of white stone towers. Do you know of it?"

"We are from there," the woman said, lifting her head in pride. "I am called Elemara, a high priestess. My companions are Neckert and Randorf my guards, my mate Horos, and the priestess Janell. You have aided us in time of need. We will protect you, and take you to Alorian." She bowed, her long dark hair sweeping the earth, and prepared to leave, stooping to touch a small sprig of wildflowers with one hand, holding a black stone around her neck with the other. Zerrick saw the transfer of power and realized she was refilling her crystal. He found another clump of grass to do the same.

"Hurry," Horos urged, cleaning his sword with a handkerchief. He was the one dressed similarly to Zerrick, and appeared to be in his late twenties or early thirties, with short cropped hair and a shaven face. "We must warn the watch that an attack is imminent." A shriek from afar punctuated his statement, and everyone began quickly gathering their things, kicking a little dust on the corpses to help disguise them. Perhaps it would gain them a few seconds.

Horos led them around the hill towards the pond, while Elemara pulled some kind of amulet from her bosom and held it to her lips, muttering something under her breath. Zerrick peered ahead, searching for the fabled city, but he could see nothing, not for miles. Then he felt magic stir.

To say he felt it stir was an understatement; there was a gigantic surge of magic all around him, seeming to come from sky and earth at the same time, making his hair stand on end. The area being affected was enormous; it filled his sight stretching from the riverside west to the desert a hundred eighty degrees, but there it did end. Nothing was happening behind them.

A shimmering in the air soon appeared to even the non-witches and they halted, watching the air suddenly become opaque as a city wall of whitewashed stone materialized in front of their faces. Above the thirty foot wall, shimmering air fell away to reveal tower after tower of shining stone--a whole city in fact, right before their eyes.

An illusion. A grand scale illusion needing perhaps more magic than the stairs on Lookout Peak had required. To be able to disguise an entire city! Here he might be able to find a master truly able to help him and answer his questions. He might even learn who had built that shrine on the mountain overtaken by Angist. And the fact they spoke a language so similar to his own--excitement surged within as he watched a great iron portcullis in the center of the outer wall being raised to allow them swift entry, so excited he hardly noticed the sounds of dragons coming closer as he and the others stepped forward to cross the gates.

Chapter Twenty-Two

"Always shall the Truth be discovered, when ye seek with open eyes."
--II Ja'hal 3:14

Inside the walls there was a flurry of activity. People hurried about, readying for battle, manning the ramparts and clearing the town square of common townsfolk, animals, and children. Zerrick noted that the technology here was behind his peoples', with crossbowmen along the ramparts rather than musket men, and catapults rather than cannons. As soon as the portcullis had shut, Zerrick felt the magical illusion enveloping them, but now he was immune. He wondered if the dragons were immune as well.

Apparently so, by the preparations.

Zerrick looked around as his group was led across a wide town square over to a series of marble steps before the edifice of a grand temple of white stone. The roof was arced into a high dome, and on each corner stood a slim rounded tower, tipped with a brass sphere shining in the desert sun. A wall ran from the building to a grove of orange trees with a gate into an inner courtyard, and over the wall Zerrick could just glimpse a full temple compound, with long dormitories, more trees, and what looked like some kind of school. The architecture was all hauntingly familiar--like his own people, but using more curving lines, more circles and arches and s-shaped curves where his people would have used angles and straight lines. He suddenly recognized the style--Western, from the spicelands and sultans' lands of the deserts. Ancient styles.

He drew his gaze back to the temple doors as a woman emerged, flanked by two muscular men with bare chests holding halberds. She strode up to them, only glancing briefly at the commotion in the square. By her white robes lined in silver and gold, Zerrick guessed she must be another priestess. By the elaborate necklace around her neck, and the grey streaking her long black hair, she was probably a high priestess. Magic glowed all around her.

Elemara stepped forward. With a low bow and a wave of her hand to indicate the group, Elemara introduced them. "Grand Priestess, this is Zerrick and Mira, born of Argessa, parents of Endersey, Mok of tribe Besprii, and Tamur of tribe Kutjari. They aided us in fighting a hoard of demons outside, and indicated a wish to enter and know of us." She turned to Zerrick's group. "The Grand Priestess Travina will determine your worthiness to stay in the great city of Alorian." With that, she bowed and stepped back.

Travina raised one hand bedecked with jewels, and a glow spread from her fingertips to gently touch and explore each of Zerrick's party. He felt a shock as it encountered him, and a million questions seemed to enter in his head as the magic searched for answers. Hirkumos had told him of this spell, so he forced his nerves to calm and carefully answered why he was here, who he was, of his travels, his apprenticeship, his successes and failures. The skill with which the priestess handled the magic, the extreme gentleness of this much power told him she was far more powerful and more skilled then Hirkumos. And pure-feeling, somehow. He had never felt magic with such . . . serenity . . . before.

Once the magic's probing had moved to Mira, Zerrick turned back to the courtyard where he could hear beastly growls. Men dressed in close fitting leggings and padded doublets with strange spectacles over their eyes lead out two enormous beasts. Griffins, Zerrick thought in amazement, seeing the bird-like head topped with a furry mane, lion-like body, and metallic golden wings shining in the sunlight, stretched out and ready to fly.

As soon as the square was clear, the men climbed onto the beasts, perched atop like children on haystacks. With three mighty thrusts, the first griffin beat its wings and took to the air. A crowd of onlookers cheered it on, then the second one took off. Zerrick shook his head in wonder. To have creatures like that tamed and trained to fight! Truly this was a city of magic.

The Grand Priestess's voice brought his attention back to the group. Several armed men had arrived, and Zerrick listened on as the Priestess instructed for them to take Mok and Tamur to the city watch tower, to learn what news there was from their ancient friends the Put-na. Next she addressed Zerrick, indicating Mira, "Is she your woman?"

"Yes," he answered immediately. This was a large city, and there was no telling where Mira would end up if he didn't claim her right now. Amazingly, she didn't protest, merely nodding in a subdued manner. He wondered if there was something wrong; never had she been this quiet.

He could not dwell long on it, however. Elemara and the Grand Priestess invited the two of them into the Temple to discuss his abilities, as the screech of dragons and the roar of griffins echoed above them. He looked up, hoping to see what such a battle must be like, but the women urged him forward, saying they had only a few moments to speak with him before they joined their magics to the city's defense.

They entered into a grand foyer with stained glass windows and a domed ceiling and Mira was taken aside by Elemara's companion Janell. Mira could see Zerrick wandering through the foyer to the temple beyond, his neck craning as he sought to take in every detail of the beautiful architecture. *He's in heaven here*, she thought, pain stabbing at her breast. She doubted he was even aware she was not at his side.

"You are not able to work magic, so you will not be allowed into the Inner Sanctum where they will test your companion. Still you must be a remarkable woman to have traveled so far, into such dangerous territory. I and my sisters are dying with curiosity. Will you sit with us and talk? I can offer you food and drink," Janell said in her odd accent, speaking slowly. Mira was getting used to the mixture of Old Tongue Endersian and Put-na, but it was still very difficult to understand.

She glanced at the great doors they had passed through, muffling the sounds of battle. "What of the dragon assault? I might be able to help somehow." In truth, she felt she was out of her experience, but she didn't want to hear that she was useless again.

Janell guided her away from the door, shaking her head. "We would prefer you stay out of sight right now. The dragons must sense that there are strangers here. That is why they attack. I would not want to endanger you or provide them with information to take back to the Dishonest One. Come. Drink with us and relax. There will time enough for helping us, later."

Mira looked to the girl's dark eyes lined with some kind of black substance, at her tawny complexion and dark red lips curled up in a smile. She looked like she could be trusted, Mira thought. She just wished all the women here weren't quite so beautiful. And Zerrick with the most lovely of all, green-eyed Elemara.

Well, there was nothing she could do about that. At least she'd been smart enough this time to keep her mouth shut when Zerrick had claimed her. She would be near his side if he needed any help. For now, she might as well try to make a few friends.

If only Zerrick's claiming of her had been true.

Zerrick looked in amazement at the stained glass dome ceiling, at the frescoes and mosaics along the walls and floors, and at the exquisitely carved wooden doors. This was workmanship right out of the Old World! True civilization! Even Mother would have approved of the beauty of it, despite the fact this was a temple of worship to the Goddess rather than Iahmel.

The priestesses led him off to a room behind the altar--the Grand Priestess's personal chamber, it looked like. Like the rest of the place, it was richly furnished with ancient-looking tapestries hung on the walls and a stained ironwood table overlaid with glass, on top of which was set a crystal ewer and two pewter goblets. Zerrick wondered at the opulence. Where had all these fine things come from? Were they made here or traded for somehow? Where were these people from?

Elemara and the Grand Priestess took seats on a low chaise across from the table. There were no other seats, so Zerrick assumed he was to remain standing. They observed him coolly, and for the first time he realized he was alone. Where had Mira disappeared to?

The Grand Priestess must have noticed his look of alarm. "Do not fear; your lady is in the other room with some of our acolytes. I wished to observe your powers in a safe place. You'll note the shielding surrounding this chamber."

Zerrick blinked and glanced around him. Sure enough there it was, a fine impenetrable shield tangent with the walls, so finely woven it was nearly invisible even to his Othersenses. Did power and mastery like this come naturally here? Or was it due to their open worship of Ainéra? He turned back to the two women and flushed as he saw them staring at him, measuring him. He couldn't help the jibe that followed, "Shall I dance for you now, priestesses?"

The Grand Priestess chuckled while Elemara glared. "Actually, I would like you to perform at least one trick. Please, if you would, catch this," the Grand Priestess said with a smile. She threw a potentially lethal bolt of lightning at him.

Hirkumos's lessons immediately kicked in; he pulled from his crystal to form a kind of net and caught the bolt, holding it in mid-air between his hands. Only then did he have time to feel the shock, the utter amazement. Never had he seen an attack so quick, smooth, and controlled. And powerful--the strength of the bolt could have killed all three of them and destroyed half the room. If she had been pulling from nature, it would have drained a small tree. Yet she'd hardly even blinked.

"What was . . ." he started to ask, but Elemara cut him off.

"It would not have killed you had you failed. Look at the magic there. What do you see?"

What? Zerrick thought, scrutinizing the energy within his net, as it slowly drained more and more power from Hirkumos's crystal. Thank goodness he'd refilled it after the *megrez*. Then he saw what Elemara was talking about. This was not a true lightning bolt--the magic had subtly altered it from a killing energy to an energy which would certainly knock one unconscious and possibly paralyze them for a time, but not burn or harm them in any way. He concentrated on looking deeper. Was that what they wanted, or was there something deeper?

He searched it with his senses, trying to see if there was anything else unusual about it. The magic was unbelievably pure, for one thing. It was also still under control by its *kumalido*--which was tied to the Grand Priestess, but also to something else--something outside the room, which was connected to . . . Zerrick blinked, and stared. The veil! This energy had its source from behind the veil! But how? He looked to the Grand Priestess with stark amazement. "How are you pulling from beyond the veil?" he asked in a choked whisper, half afraid of that holy presence from the mountaintop warning them away again.

The Grand Priestess smiled and the lightning vanished. Zerrick ended his containment spell gratefully, beginning to feel slightly dizzy.

"So you can see it. Excellent." The Grand Priestess stood and crossed to him, looking him over with new interest. "The test is over. Join your woman, refresh yourself. I must see how the fighting goes. The acolytes and novitiates here can answer any questions you may have." With that, she bowed her head at him and Elemara, then departed the room through a small door in the back corner, almost totally hidden by hanging tapestries. Zerrick realized it was from there that the Priestess's strange 'link' to the veil had come from. Another mystery.

At least he felt he was on the verge of having everything answered. These people knew about magic. They also knew about the Goddess, hopefully in detail if the legends were true. He would just have to be patient. He followed Elemara back into the main temple and to the side room where Mira, Janell, and two young women in simple blue robes were chatting amiably. He sat down on a chaise across from Mira.

"And?" she asked, leaning forward, "Do you think they can help us? And will they accept you?"

Zerrick glanced at the women. "I'm not sure yet. It seems hopeful. At any rate, they certainly know about magic."

Mira nodded. "They were just explaining to me how they brought many of their treasures here from the Old World at the time of the Flight."

"The Flight?" Zerrick asked. Apparently Mira had been gathering some information during his examination.

"Janell here told me her people come from the Empire of Al'Tuon, nearly eight hundred years ago! They are the remnants of that empire which fell after Ja'hal's forces defeated their main army and killed the sorceress leaders. After that war their realm fell into ruin, and when the barbarian hoards of the Second Age came, they fled here with the help of their magic and Ainéra's guidance. There's a lot more to the story, they say, but Janell says there is a thing here called the Book which tells it all. Incredible, isn't it?"

The ancient Empire of Al'Tuon? Truly then these were followers of the one and only Ainéra. But those sorceresses had been the enemy in the war of Ja'hal's First Coming. They had killed five of Ja'hal's brothers and had been in league with such monsters as dragons and serpents, which seemed then and now to follow Angist. They possessed undoubtedly the greatest magic known to man. But was it a pit of vipers?

Mira finished, "So anyway, that's why this temple is so richly decorate. A lot of these pieces are very old treasures from the Western Empire. I just thought that was fascinating." She smiled and sipped some tea, apparently unconcerned that she was sitting and chatting with the ones Endersey had called the Unbelievers, the Cursed, and other, worse names. That ancient Empire had tried to take over the world with its magic, and nearly succeeded. Should he be training here with these people? Again he wondered if magic were a path which lead inevitably to Angist.

And yet, these people were at war with Angist. The sounds of battle could still be heard from outside, and the magic did not feel evil here. And he could not believe the Goddess was evil. Could he?

There was the sound of something exploding outside and a hideous scream, then Zerrick heard people cheering. Janell stood and glanced out the stained glass window, squinting. "It appears we are victorious--I see the griffins landing. The dragons must have fled; otherwise we would have felt the ground shake at their demise. They crash most spectacularly."

Elemara stood before Zerrick and Mira and regarded them. "You'll soon be able to go outside. We shall find lodgings for you in our dormitory here." She smiled at Zerrick. "Then your training will begin.

Mira paused in her folding of the linens, watching out from the balcony of the long whitewashed stone dormitory which housed young witches and their families. From her vantage point she could see a corner of the Temple, the city wall, and beyond that the distant grey mountains and their continual shadows of clouds. The dragons were never far away.

She sighed. In the two weeks since they had arrived, she had been alone much of the time, contemplating the bizarre turns her life had taken.

Though she and Zerrick supposedly shared the modest room here, she had seen very little of him. The priestesses seemed almost to be training him for battle--for eight hours a day they worked him vigorously in magic, drilling him until he was a walking ghost. He ate his meals in silence then fell asleep the moment he reached the bed. He probably didn't even notice her sleeping beside him to keep the dreams away. The dreams did need to be held at bay--the one evening she was out late chatting with the acolytes, she'd returned to find him drenched in sweat, clawing at the bedcovers in terror. It took her nearly an hour to calm him, and through it all he was dead asleep.

Mira wasn't sure what she thought of the priestesses. The acolytes were friendly and fascinated by her, and they all seemed innocent and wise at the same time, but the full priestesses seemed to have too many secrets. Yes, they were helping them, but something felt askew in the city. She had gone to the market and been stared at frequently. At first she thought it was her red hair again, until she saw not all the people of

Alorian were dark skinned or raven-haired; while rare, there were some darker blondes and auburn brunettes.

On her last trip, she had heard some gossip concerning Zerrick. Two women were betting on his chances of survival. There had been more, but they had been speaking too quickly in their strange dialect for Mira to understand. It was then that she began noticing how few men there seemed to be in the city, especially in the Temple. Zerrick had magical talent as had his teacher Hirkumos and his earlier master Alden. Magical ability was not restricted to females by any means. So why hadn't she met a single male witch here? The Temple was full of women, but the only men were boys under fighting age, interestingly enough.

She wished to discuss her finding with someone, but it was rare that she saw either Tamur or Mok, and when she did they could do nothing but talk about the marvels they had seen here. Everyone seemed drunk on magic. Everyone but her.

She finally summoned up her courage and confronted Elemara one day in the courtyard, just after the priestess finished her lessons with Zerrick.

"I find it interesting," Mira said in a polite tone, "That you should find Zerrick's training so important to spend so much time on it each day. I also find it odd that he seems to be the only male *kumalido* here," she added, using the Put-na word for witch as they might not know the Endersian one, or know it and find it offensive.

"You are very astute. But your friends said that of you, that you could see things others could not. And not through magic," Elemara said, staring at her with those intense green eyes. Mira repressed a shiver.

"I only want to know the truth. I am thankful for your hospitality and your help, but I am concerned. There seems to be a shadow over the whole city." Mira had thought at first the shadow was perhaps a faint glimmer of the illusion shielding Alorian, but that pressure in her head had repeatedly told her it was not. It was not that she thought the city was evil. Like Zerrick's shadow, it seemed they were under siege, struggling but not yet conquered.

Elemara nodded with sudden understanding. "We are fighting a desperate war. Did you know there used to be a sister city of our people to the west of here? We believe they have fallen already; it has been forty years since we've had contact with them. As you saw for yourself, it is dangerous to be anywhere outside city walls, but even so, we should have had some contact. We are all that is left now of Ainéra's people."

Well, that was more than she'd hoped for from the woman. Mira decided to keep probing, "So the males died in battle? Is that why there are only females in the Temple?"

Elemara grimaced, her dark red lips twitching. "The battles account for the ratio of women to men among the non-mages. But among the mages our main fear is the Dream."

Mira's stomach turned to ice. Not that again. "What happens to them, exactly?"

"We have been talking with Mok, and we know the Dream is not unique to us now, but unlike the *kumalido* in the Put-na villages where one could ignore the summonings, the call here is too strong to resist. They must either depart to answer," she swallowed, "or go mad."

Mira gasped. "So that's why you're training Zerrick so quickly! But the dreams--I keep them from him. He shouldn't have to go. Should he?"

Elemara's eyes narrowed. "So that's how he's managed to sleep. But you haven't stopped the Dream entirely, only lessened the intensity. He is still having them, and it makes him anxious to learn as much as he can. He will have to either return back to his people where hopefully the dreams will leave him, or he must go to the Goddess."

They paused as Zerrick emerged from the training wing across the Temple courtyard, his hair in disarray, eyes turned inward. He stumbled once with fatigue and nearly passed them by before catching sight of them. "Good morning. Night. Whatever," he mumbled, raising a hand halfheartedly to greet them. He had a three day growth of stubble on his cheeks. As Mira and Elemara stared at him, Zerrick seemed to take notice of their sudden silence. "Is something wrong?"

Elemara answered for Mira, "Your woman was expressing concern for the way we have been training you. I think she now understands the necessity of quick, extreme training."

"Not entirely," Mira interjected, refusing to be brushed aside. "I still don't think training to the point of exhaustion is necessary no matter what the circumstances. How can one even retain any learning if they're asleep on their feet?"

"Believe me, it does help," Zerrick answered unexpectedly, and now as Mira looked at him she saw the shadows surrounding him growing darker, more sinister. "There has been interference every time I try to draw large amounts of magic. Him, I think. Being exhausted lets the lessons sink in without conscious thought. Helps keep the dreams vaguer as well." His speech was somewhat slurred, but at least today his mind seemed more alert.

He still wasn't thinking clearly enough for her. "What do you mean 'interference'? Why haven't you told me so that I can help? I can keep that away, you know. And there are other things we needed to talk about that we couldn't because you were too tired. Have they explained to you yet why you're the only adult male witch in the city?" She saw his eyes widen and knew she had gotten through to him, at least at the mention of being the only male witch. He blinked a few times, apparently trying to clear his head, and turned to Elemara for explanation.

Elemara was good, Mira had to note; she didn't appear flustered in any way. She merely wetted her lips and folded her hands. "Because most of our men have already left to answer the calling to the Dream, we found it most important to get as much training done as possible before answering questions. As you both are curious, however, and since the training has been going well," she smiled at Zerrick in a way Mira found all too familiar for comfort, "I think I could arrange for the two of you to see the Book. The Book will answer most of your questions about us, and about our Goddess."

Zerrick's eyes lit up and new life seemed to stir in him. He was practically salivating as he asked, "Yes, can we see that? Where is it?"

"It is in the north tower. But you are in no shape to see it right now. Get some rest. I'll schedule an appointment with the Grand Priestess to take you there tomorrow morning." She glanced at Mira. "You may come also, although there is a test that you must pass before you handle the Book." She turned back to Zerrick. "I'm sure you'll have no trouble passing." With that, she turned and left, her long silk robes fluttering behind her. Mira tried not to scowl at her retreating back. Meanwhile, Zerrick yawned.

"Well, at least we'll get a few answers from them," Mira said with a sigh. She led Zerrick back to their room before he could collapse where he stood.

The next morning they waited in the Grand Priestess's private chamber behind the main temple. Zerrick held hands with Mira and keeping a small shield of magic over her. The hand holding was not necessary for the shield to work, but it eased his mind of the way he had been neglecting her lately, and it would hopefully keep her in line, for they would be crossing potentially deadly magical traps and protections--thus the shields. Normally non-witches were not allowed inside this room, but special consideration was being granted to her, as long as she stayed right at his side. She hadn't been too happy about it, but she was complying, wearing a tight smile he knew was false.

He felt almost normal today, after sleeping a good ten hours. He felt somewhat guilty about it. He hardly had been company for Mira lately, but she'd hadn't said a word about it to him. She seemed resigned to being ignored next to his magic training. He wished he could explain the reasons for his obsessive training. He wasn't even sure if she'd been sleeping beside him or not.

What he'd said about Angist interfering was true. Just as the god had warned, whenever Zerrick used a large amount of magic, he drew that negative attention to himself. Within the city, Angist couldn't send creatures to destroy him, thanks to the shields, but he could plague him with visions, jabs of pain, waves of fear, hoping to break his concentration so that he'd lose control of the magic. Zerrick thought the god hoped magic would kill him.

Nightmares, daymares, it all seemed to be running together now, horrible messages assailing his mind at every turn. He had to be strong; he had to be able to fight. There was little question of his course. Angist would never leave him alone, no matter where he fled. And whether Ainéra was out there or not, he had to do something to stop this madness. He only wished he were certain that if he won, he could find peace.

At least he'd found a safe haven for Mira. He knew now that he loved her, but it was better that she not know. If he failed in the quest, if he died, it would be better if she never knew the pain in his heart. She was a survivor. She would live on.

The little door at the back of the room opened and the Grand Priestess, Elemara, and two other priestesses emerged. Zerrick stood straight, giving Mira a little squeeze with his hand for her to mind her manners. She had to become assimilated with these people. There was nowhere else for them to go. He hoped she understood that.

The two priestesses came to stand on either side of himself and Mira. Mira inched towards him, looking nervous. He hastened to explain.

"It's all right--in the part of the Temple where we're going, there are traps and magical safeguards to deter any evil creature who might get into the city from wandering around the Temple." He wished he had spoken more to Mira of his lessons. He had learned much of both magic and the culture here, at least within the Temple. It was formal, perhaps even more formal than his Father's Great Church in Endersey, but with that discipline came amazing feats. Magic here could make wonders like that dais on the mountaintop as well as the stairway and vision-giving basin. Here, however, it was untainted, as of yet.

He felt Mira's grasp relax somewhat, and she glanced at him, then they followed Elemara and the Grand Priestess through the small door into a long hallway. This led back deeper into the Temple complex. They passed doors here and there to the right and left, climbed up stairs, and continued around a mazelike path, finally ascending a long spiraling staircase up the north tower.

They came to a large oaken door. A flash of magic flew from the Grand Priestess's hand, undoubtedly to disarm an alarm or traps, then she gently turned the handle and entered, motioning Zerrick and Mira to be silent as she stepped through the door. The sound of heavy breathing came from one corner of a large dimly lit room filled with shelves of books and scrolls. At the far end of the room, reminding Zerrick of Alden's little library, was a great old book on a carved stand, covered with several layers of glistening magic shields.

A muffled snort warned them than something was waking up.

"Still asleep at this hour of the day?" the Grand Priestess greeted the room's hidden occupant, her voice gently chiding but somehow also respectful. Zerrick wondered if perhaps there was an old wisewoman or man living up here with these old books. But the noises the occupant was making did not sound human.

Nevertheless it did answer in a youthful, silken voice, "It is still early; the sun has hardly cleared the city wall. You have visitors, Travina?"

Zerrick blinked at the familiar use of the Priestess's first name. This was Someone or Something very important, to be addressing the Grand Priestess in such a manner. He looked at Mira and saw the curiosity sparkling in her eyes as well.

The Grand Priestess led them all into the room to stand in the center which had been left clear of shelves or furniture.

Zerrick glanced around for the source of the voice, but apparently its owner was behind one of the bookshelves. Once everyone was in the room, the Grand Priestess closed the door. "She can be a little shy. Move slowly and keep your voices lowered," she whispered to Zerrick.

"I am not. I simply wanted to see these visitors of yours for a moment. I also like a good entrance," the silken voice came now from their left, and suddenly a spell of illusion which had been masking the source dropped away. It was an *akiya*, but such an akiya Zerrick had never seen. Its hide was bright blue and faintly glowing with magic. It had apparently been born with crooked antlers--the antlers had grown the wrong direction, intertwining with each other to form almost a single horn, albeit a fairly crooked one. Its eyes were bright orange.

"What exactly are you?" Zerrick asked in a whisper, using now his other senses to gaze at the creature. This was where the Grand Priestess's great power had come from; this creature had some kind of link which allowed it to draw magic from beyond the veil. In fact, as Zerrick looked, he could see the creature itself somehow seemed wrapped within the veil, a part of it.

He realized how his inquiry must sound and grimaced, but the creature surprised him by giving a sort of giggle, sounding like the tinkle of tiny bells.

"Do I look interesting to you, human? You look interesting to me as well. Been tangling with the Deceiver lately?"

Zerrick blinked, taken aback, and turned to the Grand Priestess for explanation. He feared asking the creature itself. Was this some kind of wild beast he hadn't encountered before? Or a guardian of some kind, specially summoned by magic?

"Zerrick Dhur, let me introduce Andress, my familiar. She is a guardian spirit of Ainéra. Please show her your highest respect. Besides being my familiar she also acts as Keeper of the Book," the Grand Priestess said, bowing to the familiar and motioning that Zerrick and Mira copy. He did so, mystified but unable to ask the questions that were nagging at him. Did the term 'guardian spirit' mean what he thought? Was this an immortal spirit like those described living in Heaven? Who were there at the Beginning along with the Dual God, helping to organize things? It did seem to fit the respect the priestess was granting it. He swallowed in a suddenly dry throat.

"My Mistress appreciates the fact there are still those of her former mate's people who believe in and follow Her. She would have liked to have met you in person, but of course She is detained." The orange eyes darkened to deep red for a moment, as the familiar bowed its head.

"But come. You wished to see what they call around here 'the Book'. Her diaries." The familiar led Zerrick and Mira over to the book stand, dispelling each of the shields with a few murmured words and an intricate wave of magic Zerrick couldn't hope to duplicate. Mira was trembling at his side, but he could not stop to comfort her. His own heart was pounding loudly in his ears. The Goddess had kept a diary?

He came forward, pulling Mira along, ready to immerse himself in the enormous vellum-paged tomb, but the familiar held him back. "Wait. We must verify your worthiness and purity of heart. This goes for the girl as well. Please, let go her hand. She will be safe. Rest your hand upon the Book."

Zerrick looked now to Mira, giving her a squeeze of the hand and a heartfelt look of encouragement before letting go. She looked a little pale but was keeping a brave face. God, he loved her. But he dared not show it.

He turned back to the bookstand, noting the age of the diary. It had been rebound in thick leather but many of the pages were wrinkled, torn, and some were even a little singed. He wondered if those pages perhaps told of the Burning of Al Tuon's main city of Agrigadian after Ja'hal defeated the sorceresses. Ever so gently he laid his hand on the cover.

At first nothing happened. The leather felt cool and dry under his fingertips, completely ordinary. The next second, however, he could feel heat coming up through the leather, up his arm, to his heart. "Free me!" He heard as clearly as if She were again standing beside him in the dreams, Her frustration and fear beating at him. Then the fear seemed to subside, as if She were just now aware of his presence. A gentle searching, a friendly spark of recognition. Then the sensation faded, and it was just a book once more. He felt somehow refreshed, less burdened by the continual badgerings of his enemy. A happy sigh escaped him.

"It is pleasant to feel Her, is it not. She dreams, you know, in her coercion. Dreams while in captivity. But in any case you have passed. Please step aside and let your companion forward," the familiar said, inclining its head and pointing with its crooked horn towards Mira.

She came forward and curtsied gracefully, but there was iron in her voice, "My name is Mira, Keeper of the Book. Pleased to meet you."

Apparently she'd gotten tired of being called 'girl' and 'companion'. Zerrick hid a smile, then sobered as she went to place her hand on the tomb. What if she didn't pass?

It was too late to warn her about the possible consequences. She laid her hand on the red leather hide. Nothing visible happened, but consternation crossed Mira's face, and she looked like she was trying to pull her hand away. She did not seem in pain but she seemed uncomfortable. Zerrick debated rescuing her, but at that instant whatever had been holding her released her. She stumbled back in her haste to get away, swallowing. When she looked to him and the priestesses, she flushed with embarrassment.

The familiar seemed also flustered. "Well I guess we should have expected it, but you startled Her, girl, with your link to Her old . . ." the familiar cleared its throat. Zerrick raised his eyebrows at Mira.

"Iahmel is where I'm getting my powers to keep back your dreams and it's how I drove out Svak's demon, Zerrick. But I also believe in Ainéra. Still, I think I offended Her, reminding her of Him. I guess all the old stories are true." She looked down, shifting her feet awkwardly.

The familiar cleared its throat again and spoke. "Not offended, but touched Her in a raw spot, Mira. Still, there is no evil in you. We do not generally allow Melians to enter Her domain or peruse Her writings, but I believe with the circumstances we can make an exception."

The familiar stepped over to Zerrick, motioning for him to come forward. "Go ahead, then. Take a look, and have your questions answered."

Mira stayed back from the book, looking over Zerrick's shoulder as he carefully opened to page one.

The first pages were nearly unintelligible--they were written in what must bee an archaic tongue with letters reminiscent of present day ones but far more elaborate. Zerrick pulled a little magic hoping to translate them and make his own faulty reading skills better, and found for the first time ever, he could read perfectly. He extended the spell to affect Mira as well.

At first She seemed to spend a great deal of time expressing dismay at her situation, being self-exiled from Heaven, along with a number of her spiritual servants. There was the grief of separation, the rage against both Angist and Iahmel--Zerrick could not read such personal sentiments for long, but had to skip much of it. In Her emotion she sounded almost human. Almost. The things She had done to Herself in Her misery no human could have survived.

After what must have been several hundred years, She came out of Her depression, and began making contact with the residents of this world She had helped create. For several hundred more years She came to know all the creatures of nature, both magical and non-magical. Then She turned Her eyes to mankind. Her diary related efforts She made to teach the young human population the basics of civilization, hoping once they were educated She could use their strength to battle Angist, who had not been idle during Her years of sorrow and had gathered many men and beasts to his service.

It was a mirror image of history. But while Iahmel's followers in the Holy Book had seen her efforts as corruption and purposeful deception as She created societies of nature worshipers, She saw it as a struggle to teach respect of Creation and the proper use of Her gifts. All too often, however, Angist did corrupt what She began, and many of the societies went so far from the truth they no longer worshipped Her or Her mate at all, only beasts or gods they themselves made up. It seemed the logical thinking and planning gifts had belonged to the Iahmel aspect of the Dual God, and Ainéra, the intuitive, emotional aspect, was sorely handicapped now without Her other half, subject to making mistakes, sometimes grave errors. She could not effectively fight Angist's lies.

As in the downfall of the Empire of Al'Tuon. The Goddess wanted humans closer to Her own strength, needed more equal companionship. She was lonely and afraid, for there had already been battles between Herself and Angist, and he seemed invincible while She lost more and more of Her original divine powers with Her exile from Heaven.

The Sorceresses of Al'Tuon did grow incredibly powerful for mortals, and they began to defeat and take over some of the barbarians Angist had gathered. But then they became greedy and prideful. When their Empire touched the Melian's Emirate, they ignored Ainéra's warnings and invaded. Ainéra watched Her gifts corrupt Her people, then saw destruction claim them, when the Melians with Ja'hal as their leader counter-invaded and destroyed all that She had made.

Zerrick's magic was hardly needed for this part--while the language was archaic, letters at least were nearly the same as his own culture's from the Holy Book. He read aloud just in case Mira was having trouble deciphering these pages which were water damaged and singed.

"I realize now that my Gift corrupts; the power magic bestows upon mortals is more than most can accommodate with purity of heart and code of morality intact. I must therefore leave the world of humans, that I might avoid inadvertently harming them, for where I am, there too is the great magic."

There followed here a debate over whether She should go alone or with her closest followers who had remained loyal and good-hearted. They would face certain persecution if left behind but also an uncertain future in the wilderness if they followed Her, and would be cut off from civilization.

This internal debate lasted years, and while it went on Ainéra wandered the lands, looking for a suitable place where She could exist in peace without fear of influencing humans, especially civilized people who were more dangerous with their innovations. She had less contact with Her followers during this time, and immediately saw their views about Creation and Her change as they forgot what She had taught them.

This made up Her mind--She wanted and somehow in Her heart needed at least a few of Her created humans to know the truth about Her and Her ideas for a perfect civilization.

She found a place--a barely inhabited continent to the south, with men whose lifestyles was barely above beasts, and a place so far removed that a city could lay there undetected for many years. This was two hundred years before Ja'hal's Second Coming, a full eight hundred years from when the problem has first arisen of leaving the inhabited lands. Naturally the original followers had died, and indeed their children and children's children had suffered great persecution from the various factions that now controlled the lands, but they had managed to stay intact as a culture, wandering the lands as gypsies and traveling healers. This did not concern the Mother--She saw only the larger picture, that these people were Her children, and would be protected.

What She had seen elsewhere in the Old World had hardened her heart against staying. This was now the time of the Barbarian Hordes which swept across every land, pillaging cities and destroying order. Many 'witches' in the truest sense--untrained, half-mad people stealing Her energy were causing chaos, blind to the good they could do with such power, merely serving themselves. It sickened and appalled Her.

She had determined also that wherever She went, magic flowed from Her to build up in the rocks, trees, and plants around Her. In the southern continent, She could remain indefinitely while Her magic was slowly used up in the inhabited lands. Once used up, the men there would be free to grow as Iahmel had always wanted, by their own talents. Without magic.

For a while, it worked. With Her powers, Ainéra had no trouble transporting Her people and all their possessions and treasures, both those they had managed to keep and those the new governments had seized from them from the ancient empire. She helped build the city, weave the enchantments to conceal it, then dwelt there. Angist at this time was busy persecuting the second Ja'hal, so for a time, there was peace for Ainéra. She soon became bored, and seeing the simple beast worshipers who called themselves in their own tongue simply the People, the Put-na, She decided with Angist elsewhere, it should be safe to teach them at least a little, raise them to a higher awareness of things.

She went on yearly visits to teach the Put-na, and also built for them a holy place where they could contact Her during the times She was away. *The dais and the scrying bowl!* Zerrick thought with amazement. So Angist had taken over that place. He glanced at Mira to make sure she was still following along. She was avidly reading on her own now as the language became more and more like what the city now spoke.

Zerrick resumed reading, *"It is now winter, year 3436 by my reckoning. I returned a few months ago from the tribes Tunan, Mu-ata, and Maporlio to find my city besieged. The north wall was in ruins and fires were breaking out all over the city. And my people! They were terrified; their screams and their terror echoed within me."*

Zerrick read the detailed account of the damage and deaths. Each one was a personal blow to the Goddess, by the pain of Her words, *"Little Demora, daughter of Priestess Mariss and Stonesmith Kelson was lying upon a smoldering pile of rubble when I found her. I pressed her small body to my breast and let the rain clouds swirl above me and pour down with the tears of my grief."*

It was the dragons, those creatures Ainéra described as Angist's first friends; greedy, power-hungry and self-centered creatures who acted as messengers for Angist. Angist himself was recovering from the battles with Iahmel's avatar, the second Ja'hal. Once Ainéra was back in Her city, the dragons' attacks lost their effectiveness and there was peace, for a while. Until that time finally came when Angist recovered his strength.

"An icy wind came out of the east this morning, as I made my rounds of the city. The sun shone weakly behind a veil of grey clouds. At first I did not recognize that chill, that old cover of dimness and confusion which he uses to hide himself. After all, I had not seen him since I fled his lies in the lands of Al'Tuon. But as I watched the darkness flow over the Rundranian mountains I recognized the Nameless One's aura. He spoke to me, cursing me as his mother, laying hatred on me for his tormented existence. He is here to defeat me and my people, once and for all." Thus came the challenge, and thus the battle began.

The rest followed the story that Darya had told Zerrick. A group of Put-na came in the midst of battle when the Goddess's visits with the tribes were long overdue. Ainéra did not allow them to fight but instead only observe, saying, *"My forest children have never known the evil of war, and I will not now willingly subject them to learning the horrible art."*

The last few pages were after a particularly hard battle when the goddess lost her head priestess, chillingly enough, to the Ravenger, which was apparently real and still living from the first Ja'hal's time.

"I buried Sardara today. So many dead, so many dying every day. I am a Creator, but death is part of the Order I and Iahmel originally created. I know that their souls are untouched, but they are never the same as the mortal humans were, living. Too many I lose to Heaven, never to hear from again. My heart is heavy.

Angist is still out there, hammering us down, biding his time for a final strike. My people cannot last much longer against him. I will have to leave these protective walls and confront him. I must somehow defeat him. Yet I fear I cannot. After all, I created him. At least, he sprang from my body; I cannot see how such well-meaning intention could create such utter hatred, such rage, such suffering. He cries to me in my heart--he tells me if I could only come to him, be with him, I could reform him. But he is utterly foreign to me.

I go now to attempt a last stand against evil. Iahmel, my love, I wronged you so very long ago. I know that you shall never forgive me, but I beseech you, look after my children. I hope I can write of triumph tomorrow."

The rest of the pages were blank.

Chapter Twenty-Three

"Fear not, my children, but be true."
--Ainéra's diary

Zerrick looked up from the great Book, eyes strained and shoulders cramped. He glanced around the tower room, noting the two priestesses sitting at a small table quietly talking, and at the familiar who had gone to sleep curled up on the floor. Elemara and the Grand Priestess had departed.

How much time had passed since he began reading? He had fallen under the spell of the Goddess's words. He wasn't even feeling hungry, yet by the light of the sun, which had been slanting through the east windows and was now slanting through the western window, he knew he had missed at least a meal or two. Was it even the same day?

He stumbled away from the bookstand, blinking to relieve his eyes as Mira finished reading, looking around her with confusion.

"Do you have any questions now, my good humans?" the familiar asked, startling Zerrick. So perhaps it was not asleep after all.

Zerrick shook his head. It was too much information all at once. He needed to go think about what he had read, all the implications. Oh, what his father would have thought, reading this! To know it was all real, quite real. And now he knew beyond a shadow of a doubt that he must do as the Goddess had asked of him. She must be set free. But how should he succeed, when so many before him had failed?

"I do have a question. I know that I must complete my journey and at least attempt to rescue Her, but I don't know how I can hope to succeed with the Evil One holding Her. Am I simply destined to live on with nightmares?" Zerrick asked, kneeling before the magical creature.

Its bright orange eyes softened with sympathy. "There is help for you, if your heart is strong. That day you met Elemara fighting the *megrez*, she was trying to call down one of Ainéra's spirits from Heaven. She failed because she doubted her power. But you can try. I am a spirit, and my job is to allow my mistress a direct link to my Goddess. That is, a direct link to Her magical power."

"I saw that power, behind the veil," Zerrick exclaimed. "But when I got too close to it I heard the Goddess's voice, warning me away. She said I wasn't ready."

The familiar nodded. "Without a familiar spirit to control the amount of power flowing to you, you would have been overwhelmed. Destroyed, most likely."

Zerrick gulped. If Ainéra hadn't protected him there on that mountainside, he would have perished and Mira would have fallen . . .

"So let me get this clear--with a familiar spirit by my side, I have unlimited supply of magic," Zerrick said, standing and moving aside so the familiar could rise to its feet.

"You are limited only by your ability to shape it."

"You can't be thinking of going after Her, Zerrick! Now that we know all this, what you're up against," Mira said in a shrill voice, coming out of her stupor. She crossed the room to stand in front of him, her brows set in lines of fury but her eyes full of fear. Zerrick's heart contracted painfully.

"I must. I can't live like this, tormented by both of them." He wanted to reach out and embrace her; he wanted to imprint the memory of her touch on his soul. It was likely he wouldn't return. But if she knew that, if she saw the fear in his eyes, she'd never allow him to leave. As he'd said, he had to go, especially with this new, intimate knowledge of his Goddess. Her suffering, Her pain, all cried out to him. Truly now he could say he worshipped Her, for She knew the same kinds of alienation he had experienced, the same sense of not belonging, of being cast out. And She was good, even as Alden had said.

"Then I'm going with you."

Zerrick shook his head, and came forward to give her a quick awkward hug. "Not this time. You can stay here, or you can return to the Put-na when Mok and Tamur decide to leave. But there is no way you'll be coming with me on this journey."

Mira looked ready to argue, but she shut her mouth, her expression shuttered. Zerrick sent a prayer to Ainéra that this time Mira would do as he asked of her. He would not be able to take a step towards that distant mountain prison if Mira was with him. She must live.

There was nothing else for them to say to one another, and now Zerrick's stomach was beginning to realize how empty it was. He made his way towards the door and the two priestesses rose to accompany him. Then he remembered the familiar, standing quietly by the Book. "When should I attempt to call the spirits for a familiar?"

The familiar laughed, a gentle whinny. "Ready so soon? You are a brave one." It stepped over to him, cloven hooves making clacking sounds on the stone floor. It sniffed at him, then looked into his eyes. "You are tired and hungry. You will need to be at full strength to attempt your calling, so you should wait a few days to rest and learn the way to envision your plea. A party will accompany you outside the walls and the shields."

Zerrick nodded. "The magical protections block the call. I'll be ready then. Will you be with me as well?"

The familiar shook its head. "As Keeper of the Book, I cannot leave the city protections. That was why Elemara tried to call down another. Apparently her need was not grave enough, but I would think that yours is. Elemara will be the one to take you, and she will teach you how to call. I will you see you again if you succeed. Fare you well, until then," it said, then pressed its neck against him in a sort of embrace.

At the mention of Elemara, Mira had muttered something, but now she came forward to follow Zerrick out. She seemed deep in thought, or perhaps she was angry with him, for she kept her eyes lowered and pulled away when he reached to take her hand. She seemed to realize that he was only trying to lead her again past the magical guards for she sent an apologetic look at him, and allowed him to clasp her hand. Together, they left the tower.

Three days later, the sun rose in a cloudy winter sky, providing a bleak light upon the frost-covered landscape. Zerrick shivered in the frigid breeze as the magic shields went back up over the city, leaving himself, Elemara, and several fighters of both sexes standing by the bluff of rock outside the city. He had thought knowing of the illusion would make him immune to it, but now that he was outside the magical barrier, the city was once again invisible, except for a very faint sheen of magic which could be mistaken for normal nature.

Mira was within the city. She had not spoken to him since reading the Goddess's diary. She'd made her ire known to him, however, stomping around the bed chamber and slamming doors wherever she went. As of yet, however, she hadn't asked to move to other quarters. Undoubtedly she was punishing him for planning to leave without her. But if she thought this would make him change his mind, either about going or making her stay, she was mistaken. There was no budging him this time.

A wolf's cry in the distance reminded him that there was no time to waste out here beyond the protections. He could feel Angist's presence stronger and nearer, and aware of him, just begging him to use magic and leave himself open. Hopefully the mental guards Elemara had taught him would keep him safe.

Elemara brought out a spyglass and surveyed the distant mountains. "The dragons are taking to the air. They know you are out, Zerrick. Begin the Calling."

Zerrick sat on the ground and Elemara stood beside him to act as protector from the monsters that would surely come the moment he used magic. This was Angist's best chance to strike at him, and he would use Zerrick's spellcasting as a beacon to summon creatures just as he had when Elemara had Called. It had been no accident that her group had run into a group of *megrez*.

The fighters took up watch points around him, using hand signals to communicate with each other so their voices would not be distracting.

He began. He closed his eyes and reached up and out with his mind, as he had when searching for magic on the mountainside. Finding the Veil was much easier this time, thanks to his training and better understanding of magic. The Veil shimmered and gently waved as if in an ethereal breeze, beckoning him, but he was not going to let himself too close this time. He had been right. What lay beyond the Veil was in fact Heaven, and whatever his troubles, he wasn't quite ready to travel there.

He secured the links to his body then began to pull magic directly from the ground beneath him. The magic in crystals might be more concentrated, but only magic directly from nature would be able to keep him anchored. Elemara had repeatedly warned him that if he lost connection with his body, he would die.

Once he had the magic prepared, he sent a line of it directly into the veil and called with his mind, *"Oh great spirits of Ainéra! A servant of the Goddess requests your aid. Hear my call. I am Zerrick, born in Harrow in the land of Argessa, trained in magic by Alden who is passed on, Hirkumos of the Put-na tribe Kutjari, and Elemara of the city of Alorian. The Goddess calls me to come free Her but alone I am weak! I need a spirit to guide and assist me. Is there one who can come to help?"*

Back through the link to his body Zerrick heard Elemara warning him that the dragons were coming, and that magic was stirring along the river. Demons would soon be upon them.

He returned his attention to the task at hand, listening now with all his being for an answer. All was silent in the world of the mind. Coldness seemed to creep up over him and he was aware of a great dark presence approaching. It tried to blot out his access to the Veil. He desperately reached out despite his growing fear. He mustn't fear; Elemara said nothing would go through colored with negative emotions. He must trust her and her comrades to protect him.

"Please, any spirit who hears my call, I need your help. You must know that Ainéra is in great trouble, held by the Evil One. She has requested my help but I in turn need your help. Is there a spirit there who would agree to become my familiar?" It felt to him like he was shouting the words, driving them into the incredible barrier of the Veil. From the other side it probably came across as a whisper.

Forces were pulling him back to his body. He could hear shouts and groans, the sounds of battle. Elemara was telling him he must come back, there were too many, and the dragons were coming.

"Just one more minute. Give them a chance to answer!" He said aloud in a weak voice. That simple physical act nearly pulled him away from the Veil, but he fought with all his will to stay up, where he could hear a response.

The seconds crawled by.

Pain flared in his thigh, and fear again assailed him, a deafening roar in his ears. He blanked out his mind, he clung to hope.

He prayed.

Then a wonderful sense of peace came over him, washing away fear, warming the coldness creeping in on him. He heard a bubble of laughter, and felt an incredible sense of joy, of recognition and acceptance.

"Get back to your body, boy, and let's get to safety!" A light tenor voice said with a gentle mental tug.

With a start he opened his eyes to find himself quite firmly back in his body, holding a bundle of fur and--of all things--blue scales. He carefully lifted it to see a pair of glowing amber eyes and a small pointed snout.

"Well, don't just sit there, get up! Let's flee this carnage!"

Zerrick held the strange creature to his chest as he rose, just as a demon's axe sliced the air where he'd been sitting. Elemara threw a bolt to flatten the offending demon.

All around them there was chaos, as men battled beasts similar to those *megrez* but apparently more powerful, though they were less numerous. These creatures had horns and long whip-like tails which they used to distract their opponents, striking at the men's faces while they attacked with crude stone axes.

Elemara placed herself before Zerrick and ordered the retreat, her shield expanding to protect him. He noticed a shallow cut to his thigh, while around him, a circle of guards continued to fight, defending against a storm of blows. A shriek from above told them the dragons would soon join the fray.

Elemara pressed her talisman to her heart and muttered the prayer Ainéra had long ago made the password to Her city, and the illusion came down. The group now retreated in haste, running to where the gate was slowly opening. Zerrick squeezed through with Elemara, then one by one the fighters came through. A couple of demons managed to get past the portcullis but were soon shot down by city guards with crossbows.

Elemara put back her talisman and the portcullis slammed shut, the illusion restored. Zerrick took his furry burden to a safe area under cover lest the dragons decide to attack, and contemplated it.

It unwound itself from the ball it had been curled into and sat up on its haunches, revealing a stomach covered entirely in bright blue scales. It looked like an opossum from the Old World, with a long snout, tiny eyes and a long curling tail. Its hands were long-fingered and dexterous like a monkey's, and on either side of its neck, there was a bright pink sack, like those Zerrick had seen on the throats of some birds--some kind of voice pouch. Its back was covered in soft brown fur, but beneath that its skin was hard and scaly, especially around the tail which was black. Sitting up on its haunches, it was only about two feet tall. Zerrick touched the scaly abdomen, and a single scale came off, clinging to his fingertip. He regarded the creature's glowing amber eyes. "A karuneeb?" he asked incredulously.

The snout wrinkled in distaste. "Well it certainly wasn't my idea, but a fellow up there insisted on it." It regarded its tiny hands. "At least I have opposable thumbs."

Its voice was beautiful, Zerrick mused, just as Alden had described that day so long ago, on the day of Vera Smith's sentencing.

Strange, his magic gave him no guilt any longer. Perhaps he had at least defeated one fear within himself. Magic might be dangerous, but it by itself could not corrupt him.

"What is your name?" he asked, unsure how to address the rather diminutive familiar spirit.

It shrugged. "I don't know. I have a name among my kindred, but it isn't one you can really pronounce. How about Tibit? Fits the form, anyhow."

Zerrick bit back a smile, not sure how he was supposed to act with such a familiar. It seemed more down to earth than even Mok.

He was about to ask more of it when Elemara came with a number of priestesses. "The dragons are returning to their lairs and the demons are either slain or shut out. Come, Zerrick, come holy spirit, now it is time for celebration. There is a table laid out in the Temple courtyard."

She led Zerrick and Tibit into the courtyard which was packed with people. Zerrick saw Mira off in a corner, looking forlorn. He tried to go to her but suddenly found himself surrounded by a crowd of strangers asking questions of him and his familiar, all touching both of them for blessings. Apparently his success was a great sign to the people.

It was over an hour before he could extract himself, and by then Mira was nowhere to be seen. He didn't know how he knew, but he was sure she was really upset this time. And he was getting to know her well enough that he knew he had to confront the problem or she'd nurse it for days and come back to haunt him with it. As tactfully as possible, he made his exiting remarks to Elemara and the crowd, picked up Tibit from where he was being admired by several beautiful priestesses, and left for his room.

Upon reaching his quarters he found the door open. He crept in, uncertain. The room was tidy, with a settee, table and chairs, and a vanity by the bed in the corner. It was unlit except for sunlight streaming from the open balcony overlooking the courtyard and the festivities. Mira sat in a wicker chair by the window, her face turned away from Zerrick, half in darkness. She was crying.

Cold panic washed over Zerrick. He let Tibit off his shoulder onto the vanity where the familiar sat, regarding himself in the mirror. Once Zerrick was certain his familiar was occupied, he went to Mira.

He fought the urge to reach out and hold her. "What is it? Are people not being kind to you here? You can always go back to the Put-na with Mok if you don't like it here. You're always free to do whatever you desire." He dared not ask if he himself was the cause; he was shaken enough at the sight of her distress. He couldn't remember ever seeing her shed a tear.

"You won't let me come where you are going. You've got your familiar now, and you're going to leave me and go to your goddess. I've heard the stories. I know the chances of success are slim. And you won't let me help you!" she said with a hiccup, refusing to look at him. The trail of tears down her cheek sparkled in the afternoon sun.

Oh, she thought her tears would sway him, was that it? Though it twisted his heart to see her so upset, on this he was not going to budge. "No, I absolutely cannot allow it."

She grimaced. "Then I am not truly free to do as I want, am I? Instead of my brothers I have you."

That hurt. But deny it as he might, it was true. "I won't forbid it. But I will beg. I beg of you, do not follow me, or come with me. I beg of you with all my heart, please stay," he said, punctuating each word.

"Why?" she cried, standing. "What reason could you possibly have for making me stay? I can defend myself now. I can fight!"

Zerrick almost blurted out the truth, that he loved her, and that was why she couldn't come, but it wouldn't help her to know that; in fact she would probably insist on coming if she knew the depth of his feelings. "It's not important," he said instead, trying to keep his angry front, afraid she might see the truth if she actually looked at him. "All I can say is that I cannot have you with me in that much danger; it would interfere with my efforts. You, at least, must live."

Mira turned and stared at him, and he knew he had said too much. Before she could ask him any further questions which might be disastrous to his resolve, Zerrick dipped a bow to her and went to fetch his familiar which was now playing with Mira's brush. He could feel her eyes still on him, but she wasn't asking the feared question.

"I have to go speak with the Grand Priestess about my familiar spirit here, Tibit. I'll be back later," he said, hovering near the door. He waited a moment, wondering if he should say more, wondering if she would speak. Silence was a vast desert between them. Finally he added, "It is very important that you understand I don't mean to give orders about what you can or cannot do. But I do care about you and I will not endanger you."

With that, he fled the room.

The priestesses decided that Zerrick should make his departure in two weeks to head for the desert and the Goddess's prison, hopefully still fresh of mind and not pressed by fear into desertion. Zerrick spent again his days in intense training and his nights in the blissful slumber of the totally exhausted. He saw almost nothing of Mira, and this troubled him. When he did see her, she spoke to him only in monosyllables. He went so far as to ask the spirit what he should do, but the little fellow shrugged his tiny shoulders and said even the immortal ones could not understand a woman's mind. Zerrick only hoped she would do the right thing. He was afraid that rather than saying too much about his feelings he hadn't said quite enough--he longed to tell her everything. But it was probably for the best. Despite his familiar's cheerful demeanor and constant attempts to keep things positive, even he didn't sound terribly sure about their mission.

"We can do it, if we believe we can," the familiar said when pressed, "And if we don't make it, well, Heaven is a lovely place. I'm sure you'll like it."

After one day's particularly hard lesson on handling energies transferred directly from the Veil, Zerrick had to ask a question that had been niggling at him, "When you first appeared, you said someone had directed you to take this form. I had a dear friend who recently departed this world. His name was Alden. Did he--"

"I do not disclose secrets of the afterlife. That is something you'll have to learn for yourself some day," Tibit said gently, his whiskers twitching.

Zerrick ran his fingers through his hair which was now growing so long, it was embarrassing. Girlish, some of the priestesses said. The familiar made a chittering sound.

"And stop that frimping!" It said, then laughed, flustered. "I mean--" it paused, curling its tail round its tiny hand, searching for something to say, "--oh, never mind."

Zerrick stared at the karuneeb. It couldn't possibly be . . . no, he didn't even want to contemplate it. The spirit was right; it was something better learned later, in the afterlife.

Thereafter Zerrick and Tibit talked about many things, such as what Zerrick had seen on his travels and the ways of the Alorian people, how they seemed so similar yet so different from Zerrick's people. He did not again bring up mention of either Heaven or things Tibit knew of that otherworldly place. Tibit took heartily to his physical existence, gobbling down sweets of any kind with relish. He also sang as often as possible, delighting in the sound of his voice, singing snatches of songs in tongues Zerrick didn't know, songs from distant lands and times. The familiar kept Zerrick's spirits up where he would have been in his lowest depression.

The dreams continued on.

Finally there was no more training he could do, no more information the priestesses could offer. He was hardly eager to set off again to face the wrath of both the dreams and Angist's creatures, but there was no point in waiting. The desert would be easier to cross in winter, the people were becoming impatient, and without the training now to exhaust him, there would be little or no sleep at night. He gave notice to the Grand Priestess that he would begin his journey at her discretion. She set the day three days hence, so that a party of guardsmen could be readied to travel with him, and that a ceremony of parting could be held.

When the call went out for guards, Mok and Tamur came to Zerrick to be included. He met with them in the orchard by the courtyard among citrus trees, covered to protect them from frost.

Tamur looked almost civilized in a leather jerkin, woolen tunic and akiya hide leggings. He had kept his beard and long hair, but these were now trimmed and braided in the local fashion. Mok on the other hand still wore his full Put-na regalia down the bone rattle hanging from his neck. Both looked well fed and rested.

Mok came forward to give him a friendly slap on the shoulder and a hug; Tamur politely shook hands, then Mok began to speak, "I know you will probably object, but I want to be included in your guard party. Just think of it! To be the first Put-na to see the Mother Goddess in generations! It is the chance of a lifetime."

Zerrick frowned, wondering how to quench the scout's enthusiasm and convince him to stay. "Mok, you do realize this will be incredibly dangerous. I'm not going for the pleasure of it, but to preserve my sanity. I was rather hoping you could stay and take care of Mira. You know, in case something happens to me."

Mok surprised him by laughing. "But do not you see? That's the main reason I must come--to make sure you live. I'd never hear the end of it from Mira otherwise."

Tamur added, "She's the one who insisted we come." He looked down at his feet, reddening.

So that was it. Mira thought if she couldn't come, she could at least make these two come in her stead. Apparently she had accepted the fact she wasn't going, at least. Zerrick was so relieved he almost said yes immediately. But there was still one thing to consider.

He took Mok's arm, "I suppose you can come, but I'd prefer at least one of you stay, in case Mira decides to return to Kutjari."

Tamur shook his head vigorously. "I will not travel all the way. There has been talk that they will use the griffins to send you at least partway on your journey. I'd like to come with you to that part where you continue on foot. I can then come back with the griffins and help Mira if it becomes necessary."

Zerrick blinked, trying not to gape. Rarely had he heard so many words out of Tamur. Mira had to have coached him--that was the only explanation. It would also explain how he knew so much about the expedition. If there was ever a person who could hunt out information, it was Mira.

He couldn't think of an argument against Tamur's offer, so he simply nodded, throwing up his hands. "Well then, I guess the two of you will be coming, at least part of the way. I and the Grand Priestess will be meeting with the guard party tonight to discuss tactics and routes in reaching the 'Jagged Grin,' that circle of mountains where Ainéra is supposed to be held. I'll make sure you are both well out-fitted for the journey."

"I'm sure I'll make a splendid guard. Never too old to learn a new profession, eh? I'll make sure none of *Kormu's* minions touch you. Defend you with my life, in fact," Mok said, throwing his shoulders back, his hand fisted holding an invisible spear.

A chill passed through Zerrick's heart.

"Let's hope it never comes to that."

Mok gently patted the griffin's soft feathery fur as Zerrick adjusted his new heavy winter cloak given to him at the Ceremony of Parting the night previous. That ceremony had been one of the most boring affairs he'd ever attended, with more praying, singing, and speeches than even his father had given on holy days. It was necessary, Elemara said, because it maintained the people's ties to their lost Goddess and gave them hope. He did wish they hadn't looked on him with such desperate need. It reminded him that many of them had lost sons and brothers in previous attempts.

The gift-giving had been as grandiose as the speeches. He now had a heavy cloak from them as well as the light one from the Put-na, two new pairs of akiya hide breeches, several new linen shirts and woolen waistcoats, a scimitar--they had laughed at his thin sword--a light buckler, breastplate, helm and sturdy serpent-skin boots. He felt a bit ludicrous. After all, how much hand to hand combat was he really facing? But the priestesses had insisted, reminding him of the demons, dragons, and other creatures of Angist. He needed the protection most of all.

He'd allowed himself to be dressed as a hero out of days of yore, fussed over by townspeople, blessed with holy artifacts, and kissed by what must have been every priestess in the Temple. Thankfully, Mira had been absent. She might have kissed him too, and that could have led to another scene like that in the river. He was a little concerned, however. She hadn't slept in their quarters last night, and he hadn't seen her all morning. He just hoped he would see her before he departed.

"So where's Tamur?" Zerrick asked, watching the griffin handlers attach stirrups and flight harnesses to the animals' backs while the beasts dug into their morning meal, a freshly killed akiya each.

"He's helping to groom one of the griffins over there," Mok said, pointing to the last griffin down the line. Zerrick caught sight of Tamur's back, his long black hair streaming down his shoulders. He had been given a new winter cloak as well, Zerrick noted.

"Tamur finds these beasts fascinating. He's been studying them since we came, and he's even considering staying here permanently in hopes of becoming one of the Riders," Mok stated with a chuckle, busily checking his packs.

Trying to picture Tamur in aerial combat on such a beast was difficult, but stranger things had happened. "And have you seen Mira around today?"

Mok looked down, licking his lips. "Uh, no, not today. I did see her for a few minutes last night. She wanted me to give you this." He brought out from his pack a brooch of carved ironwood, in the shape of the star of Ja'hal, with the two agate hoop earrings of Nanna's set into the wood, creating a double hoop design while the agates formed a "v". The workmanship was exquisite--probably either Tamur or Mok helped her carve it. The agates were empty of magic from the last time

Zerrick had used them, but they could easily be refilled. A precious parting gift.

Why hadn't she come to give it to him personally? "Did she say anything to you when she gave it?" he asked Mok, trying to get a clue about what was going through Mira's mind.

Mok shook his head. "She seemed a little choked up. She just gave it to me, saying I must give it to you today, then ran off. Did the two of you have a fight?" He closed up his pack and strapped it to his back. Around them, Riders were putting the final fittings on the saddles, checking straps to be sure they were secure.

Zerrick flushed, fastening the brooch to his cloak. "Yeah, something like it. She wanted to come along and I wouldn't let her. I still won't let her, if she spoke to you about trying to change my mind." He stepped aside for a Rider to pull the griffin he had been petting away from the remains of its meal, to strap on the bridle gear.

"Ah, mmm," Mok said, rubbing at his grizzly beard.

Zerrick started to ask him what he meant by that, when a blare of horns sounded from the Temple. A procession of priestesses led by the Grand Priestess and both familiars, the smaller one riding the larger one's back, stepped out of the Temple and came towards him. His stomach knotted. Was it time to leave already? He hadn't said his goodbyes with Mira yet! Turning around, he searched the town square for signs of her lurking about among the crowd gathered to watch the departure, but didn't see even a strand of her famous red hair. She couldn't have decided to let him leave without even a glimpse of her, could she?

Apparently so, for she was nowhere to be seen. Should he delay their parting and try to find her? Should he consider letting her come?

His gaze hardened. No. This was probably a well-crafted plan to make him give in, to force him into letting her join. But this journey was too dangerous, and despite her skills with the spear she was not up to the challenge. She could be hurt, and possibly killed. He had seen it in countless dreams. After that he would die, without her. The rescue attempt would fail.

He would not back down. He would show her that one could go too far, pushing him in this way. So if she wanted to punish him by not showing up, fine. He would go on as planned.

She would probably show up at the last minute anyway.

The Grand Priestess halted the procession a few feet from the first griffin, and the Riders and guards gathered around to listen to her words. Mok and Zerrick were herded up front, and Zerrick tried not to be obvious as he scanned the lines of priestesses for Mira's face. Nothing.

He pulled his gaze back to the Grand Priestess as she came forward for the final Ceremony of Parting. He knelt, head bowed, as she pressed her palm to his forehead. Magic flowed from her into him, blanketing him in a golden glow.

"As thou art a sorcerer, and as thou hast heard the Calling of our most Holy Goddess, we name thee Nemite, follower of Ainéra, and from henceforth belonging to the city of Alorian. And as thou hast determined to undertake this quest of utmost importance, we thank thee. May thy strength never fail, thy heart never falter, and may thy quest be successful. In the name of Ainéra, Holy Mother, Amen." She raised her other hand as she spoke, releasing tiny droplets of water conjured by magic to fall on his head and shoulders.

"Amen," the priestesses and the crowd murmured. The Grand Priestess released him, and the magic settled into the ground beneath him and into the crystals he was wearing, filling the agates in Mira's brooch.

The Grand Priestess then turned to the Riders and guard party and addressed them similarly, blessing each of them by name and again sprinkling the magic and therefore holy water over their heads as a group. All heads were deeply bowed in prayer, including Mok and Tamur, though Zerrick could barely see Tamur back at the edge of the group, his face half covered by his hood. He wondered what thoughts were running through his head. He should be happy he'd be returning back to Mira alone.

Once the blessing was complete, Elemara came forward to give them instructions. "Be aware there may be pursuit from the dragons. Do what it takes to throw them off, then head for Angel Spring, preferably under cover of night."

She turned to Zerrick. "Last year we sent a party from there to try to reach the mountains you described. We've found it impossible to go closer by griffin. The closer you come to the Goddess, the more concentrated magic becomes as She has been trapped in one place, emanating Her gift. Magical creatures within a hundred miles of Her begin to act strangely, and nonmagical ones mutate. You'll find your control tested as well."

Zerrick nodded. This had all been explained to him, as well as steps he should take to protect himself and his party. She was saying it now so that the guards and Riders understood the dangers they would be facing.

Once she'd given that warning, Elemara stepped aside for the Grand Priestess's familiar to come forward. On its back rode Tibit, furiously writing on a piece of vellum. He seemed to realize where he was when silence filled the square, all eyes upon him and the Keeper.

"Oh my, it's time, isn't it?" Tibit said, raising his head. He scampered down from the back of his fellow familiar, then held up the scroll for Elemara to take. "To add to your archives, if I may presume to," he said by way of explanation, ears humbly bent back. Then he made his way over to Zerrick, who bent down to allow the familiar to climb up on his shoulder.

"Come here for just a moment, Zerrick, before you leave," the Grand Priestess's familiar called to him, waving him over with its crooked horns. Zerrick obliged, feeling Tibit's tail gently stroking his neck. Up close Zerrick could smell the scent of clover from the familiar's breath. "I wish we could have had more time with you, Melian descendant, but perhaps later, when you return, we can speak of our people's histories."

"And legends of magic in both cultures, if what you have told me about Mira is true," Tibit added at his ear. Even the familiar hadn't known what to make of the news of Mira casting out demons.

"In the meantime," the Keeper of the Book continued, "Remember a few things in your fight against evil. One, never allow hate or rage to drive your actions. That the quickest path to destruction. Second, trust in the Goddess. The more you trust in Her and the less you fear Angist, the less power he has to affect you. Third, believe in yourself. You are powerful. I see no reason why you shouldn't have the strength to be successful. And last, take care of Tibit." The familiar surprised Zerrick by winking one of its glowing eyes. Zerrick bowed, mulling over its words, and backed up to rejoin Mok. The familiar returned to its mistress, who called for the Riders to mount.

They did so, lining up the griffins--six in all. Each Rider had set up two additional saddles behind them for members of Zerrick's party to ride. The thirty-foot long griffins would scarcely notice the extra baggage. Unless they had to fight, of course.

Just let us get to the rendezvous point, Zerrick thought with a queasiness in his gut. He'd be happy to fight hoards of creatures on the ground. Zerrick stood aside as the guardsmen, many of whom had taken practice flights to accustom themselves to griffin-back fighting, now mounted on the row behind the Riders. In this second row also went Tamur, probably so he could be near the front to watch the Rider at work.

After the second row of saddles filled, it was Zerrick's turn to mount, along with Mok and the rest of the guard party. Handlers presented him with a small step ladder for him to climb up to the shoulder of the great beast, then the Rider gave him a hand up to the straps and harnesses which would be his saddle. The handler strapped in his legs and secured Tibit within one of the pouches where he would be safe and comfortable. Zerrick tied down his cloak under his belt so it would not hinder him and wrapped a scarf round his face. At the height and speed they would be traveling, supposedly the wind made it difficult to breathe.

Zerrick tried to keep his breathing steady despite his pounding heart, feeling the beast shift its weight beneath him. It seemed rather high up here on the griffin's back. He watched the enormous flight feathers separate and close as the griffin stretched one wing and glanced at the cloudless sky. Was he really going up there? He heard the Captain of the Riders give the order to take wing, then all thoughts fled from his head as he felt the muscles bunch up the beast's legs, and saw the wings begin to flap, metallic gold reflecting the sun in blinding flashes. The griffin sprang into flight, and Zerrick doubled over and hung on for dear life. He feared his stomach was left far below but he dared not open his eyes to look.

A squeal of delight--a very feminine squeal of delight--forced him to open his eyes. That had sounded like . . . he lost track of that thought as he saw the ground speeding by far below him, then his nose hit the harness of the man in front of him as a powerful stroke of the griffin's wings sent them swiftly upwards. He concentrated on keeping his balance; this ride was anything but smooth!

With that thought Zerrick recalled that the ride could get much worse if the dragons decided to attack. He craned his neck to look out at the Rundran mountains. The dragons were in the air, but if they saw them it was impossible to tell. At least they would not be immediately upon them.

His stomach was beginning to get used to the changes in altitude and the jarring motions of the griffin, so Zerrick began to check in earnest the landscape below and see how Mok and Tamur were weathering their first flight. When he saw Mok, he had to chuckle. The man was curled into a ball against the beast, clinging to his flight straps with hair in his face and his eyes screwed shut. Oh, would he have to tease the old scout once they landed! This might be one 'new experience' Mok would not want to repeat.

Zerrick had a hard time locating Tamur. His griffin was towards the back, beyond which could be seen the city vanishing into the distance. Such speed! Zerrick marveled, feeling queasy anew. When he'd again mastered his unruly stomach, he saw Tamur's griffin had come forward a little.

Now he could notice some odd details--flying in the wind along with Tamur's long black hair were little curly tufts of red. The face, like Zerrick's, was masked against the wind, and there the skin showed dark, but the hands clutching the flight straps were pale pink.

"Rider, can you swing close to that griffin there? Something is wrong," Zerrick yelled against the roar of the wind to his Rider, a burly woman whose name he believed was Raza. With a lurch, the griffin swung back in a circle to fly alongside Tamur's beast. Zerrick was upset enough he actually stood in the stirrups.

"Mira, is that you? Or has Tamur taken to growing red hair of his own!" He yelled at the top of his lungs, glaring.

He saw Tamur fumble with the hood falling back from his forehead, feeling at his temples where the red curls were escaping. Then either the wind gusted or his fingers slipped in what they were doing. The black hair slipped down over a bun of bright red hair, then was torn away in the wind to fall swirling to the ground like a stricken raven.

"Mira, how could you?!" Zerrick cried, aghast.

Her face still smudged with mud and charcoal to imitate Tamur's skin color , Mira could only pull off the rest of the disguise and smile.

Sheepishly.

Chapter Twenty-four

"Love is of the Light; therefore embrace it as a mother to son, friend to friend, lover to lover."
-- Ainéra's diary

"Tamur chopped it all off for you?" Zerrick yelled after Mira shouted her explanation.

Mok's shout could just be heard above the wind. "Tamur made a great sacrifice, cutting his hair for her to make a wig. Truly I have never seen a more determined woman than Mira. Such a woman I would keep close by my side."

"Shut up, Mok!" Zerrick shouted back. To Raza he said in a low voice, "Can we turn around? She doesn't belong on this trip. It will create extra danger for us all."

Raza turned, her face covered by her flight mask, disguising any emotions, "I'd love to oblige you, Sir, but turning around would send us straight into the dragons." She pointed.

Zerrick turned, cursing as the movement sent hair flying into his face. Behind them a mile or so back, he could see six or seven dragons flying in pursuit. They would catch up with them within soon, unburdened as they were. Zerrick snarled. "All right, Mira, you'll be coming along with us to the rendezvous. But then, just like Tamur was going to do, you're returning with the Riders!" Zerrick shouted to Mira, and bent over to check that Tibit was safe in his pouch. He pulled out his pistol and readied himself for combat.

Mira tucked in her hair and refastened the treacherous hood over her head, her hands shaking. Damn the hood, damn the wind, and damn Zerrick's stubbornness! He wasn't supposed to find out until they were on the ground after the griffins had departed back for

Alorian. Why did Zerrick have to be so adamant on this? How could she explain it to him?

It had grown slowly like a seed, the feeling that she was incomplete without him, that she was in fact miserable whenever away from him. If he died out here alone, without her, she would go mad! Much better to be here with him, even if it meant risking her life. Especially if she could somehow save him, bring him back alive.

She had tried Mok's advice, she had been quiet and patient, waiting for Zerrick to come to her, say the words she longed to hear, but with his struggle with Angist, his training and now his new familiar, she was certain any feelings he might have for her had been driven clean out of his mind. She intended to show him, in fact tell him outright that she loved him, and that he'd better damn well keep his hide safe out here!

She had been a little harsh with Tamur, bullying him, cajoling him until he finally made the ultimate sacrifice--not his hair, for he had come to like Alorian fashion and had been considering cutting it before she mentioned the idea of dressing like him, but to let her go, truly let go of her forever, to be with Zerrick and go with him into the thickest danger. If they made it back, she and Zerrick owed him.

The Rider in front of her tapped her leg, bringing her out of her musings. "Prepare; the dragons come," he said in a short clipped accent all the Riders seemed to use.

She nodded and reached for her spears. They might not be effective against dragons, but Tamur had taken these to be blessed by the Grand Priestess at the Ceremony of Parting. Perhaps that magical blessing would lend strength. She glanced behind her, and realized the dragons were closing in, shrieking their harsh battle cries and exhaling little puffs of flame. In response the griffins were becoming agitated, and Mira saw puffs of what looked like snow coming from their nostrils. Could the griffins have their own magical weapons?

The Rider patted the silken hide of the animal, speaking soothing words to it, then exchanged hand signs with the other Riders. He shouted back to Mira and her companion, "Brace yourselves, we'll be taking evasions."

Evasions? Mira wondered, then the world began spinning and her stomach rose to her throat as the griffin went into a looping dive. When she could tell sky from ground again she saw that the other griffins were following the same tactics, each in a different direction. She couldn't tell which griffin bore Zerrick, but Mok's howl of terror could be heard from a griffin to her far left.

"But Zerrick will be unguarded!" she protested as they took a sharp turn up, the beast grunting with the weight of its passengers. She wondered how much weight was too much when performing 'evasions'

No time to contemplate. They made a series of maneuvers, each one bone-jarring, then they flew low over a desert plateau, clusters of salt brush streaking past, almost close enough to touch.

"We've managed to draw at least one of the dragons. The less the sorcerer has to deal with, the better," the Rider said in response to Mira's question. Mira nodded. If there were fewer dragons fighting against Zerrick he would have a better chance of making it to the rendezvous point.

"So what happens next? We can hardly lose it in a clear sky!"

"Just a little further," the Rider said with a grunt as the griffin swerved over a cluster of thorny trees.

Mira glanced behind her and gasped. While they had been discussing strategy, the dragon, a deep midnight blue one with a streak of red feathers along its crest, had closed in on them and was on their tail, breathing short bursts of flame which the griffin skillfully avoided.

The man behind Mira loaded his weapon, a rather archaic-looking crossbow. As they dipped downward, he aimed and fired it at the dragon's head. It bounced harmlessly off its neck.

"Must hit it in the eye," the fellow said in explanation.

That the bolt had struck the dragon at all amazed Mira, but with the speed they were flying and the chaotic twists and turns, she doubted the man would hit his tiny target. Indeed as she watched, he fired a second bolt which missed altogether.

What could she do to help? These creatures were evil; they were working directly for Angist. Could the powers she had used against evil possession and dreams work against flesh and blood monsters like these? She didn't think she could harm them with prayer, but perhaps she could help the man behind her find aim . . .

As always now, when danger threatened, the pressure was there, at the base of her skull. She concentrated on increasing it, focusing it, praying fervently over and over, *Hear me, Iahmel, know my need. We are being chased by servants of Angist. I need focus, perfect aim, for the rider in front of me. Help us defeat it.*

It seemed to take forever, during which her heart pounded in fear at every buck and turn, sudden heat passing just to the side of her. She kept her eyes closed to block out the fear. The pressure built and she left herself open to it, a corridor.

The Rider warned them to brace themselves, that the griffin was going to turn and fight. Mira shouted, "Hold a moment! Take aim and get ready to fire!"

The men must have been used to taking orders from the priestesses, Mira thought, because they made no protest. The crossbowman readied a bolt and raised his arm to fire as the Rider tried to steady their flight.

The pressure was a storm now in her head, a tidal wave rushing forward. Again someone else seemed to take control of her body, as she reached out and touched the crossbowman.

He must have felt the effect, for he gasped, and then uttered a cry in the Old Tongue of the Holy Book, "To Hell with thee, thou shalt not plague sweet Erde any longer!"

The bolt flew with a flash of light, and struck the dragon's right eye, burying itself to the fletching. The dragon plummeted to the ground without a sound. Far below them Mira heard a muffled crunch. They were alone in the sky.

Flying was hell.

The minute the dragons began their chase, Zerrick lost any idea of where he was, where they were headed, or even whether he was going to be able to keep his meager breakfast where it belonged and avoid embarrassing himself. He couldn't even open his eyes, knowing the blur of ground and sky turning in circles would undo him. He had to gain control, however, for he could hear the sounds of dragons engaged in battle with what must be the griffins, and he had to make sure Mira and Mok were all right.

There was also the fact he could feel things--things Elemara and both the familiars had warned him about. He could feel that evil presence, searching for him through the eyes of the dragons, not yet sure which man he was, but aware that he was close. The other thing plaguing him was magic itself. They were traveling very fast, and he could feel the increase of magic far more than he had on foot, for now there was a tiny residue in the air itself. It niggled at him, tempting, teasing. It was not strong yet, only as strong as a tiny seedling had been back in Harrow. But the closer he came to the Goddess, the more concentrated and stronger it would grow. Like Madame Lotus's spell, it would try to overcome and consume him. Last, he could hear Ainéra s call, distant now, a whisper in his mind. He prayed he could keep control. He prayed he could remain sane.

Breathing deeply to calm his stomach, Zerrick opened his eyes and glanced around, being careful not to look down at the rushing earth. There were only two griffins near now, and they were fighting against two dragons, one bone white and the other black like the one that had killed Durnan.

Above and around him, griffins dove at the dragons, breathing icy winds which drove the dragon's flaming breath back in their faces. It was nearly impossible to see the riders, but Zerrick managed to catch a glimpse of a feather-adorned cloak and wispy gray hair on a rider upon one griffin circling the black dragon. Mok was safe, although by the way he was curled up in a tiny ball it seemed he liked flying combat about as much as Zerrick.

Zerrick checked the other griffin grappling with the white dragon, but did not see even a glimmer of red hair.

"Where are the other griffins?" he shouted up to Raza.

"They drew away the other dragons. We'll fly separately now and regroup at the camp site," she called back, tapping a short riding crop to the griffin's right side, urging it to veer left. The griffin exhaled a blast of ice crystals, blinding the white dragon so the other griffin could slash its hide with silver claws. Zerrick had the presence of mind to help; he fired off his pistol into one great flapping wing of the dragon, and was thrilled to see the bullet penetrate.

Wounded and outnumbered, the white dragon shrieked in impotent fury, and spoke in their minds, *"You think you are safe, Zerrick? There will be others coming to slay you. The Ravenger will feast on your soul!"*

The dragon then tore away from them, fleeing fast back to the Rundran Mountains. The other dragon snarled, calling its companion a coward, and attacked Mok's griffin. Once all three griffins joined up against it, however, it was forced to retreat, after inflicting a few nasty bites and burns. Mok's griffin flew awkwardly, gasping in pain from a slashing cut to the chest.

"Report conditions!" Raza shouted and hand signaled to her companions once the dragons were out of sight.

"Minor wound, flyable," replied the first.

"Medium wounds, losing blood, once bandaged should be able to continue," reported the Rider of Mok's griffin.

"Land," Raza ordered, "We'll care for that wound and throw off any eyes watching the sky." She turned in the saddle and regarded Zerrick. "Successful so far, Sir. Now we make for the rendezvous point. Should make it just after nightfall. How are you?"

"I'm fine," Zerrick answered, swallowing. "But what about the other griffins? Do we have to wait until the rendezvous point to see if they made it?" If she lived, if she made it, he would throttle her. This was exactly why he hadn't wanted her to come. The flying his stomach would eventually grow used to, but the hard pit of worry would remain, tormenting him until he saw her again.

The Rider shrugged. "Unless you want to use magic, which would reveal us. My Riders will not fail you. They will make it to the campsite."

Zerrick nodded, knowing there was really nothing else he could do.

The landscape was shrouded in darkness when Zerrick's group reached their destination: a canyon between two high plateaus, branching out from a central core into many deep fissures in the rocks. A small natural spring which supported a cluster of stunted desert trees was located near the center. They landed and secured the griffins in the largest of the fissures. Under the cover of the trees, they set up camp.

Zerrick's group was the first. According to Raza, that made sense; they had handled the dragons quickly with the odds in their favor. The others would have been fighting one to one, and perhaps even one against two. Zerrick imagined four dragons tearing off after Mira, then shook away the image. He couldn't even think about that. They would not make a fire. Although the desert here looked uninhabited, Raza assured him there was life out here, and most of it had mutated from the intense magic. Supper would be dried meats and trail bread, and they would hold watch throughout the night.

Mok was so happy to be on the ground he volunteered for first watch, then built a little shrine out of stones and brush and softly chanted his thanks to the Mother for safely delivering him back where man belonged, the earth. He took one of the more critical points at the face of the plateau wall, looking into the camp proper.

Soon after, the first of the other griffins flew in with a terrific rush of air. Zerrick ran to see if Mira was among the group. She wasn't. The Rider reported that one dragon had been chasing it, but after a great deal of fancy flying it had given up and flown off. They had made certain that no followers tracked them here.

So there was at least one dragon out there which hadn't been vanquished. And four griffins here. How many dragons did that leave for the two griffins still out there?

Zerrick stood by while they secured the griffin, searching the evening sky for signs of movement, a soft whisper of wings, anything. The rest of the camp broke out rations and began eating. He remained where he was.

After what must have been an hour or so, Tibit came over from the camp, licking his paws and humming softly. He hopped up to the rocks where Zerrick was sitting and crawled up on his knee. "Really there is no point in waiting here for them, distressing yourself and wasting precious time for food and rest. Won't you return to the camp with me?"

Zerrick regarded the glimmering eyes of the familiar and gently petted Tibit's furry back. "I've been neglecting you, haven't I? I'm sorry, but I can't help but be worried. I told Mira not to come, but she did anyway. And now she's out there, somewhere." He bent his head to examine a weed, using the movement as a distraction to blink the moisture from his eyes.

Tibit crawled into his lap and wrapped tiny arms around Zerrick in a hug. "I am supposed to be all wise, but in matters such as this I know little. I can see that the two of you very much want to be together. Though you are frightened, you should not send her away. Remember, the Goddess protects those who embrace love, courage, and endurance. Far better to follow your heart than your fears."

Well that was a new way to put it. Was that what he'd been doing all along, letting fear guide him? Zerrick was silent a moment, mulling that thought over as he petted Tibit, watching the stars. A chill breeze blew at the back of his neck.

Tibit stood in his lap. "You feel that? The magic fields just shifted."

Zerrick tried looking at the magic around him, but the levels were too high for him to see anything but a blinding mass of power. Out here he would have to rely on Tibit's perceptions.

"What do you think it is?" he asked, keeping his voice just above a whisper.

"I don't know, but I think we should rejoin the main camp. I feel vulnerable." Tibit climbed onto Zerrick's shoulder, and Zerrick could hear him sniffing the air.

Zerrick rose and walked back to the Riders. A pale sliver of moon rose to the east, shedding just enough light to see guards perched on rocks and in crevices, keeping watch. He could see Mok's profile against the wall of a plateau, sitting on his heels, a spear in hand.

A dark shadow streaked across the face of the rock. It attacked Mok.

Chaos broke out, with guards screaming warnings as shadows emerged and fell upon them. Zerrick dodged a sinuous form which tried to grab his leg and ran to Mok as the old scout cried out in pain. Tibit clung to his shoulder and from him came a steady stream of magic ready to use. Zerrick did not use magic yet, however, just in case these were not minions of Angist but merely savage beasts.

He found Mok on his back, his spear broken in pieces. His attacker was a man-like creature with a thin muscular body, naked but for a loin cloth. Its head was that of a snake, and its jaws were locked fast on the nape of Mok's neck. That ghastly head, and the fact the muscled back was covered in scales, told Zerrick the manner of creature he faced. The famous snakemen of ancient lore. Servants of Angist.

"Their fangs are venomous, and they're very strong," Tibit warned in his ear. Zerrick took the hint and used magic, first to create a small ball of light to see by, then a shield, then he increased his strength as he had when Tamur had attacked him, only this time with perfect control. As he used the magic he could feel dark attention turning to him, fully focused. It battered at his will but Tibit held it back.

The magic blazed through him and began to do its job, just in time. Another snakeman, the one who had first slunk by him, leaped out and fastened its hand on his throat, knocking Tibit to the ground. Zerrick threw it off and pulled his pistol to shoot it point blank in the chest. It toppled over, twitching.

Zerrick ran forward to pull the other snakeman off Mok, wrenching its head back and hurling it into the rock face. He heard a satisfying crunch as the creature's neck broke and threw it atop its lifeless companion. Then he reached down to pull up Mok and inspect his bite. Tibit came out of hiding from the brush he had rolled into when thrown, and resumed his place on Zerrick's shoulder.

With a groan, Mok stood, clutching his shoulder and swaying weakly. "Never even saw it," he complained, trying to smile. It was a sickly grin, and Zerrick felt certain that poison had entered the wound.

Everywhere around him echoed the sounds of fighting. He hooked Mok's arm over his shoulder and tried to lead him back to the center of camp, flinching as he heard the death cry of one of his guards. He had only gone a little way, however, when four more snakemen appeared before him, materializing out of the darkness. Mok readied his hunting knife, but it was obvious he was too ill to fight. Zerrick shoved Mok back and pulled magic from Tibit's steady stream to attack.

Four bolts of light flew from his hand to strike the creatures' eyes. As they flailed, blindly striking at him, he drew his sword to give each a wound to the heart. Three of the four immediately died, but the fourth managed to duck away and vanished again like the shadows. Zerrick cursed.

"Slippery, aren't they," Mok said with a gasp, staggering to his feet. He was looking worse, and Zerrick knew he had to get help.

Out of the night sky, bats attacked.

Tiny claws and teeth nipped at Zerrick's head and torso, inflicting a dozen tiny wounds before he dropped Mok and ducked, covering the injured scout, his familiar, and himself with his cloak. From above he heard the cry of a wounded griffin and Mira's desperate call.

"Zerrick, are you down there? We need light here--the bats--we can't see them enough to defend ourselves! We have wounded!" She was cut off and Zerrick could hear the screech of dozens of bats as they flew up to attack, attracted by the sound of her voice.

Fortunately that left a little space for him, though at what cost he dared not think. Was she one of the wounded? Staying crouched with Mok under one arm and Tibit under the other, Zerrick drew magic, and this time instead of using it to make a single light for himself, he set the magic out to activate all the tiny droplets of magic saturating the air. Everywhere around her, the suspended magic began to glow like tiny fireflies, creating an overall effect of a glowing fog just bright enough to reveal a swarm of bats attacking the griffin flying above. Zerrick could make out five humans on its back, and felt a chill. What did that mean?

The griffin, a day flying creature, could now see its tormentors and breathed cloud after cloud of ice at the bats which froze their wings solid, sending them plummeting to the ground. Zerrick could also see the camp, and gasped at the carnage. Three of the four Riders were still standing, grouped together with two guards who had not been on watch duty. The other guards, however, and the fourth Rider, had been butchered by the snakemen and bats. Around their corpses, the creatures were busy gorging themselves. A wave of flame from Zerrick swiftly changed their minds about that. In moments all the creatures had either fled or been killed, and the griffin landed to limp over to its brethren.

Zerrick met Mira as she dismounted and reached out a hand to help her pass down a wounded Rider. The Rider that had been in command of the beast set to tending the beasts's wounds, leaving the guard who had ridden with Mira aiding a second wounded guard.

"We rescued these two from a griffin who crashed," Mira explained as they helped the wounded over to the camp. Her face was smeared with blood and the leftover mud from her disguise but apparently none of the blood was hers. She walked straight and her voice sounded strong and assured.

She continued, "We got the dragon that killed their griffin, but not before it killed Syran, their crossbowman. It got our griffin too, in the leg, but she should be able to make it back. What happened here?

Mok, you look terrible!" She gasped as Mok turned to show the fang marks in his neck, and paled.

They reached the camp and Mira brought out her knife and herbs, setting to work on Mok. Zerrick would apply his magic to the task as well, but not before he secured the camp. Another attack now could be disastrous. He set a series of spells around the perimeter set to light up in flame if they detected magic--something he wished he could have done before but couldn't for fear of revealing their location. Now it was known where they were, so the more protections the better, until the griffins were rested and ready to return.

After following up his detection spells with a few shields, Zerrick returned to a small campfire and the remainder of his party. Apparently they had decided hiding was useless. The fire would keep the wounded warm against the winter chill and hopefully keep at bay the bats and shadowy snakemen.

Mok struggled to remain conscious.

"I removed some of the poison, but his condition is growing worse. Can you use your magic on him?" Mira pleaded. She had washed her face and removed her hood to allow the fiery curls to fall loose down her shoulders. Looking at her, Zerrick wasn't sure whether he wanted to strangle her or embrace her.

He knelt down and put one hand on his familiar, and the other on Mok to get the purest connection to power. He pulled, and let the burning sweet magic pass through him into the old scout, praying to Ainéra to save her devoted follower.

He was not aware of time as the spell progressed, but suddenly he could hear his goddess. It seemed She was aware of his growing proximity, *"Yes, this way, come to me, you must come. I cannot fight him, you see . . . I created him."*

With a shock, Zerrick lost concentration. He hurried to dispel the excess magic, and gently checked Mok, trying to still his shaking hands. Indeed he was growing close, to have Her speak to him directly through the magic. And again that admittance of having created

Angist--did that make his father right? What was he doing here, what was he headed into, really?

Triggered by his sudden doubts, a message slipped past Tibit's protection in that all-too familiar voice, *"You are headed for me. I will have you, one way or another . . ."*

"Close your mind, Zerrick. You do not understand the full situation. Don't let the Liar weaken your faith," Tibit said in a grave voice, digging claws into Zerrick's hand to snap him back into the physical world.

"What's happening? Is it him?" Mira asked, leaning forward to lay her hand on his shoulder. The voices receded, blown away by the soft whisper of her breath. He found himself staring at the depths of her eyes and turned away, struggling to remember what he was doing.

"Mok looks better. I think he's recovering," Mira commented, reaching out her other hand to check Mok's forehead.

Zerrick nodded, feeling Tibit's shielding once again over him. He breathed deeply, working to calm his heart, steady his mind against the barrage of different powers. One task at a time. Check Mok.

Mok would recover now, but it would take several days. He needed care, bed rest, and probably a few more magic treatments. He could get all that in Alorian, but out here, with Angist's servants attacking, he was as good as dead.

"I don't think he'll be able to continue with us. He'll accompany you back to the city, and you can keep watch on his condition, Mira," Zerrick looked hard at her, waiting for her to challenge him, or for tears and hysterics.

She remained calm, but there was defiance in her eyes. "Zerrick, I'd like to discuss that with you, but I'd prefer to do it in private. Is there some place we can go?"

Zerrick glanced at the camp, Riders were sprawled out in slumber around the fire and unwounded guards stood guard in a narrower perimeter around camp and griffins. The griffins were lying close together, but between them was still enough room for two to walk abreast. "By the griffins. If they can't protect us, nothing can," he responded, rising to his feet.

They left Tibit to watch Mok and strode into the crevice between boulders where the griffins were softly snoring away in exhausted slumber. One beast's tail twitched at their passing, and it raised a huge paw to swipe at its tufted ear, then it settled down again.

Zerrick stepped over the hind paw to stand in the space under its arm where the wing was joined, forming a sort of hollow. Mira stepped over to join him. He opened his mouth to speak, but Mira silenced him, placing a finger on his lips.

"Before you say anything, let me say this. I have to stay because I love you, and the only way I can be sure you're going to come back is to be here to protect you, use my own special power to make sure you succeed and come back safe. I don't want to be alone without you, I really don't. I love you. I want to be with you." She took a shuddering breath, her hands clenched in front of her. Moisture glistened in her eye but she blinked it away and looked straight at him, defiantly.

She thinks I'm going to reject her! Zerrick thought, his throat tightening. She was standing there, offering herself to him, totally unaware of his feelings for her, and the reasons he'd tried to keep her away. His heart was expanding in his chest, his head growing dizzy.

She had made the ultimate argument, for now he couldn't send her back--it would tear him in two. She loved him! Enough to brave the dangers here, enough to face his anger at her coming . . . enough to go with him to the end and back.

As he stood trying to fathom such a notion, that someone could love him so deeply, Mira lowered her head and turned to leave. Her back was painfully straight, but her hands here trembling. The sight of her pain and the realization that she was leaving shocked Zerrick into action.

"No wait! Don't go," he yelped, diving forward to catch her arm. The squeak in his voice caused the griffin to rumble in annoyance, but apparently it was used to humans; it shifted its position a little and returned to sleep.

Mira gulped. "Look, I know you do care about me, that you're trying to keep me safe. And if you don't feel the same . . . it's . . ." the words died on her lips, but before he could see those lips quiver or a tear splash over them, Zerrick pulled her back to him and wrapped his arms around her in a tight embrace.

He held her head cradled in both hands as he kissed her hair, the side of her neck, her cheeks which were now salty with tears, and finally her lips, whispering over and over "I love you too, don't leave--I really do love you." The intensity of emotion was finally too much for him; he began crying also, burying his head against her shoulder, against her hair. He whispered, "I was too afraid to tell you, I didn't want to put you in danger, or let harm ever touch you. I know you had too much of that from your brothers, but I couldn't help it. You're too precious."

Now it was his head cradled in her hands, her lips pressed hard against his cheek. She removed them long enough to say, "You are nothing like my brothers--they never allowed me to live. You just don't want me to die."

Zerrick nodded, and held her even tighter. "If you die, I die."

Mira cupped his chin with one hand and turned it so that he was looking at her face, into her deep dark eyes. "Do you think it would be any different for me, without you? You showed me so many things I'd never seen, never known about. You are my world, Zerrick."

Finally the words felt natural. "Will you marry me?" Zerrick asked in a half whisper. His whole being waited for the answer.

Mira's response, while not verbal, was definitely affirmative.

Chapter Twenty-five

"Doubt is the ultimate evil."
--Ainéra's diary

Perhaps because of Zerrick's spells or perhaps because of the success of the first battle, no further attacks occurred that evening. Zerrick and Mira woke up lying against the griffin's hide, clothing a little more rumpled, both smiling, their eyes aglow with happiness. They walked back into camp as breakfast was cooking, trying to ignore the curious stares of the guards and Riders. Mira went to help prepare the food while Zerrick went to check Mok's condition.

Mok was awake, fighting a slight fever and still in some pain. He looked far better than he had last night, however; his color was back and he was complaining about his forced return.

"I am not taking one of those flying monsters back to Alorian. I'd rather walk," he snapped, waving a hand at the griffins. "I'm old, I've lived a full life. Just let me continue until I fall, then leave me. If the Mother thinks I'm worth saving, She'll protect me."

"The Mother has enough problems right now. Zerrick is hardly going to leave you and we can't take you along, slowing us down and posing a vulnerable target. The Mother will protect you just as well on the griffin, so swallow your fear and get ready to remount. They'll be leaving within the hour," Tibit said in a commanding tone Zerrick had never heard him use before. Mok bowed his head in a apology and murmured a prayer of forgiveness.

"Because you ask it, I will go. Shall I be taking Mira with me?" Mok asked, turning to Zerrick. Pain deepened the wrinkles around his eyes, making him look aged. This was another hard decision for Zerrick to make, sending him home, making him feel useless, but far better for him to feel poorly now and live to scout another day.

"I'm glad you agree to return--I don't want to lose a friend like you. Mira, however, will not be returning." Zerrick said, flushing.

Mok smiled. "Really. What changed your mind?"

"She told me she loved me. And you were right. She does have power that might aid me. Since she insists, and since I'd rather be with her, I've decided she's coming."

Mok grinned. "Good. Then I know you'll return. He glanced once more at the griffins and grimaced. No breakfast for me. I'd ask you to spell me to sleep for a while, but I suppose I'd better keep my wits about me."

Mira came with the morning repast, and everyone but Mok ate, keeping watch for attack from the shadowed canyons. Travel would be safer by day when they could see trouble from a long distance off, but no time was completely safe out here. They suited up the griffins and quickly buried those who had fallen. In all, they had lost one griffin, one Rider, and five guardsmen. Another guard was severely wounded and would be returning.

That left Zerrick, Mira, and two guards, Landor and Drue. These four would ride on the griffons to the top of the plateau about five more miles west, then they would be on their own to walk the seventy or so miles to the Jagged Grin. According to the Riders, the land was flat except for a few scattered hills and canyons.

Zerrick climbed onto Raza's griffin with Mira in front. If she was going to travel with him, she was going to be right by his side--not on another griffin where she could run into more trouble. While eating, he had asked her exactly what had happened while she was separated from the group and learned of the mysterious power making yet another appearance. As they were being strapped in for the short flight, he continued his questions, "So how did you come upon the wounded Rider and guard?"

Mira's response was delayed a moment while they took to the air, and Zerrick noted with satisfaction that she too clutched at her stomach during the first seconds of becoming airborne.

"We found the other griffin in a death embrace with a pair of dragons--all three had apparently fallen to the earth locked in combat. The impact of their landing is what killed the second guard and wounded the Rider and crossbowman. There was little danger, but I had to bind their wounds and stop the bleeding before we took off again, and with all that extra weight we were slower."

Zerrick nodded, but he could not suppress a shudder. So two dragons had teamed up against one griffin. It was only blind luck that the griffin hadn't been Mira's.

They landed on the plateau, sparsely dotted with saltbrush and thornweed clinging to life in the hard-packed clay soil. Zerrick unfastened his straps and dismounted as soon as the beast settled. As his griffin landed, Mok waved Zerrick and Mira over to say their farewells. He was a little green already from the first hop, but looked resigned to endure the flight ahead.

Zerrick climbed up on the griffin's shoulder blade to clasp Mok's arm. "I'd like to say I'm sorry you're not coming with us, but that wouldn't be true. I'm glad you'll be going back to safety. You are a true friend, and I never want to lose you."

Mira added, "Thank you for all the help in getting us to Alorian. We never would have made it without you."

Mok coughed once, swiping at his eyes, then reached out to hug first Zerrick then Mira. "You'll have to pay me back. Return safely, and we'll discuss terms." He tried to smile.

Mira hugged him once more, wishing him good luck, then climbed down to join Zerrick.

They backed away so the griffins could take off. Raza saluted them and added, "If you are successful, you may not need our help in returning, for you will be with the Goddess, but should you need us, send a Calling to Elemara or the Keeper of the Book. Good luck, Master Zerrick. All our hopes go with you." The Rider gave him a smile, then lead her party up into the sky with a rush of wings and an excited roar from the griffins, eager to return home. Zerrick watched them until they were far above, then he pulled out a spyglass and looked west.

Off in the distance he could see a thin line of mountains—buttes, really--formed of black jagged rock, as haunting in real life as they had been in innumerable dreams. He knew the way there by heart--follow a dry stream bed to the base, up a small rocky rise, to the steep cliffs of the unnatural-looking mountains. And what would happen there on that small rocky rise? He had seen so many possibilities, he could say nothing with certainty. That was the rise where the ring of fire and his father had appeared when he first began having the dream. Then the Ashwa-grippa had attacked him, or dragons, or a dozen other hideous creatures. In some he had even had to face the God himself, or his highest demon, the Ravenger. In some Mira had been alive and well, but in most she had been dead or dying. One thing he knew for certain--there would be a confrontation of some kind before he climbed that final barrier to his Goddess. He willed his fear to stay back. One way or another, he was going to do this, and he was going to protect Mira as well.

Zerrick lowered the spyglass and lead his group into the desert.

They made progress through the day, only needing to hide once from a flock of something--dragons, perhaps, although they did not look like any dragons Zerrick had ever seen, with four sets of wings each and twisted bodies streaked with violent colors of orange, purple and red. He could see the magic at work on them, working its mutations. He could also feel the magic trying to gnaw at him and his party, but his training with Elemara and his link with Tibit continued to hold the ruthless magical forces at bay.

By sunset they could see the Jagged Grin on the horizon, growing nearer with every step. As the sun dipped behind the toothy spires, they found a shallow canyon to camp in for the night, setting two to watch and two to sleep. Tibit went into trance to best monitor the magical fields. He would not sleep until the first light of dawn.

The attack this time came late in the night, only hours before dawn. Zerrick and Mira were on watch together, although the watching part was somewhat difficult between whispers of endearments and stolen kisses. So much time had been spent trying to keep Mira away, trying to deny his feelings for her. Now that now that their love was real and she was unequivocally his, he had to spend as much attention on her as possible, despite the danger.

Besides, there was always Tibit.

"Zerrick!" the familiar whispered as Zerrick and Mira huddled closer in the blanket they were sharing. "I think you may want to--"

An unearthly howling and barking cut off the rest of the familiar's words, as a pack of what looked like desert foxes suddenly charged the camp from all sides, eyes aglow with magical power. Tibit squeaked in surprise and ducked into a tight crevice just in time as a grinning fox snapped at his tail, curling into a ball with his scaly hide out to protect himself from the snapping jaws.

Zerrick almost threw a bolt of magic when he saw a glow surrounding each fox. "They have shields! Everyone to arms!" he shouted as he pulled the guards to their feet, helping them to avoid the sharp teeth of their attackers. They took up their weapons to combat the foxes, but the blades bounced off the shields harmlessly.

"The blades were blessed! They cannot penetrate the magical protections," Drue cried as blow after blow rebounded. Six little foxes all leapt for his throat. Together, they caused him to lose his balance and he fell, cursing. Before he hit the ground, his throat was torn out by six snapping mouths.

Mira cried out in horror, but there was little else she could do. Four of the little demons were nipping at her ankles, and try as she might to spear them, they were too quick, leaping and darting away from her thrusts. Teeth marks already showed on her legs above her boots.

Zerrick was having a little better luck, if only because he had never allowed his old sword to be blessed or even touched by magic. With a quick succession of parries of their flashing teeth and thrusts to the fast moving tufts of fur, he managed to kill seven of the ones closest to him.

Unfortunately that didn't help Mira. Even as he thrust and killed one of the foxes, Zerrick saw her fall back unable to reach an area where she could use her spear. She had wounded two but her weapon was too long for close combat and small targets. As he tried to reach her, a pair of foxes leapt up in attack; one bit her right arm, hampering her, while the other went for her throat.

"Mira, look out!" Zerrick shouted, running to defend her. He was too late. The fox missed her jugular vein, but had the side of her neck in its jaws and was tearing into her shoulders and chest with its claws, trying to cause as much damage as possible, while the other hung from her forearm, jaws locked tightly into her flesh. Zerrick leapt through the tangle of foxes to wrench both away from her and throw them with all his might into a gully filled with thornweed. The sight of so much blood coursing down the front of her shirt nearly drove him mad. Mira fell to her knees, clutching at her throat. All he could see was red--the red of blood on the ground, matted in the fur of the possessed foxes, the red of their unholy glowing eyes . . . .

With a cry he began stabbing at them, at every tawny bit of fur, at anything that moved. A fox which pounced at Mira's good arm was sliced almost in half by the strength of his fury; another one gnawing at her boot received a thrust through the heart.

"You will not take her from me, Angist!" Zerrick shouted at the night, panting heavily. He caught sight of one of the wounded foxes beginning to stir and hacked it to pieces.

"Don't give in . . . to rage, Zerrick," Mira's soft whisper stopped him cold to stare at his handiwork.

An accompanying plea came from an equally gifted voice, "Steady, Zerrick, they've all been vanquished. The magic feels whole and undisturbed again. Here, I've brought bandages."

Tibit had a jagged scratch across one eye and was limping, but otherwise seemed all right. Zerrick forced his rage and fear to cool, belatedly noticing he had been clawed in several places as well. He glanced over at their camp. The two Alorian guards were dead, though in their dying they had slain nearly a dozen foxes. And Mira . . .

He fell to his knees by Mira, trying to stop the flood of blood with his hands and with the bandages from Tibit. His reserves were full; he hadn't used even a trace of magic against the foxes, so it was easy to draw some to him to heal her.

"No, you mustn't, Zerrick," Tibit said, grabbing his hand in his tiny paw, "These creatures were not intelligent. They were not able to communicate our location. It's possible they were merely a scouting party who happened on us by accident. If you use magic now, a much larger and more powerful group will come."

"Just get me my herbs," Mira said between breaths. The blood was slowly congealing around the jagged cuts down her front, her legs, and her arm. She looked waxen, but she seemed determined not to swoon.

Zerrick could feel the rage, boiling just below the surface wanting to strike out at something, anything. He beat it back down but the fear and worry were there to replace it, nearly choking him. "This is insane! You're hurt! And you're saying I can't use magic to help you? How are we supposed to continue if you're wounded?"

What do I do if you die? His hands shook as he pressed the bandages against her throat and chest, praying nothing vital had been hit, that it was not as bad as it looked.

Tibit ran to fetch Mira's things as Zerrick carried her back to the camp, ever so gently laying her down on the blankets, her upper body resting against his chest.

"Mira, are you still awake? Tell me you are all right, don't make me insane," Zerrick said when he noticed her eyes close and her breathing slow. Panic threatened to engulf him.

She licked her lips and squinted up at him, trying to smile and failing dismally. "I'm fine. Probably barely bleeding now."

Zerrick checked. It was true, the bleeding was slowing, but she had lost a lot of blood. His clothes were soaked with it. "Will it take you long to recover? Are we trapped here for a while?" He tried to keep the desperation from his voice.

Mira shook her head. "The blood won't matter much; if I mix up a few strength-building drinks. Too bad we don't have any fish oil . . ." she chuckled at the desert landscape around them, then grimaced. "The problem will be infection. Tibit? Do you have my herbs?"

"Right here," the familiar said, dragging behind it a pack twice its size. It placed the pack next to her and helped her open it so Zerrick could begin to clean her wounds.

"Pitchu, berrywort, leatherwood resin, barror bark," she muttered, digging through her things with her good hand.

"Let me help. I may not be as knowledgeable as you but I did have my training. Lie back, rest. Tibit, the area is safe now? No disturbances?" Zerrick took the herbs from Mira's trembling hand as she swayed, falling back against him.

"It's safe, for the moment, and it's too close to dawn for another attack, I think. Daylight lessens his power. He works best in the dark." Tibit pulled over a blanket to cover the three of them; a trace of frost now lined the stains of blood on the ground. Mira was too spent to even shiver, and it would have taken a blizzard to get Zerrick's attention away from the task of tending to her.

She sighed and snuggled closer to Zerrick, softly petting Tibit with her left hand. "I'm so sorry. This was just what you feared. I wanted to protect you, but now I'm just a burden again." She seemed on the verge of tears. With difficulty she wiped at her cheek with her bandaged hand. By the grimace just that simple movement produced, it was obvious she wouldn't be fighting any time soon.

"During the day, I'll heal you. If we keep moving, it shouldn't make a difference. We're easy to see in these lands anyway." Zerrick spread on the healing poultice very thickly, saving only a small amount for future use. If trouble were not stopped now, there would not be a need for the rest.

Mira nodded wearily. "May I sleep a little? I'll need my strength for the morning."

Zerrick finished his ministrations. He made sure she was comfortable, while he sat gazing at the landscape of rock and starlit sky. "Yes, rest now. I'll keep watch. Nothing is going to touch you. Nothing."

The following day's march was grueling. Mira walked with a limp, hanging onto Zerrick's arm to support a body gnawed by fever and drained of strength. The desert landscape before her danced and wavered with her lightheadedness, and every wound burned. Despite their efforts from last night, infection had set in. She refused to tell Zerrick of her suffering, plodding along, one foot before the other across the wide plateau. The mountains were growing nearer, near enough to see their unnatural structure of what appeared to be black obsidian ripped out of the earth and piled high in furious energy. They would reach them in perhaps two days. That was two days normal marching, providing she allowed Zerrick to risk the magic to make her well.

"I have a question, Tibit," Zerrick said, helping Mira down a rocky stream bed. Mira regarded the struggling plant life there, hoping to see something she recognized as medicinal, but the only plants living were thornweed and gnarled mesquite.

Tibit was a few paces ahead of them, running along on all fours, sniffing at various plants, most likely to keep track of the increasing strength of the magic which even Mira could feel now, a pressure like an oncoming storm in the air. He paused as they climbed the bank of the dry bed. "Go ahead."

"What exactly am I supposed to do when I reach Ainéra? I understand I must awaken Her, but how? Why?" Zerrick motioned for Mira to lean on his other arm, transferring their packs to the one she had been holding. She tried to take one of the packs to ease his burden, but he shook his head. "Just take it easy, Mira. I can handle the weight." He kissed her brow tenderly, making her writhe inside anew at the anguish and worry she was causing him. How could she have let herself be wounded?

Tibit exhaled a puff of steam into the chilly air. "When the Two were joined They were omnipotent, but now Their powers are much reduced. And together They held all talents, but divided now, so are Their gifts. While Iahmel retained the powers of logic and orderly thinking, Ainéra kept the talents of dreams and imagination. These talents of Ainéra are very powerful, but unfortunately make Her vulnerable to Angist and his lies."

Zerrick's eyes grew haunted, and Mira was sure he was reminded of his own dreams. "So he holds Her by fear, then."

"And shame," Tibit added, nodding. When Mira and Zerrick stared at him, he turned away, smoothing his fur. "My Goddess feels responsible for the creation of Angist. In a skewed way, She is his mother. She cannot bring Herself to destroy him, in fact has difficulty raising a hand against him."

Zerrick nodded. "I understand. What I have never fully understood, what even the Grand Priestess failed to make clear to me, is what exactly do I do to free Her? He can swat me down like a mere fly before I ever reach Her." Despite his efforts to sound nonchalant, Mira felt a shudder go through him. She squeezed his shoulder where she was holding him for support.

If Tibit was aware of Zerrick's fear, he did not show it as they began walking again, "The Goddess protects like a mother, and will fight for Her followers where She will not protect Herself. If you fight Angist, She will do all She can to assist you, and in that way fight to free Herself."

He regarded Mira thoughtfully, a half-smile on his long snout. "With two of you She should be even more encouraged to aid, and with love blossoming between you," he grinned, "She shall be greatly roused."

Zerrick nodded, his eyes lighting up with understanding. "She dreams Herself in captivity! Just like Andress said. So our task is to waken Her to Her own powers."

Tibit nodded. The three continued for several moments, each deep in their own thoughts. The ground here rose a little and was rockier, so Mira was forced to put all her concentration on negotiating the terrain. Heat grew in her and made her more and more unsteady, sapping her strength and making her head spin. The familiar went ahead a little as Zerrick helped her up a rocky incline littered with the bones of some long dead creature.

While Tibit scouted ahead, Zerrick paused to glance at the sun, now directly overhead, shedding a pale light over the frost-swept desert. A cold wind out of the west was blowing, cutting right through Mira's cloak. She moaned, clutching it tighter to her.

Zerrick turned to her. "I think I need to heal you. The shadows are at their lowest, so hopefully nothing can ambush us, but I don't want to chance the night with you wounded." With his help, Mira sat down. The pain throbbed in her chest and up her neck, choking her. It was true they might attract attention, but they might find them anyway as they had last night, and Mira wanted to be capable of helping, not hindering.

"I just want to say I'm sorry again," she managed to rasp through the dryness of her throat.

He glanced worriedly at her. "Don't worry. Relax. Close your eyes." He put a hand to her brow over her eyes, similar to the way she had when she'd tended him in Darya's tent. That hum in the air she recognized as magic suddenly seemed to become sharper and stronger. A spark seemed to strike where Zerrick's hand was pressed to her, then sensation blurred into blissful ecstasy. There was only Zerrick within her, beside her, his magic coursing through her body, making her cheeks blush and her heart race. The pain was subsiding, the intense heat in the wounds cooling, but before it could go away completely, a terrible screech pierced her ears--not like a dragon's, but even worse, an ungodly sound of fury and pain. It pressed the air with hatred so profound, it froze even her thoughts. Zerrick's spell abruptly ended. She opened her eyes in terror.

A great black shape descended from the sky, seeming to come right out the air itself. At first all Mira could see were wings: four black-feathered wings, each about ten or twelve feet long, all flapping in a blur of movement. Then the head of a horse, also black, reared up out of the tangle of wings, and four cloven black hooves appeared, each hoof chiseled into a razor-sharp point, churning at the air as the creature landed in a cloud of dust.

It reared up, shrieking again, and struck at something--Tibit, Mira's mind sluggishly registered, trying to fight the terror of the creature's ghastly voice. She saw the familiar sent flying by a powerful kick to lie unmoving, a little bloody heap.

Beside her, Zerrick whimpered, but he too seemed frozen, all his color suddenly fled from his face. Very soon Mira understood why. The pressure of the magic was all around, making it difficult to breathe, difficult to think. It seemed to whisper fell things, of woe, of destruction. She could feel it seep into her skin, trying to change her. She gripped Zerrick and the sensation lessened somewhat, at least enough to be able to see clearly again.

The four-winged horse strode up to them, and horror struck Mira anew. The eyes that gazed out of the equine features were human, opened wide in a semblance of hate, but clouded with pain and fear, as if within the beast cringed a poor human, trapped. The voice which came from the creature's mouth, however, was steady, calm, and arrogant. "You have been allowed to live long enough. Since you continue to foolishly use your magic in my Master's domain, you will now face the Master's wrath."

Zerrick struggled to stand, and Mira saw the air around him shimmer, as he tried to call forth magic to defend them against this terror. Not quick enough. A streak of movement from the sky dove straight into him, knocking him on his back as it flew past. A second blur flew past Mira, and sent her flying, landing hard on her wounded arm. She groaned, trying not to black out, and rolled to her hands and knees to check on Zerrick.

Two creatures landed by Zerrick and stood over him, regarding his prone form. They were humanoid with grayish skin, their bodies corded and nearly contorted with muscle and sinew, and like the horse, each had two sets of feathered wings. Mira recognized them from children's horror tales and the Holy Book. Gargoyles.

Each held a spear, and as Mira watched, one raised it to stab at Zerrick's leg, a gleeful look on its face . . . "No!" Mira cried, leaping to thrust herself in the way of the attack. She was wounded; he was not. It was important it remain that way.

She landed hard on Zerrick's body and stretched to cover it with her own as the spear point drove down into the back of her thigh. It nearly went through to hit Zerrick even with her intervention, but was stopped by the bone. She blacked out.

"Mira, no!" Zerrick groaned, struggling to get out from underneath her. He lunged to his feet, blinking his eyes to clear them, and saw the deep wound in her leg, and the demon standing before him, trying to tear its spear from her. He had barely seen it come. They had tried to kill him, and Mira had somehow taken the blow. They would die. He drew his sword and swung at the gargoyle, but before he was halfway through his swing, the second gargoyle ripped the sword from his hands and pinned his arms behind him against its hard chest. While he struggled to break free, the first one leisurely pulled out the spear, drawing another groan of pain from Mira. Then it pulled her up by her arms, trying to make her stand. She cried out and flailed, trying to claw at its face, but it seemed only amused by her efforts. A low rumble of laughter reminded Zerrick there was still the third creature to contend with.

It stood before him, gazing with its infernal eyes at him, at his soul, searching his memories through the magic, laying bare every hope and fear. Too many dreams of this one had plagued Zerrick; he felt he knew it as well as it knew him. The Ravenger would take them to the mountain to be interrogated and either converted or neutralized. Death would be the simplest solution, but Zerrick doubted they would let him off so easily. He glanced at Mira to check her condition. She was pale and growing paler with the blood streaming down her leg, and was in severe pain, but alive. Still alive.

He couldn't worry about her, impossible though it seemed not to--any attention paid to her now the Ravenger would use against him. Angist probably wanted him alive right now, but Mira was another matter.

"Now you see how foolish it was to come. Did you really think you could challenge a god? You will pay for your pride with pain, endless years of pain, unless you want to bow now to me. Plead now, on your knees, if you want to save your hide." The Ravenger came close to deliver its ultimatum, snorting steam in his face. Its foul breath made his eyes tear, but Zerrick stared back at it bravely. Inside, he quaked.

"I will not bow down. My Goddess will protect me," Zerrick stated, throwing insolence into his voice so that any thoughts of Mira would be erased from the mind of this infernal being. Out of the corner of his eye he saw Tibit crawling towards them, dragging one ruined leg behind, his tiny face a mask of concentration. Gradually the shields were being reinstated over Zerrick and undoubtedly over Mira as well, protecting their minds once again from the intense magic. He also felt the almost infinite supply of magic at his command through the familiar, ready to do battle. Desperately he focused on keeping attention to himself, prepared for any action the guardian spirit might make.

"I've gained power since your master began tormenting me with his dreams. Perhaps I cannot defeat him, but I can cause damage before I fall. If I awaken the Goddess, Angist may find more trouble than he can deal with. Perhaps it is you who should fear." The sheer will it took to say those words without letting his voice falter or his gaze drop! He was amazed to see himself standing tall rather than melting into a puddle of helpless flesh. How could he do this? Why had he ever dreamt he could do this?

Steady, a voice within said--Tibit's presence. His heart clung to the assurance of that presence, bolstering his courage. This was why he'd Called for the familiar. Tibit would see him through this fight; he wouldn't let him face this terror alone. He tried to look for the familiar out of the corner of his eye but was afraid any attempt to locate him would ruin his subterfuge. He concentrated on the baleful eyes before him, curling his hands into fists.

The Ravenger took another step forward and snorted another blast of foul steam, challenging him to lower his gaze. "I will eat your bragging tongue, mortal. I will design such tortures for you and for your woman there that will test your limits of sanity. But never beyond, I assure you. You will pay for your insolence with the agony of a competent mind."

"You dare speak of insolence, demon?" Tibit spoke again in that stern otherworldly voice, and suddenly the magic in the air and from the ground convalesced into a great hammer to strike at the Ravenger, hitting hard enough to send it staggering.

The magic was there for Zerrick to pull, yet he couldn't pull it for fear of what the gargoyles would do to Mira. A stream of learning coursed into him from the familiar even as he fought the Ravenger, telling his how to build shields against magic at its highest intensity. Zerrick struggled to stand to aid Tibit, but before he reached his feet, he was thrown to the ground by an unbelievably fast and powerful gargoyle, then pinned there against the sharp point of a spear. Out of the corner of his eye, he saw Mira held in a similar manner. A warning.

Tibit dodged another kick from the Ravenger and threw a lightning bolt at it of such strength that the force of the blast sent the gargoyles, Mira, and Zerrick flying, creating a crater in the earth. As the dust settled, Zerrick blinked and saw that the Ravenger still remained, untouched.

Tibit panted, looking spent as he favored his good leg. He raised a tiny arm, almost as if in farewell. He couldn't be leaving, Zerrick thought in a panic. He couldn't face Angist alone--he needed Tibit! "You can destroy him, I know you can!" he shouted, struggling against the gargoyle's hold despite the spear point grazing his Adam's apple.

The Ravenger recovered. Zerrick felt a peculiar sucking sensation and watched as the magic in the air began to fade in intensity. The Ravenger seemed to absorb it completely, sending out a painful buzz which seemed to echo inside his head. It effectively nullified Tibit's conjuring, and with a furious shriek, the Ravenger leapt across the brush to trample the familiar. This time when the Ravenger stepped away, all four hooves bloody, Tibit did not stir. All protection vanished, leaving Zerrick again bare to the intense and now faintly tainted magic. With a terrible awareness, Zerrick knew his friend and guardian was dead.

Only a physical form, my boy. I'll be back, that I promise you. Remember, no hate, no fear, no doubt. Be steady and strong. I will fight to help you from Beyond . . . A whispering voice, Tibit's voice, but somehow altered, aged perhaps or somehow more human, sounded in his mind and heart. It faded into the wind, leaving only the sounds of Mira's moans and the heavy breathing of the Ravenger.

"Bring them before the Master. It is time they paid in full for their sins," the Ravenger commanded.

Each gargoyle grabbed hold of its charge and Zerrick found his arms pinned by a powerful arm while it maintained the spear point at his throat with the other. He saw out of the corner of his eye its double wings unfold, then it propelled them into the air flying fast and straight for the Jagged Grin.

Beside him he could see Mira carried in a similar fashion, her head lolling on her shoulder, her eyes open but only barely. She was white as parchment, obviously in great pain. Fear threatened to engulf Zerrick again; he squashed it. He must not think of her.

But what of Tibit? His link to Ainéra had been severed, his power now diminished. He'd been counting on that link not only for the added access to magic, but for communication as well. He was doomed. Loss and terror closed his throat until he was gasping for air, his vision blurring. No fear, no fear--that was always Tibit's teaching. He had to be true to that small but mighty instructor.

He concentrated on the landscape, at the plateau gently rising before the hard edge of the mountains of black obsidian, breathing deeply to push down the fear. He tried to look within the circular valley the mountains formed for a glimpse of the Goddess's prison, but a thick bank of clouds obscured his vision. They dropped beneath a few clouds of the bank as they grew closer, and he glanced down, noting a thin dry streambed trailing out from the dark mountains, a hauntingly familiar streambed . . . yes, there it was now, the site of so many dreams. . .

Even as he felt a shock of recognition, gazing at the fast approaching base of the mountain, a chill breeze blew past and he knew he was being watched, that Angist was near, studying him with gloating satisfaction. The awful sensation swept over him, making bile rise in his throat. The gargoyles let go of him to let him fall the last ten feet or so, and he landed hard on his side to immediately roll over and be sick on the hard-caked earth. The magic was overwhelming--it twisted his insides and screamed in his mind, demanding to be pulled, commanded, used. For several minutes he could do nothing other than fight with it, trying to preserve his sanity.

Tibit's teachings and concern for Mira saved him--the knowledge of what she would face if he were not there to protect her. He raised his head to look for her. Despite the magic which made his vision waver and swim, he was able to locate her perhaps twenty feet off, sprawled on the ground where she'd apparently been dropped.

She seemed delirious, waving her hands at unseen things in the air around her, sobbing and calling out for him. The magic, he realized. He created a shield for her to block out the terrible energy. She began breathing easier immediately, and stopped her flailing to look around her. Their eyes met.

I love you, Zerrick put the message into his gaze, lest it be the last time he could express it to her. Then he stood to confront the gargoyles and the Ravenger. At least he knew how to save Mira now, if all help failed him. Taken over by magic, she would never be aware of anything they did to himself or her.

He thought the gargoyles would fight him first and he was ready, drawing now his scimitar from Alorian. It was blessed and might not work, but with the concentration of magic here anything would be saturated. The gargoyles however, seemed to take no interest in him.

Instead they stalked towards Mira, raising their spears. Zerrick's heart leapt to his throat. He felt that presence again, testing him, watching what he would do. He challenged it.

"That's right, Angist, go and torture the one who has Iahmel's gifts, as well as Ainéra's blessings. Go and stir up both gods against you." The old stories of Ja'hal had said the Master of Lies was a coward, that standing up to it, one could defeat it. He desperately hoped that was true. The gargoyles paused a few feet from Mira and lowered the spears. They did not back away, however, and the presence watching over did not waver. Indeed it seemed to become more powerful, heating up the air with its fury.

Only the barest shimmer in the air warned Zerrick. A ring of fire leapt up around him, cutting him off from Mira, the mountains, and the gargoyles. Only the Ravenger was included in the tight ring of red flame, the light dancing across the sable coat. Behind the Ravenger, part of the flames formed itself into a pair of glowing eyes.

Zerrick gulped. He was looking at the face of a god.

Chapter Twenty-six

"I am my Lord's messenger."
--II Ja'hal, night before execution

Pain wracked Zerrick's body: heat upon his skin, cold ice in his lungs, blinding knives in his head and muscles contorting as if a giant hand were crushing them . . .

"I will not submit!" he screamed, though his will was in tatters, his faith in shreds. Where was the Goddess? Why hadn't he felt even a glimmer of Her? Would he simply stay here for eternity on the edge of his destination, ringed in fire and writhing in pain?

"That's right, resist, Zerrick. Fight him--just a liar," Mira's voice was barely a gasp. Through the flames, her face looked pale with fever, and she lay in what appeared to be a dark red puddle--but that could just be illusion. His insides quailed at the sound of her voice. He'd tried to keep her forgotten, keep the attention and punishments to himself. He couldn't say how much time had passed since he first glimpsed Angist's all-seeing eyes. Perhaps an hour, perhaps a day; it was impossible to tell with the cloud cover and the dimness, making it appear like a continual twilight. The god had taken different forms to frighten him--a dragon, a swarm of snakes crawling over him, a cloud of malaria flies, a decrepit old version of himself trying to strangle the life out of him, but the god's favorite by far was fire. Over and over flame swept from above, below, every direction to sear at his flesh, taunt him that at any second he could be utterly destroyed.

Yet he was still alive.

Even as he watched, the god took a new form, sitting astride his mount, the Ravenger. A long black cloak swept back from a human figure, one Zerrick had not thought about in weeks. His father.

"And here you fail again. Only inches from your goal, only inches from your woman, and quite unable to reach either. And you couldn't even keep the little woman safely back in Alorian," the image of his father said with a laugh, the superiority of his tone and the condescending tilt of his head so like the real father Zerrick had left in Harrow, that it chilled his heart. He struggled to remember Mira's words.

"Liar. I have succeeded in coming where no one else has, I have succeeded in controlling my talents. The fact I could not hold back friends from danger shows their strengths, not my weakness. The fact you are here before me proves my success. I frighten you! Otherwise, why torment me, why send all your creatures to stop me, why bother with me at all, when you could just kill me? I know my powers now, and I will stand up against you! Until you release Ainéra and *leave me alone!*"

He screamed the last words, despite the pain of an aching throat and a pounding headacheThis was stupid, but he had to get the Goddess's attention. He had to end this play the god was having with him, wearing him down. The Goddess had to see his peril. She had to respond, or he would finally know the that the truth about magic was that it was, after all, truly evil.

Please let it not be. Please, Ainéra, we need you! Fight your slumber! He prayed, throwing his mind into that place he had called for the familiar, not that he thought She could hear . . . She had to. Or he was doomed.

"She can't hear you," his father--Angist--stated. He leaned back against the folded wings of the Ravenger, a slight smile playing on his thin lips.

"You're still afraid, Zerrick! She can't hear through the fear," Mira cried out, every word clipped with agony. Zerrick could barely see her through the magic and the flames, but the red puddle seemed to be growing beneath her. The wounds the desert foxes had inflicted were bleeding as well, running in rivulets down her front.

"You have been allowed to live long enough, woman. He finds strength in the fact that you live. Therefore, die," Angist commanded, his voice the sound of rumbling thunder.

The gargoyles raised their spears to strike. Zerrick cried out and dove into the flames, determined to save her--he passed through unscathed. He ran to attack, but as he neared them, he saw her head fall back, her eyes close . . . . A smile formed on her lips.

A blast of white light threw him on his back. Something screamed in pain and he felt a change in the air, a sudden waver in the darkness. Dazed, he sat up, blinking away spots, then leapt up to check on Mira.

She lay prone, not moving, not breathing, clothes black with the blood of her many wounds. For a moment all he could do was stare at her pale cheek, untouched by the violence which marked the rest of her body. Then he realized she was not alone lying there. Both gargoyles lay to the side of her, flesh burned away, only skeletons remaining. She had destroyed them by the power of . . .

Him, Zerrick thought, awed. So one other deity was watching. But to leave her there, slain . . . rage boiled within. He felt for the magic, ready to pull it all to him, preparing his mind for a final strike. Now that she was dead there was only one thing to do. He glanced at Angist's form, hatred and fury making him seem to glow with an unholy light.

Angist laughed.

That was a mistake. Zerrick released the magic back into the air and stopped the flood of emotions to think for a moment, consider his actions. He had been prepared to attack with worst spell he could imagine, but he saw that was exactly what Angist wanted. Mira had died to allow him a chance to succeed. He owed it to her to try, before he ended his life and joined her.

Grief threatened for a moment to overcome him. He stomped it out, ruthlessly. He must be stone. His mind must be clear. A thought occurred to him, as he released the magic that had been Mira's shield. All this magic here was emanating from the Goddess. What if he talked to it, as he had in Hirkumos's tent, seeking to do the impossible? He could worship the Mother, pray to Her, through Her magic.

My love--anguish threatened to stop even his mental voice--*my love has been slain by the god of evil, by Angist. I am here for You, Goddess, come to me, aid me against him, so that You may go free. The magic is too concentrated!* He spoke to the magic; he was the magic, full of ancient secrets of creation and destruction, energy and nothingness. Angist was not here. This was before Angist. Through the magic, he felt a direct line to the One who had existed with the magic, in the Beginning. His loss, his pain and his love pulled him through with his message.

He felt the Goddess stir.

"No, you will not wake Her!" A thin voice--his grandfather's? No, it was Angist's--cried out, and with a jerk Zerrick was back in his body, the magic a bright glow around him. Angist appeared in the flames again, but he seemed translucent now, without much heat from this side of the barrier. The flames disappeared and he felt the presence withdrawing as the Ravenger stepped forward and screamed in challenge.

It charged Zerrick and he dove to avoid pointed hooves clawing up the earth as the beast rushed by. He leapt to his feet and readied his scimitar as the beast pivoted with the aid of its wings and charged him again, screaming in fury, its eyes aglow.

Zerrick swung his sword and felt it contact flesh, slicing neatly through, but the force of the beast's passage ripped the sword out of his hands as it galloped past. With an inhuman laugh it shook the weapon out its flesh, rearing on hind legs and beating its wings to send dust into Zerrick's face. Before he was forced to shut his eyes, Zerrick did manage to see that where the blade had been.Not a trace of blood showed.

So weapons wouldn't work against it. Perhaps magic, thought Zerrick, pulling power to create a spell similar to the one Elemara had used against the *megrez*. A shield of flashing scythes and light materialized around him, able to attack and defend at once. Still, the Ravenger did not seem daunted. With another half-human, half-animal cry, it charged him again, ignoring the flashing blades.

The strength of its physical attack knocked out Zerrick's spell, and the backlash of that magic together with the magic of the air threw him sideways, just as wings and hooves beat at the air where he had been standing. The breath was knocked out of him but he forced himself to roll out of the way of the dancing hooves and stand again, thinking furiously. What would possibly stop this thing?

The magic would know. He asked it, but he was so exhausted, it nearly overcame him again, as it had when he had first been dropped on the hillside. It was far too potent, trying to take control of him, Dimly he heard the Ravenger prepare to make another run. Again he prayed to the Goddess.

Help me! He pleaded, throwing a flaming sphere as the creature charged him again. The flame passed through it. Where the beast should have been blackened and charred with the power of his spell, it was merely singed. He felt the impact as it slammed into him, throwing him back, but he managed to again roll out of the way of the murderous hooves. Zerrick struggled to stand, groaning. His body was beginning to feel like one giant bruise. As he got to his feet he could see the beast watching him from several feet off, taunting him with its blazing eyes. Despair pummeled him. It seemed utterly invincible.

The magic--trust it. I know you do not, but you must this one time. It is all right. I am with you. Release your fear and embrace the magic.

Zerrick didn't know have time to worry if what he was doing would be fatal, or if he would lose himself forever as Madame Lotus had. This voice felt so pure, so full of loving care and guidance, and it was the voice from his dreams. He decided to trust it.

The magic was already with him; it was impossible to keep out at this concentration, and it was probably mutating him, but how long that would take he hadn't a clue. Its pseudo intelligence was there as well, the chaotic instincts of nature. As he gave in to let it take over, he seemed to step outside himself, as if his consciousness were being set aside as the new 'mind' came in.

To preserve your sanity . . . He didn't know if the voice was that of himself, the magic, or the Goddess. All seemed to blend into one. He saw the magic of the air blending with the magic and soil of the earth, thought with matter, reality with dreams. When he looked at the Ravenger charging at him, he noticed he could see right through it.

He understood. It was an illusion! All that was needed to cancel the illusion was to know the truth: that it was, in fact, unreal.

The Ravenger came at him, and with his attention focused on disbelieving it, he had no time to duck. It hit him hard and he heard a crack as one of his ribs broke, but with the magic the sound seemed somehow distant, and without pain. He landed on his back unable to mov,e but the magic again acted to protect him. Somehow the hooves did not connect with his flesh. A moment of dizziness passed, then he found himself standing several feet back from where he had fallen. The Ravenger looked at him in confusion.

I will protect you as much as I am able, but only you can defeat the Ravenger. Remove all fear. The voice came from within and without at the same time, comforting him. He knew what had happened. He still feared the creature, so it still had power to hurt him.

No fear . . . he looked to Mira's prone form. She hadn't been afraid to sacrifice herself. She hadn't feared much of anything in the time he had known her. He owed it to her to defeat this monster. After all, if he failed, he would only be going to join her.

"Try that one more time, Ravenger," he challenged the beast, picking a spot away from Mira to make his stand. The magic moved his hand, reaching up to take hold of Alden's pouch which he still wore, now more for sentimental reasons than for the weak little amber it held. He felt himself yank free that pouch and hold it out in front of him, and was surprised to see the sign of the triangle within a triangle, Ainéra's sign, was glowing, as it had in his first encounter with the *Ashwa-grippa* in the jungle. Since then, he'd assumed the glow had come from the magic in the amber, but now he saw it was not so. It seemed to possess a magic of its own, though how such a thing could be possible, he didn't know.

I have always watched over you, as I watch over all my children. Be at peace, dear pupil. Your success is at hand. The words were all about him, deep through his soul, and he could feel a stirring in the air, a glow in the magic like the eastern sky in predawn. The Goddess was waking.

The Ravenger snorted, red eyes opened wide, nostrils flared. It sensed his resolve, he was sure of it. Darkness seemed to emanate from it, winged shadows of bats, crows, hate, nightmares, spreading out from the beast towards him. He saw through the magic that it was preparing to make a final strike with its magic.

He stepped through the shadows up to the beast and touched Alden's pouch to its hide.

It passed straight through.

The Ravenger screamed, but its screaming faded as it began to disappear. Zerrick redirected the magic it had been pulling to strike him, trying to avoid another maelstrom like the one that had engulfed Madame Lotus. The magic flared around him in a series of explosions, pulled too many directions at once, confused into simple detonation. With a wave of agony, the magic that had been inside of him rushed out. He fell to his knees, his senses blurring.

Silence fell upon the desert. When he felt once again in command of his senses and body, Zerrick stood and looked around. A charred circle of earth lay where the ring of fire had been. Before him towered the black mountains, and at his feet were the skeletons of the gargoyles and Mira's pitiful--he could not bring himself to call it a corpse--her body was still there as well. Of the Ravenger there was no trace, and the shadows flowing from it had disappeared as well. High above, the clouds spilled out from the mountains, but the sense of shadow that had pervaded this area seemed somehow withdrawn. He could not feel Angist's presence.

Zerrick limped to Mira, holding his side where the broken ribs smoldered with pain, one pain among many. His leg was bleeding where a glancing blow from a cloven hoof had connected. Burns covered his arms and face, and there was even a snake bite to one ankle from one of Angist's attacks. His insides were in agony from handling too much energy. And his heart--there was only a terrible ache there, a deep empty chasm.

He had one last task, before he ended his pain. Ever so carefully, he lifted Mira's body over his shoulder. There was a tiny hope in him that perhaps Ainéra could help. At any rate he would not leave her for varmints.

It was difficult to see a path up the mountainside, especially with the tears blurring his vision. Strange that they should leak--in his heart he strove to be frozen stone, bent on his task. As he began his climb, he noticed the stones cutting his hands even as they had in numerous dreams. Grief threatened to overcome him. Yes, he had seen this future once, a lone figure struggling up a mountainside, desperately pulling a red-haired body drenched in blood . . . . The world threatened to plunge into darkness.

Yes, come to me. Free me.

Zerrick pulled, arms straining, to bring Mira up to a ledge with him. At the sound of that all-powerful voice, he shook his fist at the heavens.

"You're no longer trapped, Ainéra! You never were! Wake up and see! See what it has cost me to reach you and tell you this!" Anger filled him, but he could not rest it all on Her. He understood Her now. She had never had a chance to fight alone against Angist, because Her power was not aggression; it was as foreign to Her as killing to a butterfly. She was not capable of it. She was, after all his worries, wholly and undeniably good.

She did not materialize before him, so he knew She was still not fully awake, that She still believed Herself trapped. Wearily, he continued his climb, dragging Mira up from rise to rise and cliff to cliff through the night. The first light of dawn rose up in the east to help him negotiate the treacherous path, and he tried as best he could to see that no more cuts from the rocks joined those already marking both of them. As the first rays of sun hit the rock-face he passed over a particularly difficult crossing over a deep chasm. He slipped on the slick surface and nearly lost his grip of Mira. When he pulled her up to him, he saw new cuts in her skin from the black slate.

Blood slowly pulsed forth.

Zerrick's breath caught in his throat. Could it be? He gathered her up in his arms and felt at her temple, at her throat and at her lips, trying to find a pulse, a breath of air, something. Her body was so cold. There wasn't a sign of life in her. He pressed his head to her heart and held his breath, waiting.

After a moment, he heard a faint thump, a single heartbeat. Then another. And another. Spaced so far apart, it couldn't possibly be enough to keep her alive, and yet . . .

She was alive. For the moment at least, she was alive. Zerrick wanted to hold her for all he was worth, sob with joy, with hysterical relief, but he hadn't a moment to lose. It was a miracle she lived, but she would not live long without healing. His own magic could help, but he didn't think he could pull any more without succumbing to it, in all its primal fury. The Goddess was the only answer.

He plunged ahead again, climbing, pulling, lifting, dragging Mira and himself to each ledge. Foot by agonizing foot they reached a pass between the peaks.

After the dry lifeless desert, Zerrick was surprised at the lush growth in the valley, a valley formed by the perfect circle of mountains. The black clouds hung over the valley blocking out the light, sending down a steady drizzle of rain. Jungle life ran rampant with that abundance of water, trailing up the steep sides of the cliffs.

Zerrick listened to the sounds of the jungle, sounds he realized he had missed in the long trek since leaving Harrow. He was startled by the flapping of some giant creature down below. Out of the misty treetops a pair of galundren, the flying deer rabbits, flew to alight on a nearby ledge. They glanced at him, large brown eyes looking him over with curiosity while he stayed perfectly still, unsure if he could defend himself right now against their sleeping magical breath. They seemed without fear of him, however, and after a moment took to the air again, flying down to the valley and disappearing into the dense foliage.

Zerrick fought a wave of despair. Such a long way to go, down the mountainside.

He blinked as a full-sized griffin swooped up towards him. It too landed on the ledge just below, and gave a low rumble of greeting. This one did not fly, but crouched in a position suitable for mounting, watching him, the fur of its mane smooth and flat on its neck, no hackles raised as Zerrick would expect from a wild one unused to human contact.

"May I?" Zerrick asked aloud. He should use magic to make sure the creature understood, but he was so tired, so very tired. He prepared himself for the fact that with the sound of his voice he would probably startle the creature off.

Instead, it inched towards them, claws scraping off the slick black rock. It tilted its head and from its beak gave a low friendly mewl.

"Ainéra?" Zerrick whispered. He heard nothing, but he suddenly envisioned himself on the back to the griffin, speeding towards the Goddess. A visual message, then. He nodded and made his way to the griffin with Mira.

It trembled as his foot came into contact with its flesh, unused to a human's touch. Zerrick soothed it with a few quiet words and very carefully lifted Mira up to the scruff of its neck, ready to pull her back if it leapt away. It growled nervously, shifting its weight, but stayed still for him.

Once Mira was up, he climbed the beast's back. Now it snorted and moved about beneath him, but he was able to grab hold of Mira with one hand and a great tawny clump of mane with the other as it spread its wings to fly. The next second his stomach was in his throat and they were flying swiftly in a downward spiral, through the treetops and vine-clad forest, down to a dark cavern formed of vegetation and moss. They landed beside a deep dark pond, surrounded by the sound of creatures, muffled as if something heavy were covering the area. As if the animals were trying to keep quiet.

As soon as the griffin touched ground, Zerrick dismounted, carrying Mira in his arms. The griffin took to the air again, leaving them alone in the jungle.

Zerrick went to where the shadows lay thickest, where he could feel an evil presence pervading the area, both the physical and the magical. He blinked. The magic--it was again affecting him. Tightening his shields, he strode forward.

Visions danced at the periphery of his vision in the shadows beneath the dense foliage, but when he turned to stare directly at them, there was nothing. He ducked under the root of a mangrove--mangroves, here, out in the desert!--and found a small clearing ringed with ancient trees and carpeted with moss. Ferns covered the trunks of trees and much of the ground, creating a high bed of plants at the far end. Upon that bed lay a shrouded figure.

His heart leapt. The magic here was so thick it had a smell, a sharp scent of electricity. In the corner of his eyes the visions continued, and he realized they were snatches of dreams--some of them nightmares similar to his own. He saw them when he stared straight ahead, in the very corner of his eye. Some dreams seemed entirely inhuman--these must be the nightmares of an immortal one, along with dreams of thousands of humans, all in one place.

He dismissed the phantom images and crept up to the bed of ferns. A layer of delicate spider webs covered the female figure lying in calm repose, undisturbed for many years. Zerrick set down Mira to lie among the ferns at the feet of the figure, then bent to brush aside the cobwebs.

Darkness blacked out his vision and he felt Angist suddenly very near, warning him to step away, depart. A pair of glowing eyes materialized just above the figure. His heart thundered in his chest.

"No," he whispered, fighting to speak against the terror. "Not this time. Not any longer," he said in a louder voice, glancing at Mira. She was dying, and not Hell itself would keep him from bringing life back to her. He reached through the eyes and lifted away the webs to brush the cheek of the Goddess.

The glowing eyes vanished, the evil presence fled. The Goddess's eyes opened and came to focus on him, eyes black as night, filled with stars.

Zerrick was frozen. Incalculable depths lured him in, unimaginable tenderness probed at him, learned who he was, what he had been through. She blinked, and suddenly her eyes became normal, human-looking. Zerrick found he could move and think normally again. He tried not to be rude, but he couldn't help staring.

He hadn't thought she would look so *human*. As if all of humanity were in Her visage, all of perfection and grace. He beheld two violet eyes in a perfectly oval face, pouting red lips, and golden hair falling down the shoulders past the waist to mingle among the ferns at Her feet. She was dressed in a robe of some kind which seemed to be made of the earth itself, colored russet brown, gold, and green and adorned with leaves and flowers. Like a mother, She reached up a pale hand to cup his cheek and kissed him on his forehead.

He didn't know how to respond. At last he had done it; he had finally made it to his goal; he had woken the Goddess.

He was at a loss for words.

"I've been dreaming, haven't I, Zerrick," She said, and the fact She knew his name did not shock him as much as the sound of Her voice, so deep and melodic, it reminded him of . . .

"Mira!" he said with a gasp, remembering the reason he had fought so hard to reach this place so quickly. He bowed low and hurried to lift Mira up in his arms. He noticed while still cool to the touch, she was warmer than she'd been a few moments earlier.

"Can you help her, please? My--" he hesitated, unsure how he should address Her, "--my Goddess," he said, keeping his eyes lowered now, trying to be the humble worshiper.

He started at the touch of Her hand on his head, smoothing back a sweat-damp strand. "You have gone through great pain to arrive here. I was foolish to let Angist take me, but blessed to have a soul determined as yours to awaken me. I will see what can be done."

Her touch was incredible. Magic poured into him from just that small brush of Her hand, magic rushing energy to his limbs, healing him even as it had that day by the lake after the serpent attack. And the emotion in Her voice, the heartfelt apology and compassion he had glimpsed in Her diaries was so potent in person, he found he could not voice his thanks for the knot in his throat. He could imagine now the loss the Put-na and the Alorians had endured when She was captured.

He gently set Mira by the Goddess and held her head up as She laid a hand on Mira's brow. Immediately Mira's body twitched, as if disturbed in slumber, and he could see the magic pour forth, magic of such intensity and purity it was a wonder it did not simply burn away all it touched. It gently healed all the cuts and bites and bruises, bringing color back to Mira's cheeks. In less than a moment, all trace of injury was gone. He waited, but even after several moments, she did not wake.

Fear creeping into his voice, Zerrick asked Ainéra, "Why doesn't she--"

"I cannot wake her. She is hiding with Him, and I dare not tread there and awaken old pains . . ." Her whole countenance changed momentarily, and Zerrick thought he saw hairs of gray intermingled with the gold, a scarring of the flesh along her right cheek. He blinked and the moment passed; She was radiant.

He did not wait to hear any more, whether She believed Mira could be woken or not, but began gently shaking Mira, burying his head against her throat and pleading, "Mira, it's over--please wake up! I've made it, I can go back in peace now, but I won't without you. Please, Mira, I love you, come back . . . ." Grief stopped his voice and he simply clung to her, reaching now with his mind, with his magic, with every fiber of his soul to find her and bring her back, calling against the gossamer barrier of the veil.

His magic told him nothing of whether he was successful or not. After a moment the Goddess again brushed him with Her touch. He straightened, opening his eyes. As he did so, Mira's eyelids fluttered, then slowly her eyes opened, and her hands clung to him. In a ghost of a voice, she whispered, "We can go back?"

Zerrick nodded, two large tears rolling down his cheeks to fall into her hair. She reached up and he reached down to embrace fiercely.

An evil laugh stopped him cold.

"You think me defeated? You think that I will lie low and slink away?" Angist's voice rang out in the valley, beginning as a sinister whisper and quickly gaining in volume to an echoing shout, "I will destroy you sorry mortals, and Ainéra, you will see my traps still hold you here; you cannot leave so easily! I will not--"

"Silence!" Mira bellowed, and her voice was not her own, but that otherworldly tone Zerrick had heard her use when she banished the evil spirit from Svak. He felt something--a presence, or a pressure in the air which the magic began to react to in a most peculiar way, sparks bursting from the tree tops and along the vines. Through the magic he could see the trap Angist spoke of--a complex weave he could not begin to decipher, except to see that it was a coercion suggesting the body to sleep, just as the dais on Lookout Peak had pulled him to look into the basin. So this was what held Ainéra. It wasn't affecting him, so he assumed it was designed solely for Her. Which meant he could probably disrupt it . . .

Magic leapt to his command, and he sent a counter-spell sweeping the valley to interfere with magic under anyone's control besides his or Ainéra's. At the same time Mira raised her right hand, and again that white light which had destroyed the gargoyles which was *not* magic, flew from her hand. It illuminated the entire valley. Zerrick felt his magic contact with something, knocking it out . . .

A horrible scream pierced the air and the shadows suddenly were no more. The heaviness in the air lifted, and as the valley brightened, Zerrick looked at the Goddess. For a second he saw a second spell being interfered with by his magic--a powerful illusion covering Her features to make Her beautiful. Underneath, the reality was horrible-- the left half of Her face was indeed beautiful, even as he had first seen Her, but the right half was nothing but gruesome scar tissue from an ancient wound traveling the length of Her right side, as if half of Her body had been torn away--with a snap, the magic reasserted itself under Her control, and She seemed whole again.

Zerrick looked away, rage tearing at him that She had suffered such harm, and pain at the knowledge She had never healed. But such emotions could not endure long.

Above them the clouds were breaking up, and the first rays of sunlight struck the forest floor, illuminating the valley in brilliant detail.

Ainéra smiled, and Her smile was as radiant as the sun's rays. Zerrick saw the illusion in this case was more true than reality--it reflected the beauty of Her essence of goodness. The Goddess of earth and magic and love should be beautiful and whole.

"He has fled. Thank you both." She stood, brushing away the last of the cobwebs. A chatter of bird-like calls sounded form a nearby tree, and a pair of flying lizards flew down to perch on Her shoulder.

Zerrick helped Mira stand up and together they surveyed their lack of hurts, each looking pale with exhaustion, but alive, so amazingly alive! He had to keep holding Mira's hand just to know that she was really there, that everything around him was real.

The Goddess wandered around, touching plants as if in greeting, laughing at the sight of magical creatures darting through the treetops. "I cannot believe I was so foolish, so gullible and ignorant, to let him ensorcel me!" She cried, opening Her arms as if to embrace all the jungle. A griffin roared from a distance, greeting them, Zerrick realized. She closed Her eyes and breathed in deeply, seeming to absorb all the life that was around Her. Then She opened Her eyes and looked at Zerrick, and he could swear he saw a sparkle of mischief in Her.

"Let us return to my city."

*   *   *

Glossary of Put-na Words

Ainji : hear

Akiya: deer, antelope

Anka: to speak for, vouch

Ashwa-grippa: Two deaths (of an evil nature)

Bialilla: daughter (of)

Borderima: white man, stranger

Inyamina: your

Jamenenu: hunter

Kormu: Angist, god of Evil

Koyda: negative/ not

Kumalido/ kumalida : a magic user, witch. (male/female)
kumalida also refers to magic itself.

Kumara: Ainéra, goddess of magic

Kuri: to weep; to cry

Ngai/ ngaiya : I (male/female)

Mapo: grass

Maring: life

Megrez: demon

Miborigi/ miborgia : know/am familiar with (male/female)

Mibu: future participle "will" Muniyana: us

Moibu: shelter

Ngainma: my

Ngandiddo/ ngandidda: good/goodness

Nginya : you

Owei: yes

Pikkai : faster

Poko: debt

Poru: heart

Put-na : a person/ the People

Rlia: in, inside of

Taktata: to call

Wariji: to to end, to finish. Death.

Wo: to give

About the Author

Judy Goodwin has been writing since she was a child, when her fourth grade English instructor told her, 'You should be a writer." She earned her Bachelor of Arts degree in Creative Writing from the University of Arizona, and a Masters in Education from Argosy University. Over the last ten years she has appeared in several small press magazines and anthologies with her fantasy and science fiction short stories and poetry. This is her debut novel.

When not working on her fiction, Judy works at a local college and also does technical writing as a consultant. She is proud to say that her daughter has the writing bug as well. They live in a house full of life in the form of three dogs and four cats, and always try to appreciate the beauty of nature.

You can connect with the author at her blog here: http://judygoodwin.wordpress.com or at her Twitter account, judygoodwin6. She is also a Goodreads member.

Upcoming and Other Works

You can find other works by Judy Goodwin at Amazon, Barnes and Noble and other retailers, including these short stories:

Purple Irises
Noon: A Paranormal Short Story
A Troll Under Golden Gate Bridge
Name of a King
Eight Minutes Until the End of the World

Also look for her next upcoming novel in a new series, the *Spirit Mage Saga*, with the first book scheduled for 2014: *Journey to Landaran.*